RENOWN

Books by Danielle Novotny

The Remade Series

Remade

Renown

Renown

By Danielle Novotny

Renown

Copyright © 2020 by Danielle Novotny

First published February 2020

Cover design © Danielle Novotny

The names, characters, locations, and scenarios in this book are entirely fictional. Any resemblance to actual persons, places, or events is entirely coincidental.

ISBN: 978-0-578-63991-8

To Adam and Lauren,

I couldn't have asked for better siblings and friends.

Thank you for helping me reach this milestone.

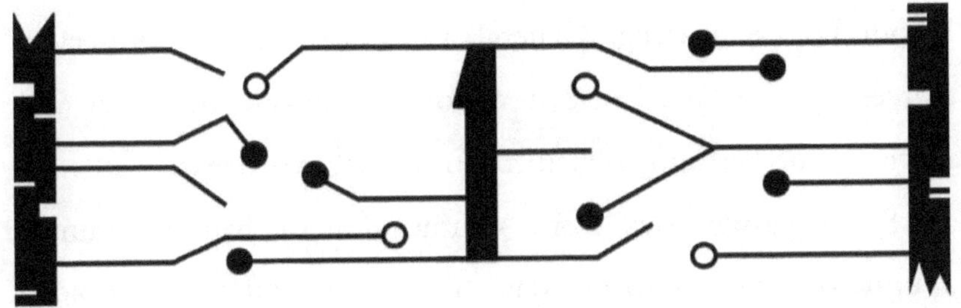

I hated waiting.

After staring death in the face, not just once but at least three times now, one would think that being told to wait couldn't possibly be the worst thing to happen to me. But right now, it was.

I paced back and forth across the sparring mat in one of the Protective Forces' training centers, annoyed that whoever I was supposed to meet was running late. My combat boots made soft squishing noises as I stomped around the large, rectangular mat, and I tried to focus on those sounds instead of the questions swirling around my brain.

It wasn't like I had places to be, but I was impatient. There had been so much downtime these past two weeks that I desperately wanted something to happen. Well, anything except a call for aid from another planet.

But seriously, whoever wanted to meet with me was taking a long time to arrive. Slowly my thoughts turned to possibilities of whom I'd be meeting. General Vinculus? Another Protective Forces captain? King Locklyn? It could be anyone, but it was odd since no one had approached me in the last two weeks.

Since getting back from Vanthurium, we had no training routine or structure to our days. Doctors attended to the Nova squad's various injuries, we rested, and Gunther and Gráinne went to work repairing the *Starfire*.

And then we were told to wait.

Other squads had been sent to Vanthurium to assist in the cleanup from the attack. Or, as everyone seemed to call the whole incident, the Battle of Vanthurium.

The battle had only occurred at the palace, but the shock wave that rippled through the King's Galaxy afterward had rocked many people to their cores. After all, the last major war this galaxy had seen was the one with the Krech. And that had taken place one hundred years ago.

Until recently, everyone thought the Krech had been eradicated. Everyone had been wrong.

The myth of the Krech had been shattered – both by their appearance on Charra and their orchestration of the cyborgs' attack on Vanthurium – and the possibility that another attack could happen at any time had taken root in everyone's minds.

Caspian, who remained a captain even as we considered King Locklyn's request, relayed news from the outside world to us: King

Locklyn and all the other nobility were increasing the number of guards and standing armies around their homes, travel to the Outer Rim was being closely monitored, and galactic citizens were being warned to proceed with caution. It wasn't a lot, but considering what we all knew about the Krech and their motives – which was next to nothing – those small actions were a good start.

On the Protective Forces base, squads trained harder than ever, ensuring that every single trainee and soldier was ready for combat. Sparring and shooting lessons became the most requested, and new class sessions on a multitude of defense strategies had been added to the Protective Forces curriculum. Several captains even approached Caspian to ask that he or members of our Nova squad attended drills so that we could share our experience and constructive criticism.

Thankfully, Caspian had said no.

He insisted that the Protective Forces' lessons would be good enough, coupled with a soldier's intuition. His squad had been through enough, he said, and we didn't need to relive the battles – and the fear we had experienced – over and over just for the trainees' benefit.

I was immensely grateful that the captains accepted Caspian's answer and backed down.

After training with the Forces for only a couple months, I hadn't been remotely prepared for our first fight on Charra. The shooting, running, and overwhelming sense of panic… it had been unstructured chaos. And you can't teach someone to prepare for chaos.

My only blessing had been the modifications that Doctor Givray had made to me when he saved my life. I had the speed and agility to outmaneuver the Krech when they cornered us in the storage hangar on Charra, thereby saving my team's lives.

And then, not even a week later, we found ourselves in the middle of another battle, this time in the palace on Vanthurium.

Some nights I still had dreams in which I found myself running for my life in underground tunnels or cornered in a dead-end hallway. The worst nightmares, though, were the ones where I could only watch as the cyborg held his knife to Caspian's throat because I couldn't move. In those dreams I was never able to save Caspian, and I always woke up sobbing.

On those nights, Caspian would leave his bed to hold me until I calmed down. He never asked what I dreamed about, but I had a feeling that he knew. His sleep was restless in the bunkhouse, so I guessed that he probably had similar nightmares.

My cheeks heated as I thought about him holding me, and I was thankful I was alone. From there, my thoughts shifted to the kiss that Caspian and I almost had in the tunnel beneath the palace. Our lips had been a hairsbreadth apart when shouts of dismay over the wrecked escape ship had shattered our moment.

Now those late-night comforting hugs were the only slightly romantic interactions we had, and I couldn't help wondering why. Did he not mean what he said in the tunnel? Or was he embarrassed by his display of affection since I hadn't exactly confirmed how I felt?

I desperately hoped that he hadn't changed his mind about me because I couldn't deny the feelings I had for him.

He had been my liberator, my defender, and my biggest supporter since I joined the Protective Forces. Caspian cared more than anyone else I had met since this wild journey began, and that had certainly left its mark on me. I trusted him, felt deeply for his own losses and struggles, and twice I had put my life in danger to protect his.

Which I would do again in a heartbeat.

But today my trust for him was wearing thin. I had been pacing inside the sparring room for half an hour waiting for my visitor. Caspian had refused to tell me who was coming and had simply smirked when I tried to pry an answer out of him.

Whoever this was had better show up soon, or I was going to retreat to the Nova bunkhouse. A cold shower sounded heavenly right now.

Midsummer on Callais was warmer than what I had experienced on Terra. The heat in this region was the dry, stifling type, and beads of sweat rolled down my neck where they soaked into the neckline of my white shirt. I barely felt the breeze from the dated cooling system in the sparring room.

I stopped my pacing as gravel crunched right outside the door. It inched open while the metal hinges protested loudly, and a familiar face peered around the door's edge.

"Doctor Givray?" I hadn't seen or heard from him since being handed off to General Vinculus, and I was pleasantly surprised to see him now.

"Aliya, darling!" He shuffled into the room as the door squealed shut behind him. It had only been a few months, but it felt like years since I had seen him last. "I am so relieved to see you're well." Soft wrinkles formed at the corners of his mouth as he beamed from ear to ear, and I couldn't help smiling in return.

"It's good to see you, too," I replied.

And it was good. When we had parted, I was angry at him for changing me. I had hated him – and myself – and was in complete denial over what I had become. I remembered how horrified I had been the first time I saw my new nerve-circuits light up and how I had attacked Doctor Givray only moments later.

These memories were almost like looking back in time at another person. I had come so far from those horrible and confusing days, and I almost felt bad for overreacting.

"I told you," he said as he wagged a finger at me, "I told you that you would do great things!"

He hadn't used those exact words in the healing facility when he'd tried to convince me that I should join the Protective Forces, but I understood what he meant. Thanks to my remade body, I'd saved lives. And after the stories from the battles on Charra and Vanthurium's had been told all over the base, every captain, trainee, and soldier expressed awe over me, even going so far as to call me the "Hero of Vanthurium."

"You did," I said with a laugh. "And I can't thank you enough for all that you've done. I… I truly appreciate it now." I knew I didn't need to say much more than that. This male had saved my life in more ways than one, and I would forever be grateful for him.

He beamed down at the floor as a blush rose to his cheeks.

"I'll admit that I am curious," Doctor Givray said as he knotted his fingers together and looked back up at me, his baby blue eyes filled with curiosity, "how your shoulder is healing."

I almost laughed at his implied question. Naturally, the doctor would be curious about my injuries.

"It's healing much faster than I expected." I tugged my collar as far to the side as it would allow to show him the reddish-pink mark which remained as the only indication of my injury. A shot from a cyborg's blaster had clipped my shoulder during our escape from the tunnels under the palace of Vanthurium, and it had been pure agony. I'd expected that fiery pain to take longer to heal, but all that remained was a jagged, fading scar which was roughly the size of my palm.

Doctor Givray took a few steps forward and gently pressed his fingers against the mark. "Good, good," he said as he continued to probe.

"I was worried for a while that my nerves wouldn't work right," I admitted. I never understood the medical procedures he had used to heal me, especially the advanced circuits he had used to repair the extensive nerve damage I had suffered in my fatal car crash. "But I haven't had any issues with movement or sensation."

"Good," the doctor droned again, lost in thought while staring at the scar. When he realized that I was waiting for him to say more, he stuffed his hands back into the deep pockets of his white coat and took a step back. "Right. Well that is very good news. It means that your body accepted the synthetics better than I had previously thought they would."

"What does that mean?"

Doctor Givray ran a hand through his short salt-and-pepper hair and turned to look at the sparring room. "It means…" He cleared his throat while searching for the right words. "The synthetics are made from materials that naturally occur within your body – carbon, oxygen, and so on. While the exact nature of the synthetics was foreign to you, the chemical makeup wasn't completely unfamiliar. The fact that your body is repairing itself without any issues to movement or sensation, as you say, means that your body has learned to repair the synthetics."

"Even the circuits?" I couldn't imagine my body reproducing the circuits that lit up under my skin every time I exerted myself.

"Oh, yes," he said as he focused on me once more. "They aren't the circuits you're imagining for a ship or for lighting a room. I suppose you could say they're quite natural as well."

My head spun with all the science talk, but I had learned what I needed to know. Nothing added to me after my accident was unnatural, and my body could heal itself – which included my new muscles and circuits – instead of needing to be repaired.

"That's good to know," I replied. "And speaking of… Doctor Givray, do you have any news on Adís?" She'd been sent off for medical help after the battle. I assumed since he was a doctor that he had to know *something* about her.

"Ah." Doctor Givray paced away from me and sat heavily upon the mat with his legs stretched out in front of him. "Unfortunately, I do not. Her case was not given to me. In fact, I'm not entirely sure whom she was sent to."

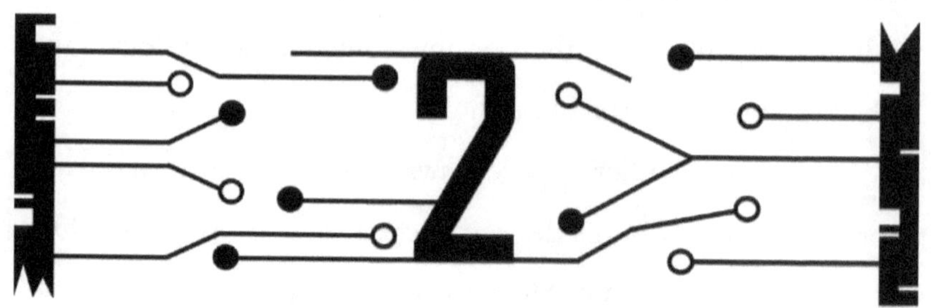

I sat on the floor as my stomach sank. No one knew where Adís was and if she had been healed. I was starting to feel like she had been taken from us, and we would never get her back.

I thought back on one of my first memories of Adís. She had walked me to my room on the *Starfire*, and right before she left, she'd asked if I thought I was going to stay. I remember how hesitant that question had been.

The Nova squad hadn't given me the most welcoming of receptions after learning that I was a modified Terran. Adís had even snapped at Caspian for withholding information since he'd only told them that I was modified.

It was funny now, thinking back on Adís' question if I'd stay. At the time I had said yes, that I'd stay with the Nova squad, just because I didn't want to go back to the Protective Forces. Now I saw the question on a broader scope: if I'd stay and be a part of this bigger galaxy.

I still ached for my home from time to time. I felt horrible thinking of my family mourning my death, but the longer I was away from Terra, the less I found myself missing the planet as a whole. "Immature" had been the word Doctor Givray used when he explained why the greater galaxy didn't interfere with Terra. The planet was a study in human development, to see if they'd eventually make the advances in technology, medicine, and travel that the rest of the galaxy had.

I'd been enraged when I had first learned that the king and his council knew about Terra's existence but refused to help them along, but now I understood. We had countless books and movies about aliens, superheroes, and space travel, but there were many more examples throughout the planet's young history where shocking information was released and people panicked. But something such as this, that there *was* life in the galaxy, would really make everyone freak out.

Despite missing my home, I knew where I belonged now, and it wasn't on Terra.

Adís had been the first one to make me feel like I was becoming part of a family, of something bigger than myself and my troubles. And now she was the one in trouble.

I just wished there was something I could do to help.

I snapped out of my memories to find that Doctor Givray had rambled on. "Of course, I could try to do some asking around the next time I get a break from my new work…"

"New work?" Was he no longer employed at the healing facility where he'd saved my life?

"Oh, yes!" He brightened up considerably at the new topic and awkwardly scooted closer to where I sat. "Your successes have brought quite a bit of attention to me and what I did for you. Perhaps too much attention."

"Oh, no. What happened?" In the heat of battle, I hadn't even thought about the impact that my actions would have on the doctor's reputation.

"Well, first the entire king's council approached me—"

"The *entire* council?"

"Yes, yes, all of them." He leveled a cool look at me that dared me to interrupt his story again. "They were quite concerned that I had created a monster, one who could fight off four Krech on her own. But after a… good deal of questioning and debating, they came to support my actions and, ultimately, you."

They thought I was a monster. How was that fair? I had fought off multiple Krech to save the most skilled and respected captain in the Protective Forces, and they thought I was a monster?

But I thought I was a monster at first too…

How could I be angry at the council for thinking I was a monster when I had initially hated my transformed self? I hadn't understood it, and I had even shied away from my abilities. I had stifled my true self because I was scared of what I could do, and, if I were to truly admit it, during those first few months I was embarrassed that I had been changed without my consent. Nothing had been more shocking than realizing that I was myself, but also not myself.

In the end, I really couldn't fault the council for the way they first saw me. Thanks to Doctor Givray's persuasion, at least they accepted me now. If only accepting myself had gone that smoothly.

My anger dissipated as Doctor Givray continued.

"Once they realized that I wasn't in the business of creating monsters, the Master of Medicine came forward with a… proposition." A proposition? I wasn't sure I liked where this was going. "She wanted to see if I could recreate my success with you." He paused and looked to me for a response.

Was I the only one who saw how terrible of an idea that was?

Sure, Doctor Givray took a risk in creating me the way he did, but it was a risk that eventually paid off. I hadn't become a menace to society. In fact, I only used my strength and speed when it was absolutely necessary.

But to try to create *others* with my abilities? Others who might not be as considerate and restrained as I was? Others who might get the wrong idea about what they can do with their new skills?

It sounded like a nightmare waiting to happen.

Something in my expression must have given away the horror I felt because a look of surprise crossed Doctor Givray's face.

"What's wrong, Aliya? I thought you would be excited to have others like you?"

Ignoring the fact that his question made me sound like the only one of my species, I thought through what I could possibly say to him. He had saved my life, after all, and I didn't want to offend him, especially since he seemed excited by this offer from the Master of Medicine.

"Doctor Givray, don't… well, don't you see how this could go wrong?"

He was confused for a few seconds. "Ah," he said as understanding erased the concern from his face. "Yes, it would be a dangerous procedure for the subjects, but since it is on a volunteer basis—"

"That's not what I meant," I interjected. "What happens when you succeed with someone who isn't like me? Someone who's— well, a bit more careless with this type of power."

He looked dumbstruck and blinked several times as my words sunk in. Had he never considered this outcome? There were times during my early training where I had scared the doctor in a flash of anger. Did he ever think about what might have happened had I not held back?

"I see," Doctor Givray murmured, as if to himself. Then the corner of his mouth lifted in a half-smile as he said, "I guess we would call you in to help handle the situation."

Lovely. Not only was I the "perfect soldier," as Doctor Givray had once called me, but now I was also the perfect solution to any mistake that he might create. It was a struggle not to roll my eyes at him.

"We have put certain qualifications in place for our participants," he continued. "I'm still not sure why my procedure worked on you as well as it did, especially when you were in an extremely critical state. Therefore, I've been looking for participants in a similar state, to certain extents. Someone for whom there is no other option for a chance at survival."

That was a slight relief to hear. I didn't know what kind of a conscience this male truly had, but in my first conscious days on Callais, he had been adamant that his actions had been to save me, not to experiment on me. I knew there was no way he would feel comfortable working on volunteers who were perfectly healthy when things could go wrong.

And there was the chance that someone who saw their life slipping away and received a second chance with this procedure would be grateful for Doctor Givray and ultimately more willing to listen to his advice should they develop the abilities that I possessed.

At least, that's what I hoped.

"That could work," I hedged. "You mentioned you've already begun working on this project?" Seeing how I hadn't been called in to help him meant that he probably hadn't succeeded yet, but I had to ask anyway.

"Yes, I've worked with a handful of volunteers so far, but I've yet to see success." He looked down at his hands for a moment, quiet and lost in whatever thoughts occupied his mind. "I haven't lost the volunteers, if that's what you're thinking." I wasn't. I could tell that he was letting something off his chest, so I didn't interrupt to correct him. "However, I haven't quite figured out what made you so different. Why you not only survived but also developed these abilities…"

I understood what he meant. The lack of evidence and data for my specific case was probably quite frustrating when he was being asked to recreate my miracle on others.

"Wait a minute. You said you haven't lost a volunteer but that you also haven't had success?" When he said that his volunteers were those facing dire situations, I thought he meant that they were dying. If his procedures weren't successful, how were they still alive?

"Correct." He brushed some imaginary dirt off one khaki pant leg before continuing. "My subjects so far have not been on the brink of death. Most have simply had grave injuries for which typical treatments would not suffice."

"Such as?"

"You know I can't name names," he said as if I wasn't already the least connected person in the King's Galaxy, "but one was a female from Vanthurium. She had quite severe burns down her left arm, presumably from an explosion."

"Or a flamethrower," I mumbled, thinking back to the cyborg with the sword arm that had burst into flame.

"What the other doctors originally thought would be an easy wound to repair became quite dire as they cleaned up the…" Doctor Givray paused as he caught my grimace. I didn't need to know all the details about the injury and procedure afterward. "Right. Anyway, I applied my technique to repairing the injury using the same synthetics and circuitry that repaired your injuries."

"But it didn't work?"

"In a sense," he said with a sigh. "Her arm healed beautifully, without a single mark to show from the original burns. Even she was surprised with the results. But when I tried to test her for new strength in the limb… nothing. She could do no more or less than before." He scowled and shook his head.

I was struck by a thought. "During my first few days in the healing facility, you said that you hadn't expected me to demonstrate as much strength as I eventually did. And you said…" For a moment I fumbled around inside my head for the correct words. "You said that in the times before you hadn't changed as much as you did with me. Did those earlier patients have any abilities like mine?"

"I had only used synthetics when I healed those individuals, Aliya. And that's not a radical or new procedure by any means. The nerve circuitry, and how extensive it was, was the difference with you. I used it on this particular female, but it didn't make a difference."

"But you healed her. That, in itself, should be a breakthrough, right? After all, you said that traditional treatment wasn't going to heal her injury."

"Well, yes." Doctor Givray waved his hand to brush away my praise. "But, you see, that isn't the intent of the procedure. I'm being tasked to create other beings like you, and so far," he looked down at his lap with genuine disappointment in his eyes, "so far I can't."

I reached over and put a hand on his shoulder. "I'm sure you'll figure it out. You did it once, and I'm sure you can make it work again."

"Yes, but what if I *can't?*" He pushed up from the floor and began to pace the interior of the mat's sparring circle. "What if the Master of Medicine realizes that I had no idea what I did to give you this strength and speed, and then…" Doctor Givray's shoulders went rigid, and his eyes unfocused as whatever thought that had just occurred to him gave him pause.

Slowly, I rose onto my feet, a bad feeling pooling in my stomach. "And then what?"

I counted three full breaths before Doctor Givray answered me. "And then they come for you. To try to understand why you're different."

My body tensed, and I had to resist the urge to flee. The Master of Medicine and whoever else answered to her would come for me? What would I do? I couldn't fight them and run away. That would make me a fugitive.

I took a slow, deep breath. This wasn't happening right now; no one was coming to collect me and examine my synthetic muscle and circuits.

With measured steps I made my way over to where Doctor Givray still stood and planted myself directly in his line of vision.

"You'll find a solution long before that happens. I believe you will." Even though I would now worry about this possible future, I had to show the doctor some hope. "You did this once. You can do it again."

His posture relaxed, and he slipped his hands into the pockets of his doctor's coat. "I won't let you down," he said as he finally met my eyes.

"Who knows," I said, "you might just need a little help. Do Gunther and Gráinne know that you're on the base? They've been incredibly curious to figure out how my circuits work."

That finally coaxed a small chuckle out of him. "While I haven't had the pleasure of meeting the twins, that will have to wait for another time. I really should get back to my facility."

"I understand," I said as we walked to the door. The twins would be disappointed, but I could tell that Doctor Givray was worried about his so-called failures. "Thank you for coming to see me."

"Aliya," he replied, reaching for a quick hug, "it's always a pleasure to see you. Perhaps next time you could visit me, hm? The general still doesn't like me much."

We both laughed, and I promised that I would try. And then, once more, we parted ways.

The last time I had walked away from him, I was a trainee in the Protective Forces. I had hated him and myself. I had felt forced into my situation, and I had no idea what kind of a life had awaited me.

So much had changed.

I still didn't know what was in store for me and the rest of the Nova squad. I wasn't sure if we would all accept the king's offer to serve him or if we would choose another path. But as I left Doctor Givray, I felt no hatred for him or myself. I didn't resent the Protective Forces because if I had to do it all over again, I knew that I would pick the same path.

And this particular path, I thought with a laugh, led back to my squad. A squad who needed to hear the information I had just learned.

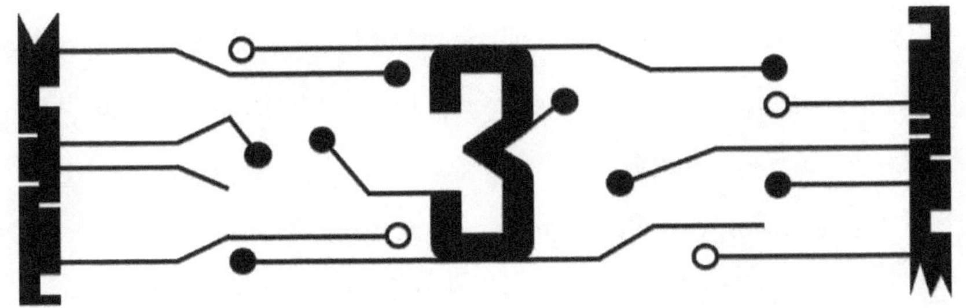

I found Caspian in the Nova bunkhouse with the rest of my squad. None of us had duties to perform today, and due to the midsummer heat, Caspian wasn't making us go through drills. Instead, everyone lounged inside the cool bunkhouse.

The twins sat at a table in the farthest corner with their backs facing the front door. They had been tinkering with some new tech for days now, but we knew better than to try and get information on what it was out of them. Ki'ran scrolled on a dataport, and Jorl sat beside Lem on the floor. And Bragdan... He was curled up in his bed, ignoring everyone else.

"Aliya!" Caspian called from where he sat on the floor. He and Lem were sitting cross-legged, cleaning their blasters. It was a normal habit for Lem – indeed, one that she did nearly every day – but it was strange to see that Caspian had joined her.

Aside from the fierce protection he displayed for us in the face of the other captains, something was bothering Caspian. I couldn't tell if it was concern for the well-being of his squad or the days we had spent waiting to hear from King Locklyn, but something was making Caspian antsy.

Antsy enough to clean blasters that were already pristine.

A small part of me felt guilty that I was about to share news that might only make Caspian more agitated, but it was something that everyone needed to hear.

"How was your visitor?" Caspian asked with a conspiratorial smile.

I glared but couldn't hold back the smile that crept across my face as I sat down beside Caspian. "Seeing Doctor Givray was great, thank you." A metallic *plink* sounded from the back of the room, and I chuckled as I imagined the irritation that must have been on Gunther and Gráinne's faces. I couldn't explain my circuitry to them, so they wanted to meet the doctor to learn about it from him. "It was good to see him," I continued, "since we had parted under less than ideal circumstances."

Caspian knew all about my first few days on Callais and how I'd learned to use my abilities. He heard about the deep resentment I had felt for Doctor Givray when I'd been dumped on the Protective Forces' base. But Caspian had seen me grow to accept my new limits, and he was smart; he had probably been the one to set up my meeting with the doctor, knowing that I would eventually want to reconnect and smooth things over.

Of course, he'd been right to do so. Until now, I hadn't realized just how much it meant to have things patched up with Doctor Givray. After all, he had saved my life and, in turn, had gifted me with abilities that I could use to save others.

"I'm glad," Caspian said as he continued to wipe down the blaster.

"Hey!" I said as I noticed something. "Isn't this mine?"

Caspian just laughed and placed it out of my reach. "So, what did the good doctor have to say? You were gone for a while."

I rolled my eyes but continued with the change in topic. "He wanted to check up on me after hearing that I'd been injured on Vanthurium. Apparently, I've healed better than he anticipated. And then I asked about Adís..."

Everything in the room came to a halt. The sounds of the twins' tinkering ceased, Caspian's hand stilled on the blaster, and the weight of every eye in the room fell on me. I cringed as I anticipated how my next words would be received.

"...and he didn't know anything." Several people sighed and activities resumed. "I'm sorry," I said as I dropped my voice, "but I really tried. She wasn't sent to him, and he's been too preoccupied with other work to have heard anything."

Caspian reached over and took one of my hands. "It's okay. Thank you for asking him. Maybe now that he knows we're curious, he can do some digging around for us."

"Maybe," I hedged. Now I had to drop the bomb. "He's been working on something..."

"Working on what?" I had Caspian's full attention now as he shifted to face me. Even Lem put down her cleaning tools and watched me carefully.

"He's... well," I secretly hoped that Doctor Givray had already left the base so that he wouldn't have to face the of fury my squad. "Doctor Givray has been trying to... um, recreate the success he had with me?" I immediately tensed.

The bunkhouse had quieted slightly when I mentioned that the doctor was working on a project, but now it was completely silent. I felt extremely uncomfortable and could only meet Caspian's eyes, even though I knew that everyone's were on me.

Caspian's dark eyebrows were arched, and his mouth hung open just slightly. His jaw worked a few times, as if he was going to say something but changed his mind. He leaned back on his free hand but also released the hand that had been holding mine. The move stung, but I knew that the news I'd shared only added to whatever burden Caspian previously carried.

Raking his now-free hand through his hair, Caspian sighed and said, "Well... that's unexpected of him. I suppose seeing how well you've done has inspired him to try again." He paused. "Is he working alone?"

"Not entirely. The Master of Medicine put him up to the task, but from what he told me, Doctor Givray is the only one working on this." Thankfully. I was already worried enough about Doctor Givray understanding how I had been healed and changed. To have multiple doctors going about their work with that type of knowledge at their fingertips? I couldn't even imagine how that would impact the galaxy.

"The Master of Medicine?" Caspian's brow furrowed as he pieced the information together in his head. "That means the council is directly involved with, or at least monitoring, his work now."

"Yes," I said, feeling the nervousness from earlier return and pool in my stomach at the mention of the council. "They're watching him closely now in order to understand what he did to me. And Doctor Givray mentioned that if he didn't succeed soon… they might want to talk to me."

"They…" Caspian drifted off in thought, trying to understand what I'd just told him. It took a few moments, but I knew the instant he figured it out: his face paled and his eyes went wide as they slowly slid to meet my gaze. "They *would* want to talk to you," he said absently while nodding his head.

No doubt he was already coming up with scenarios for how he could whisk me away and protect me if the council ever came knocking. But would he really stand against the king's closest advisors — the group to which he had almost belonged — if it came down to it? Would he really pick me?

Suddenly a slight, light blue hand closed around mine and gave it a brief squeeze. "They won't have to come for you," Lem reassured me. "The doctor will figure it out, and if he doesn't, well…"

My chest tightened with emotion at her implication. She'd

stand with me too should the council come and demand to "examine" me.

I glanced around the room and caught several serious expressions on the faces of my nodding friends. To refuse the council could be considered treason, but my squad wouldn't let me go without a fight.

I hadn't been part of the Nova squad for long, and I still couldn't believe the bond that had formed between us. True, everyone else had been together for a while before I joined, but these moments – where everyone else showed just how much they cared about me – still took me by surprise.

I quickly blinked back the slightest prick of tears in my eyes. No need to get all weepy over friendship when there were bigger matters at hand. "I believe that he'll make a breakthrough. He's done this type of work for years, but he's feeling rushed now with the council breathing down his neck. Sooner or later, he'll make it work."

"But what happens then?" Ki'ran asked.

My head snapped up to look at him; I wasn't expecting his input since he was normally so quiet. Ki'ran was a protector, quite literally the Nova squad's muscle. So clearly, it would make sense that he was already imagining how he might have to protect us in this new scenario.

"I'm… not sure." It was better to be honest since I was also concerned with Doctor Givray's work. "Believe me, I voiced my concerns about this. I don't like the idea of him giving other people the strength and speed I have because… Well, who knows how they'll turn out?" All of a sudden, my concerns started spilling out. "I really think he got lucky with me – I didn't even *want* these abilities, and I tried for so long to hide them. And now, to think that someone could be gifted like this and then do who knows what…"

"Aliya." Caspian's voice broke me out of my terrified thoughts. "We're all thinking the same thing. There are major benefits and drawbacks to Doctor Givray's work, and yes, what you're describing is definitely the darkest option."

I dipped my head, feeling uncomfortable by the words that spilled out next. "He implied that I might have to 'help out' should one of his subjects abuse their abilities."

I'd fought Krech and cyborgs because they were evil, but I didn't want to be responsible for ending someone's life, especially when they thought that Doctor Givray was giving them a second chance.

"We'll be right there beside you," Caspian said as his hand closed around mine once more. I nodded my thanks as he returned his attention to cleaning my blaster. "So," he said with a chuckle to diffuse the tension in the room, "did you two discuss anything else?"

I couldn't resist laughing. "No, those were the only surprises he dumped on me." *Thankfully.*

We drifted off into a slightly awkward silence for a few moments. The only sounds were the swiping of cloth over already-clean blasters, the metallic *clicks* and *plinks* coming from the twins' work, and an occasional rustle from Bragdan as he tossed and turned in his bunk.

But after a while that feeling started to sink in again – the feeling that I was being forced to wait and wait for *something* that may or may not happen. I really wished King Locklyn would send us an update on whether or not he still wanted us to join his guards.

I tried to relax and enjoy the peacefulness that filled our bunkhouse. There was nowhere to rush off to, no crisis that we had to solve, but I still felt like I just *had* to be doing something. Sitting around right now just felt wrong.

Perhaps that was why Caspian was cleaning my blaster.

With a loud sigh, I turned and strode toward the door.

"Where are you going?" Caspian asked.

I hadn't even thought about my destination, but I was going to do something other than wait in the bunkhouse forever. "I don't know yet. Maybe I'll just take a walk," I replied as I faced him.

He tilted his head to the side and studied me for a moment, his blue eyes reading me far more than I would have liked at the moment. I didn't need him to see how worried I was about what Doctor Givray was doing. I didn't need him to see my anxiety over having to wait for the king's word. And I didn't need him to see just how uncomfortable I was starting to feel in the confines of this bunkhouse.

"Want another flying lesson?" he asked with a soft smile.

"I'd love one."

✳

"Harness?"

"Check."

"Power levels?"

"Full and holding steady."

"Passenger secured?"

"Not yet, since he's giving me orders instead of strapping in," I teased. Caspian joined in my laughter as he settled into the metal seat next to me.

After the first few days of boredom on the Protective Forces base, Caspian remembered that I didn't know how to pilot a cruiser or space ship. Thankfully, instead of handing me off to another instructor on the base, he'd taken it upon himself to teach me.

The controls for a cruiser were fairly easy: a palm scanner and passcode combination started the engines, a large red button just above the palm scanner initiated the vertical thrust off the ground, a two-handed control wheel directed the vessel once we were in the air, and a handle similar to a gearshift was responsible for our speed. Of course, there were a bunch of other controls and buttons whose use I couldn't fathom, but Caspian was just getting me used to the basics. For now.

This particular cruiser – which I had secretly dubbed the *Dragonfly* since its shape was reminiscent of the insects back on

Terra – held two passengers and was typically used to teach first-timers how to fly because it was smaller than other ships and easier to maneuver.

I was very glad that I didn't have an additional audience inside the ship with me because even though this was our fifth flying lesson, I was still extremely nervous. Caspian's seat was what he called the "alternate pilot's seat" since he could take control if something went wrong. So far, he hadn't been required to wrest the reins away from me.

"Ready when you are, captain," he joked as his harness clicked into place.

I let out a slow breath. The initial takeoff was my favorite part, but after that everything was up to me.

"Initiating launch," I said as I pushed the red button.

Gravity forced me down into my seat as the cruiser pushed off from the ground, yet I felt a weight leave my shoulders. The stress of waiting around on the base was wearing on us all, and more often than not, the Nova squad felt useless.

But in the air… I actually felt like I had a purpose. I was learning something new, something that was extremely useful here in the King's Galaxy since space travel was the only way to get around.

I knew that I wouldn't be able to get far without learning how to fly, and Caspian was a great teacher. His lessons were patient and methodical, although he liked to attribute my progress to me being a quick learner.

The initial thrust only took a few seconds, and then I was free to direct the *Dragonfly* wherever I wanted to go. Unfortunately, I still wasn't very knowledgeable about Callais' landscape.

"Where to?" I asked Caspian.

Our first three flights had been local – only cruising at a low altitude around the edges of the base. The last trip we took a few days ago was over the enormous forest to the south of the base. I hoped that our trip today would bring us somewhere new.

"Head northeast. You'll know where we're headed when you see it," he replied with a smile.

"Okay," I said as I gently eased the cruiser forward. As badly as I wanted to whip away from the Protective Forces base, it was a reckless move and could potentially be dangerous for other pilots entering or leaving the airfield.

"Good work," Caspian praised me as we flew out over the plain where Captain Sansish had once made me run.

The copse of trees that had served as the run's halfway point passed beneath us in an instant, but I continued to feel nostalgic for several minutes afterward.

How could I not? Somehow the entire base felt like something out of the distant past – a past life that an older version of myself had experienced. At least the second half of that thought was true. The older, confused, and angry Aliya had hated everything about this base and its occupants. It had been something to be afraid of, to resist.

I felt the cruiser wobble slightly as I lost my focus.

Instinctively, Caspian reached toward his set of controls. "Everything okay?"

"I'm fine. Sorry," I mumbled as embarrassment set my cheeks ablaze. I needed to focus. My mind was a mess today, and here I was, piloting a cruiser and responsible for not only my life but Caspian's as well.

Somehow that thought – worrying about Caspian's life – set me off.

I was suddenly back in the tunnels again. I could see the cyborg standing behind Caspian: a weak light reflecting off the metal spikes protruding from his head and the thin dagger that he held to Caspian's neck. The earthen smell of the tunnels filled my nose, and the interior of the cruiser began to feel too small.

We were thousands of feet up in the air, and there was nowhere for me to go. My chest felt tight, and my breathing accelerated. Trapped inside the terrifying memory my mind insisted on replaying, my focus on flying really slipped.

The cruiser dipped dangerously toward the ground, and gravity forced me back into my seat. Beside me, Caspian jumped into action and punched the button that would allow him to take over steering. Our descent immediately leveled out.

"Aliya, breathe. Just close your eyes and focus on your breathing." But I couldn't – I just *couldn't*. When I closed my eyes, all I saw was Caspian in danger and tunnels that seemed to stretch off into the darkness forever.

My hands were clenched around the useless wheel, but I

couldn't make them let go. "I need to get out," I squeaked.

"It's okay now. I've got us." His reassurances fell on deaf ears.

"Please land *now*," I begged him.

The cruiser banked toward the right and descended – but at a controlled rate this time. Caspian didn't speak, and I knew he was worried. None of our previous flights had produced this reaction, and he was probably trying to figure out what had happened.

I desperately tried to pull myself from the terrifying memories, but instead my thoughts shifted to the horrible dreams I'd had – the ones where I watched Caspian die at the hands of the cyborg because I couldn't move. What if I *hadn't* been quick enough to save him? Would the cyborg truly have killed us all, or would he have taken me as a prisoner for the Krech?

"Aliya!" Caspian's firm hand gripped my shoulder and shook me roughly. "Look at me."

Somehow, I managed to turn my head and meet his eyes. Caspian knelt on the ground beside my seat.

I didn't remember him landing.

We'd landed. The realization was like a breath of fresh air. Still feeling claustrophobic, I frantically fumbled with my harness until it snapped open, and I flew past Caspian in a blur. He tried to catch my arm, but I couldn't stay inside the cruiser for another moment.

Luckily the ramp was lowered, so I didn't need to wait to make my escape.

Still taking gasping breaths, I stumbled out of the cruiser and into the sunlight.

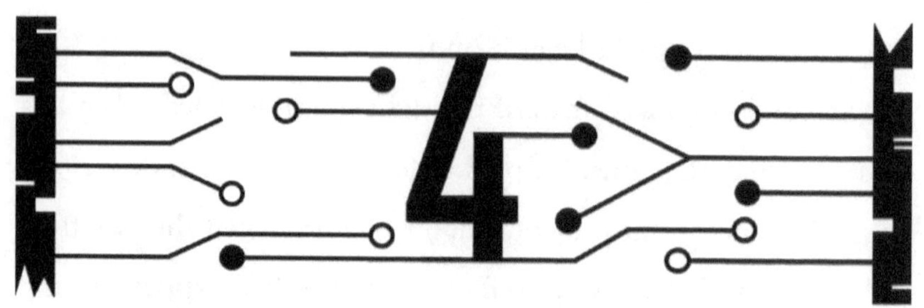

My breathing was ragged and my whole body shook as I lurched off the end of the walkway. Before I'd taken even a few steps onto the low green grass, my legs gave out from under me. My knees crashed into the ground, and my palms flew out to keep my face from smacking into the dirt.

Why was this happening to me? Sure, I'd taken a few hits in our battle under the palace, but nothing serious enough to give me any type of emotional trauma. Definitely not as bad as Bragdan had it. My previous flying lessons hadn't caused panic like this, so where had this come from?

Head spinning, I closed my eyes and furiously shook my head in an attempt to dispel the vertigo.

But that only made it worse.

We were told that most of you would be easy to kill. Once more the cyborg leered at me from my memories. *Except for you, darling.*

It was over. What I was seeing – remembering – wasn't real. Was it?

Drop your weapons and kneel. And this will all be over.

My fingers tore into the soft dirt I knelt upon. If it hurt, I couldn't tell because I was trapped inside my nightmare.

Don't, Caspian mouthed at me while the blade at his neck gleamed. The smell of blood and dirt surrounded me, and I couldn't breathe.

Not real, not real, not real. Why could I see this all so clearly? I couldn't see straight or take a deep breath, even as the memory-cyborg's knife began to move.

"Stop!" I shrieked, finally collapsing forward as my tears surged forth.

"Aliya!" And then Caspian was there, kneeling beside me. Two strong hands gripped my shoulders and lifted my limp body from the ground. For a moment they released me, and then Caspian held me to his chest as we knelt on the grass.

It was his gentle touch that caused me to fully shatter. Twice I'd saved Caspian and the rest of the Nova squad from enemies set on killing us. Twice in dire situations I'd been the one to come through with a miracle.

But now I was a mess, sobbing into the front of Caspian's gray Nova jacket. His arms were the only thing holding me up even though mine had snaked around his back.

He didn't say a word. Caspian offered no reassuring pats on

my back, nothing more than holding me in place against his chest.

I had no idea how much time passed until my tears stopped. Like a faucet suddenly run dry, one moment they were streaming down my face, and in the next they were gone. Shortly after, my heaving sobs abated as well.

The first thing I felt was monumental embarrassment. What would Caspian think of me? I'd held up so well during the last two weeks, oftentimes being the one to support Jorl or Ki'ran or Caspian when they were consumed by their own recollections of the battle. Would Caspian think that I was as damaged as Bragdan?

Would Caspian refuse to let me join him when he went to serve King Locklyn?

The question caused me to tense as fears of being separated from Caspian crept into my already overloaded mind.

He wouldn't. In fact, he had been the one to ask *me* if I would go. *We'd get to stay together*, he'd promised.

My breathing hitched again, and this time Caspian's hand began to slowly, gently rub my back. I wasn't going to fall apart a second time, so I closed my eyes and breathed in and out to the count of four.

When I finally felt like I could breathe normally, I opened my eyes and leaned back.

"I'm so sorry," I said as I met his eyes.

In his deep blue gaze I saw no anger, fear, or concern at my outburst. Instead all I saw was genuine concern.

"What happened?" he asked softly. Slowly his arms unwound

from behind me, and his hands trailed down my arms. When he reached my dirt-stained hands, he folded his fingers through mine.

"I felt… trapped," I said, struggling for words. "It was like we were in the tunnels all over again, and I was so scared." I broke our gaze and dipped my head toward the ground as chagrin stained my cheeks pink. My words barely explained the episode that I'd just had, but how could I really describe that the attack on Vanthurium still terrified me?

"What happened in the cruiser to make you feel trapped?"

I lifted my head, brow wrinkled in confusion. "I don't really know. It—" *It had been worrying about Caspian.* The fear of hurting Caspian after I'd made the cruiser wobble was what had set me off.

I blushed again. I couldn't exactly tell *that* to Caspian since I didn't exactly know what we were.

"Aliya, what was it? If it was something that I said or did, I'd like to prevent it from happening again."

Stars, he was blaming himself for upsetting me.

"No, it… it wasn't you." I had to explain it now so that this didn't add to the concerns already plaguing Caspian. "When the cruiser wobbled, I realized that I was being careless and that could hurt you."

Caspian shifted closer to me. "You were worried about me getting hurt?"

I started to see it again, the blade at his neck, but I banished the memory before it could fully form. "It made me think of the tunnels again. How small they were… and the small cruiser…" That was all I could say without drudging up the memory that lingered at the edge of my thoughts, threatening to overtake me once more.

We were both silent for a few moments. Even the forest around us had a pleasant quietness that didn't interrupt our moment.

I felt like I should apologize. Making the cruiser wobble once in the air wasn't a dangerous act, but having a meltdown while at the controls? *That* would have caused far more damage than the brief lapse in concentration. I was lucky that Caspian could take over.

Bolstering my courage, I opened my mouth to say sorry, but I didn't get the chance.

"My first mission with the Protective Forces was to retrieve stolen cargo. Rogues, likely from Charra or some other outpost in the Outer Rim, took a shipment of weapons that were being sent from Xenda to Callais." Caspian was telling me a story? I recognized the planet he spoke of, Xenda. Located on the innermost edge of the Outer Rim, the best technicians in the King's Galaxy lived there to develop weapons and ships.

"Fortunately," Caspian continued, "the Xendans had thought to put a tracker within their shipment and located the goods on a large asteroid called Muldon. Very few of us within the squad were familiar with Muldon, so we had to approach it with extreme caution."

He looked off into the woods, and his expression darkened. "We came to realize that Muldon was a cavernous orb, and the thieves had planned very well to prevent anyone from retrieving their stolen goods. Once within a tunnel system, there was no light, and our torches weren't bright enough to help us see the nightmarish traps they'd set for us." Caspian paused for breath and, releasing my left hand, pulled down the neck of his white shirt to reveal thick, ragged scars running across his collarbone until they disappeared under his shirt. "The floor beneath an archway had been rigged to collapse, and I fell through it into a net of sorts made from barbed wires. My squad had to cut the net apart just to pull me back up, and then to remove it…" He shuddered. "Twelve of us went into that booby-trapped hell. Six of us made it out with the stolen weapons, but only two of my squad members were unscathed. What should have been an easy retrieval mission turned into a nightmare with serious casualties."

For a few moments I couldn't say a word. Compared to Vanthurium, Caspian had *literally* gone through hell.

"I'm so sorry," I whispered. He still hadn't looped his fingers back through mine. Instead, his hand rested on his thigh while he knelt in front of me. I ached to pull him into an embrace, but I wasn't sure if he wanted my touch.

"My point is that I understand because but I've been there too. It took *months* for me to feel relaxed in the darkness again. Every time we had a night shift, I became paralyzed with fear that I was going to fall into another trap. The first few times it happened my squad leader just left me in our bunkhouse. And," his jaw clenched as irritation flashed across his face, "I was nervous to walk through doors for a while too."

"You didn't seem nervous in the tunnels on Vanthurium." Had those unnerved Caspian as well? Or was he well past his fears?

"Those very nearly put me into a full panic," he admitted. "The look, the smell – it was Muldon all over again. Even though the idea of heading down into those tunnels scared me, I had to go because it's my job to keep the Nova squad safe."

"I couldn't tell. That you were scared, that is."

"I've had years to conquer my fears," he replied with a small laugh. "But – getting back to you – you were scared of me getting hurt?"

Embarrassed again, I struggled to find the right words. "I was so scared that you would die because I didn't know if I could get those shots off in time. Everyone was watching, and if I had been the one to let you die… You mean so much to me – uh, I mean the squad."

My cheeks flamed at my slip up. He already knew this – we'd shared our feelings in the tunnels just before we all discovered the wrecked escape cruiser – but reminding him that I feared for his well-being because of how much I *cared* was like baring my heart all over again.

"That day still haunts me too, Aliya." I looked up to find raw emotion smoldering in his eyes, and I felt butterflies erupt in my stomach. "With every fiber of my being I wish it hadn't come down to that. But at the same time… I'm glad you were the one in the position to save me. I was scared, but I also knew that you would make the shot. I just knew it."

My tears started again, but this time they weren't a flood. With his life on the line, Caspian had trusted *me* to save him. That touched me more than he probably realized.

"I'm so sorry that your first missions with the Forces have been so dangerous. This should have been a time of peace, but somehow we've been present for the worst events in the past century." His free hand came up under my chin and lifted my face toward his. "You weren't a soldier on Terra, and somehow your life has been in grave danger twice in the past three months. I worry about you and how you're holding up," he whispered as he leaned forward to touch his forehead to mine.

"You're right," I whispered back. "I can't even begin to comprehend all of this. I've been trying ever since I woke up in Doctor Givray's healing facility, but honestly… I still feel so lost. Planets with life, spaceships, being in combat… it's nothing I *ever* thought I'd experience."

"Don't try to hold it all in," Caspian said. "I'm here. We're all here to support each other."

"How did you do it?"

"Do what?" Caspian pulled back to look at me.

"To overcome your fear of the dark." He'd admitted that the tunnels on Vanthurium had unsettled him, but he hadn't been paralyzed by fear the way I was in the cruiser.

A small smile lifted the corner of his mouth. "I started small. I got a member of my squad to take short walks with me at night. Eventually he helped me get to the point where we would walk through the woods all night, and I wouldn't be in a panic to return to our bunkhouse."

"Who helped you?"

Caspian's smile grew. "Captain Sansish."

That explained the camaraderie the two displayed when Caspian had come to watch my trainee squad. They had a powerful history connecting them.

"If you want," Caspian said as he cupped my right hand in both of his, "I can be there for you. It might take weeks, or months, or even longer than that. But if you're willing, I'll walk this path with you."

I didn't want Caspian to be in danger ever again. He'd almost willingly sacrificed himself on Charra so that we could escape, and because I hadn't wanted to lose him, I'd learned how to… well, to be me. To use my abilities to save those around me. And then on Vanthurium… Well, I realized that I would never be okay without him.

Unfortunately, our occupation required us to handle dangerous situations. The Krech were likely on the rise, and who knew what would happen when we went to protect the king. But if I was able to conquer this fear, this worry over losing the man I couldn't live without, I knew that I would be able to help when danger arose.

He trusted me to save his life on Vanthurium, and right now, I trusted him to help me piece mine back together.

Just like the times before, Caspian and I would get through this. Together.

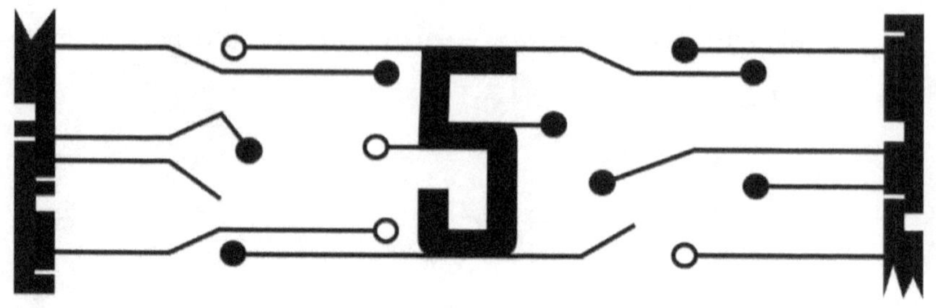

I laid on my back, sheets bunched at the foot of my bed. Just the thought of them wrapping around my body made me sweat. I wore a white tank top provided as part of the base's uniforms, and I'd rolled my black pants up as high as they could go.

We had yet another day of languishing in the bunkhouse, and today's heat felt more miserable than yesterday.

I wasn't the only one wearing as little as possible. We'd all discarded our jackets and boots, rolling our standard issue pants up as high as they would go. Lem had sheared her white tank top in half just above her stomach, and I was surprised she wasn't embarrassed to show off the dark blue scar she'd earned on Charra.

Somehow the temperature didn't seem to bother Gunther and Gráinne. They both wore t-shirts but kept their pant legs unrolled. I envied them as they incessantly tinkered away on the workbench.

Jorl sat on the bed beside Lem's, half paying attention to the blaster he was reassembling and half paying attention to the female sitting a few feet away from him.

Ki'ran had actually cut his pants into shorts and sat at the foot of his bed plucking at the loose ends of the fabric.

Like the other males in the bunkhouse – minus Gunther – Ki'ran was shirtless. It was… slightly distracting to have so many shirtless soldiers sharing the same bunkhouse.

Caspian, lying on the floor beside his bunk, was tapping away on a dataport. Even if I turned my head in his direction, I couldn't see him, but I occasionally heard voices from what I guessed was a news stream. He'd listen to one report for a while, and then he would switch to another.

I would have asked what he was hoping to hear, but I was too hot to do much more than lie on my bunk.

But every now and then I would sit up to check on Bragdan. Today seemed like one of his less responsive days, and I needed to make sure he wasn't becoming dehydrated or weak from hunger.

Something about the battle had seriously shaken Bragdan, and he had only gotten worse after getting back to the base. He'd go silent or stare blankly into space for hours at a time. And he would completely lose it if someone approached with a visible weapon. Ki'ran had completely hidden his sword because Bragdan had screamed after seeing it.

Caspian had gotten Protective Forces specialists to come look at him, since his shock was far worse than any of ours, but they said that the trauma he'd suffered – most likely caused by nearly dying at the end of a cyborg's blade – would take time to heal.

As a squad, we decided that we would all take turns looking after him. We brought Bragdan food when we couldn't get him out of the bunkhouse, helped him dress when he woke up in one of his immobile phases, and checked him regularly to make sure he wasn't coming down with some other illness.

I felt horrible for him.

I'd saved his life, but now… it was as if he wasn't even here. None of us knew what to do other than help him with day-to-day tasks and give him space.

At the moment, he was laying on his back with his eyes closed. I watched his chest rise and fall a few times before determining that he was still all right, and then I laid back down.

Even with this heat, I just wished that there was something to *do.*

"…several reports of missing people. Horval Bazlit, along with his trading ship, the Venture, *has been reported missing for five days. Authorities were notified when his scheduled shipment failed to arrive on time."* The voice from Caspian's dataport sounded tired, like she'd given this report many times.

"What was that?" I asked, sitting upright.

"There's been an increase in missing people and ships in the Outer Rim," Caspian said from the floor. "Entire crews just vanishing without a trace. That was the latest disappearance."

"I thought King Locklyn had restricted travel in the Outer Rim."

"For civilians without adequate guards. All major trade routes are still operational since the increase in soldiers and armies requires more weapons and ships." Caspian sat up, and I could see that the haunted look had returned to his eyes. "This report bothers me, though. Bazlit was a former military captain who was transferred into trade years ago. If he was attacked, he was more than capable of protecting himself…"

"Unless the attacker was someone he wasn't prepared for," I murmured.

Caspian turned to me and gave a grim nod let me know that we suspected the same source.

The Krech.

None had been seen since the encounter on Charra, but the rising number of disturbances in the Outer Rim made the Krech a likely suspect. Their home planet was located somewhere – unfortunately no one knew exactly where – out in Kääs, which placed the Outer Rim right in their backyard. Their metaphorical space backyard.

"Why doesn't the king send more troops to patrol the Rim?" Surely a large military presence would deter any further attacks.

Caspian shook his head. "Then we'd be spread far too thin inside the King's Galaxy. If even one Krech ship got past our defenses, it would take too long to recall a large enough force to defend whomever they attacked. Even with all the new soldiers we're training here… it wouldn't be enough."

"They're that bad?" A few times in the last few weeks I'd tried to find information on the last major battle with the Krech. You'd think that such a technologically advanced galaxy would have some kind of record of the event. Instead, I'd found a whole lot of nothing.

Right after the skirmish on Charra, Jorl had given me a short history on the war a hundred years ago. He said that major trade lines had been disrupted, several planets along the Outer Rim had been attacked, and that the battle had been the bloodiest that the King's Galaxy had ever seen.

Unfortunately, those scant details were more than I had uncovered during my research. Whatever had happened, it seemed like the chaos had been so widespread that no one was able to record the events that had occurred, or historians were trying to erase the war from public records.

"Yes, they're that bad," Caspian said in a tone indicating that he, too, didn't wish to speak of the event.

How was I ever supposed to understand what we were up against if no one had information on the last major event involving the Krech?

I was about to prod for more details when a knock sounded at the door.

Every pair of eyes in our bunkhouse fixed on Caspian as he lurched to his feet and padded over to the door. A wave of heat spilled into the room as Caspian pulled it open, and in strode General Vinculus.

"General," Caspian curtly greeted our visitor and stepped to the side.

I moved to stand and salute the general, and I could hear the rest of the Nova squad doing the same.

"At ease," the general snapped, not that any of us were close to properly saluting him. He surveyed the room with a grimace, as if we were the unruliest squad on the base.

He stood in his long, gray general's coat. A few beads of sweat rolled down his temple and disappeared underneath the high collar. Even on the hottest of days, General Vinculus was stringent about his attire, and I didn't feel bad for how uncomfortable that must have felt.

I still hated him. In fact, I hated General Vinculus more now because of the role he'd played in the Battle of Vanthurium.

Honestly, I was surprised that he still held his position after ignoring our initial call for aid. I couldn't fathom why King Locklyn still saw this male as fit to lead the Protective Forces.

I wasn't the only one who still held a grudge against the general. Caspian had a calm expression plastered on his face, but I watched his hands ball into fists right before he shoved them into his pockets.

"How can we help you?" Caspian asked in a pleasant tone.

"I have word from King Locklyn," General Vinculus replied, turning to look at Caspian. "For some unfathomable reason, he's still extending the offer for your squad to join his personal guards. He'll be here tomorrow at noon to collect anyone who wishes to go." Message delivered, General Vinculus began to leave the bunkhouse.

"Anyone who wishes to go? I thought he wanted us all."

General Vinculus replied without turning around. "Yes, captain, anyone. The king doesn't require you all to join him, as he knows you've been through an… ordeal." Heavy scorn laced that last word.

"I see. Thank you, general." Caspian's voice had gone flat. "May I ask you a few questions?"

The general sighed and turned back to face Caspian. "What, captain?"

"Adís, sir. Do you have any update on her? We haven't heard anything…" Caspian's voice trailed off.

"Of course. I thought you would have heard by now." He taunted with a smirk. "Your first mate is already with King Locklyn."

"What?" I gasped. "Why hasn't she reached out to us yet?"

"How would *I* know?" the general snapped.

I hesitated, embarrassed by my outburst, but I was quickly becoming annoyed with General Vinculus' treatment of this squad. We defeated Krech on Charra and saved the rulers of Vanthurium. We deserved to be treated with *some* respect.

Beside the door, Caspian was taut, like a bowstring about to be loosed. He wasn't happy with the general's attitude either, but

I knew that Caspian couldn't do anything about it.

He caught my eye and mouthed, *Stand down.*

I couldn't let General Vinculus get the best of me, as badly as I wanted to snap back at him. *You should know everything, general. Just like how you* knew *what the best course of action on Vanthurium was, right?* I couldn't even imagine how much trouble I'd cause if I said that to him. No, I'd save this battle for another day.

"I understand, general. I'll take that up with Adís when we see her again," Caspian cut in. "One last thing… The Krech prisoner. Have you gotten anything out of it?"

I almost forgot that we'd taken a Krech captive on Charra. Part of me was surprised other Krech hadn't come for their companion, and the other part was curious *how* exactly he was being held here. During my time with Captain Sansish, I was never told that we had prison cells.

General Vinculus stiffened and clenched his jaw. "It's been rather… difficult to work with," he said slowly. "Refuses to speak unless it's throwing curses and threats at us. Since it isn't being helpful, we're not sure how much longer it will last." He finished with an indifferent sniff.

They were going to kill it? Surely Caspian wouldn't stand for that. Would he?

I knew that Krech were dangerous and potentially evil beings, but to kill one who was already a prisoner? That didn't exactly seem right to me.

"Thank you for the information and your time," Caspian said.

Without another word, General Vinculus marched out of the bunkhouse, leaving the door wide open.

That's it? I wanted to snap at Caspian. *You're not going to at least try and get more information out of him? He barely answered your questions!*

But it seemed like Caspian didn't want to deal with the general's partial answers any longer because he shut the door and stood facing it for several seconds in utter silence.

There was a good deal to take in: not all of us were required to serve King Locklyn, Adís was alive and already at the palace, and the Krech prisoner was still on the base.

I wasn't worried about the captive – if he was being uncooperative, there was nothing I could do to change that because I wasn't an interrogator. But Adís and the future of this squad now loomed in my mind. Why hadn't she reached out to us? And would we all serve the king, or would some of us go different ways?

When Caspian finally spoke, his voice was soft, as if he was in shock. "It seems like we all have a decision to make."

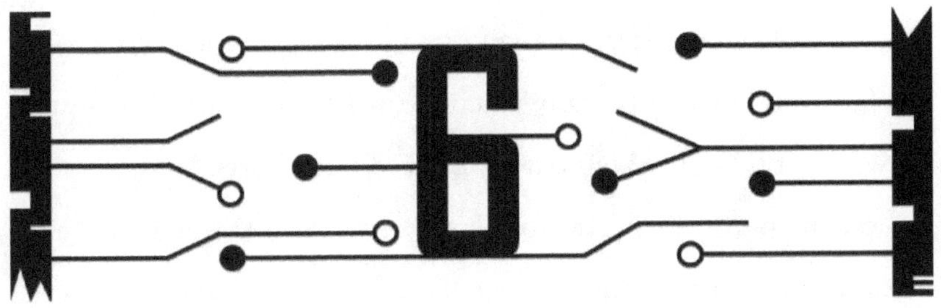

No one immediately responded to Caspian's statement. I think we were all thoroughly shell-shocked from General Vinculus' visit.

He'd been a jerk, but at least the general was consistent in his behavior toward us. I just wished that he had been more forthcoming with the answers to Caspian's questions.

At least his visit had been helpful for me because now I really knew what I was doing next: accept the king's offer. I didn't know what he expected from his guards or how much I'd fit in since I was so inexperienced with the workings of the King's Galaxy, but since the offer was open, I was going to take it.

Because I would not serve under General Vinculus any longer.

From the start, he had been a rude and condescending individual, and in regard to his ability to command the squads on this base, I felt his "skills" were nothing but annoyed bravado.

He'd made a grave mistake by denying us backup on Vanthurium, a decision that had cost the lives of dozens of Vanthuri soldiers and the well-being of more than one Nova squad member.

He didn't care, especially when it came to this particular squad.

At least King Locklyn readily praised our efforts. He had asked for our help and respected us. In my mind, he seemed like a far more rational leader than the general, so it made more sense to work for him.

And then, of course, I would be able to see Adís. I'd be able to figure out why she was staying away from us, her family, and hopefully make things right.

"I think," Caspian said, interrupting my thoughts, "that we should take the rest of the day to think through the king's offer, now that we know everyone isn't required to move to the palace. I… Well, you know how I feel. Should you wish to go a different direction, know that you'll have my full support." He slowly walked over to his bunk, pulled on a white t-shirt, and left the bunkhouse.

The silence that descended after Caspian's exit made me uncomfortable. There were serious decisions to make, but I wasn't sure if anyone felt safe voicing their opinions just yet. After a few minutes of waiting for someone else to speak up, I finally decided to be the first one.

"I'm going to accept the king's offer."

Lem dropped her gaze to the floor as she nodded. "As you should."

"What do you mean?" I asked, crossing my arms over my chest.

"I don't mean it in a rude way!" She genuinely looked concerned that she had offended me. "I mean that… well, staying here is probably the last thing that you want to do, right?"

"Yeah, I don't want to be around General Vinculus any longer than I have to be." I didn't feel bad admitting that out loud. Pretty much everyone knew my story and how I felt about the general. "But I also have nowhere else to go."

She looked up at me, and I was shocked to see fire in her eyes. "You have *everywhere* to go, Aliya," she said with immense passion. "There's an entire galaxy for you to explore. You don't have to be in the Protective Forces any longer if you don't want to!"

She was right. I hadn't even seen that as an option until it came from her lips.

I could be *free*. I could fly a cruiser now – Caspian said that upgrading to a ship wasn't that much more difficult, especially if I had a full crew – so I could travel the planets of the King's Galaxy until I found somewhere I wanted to settle.

It wasn't that hard to imagine. Days spent discovering new people and places, learning about the galaxy, and finding a place that finally felt like home sounded wonderful.

But it was also the wrong future to imagine.

"You're right," I replied, "but I can't do that. The things I can do… I'm the only one who can do them, and it would be wrong to run off—"

"But you're *not* running off!" Lem cut in. "You'd be living your life, exploring new possibilities now that you've been given a chance to live on your own terms. I'm sure you could even find a smuggler who would get you back to Terra if you wanted!"

"That still doesn't make it right. You know what the cyborg told me. The Krech *warned* them about what I can do! They knew who I was and expected to see me on Vanthurium. If they attack again and I'm not there…" I shuddered imagining the amount of destruction that another attack from cyborgs could cause. "I need to remain a soldier. I hated it when I first joined the Forces, but that's because I didn't understand who I was. Now, after learning what I can actually do to help, I can't imagine doing anything else."

"Aliya is right," Ki'ran said. "She has no reason to be elsewhere, and she's a good soldier. That is why I will be accepting the king's offer as well."

We shared a brief nod. I was glad that he had backed me up and to know that he was coming with me. If Caspian was the heart and soul of the Nova squad, Ki'ran was the armor that kept us safe.

Lem stood and crossed the room to where I lingered beside my bunk. Awkwardly, she thrust out her hand, waiting for me to take it. "Then I wish you both luck because I'm not going."

I was so shocked that I didn't shake her hand. "*What?* Lem, why?"

She scowled at me questions and thrust her hand into the pocket of her cargo pants. "You feel like you don't have anywhere else to be, but… well, I do." She glanced over her shoulder to where Jorl lounged on his bunk. He was the picture of relaxation with his arms folded behind his head, but his eyes were locked on Lem. "I need to go back home. Lord Galven and Lady Kalina need my help reinforcing their lands, and even though I left Vanthurium under less than great circumstances…" She turned away from Jorl and stared at the floor, her blush deepening to violet.

"I get it." Lem looked back at me, gratitude showing on her face. She had a duty to help her home, her people. She knew that she belonged with the Vanthuri during this time of recovery, and I respected her for making that tough decision.

Even if it took her away from us.

"I wish you and the Vanthuri luck," I said, holding my hand out to her.

Tentatively, she accepted the handshake. "Thank you."

"When do you leave?"

"Hopefully tomorrow, since some of you will be leaving then too." Lem turned to head back to her bunk. *This might be the last time you get to talk to her*, I realized.

"Wait, Lem," I called out. She stilled and turned halfway to face me. "Why *did* you leave Vanthurium in the first place?" I knew she had a father and a few brothers on Vanthurium, but I'd never heard why she left them for the Protective Forces.

"Oh." She seemed genuinely surprised at my question and took a few moments before replying. "They're all royal soldiers — it's almost a tradition at this point. And I… I didn't want to follow in their footsteps. I didn't want to stay on Vanthurium forever."

"So, you went to be a soldier elsewhere?" I asked with a laugh.

She smiled. "I guess I did. And now I'm going back to make things right."

That reminded me. Caspian had probably been to the palace at some point when he was being groomed for the council, and he hadn't returned after Leila's death. Would he be okay returning after all these years?

I really didn't want to head outside into the heat, but I knew that I should find Caspian to see if he was okay.

It was downright *awful* to have my pant legs rolled down in addition to wearing boots and socks. At least I could mostly walk in the shade of the other bunkhouses and buildings as I sought out Caspian.

After a few passes between the bunkhouses, I stopped and leaned against the wall of the mess hall, debating where I should search next. Caspian hadn't been in any of the five sparring buildings, he wasn't in the mess hall, and I knew that he wouldn't be on any of the training grounds.

I wasn't above marching up and down every row of bunkhouses, peeking into each one and asking after Caspian, but that also meant more time spent traipsing around outdoors.

Where would he have gone?

I took a left around the side of the mess hall and headed to the airfield. Maybe Caspian borrowed a cruiser for a quick trip.

Just as I left the shade of the building, cringing as the sunlight beat directly on my bare skin, movement in the tree line to the right of the field caught my eye. It was Caspian, pacing around a tree just beyond the forest's edge.

I adjusted my course and strolled toward him. Whatever he was contemplating, he was deep into it because he didn't notice my approach.

"Caspian?" I called out as I neared his tree.

He ground to a stop and looked toward me in surprise. His black hair was matted in sweaty clumps that clung to his forehead, and his white shirt was damp. For a moment I was surprised to see him barefoot, and then I realized that he'd been barefoot in our bunkhouse but hadn't put shoes on before leaving. Even the bottoms of his pants were still rolled up around his calves.

Caspian was a mess. In addition to the sweaty hair and clothing he just looked… wild? That wasn't quite the right word, but there was a panicked look in his eyes that made it seem like he wanted to bolt off into the forest.

"Aliya. What are you doing out here?" He hurriedly began to wipe drops of sweat off his forehead and flushed cheeks.

"I came to check on you. You pretty much rushed out on everyone…"

"Oh." He glanced away, embarrassed, and rubbed the back of his neck with one hand. "I guess I shouldn't have… Are they okay?"

"I'm not fully sure," I admitted. "I think a few of us already knew what we were going to do, but this came as a surprise to everyone because we thought we were all expected to transfer over to King Locklyn's guards."

"I thought so, too," Caspian mumbled as he turned for another lap around his tree.

Unsure what to say next, I sat at the base of the tree, opposite Caspian, and stretched my legs out. Since there wasn't anyone outside besides me and him, I decided to roll my pant legs up again too.

The grass wasn't very long, and it made my exposed calves itch. Despite having wider blades and being a darker shade of green, the grass evoked memories from Terra. The smell of a fresh-cut lawn. Kicking a soccer ball across a verdant backyard.

These were much more pleasant memories of home than I usually found myself remembering, and for a few moments I allowed myself to get lost in them while I waited.

One minute bled into two, and then a rustle alerted me to Caspian circling to my side of the tree. He leaned heavily against its side and then used it as a support as he slid down to the ground.

Despite the temperature, Caspian sat with his right leg barely an inch away from my left. I could feel the heat radiating off his body and wished I'd thought to bring him some water. Drops of sweat glistened on his arms, and his hair was completely saturated with sweat, now that I was close enough to really see it.

He tipped his head back and closed his eyes, exhaling deeply through his nose.

Even in this stressed and sweaty state Caspian was attractive. His dark hair and his bright eyes, the faded scars that were sprinkled on his face and arms… Everything about his appearance made him seem strong, in charge, or at least someone who commanded attention.

I hated seeing him this distressed, and at this moment, I had no idea how to help him.

"I probably shouldn't have left like that, right?" he asked.

"Well…" For a moment I scrambled for the right thing to say. I didn't want to upset him further, but in the end, honesty won. "Probably not. You *are* still our captain."

He was silent. His right hand, resting atop his leg, brushed absently at the material of his pants. *What are you thinking, Caspian?*

When he finally spoke, it was in a whisper, and he kept his eyes closed. "I did everything I could to keep them safe and together. It was all I wanted…" Caspian stopped and swallowed, much louder than his voice had been. "And now I'll lose them all."

"Everyone isn't leaving, Caspian."

Somehow, that seemed to surprise him. His eyes snapped open, and he turned toward me. "They're not?"

"Of course not! I'm going with you, and so is Ki'ran…" I stopped as his jaw dropped slightly. "What?"

"You're coming? Really?"

Why was this such a surprise to him? Like I'd explained to Lem, I might not have initially joined the Protective Forces wanting to be a soldier, but I saw the reason I should remain one now. I had a duty to protect others because *I could.*

But what I hadn't mentioned to Lem was how I wanted to stay near Caspian. He was a kind and genuine person, and I'd developed some serious feelings for him.

I didn't want to be that silly, dependent girl who gave her heart away to a man she barely knew, and part of me worried that my feelings were unfounded. That he'd simply been the first person to care that I wasn't just a super-soldier, and I was misinterpreting his kindness. Or, another part of me argued, that he was the first and easiest person to latch on to in my new and vastly expanded universe.

But neither of those were right. This wasn't just blind puppy-love. He was honest and cared not just for me, but for the rest of the Nova squad. He'd turned down a role on the king's council in order to directly protect others throughout the King's Galaxy. There was so much more to my captain than being a good leader and dutiful soldier.

I'd seen him at his worst – drunk and disheveled after he'd destroyed his room aboard the *Starfire* – and didn't think any less of him for it. In fact, seeing how determined he was to protect others from suffering a loss like the one where he'd lost his parents and Leila proved how much Caspian cared for others.

And twice now Caspian and I had almost had… something, some kind of tense moment between us, so unless I was gravely mistaken, he had feelings for me too.

But this wasn't the time for that kind of heart-to-heart.

"Really. I'm coming with you to help protect King Locklyn," I told him with a smile.

Some of Caspian's distress faded; his shoulders lost their tension, and his hand stopped tracing random patterns on his leg. With a small smile, Caspian leaned his head against the tree once more. *Was he worried about losing everyone or just me?*

He stared up at the branches above our heads, that small smile lingering on his full lips. "I'm glad. I was worried that you'd want to go elsewhere now that you were free."

"I have a duty to protect others," I replied with a shrug. "There's nowhere better for me to be if I want to uphold that duty."

"Good," he breathed as his eyes drifted shut. "Then perhaps you'll want to accompany me on a quick trip tonight."

I cocked my head to the side. "Where?"

"To see that Krech. There are questions I want to ask it."

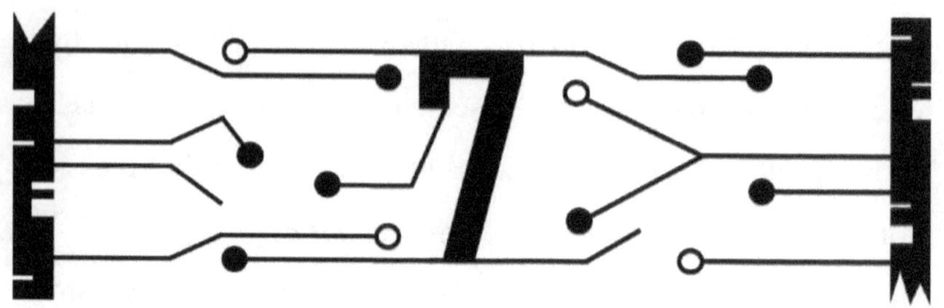

It was very late when I heard Caspian rising from his bed.

After Caspian had mentioned his desire to see the Krech, he'd outlined a brief plan – really, nothing more than telling me we'd have to sneak out later tonight and that he knew where to go – before we returned to the bunkhouse.

Most of the squad had dispersed, so there were no awkward confrontations about who would be going to serve King Locklyn in the morning. It seemed like we'd find out right before the royal escort arrived.

Around us were the deep breaths and snores of sleep. Innocent sleep, without a hint of knowledge that Caspian and I could potentially get into a ton of trouble tonight.

Before Caspian could nudge me awake, I sat up and slipped on my boots, lacing them slowly so that I wouldn't wake my other squad members. Caspian tugged a clean, white t-shirt over his head, and I glimpsed some of the ragged scars he'd earned on Muldon.

I actually wished that I'd retained scars from my car accident. At first, I'd been horrified that I'd come out of the crash without a single mark to show for it. How could I believe that it had actually been real if I didn't have proof?

Then, after joining the Protective Forces, I was glad I didn't have any distinguishing marks. It had helped me lay low once people stopped expecting me to perform some amazing feat. Perhaps it was because they, too, didn't believe that I'd been changed.

At least I had two scars now – ones that proved I'd been through the mess on Vanthurium.

I absently brushed at the scar on my shoulder, invisible under my shirt. I'd survived Vanthurium, and I could survive anything else that came our way.

Like visiting the Krech tonight.

In my mind, this plan had three phases: sneak out of the bunkhouse, locate and get into the prison cells, and then sneak back into the bunkhouse. Questioning the Krech was just a bonus if all of our sneaking went well and it was still alive.

I had no idea how much trouble we could get in if we were caught. Clearly, this wasn't allowed since we had to be secretive getting to and from the cells. General Vinculus hadn't sought out any member of Nova when he started questioning the Krech, and absent invitation made it seem like the prisoner was supposed to be a secret.

That made me deeply concerned. Prisoners who "went missing" on Terra rarely fared well, and I had a feeling that this prisoner – especially being from the race responsible for starting the last galactic war – was going through hell.

With painstaking slowness, Caspian turned the doorknob and quietly eased the door open. I breathed a small sigh of relief. On some days the hinges really squealed, but it seemed that today wasn't one of those days.

On silent feet, Caspian and I slipped out of the bunkhouse.

Sometime after the sun had set, clouds had rolled in, throwing the entire base into near-pitch darkness. Bunkhouses and other buildings didn't have an outdoor light, but in his planning, Caspian mentioned that the patrolling guards would have some sort of light with them.

"Where are we headed?" I whispered.

"Southern edge, near the shooting range," he replied, brushing past my arm as he took the lead. "Just look casual. You're with me, so at most, anyone we run into will have questions for me. You're just following my orders."

"Okay."

We wound around the side of our bunkhouse and headed for the shooting range. Several times as we passed windows, I had to remind myself not to crouch. I didn't want to be seen and have an alarm raised, but being caught crouching would raise suspicion.

We passed five bunkhouses before Caspian held a hand up. "Wait," he breathed.

I stood like a statue, hidden in the shadow of the bunkhouse on my left, as a patrol of three guards approached in the alley across from us.

I retreated around the front of the bunkhouse with Caspian, sticking to the shadows. He lounged against the wall, the picture of nonchalance. I tried my best to look relaxed, but judging from the smirk on Caspian's face, I failed to appear calm.

The guards' footsteps crunched on the gravel path, and the alley gradually became brighter as they approached. They walked in formation – one in the front with the light while the other two trailed slightly behind – and didn't speak a word. I was curious what squad they were from, but I couldn't get a good look at the symbols on their jackets without being seen.

The light didn't come from a lantern, as I'd expected. Instead it was some type of small white orb that the lead guard held in his hand. At the intersection, they turned left and continued on their patrol, oblivious to the fact that Caspian and I lurked in the shadows.

Caspian waited until their footsteps faded before edging back around the side of the building and continuing forward.

My heart hammered inside my chest. *That was too close.* "How far are we from the cells?" I whispered.

Without breaking stride Caspian answered, "Just beyond the last bunkhouse."

Thank goodness. Hopefully we wouldn't cross paths with any other roaming patrols.

We didn't encounter another soul as we strode past the two remaining bunkhouses, and that struck me as odd. If we were so close to the prison cells, shouldn't there have been more security? Where was this place anyway? Because just beyond the last bunkhouse was… nothing.

The lands to the south of the base revealed nothing but rolling hills, spotted here and there by a solitary tree. They weren't even tall hills – no, these were the kind that, in daylight, would look like an undulating sea of grass.

In the dark, however, the overall effect was creepy. I felt that at any moment a guard could come charging around a hill and see us.

I couldn't see a single building that might secretly house prisoners, but I did see two guards doing a slow patrol behind the hill directly in front of us.

"Caspian, where—"

Still facing forward, he held up a hand to quiet me. With a flick of his wrist he motioned me forward, and we continued out into the rolling hills.

Caspian circled to the right of the small hill and came face to face with two guards. Dressed in black pants and jackets, they blended into the night very well even as they raised blasters at us.

I immediately tensed, preparing for shouting or a fight, but Caspian actually *sighed.* "Well, well. Look who it is."

"Captain Caspian!" the one closest to us said as he snapped into a rigid salute.

The male was slightly shorter than Caspian but far more sturdily built. His brown skin was a dark enough shade that it very nearly matched his uniform, but his white hair – done up in a bun – stood in stark contrast. A long blaster was clipped to his left hip, and he slid the other into its holster as he and Caspian clasped hands.

I had never seen him before, and indeed, he'd never seen me either as he gave me a look that landed somewhere between curiosity and distrust.

"She's with me," Caspian said.

"Obviously," the guard said with a roll of his yellow-gold eyes. "What are you doing here? You know no one is allowed in this area."

"Roth," Caspian addressed the guard as he stepped closer and folded his hands behind his back, "I'm leaving the base tomorrow. I don't know when I'll be returning, and there are questions I need answered."

Roth turned to his partner, a long-limbed Schlee male with red locks that hung down to his shoulders, and said, "Take a lap."

Without a word the second guard complied, loping off further south among the hills.

I shifted uncomfortably as I stood in the warm evening air. Was the Schlee guard being sent off to retrieve reinforcements? Why hadn't Caspian been mad at Roth's disrespectful eye roll?

Once the Schlee was out of earshot, Roth leaned toward Caspian and whispered, "You know I have orders not to let *anyone* in. Especially nosy, know-it-all captains such as yourself." Then Roth chuckled.

"Is that actually how he described me?" Caspian replied with quiet laughter of his own.

"Honestly, that's not the worst he's said about you." They laughed harder.

My hand shot into the air. "Excuse me? I have a lot of questions about what's happening here."

Caspian took a step back from Roth and gestured toward the guard. "Aliya, this is Captain Roth Kumryn. We both started in the Forces around the same time—"

"Unfortunately, soldier extraordinaire over here rose through the ranks well before I did," Roth finished for Caspian. "We… uh, go back a bit." Roth gave Caspian a questioning glance, and Caspian nodded.

"Roth was part of the team that pulled me and my remaining crew off Muldon."

Ah. Roth probably hadn't been sure if Caspian had shared that part of his past with me. "I see."

"Roth knows how much of a jerk Vinculus can be." Caspian paused as Roth scoffed and used a few choice words to describe the general. "And somehow after all that, he *still* ended up as part of the general's extended guard."

Roth shrugged. "It pays well."

"And it seems like Vinculus warned the guards that I might try to come visit the cells, given how I questioned him about the prisoner earlier today."

"Are you really surprised by that?" Roth asked Caspian.

"Truthfully, no. Although I was anticipating him having someone watch me in case I did try."

Roth grimaced and shook his head. "Oh, he considered it. Until he realized that he would have to pull someone off rotations just to shadow you. I guess he finally came to the conclusion that it wasn't worth it."

"Of course. Now, Roth…" Caspian's tone took on a hint of pleading. "This conflict is far from over. Vinculus has all but washed his hands of me, so once I leave, I'll never hear another word about this prisoner or the information it might have. Please? Let us try to speak with it."

Roth crossed his arms and deliberated for several moments before he sighed. "Fine, and only because you're leaving tomorrow. Just don't… don't do anything stupid." Then he turned and pressed his open palm into a seemingly random spot on the grassy hill behind him.

There was a brief mechanical whirring, and then part of the hill slid sideways to reveal a doorway. The immediate entrance was very dim and slanted downward – stairs perhaps?

Roth fished in his pocket for a second and came out with a thick, metal key which he handed to Caspian. "Last cell. Don't let it out because I won't be able to cover *that* up."

"You've got it." Caspian nodded solemnly as he accepted the key.

Caspian crossed the threshold of the doorway and proceeded down a narrow set of stairs.

I'm glad Caspian got over his fear of walking in the dark, I thought as I followed. This set of stairs was unpleasant even for me to walk down because they were barely wide enough for one person to walk down – someone like Thun would have had difficulty on them. Additionally, the lighting became progressively worse as we descended. No lamps or glowing orbs lit our path, and I had to be extra careful not to trip.

There were no rails to hold on to, and the switchback halfway down made me feel claustrophobic. The panic I'd felt in the cruiser returned, and I came to a full stop, unable to make myself take another step.

"Aliya?" Caspian retraced his steps until he stood in front of me.

"I can't do this," I whimpered as the stairwell seemed to close around me.

"Open your eyes." Caspian took both of my hands. "I'm right here, and I'll be with you the whole way. Okay? We're in this together."

Forcing myself to look, I memorized the image of Caspian before me – tall, strong, and *safe*. We weren't in danger here, and I wasn't alone.

Nodding, I allowed Caspian to lead me onward, and after three more minutes of descending darkened stairs, Caspian and I finally reached the bottom.

What lay before us was a long, straight hallway which was just wide enough for two soldiers to walk abreast. I couldn't tell how far the brown stone floor stretched in front of us because of how dark it was. I felt like I was staring into a bottomless pit.

What I could see, though, was that the hallway was lined with door after door on either side. Each one reached all the way to the ceiling and was nothing more than a giant slab of gray metal fastened with hinges that were longer than my hand.

Each door bore a large number at head height made out of a coppery metal, resting above a sliding panel that would allow a guard to see into the cell.

"Welcome to the Protective Forces prison cells," Caspian said grimly.

He fished something out of his pocket and eventually came up with a palm-sized orb that looked to be made of glass. Caspian rested his thumb against it for a moment, and then it began to emit a soft, white light.

I wasn't sure if I preferred the darkness or not. The prison appeared far gloomier by the light of the orb. The floor was polished and bare, no lighting or decoration hung on the walls, and nothing broke the monotony of cell after cell after cell… What an awful place to be locked up.

I had no idea if there were even other prisoners here. The cell doors were too thick to let any sounds through, and I wasn't going to open a viewing panel to check.

Caspian trudged onward, one hand holding the orb aloft while the other pulled me along. The only sound was the soft thud of our boots on the stone floor.

Finally, the last door came into view. Unlike the other doors in the hallway, this one was set into the back wall. The number on the door, "50," seemed larger than the other numbers had been. Perhaps that was because this particular door didn't have a viewing window.

Caspian pulled the thick key from his pocket and placed it into the lock.

"What are you doing?" I cried. "Roth told us *not to let it out!"*

"Relax," Caspian said as he turned the key. The lock clicked open, and Caspian turned the handle. "This is a different type of cell."

My entire body was tense as Caspian slowly tugged the door open. I expected the Krech to come flying out of the darkness, its claw-hand extended toward our unprotected bodies.

Caspian let go of the door when it was wide enough for him to slip through. The room beyond was dim and silent. No heavy breathing, no telltale Krech hissing. Just… nothing.

What if the Krech is dead?

It was entirely possible that General Vinculus had lied to us, and the prisoner was long gone. I had no idea how it might have been "interrogated" or how long Krech could endure aggressive methods of questioning.

Calmly, Caspian stepped into the room. Now that the orb was inside, I could see what he meant by this being a "different" cell. Where a normal cell, in my mind, would have held a prisoner's bunk and little else, this one was almost like two cells put together.

The half we stood in was some sort of viewing area. Two wooden chairs were pushed up against the wall, facing metal bars that divided the room in half. Beyond the bars, a ratty mattress and a lump of rags sat in the corner.

I stepped into the room, stopping beside Caspian. He didn't advance toward the bars, but he held the orb out toward them, illuminating the rest of the room for me.

Wrapped in rags was the Krech. The black clothing he had worn on Charra had become tattered beyond repair and was stained even *darker* than the shade of black they had been before. He lay curled on its side with his back against the far wall, the left half of his face peeking out above what I assumed was his arm.

Scales were missing from his forest-green, lizard-like face, and a long gash stretched from above his closed eye and ran diagonally off the side of his face. It didn't look like a fresh wound.

The miserable creature looked dead.

The rags he wore didn't rise and fall to indicate breathing, and he didn't move, even when I softly gasped.

"Is it…?" I whispered.

"No," Caspian replied. He hauled one chair forward and slumped down into it. "It wouldn't be here if it was dead. Isn't that right?" he called loudly.

It was then that the Krech's slit of an eye cracked open. The black iris faintly reflected light from Caspian's orb as the Krech studied us. Aside from a few slow blinks, it remained motionless.

Caspian snorted derisively. "It looks like you have nowhere else to be, and I've got questions. Let's get started, shall we?"

I drifted back behind Caspian's chair as he leaned forward and placed the light on the floor. Our shadows elongated, stretching up the walls to loom over the Krech as he remained in the fetal position.

I actually felt bad for the Krech. He had been defeated on Charra, tied up and sent here, and who knew how many terrible things he'd been subjected to? And to top it all off, I – the person who'd killed his companions – was here with Caspian to question him further.

Caspian leaned his elbows on his knees and folded his hands. He was silent for a few moments, as if debating which question to ask first.

"Why were you sent to Charra?" A lazy blink was the only indication that the Krech was still alive. "Were you ordered to attack Charra? Are there more of you on our other planets?"

The Krech's lidless eye slid closed, and Caspian sighed in exasperation as he ran his hands through his hair.

Did he really expect to get answers that quickly? I figured General Vinculus hadn't lied about not being able to get information out of the Krech, yet somehow Caspian had come here tonight expecting different results.

"*Why* were you on *Charra?*" Caspian asked again. He glared at the Krech, his mouth set in a grim line.

"Caspian, relax! He's not going to answer you! He's been through all of Vinculus' torture without cracking, so why would he spill his secrets for you now?"

With a crash, Caspian stood up and kicked his chair over. "They're *killers*, Aliya! They tried to shatter our galaxy once, and now they could be trying again!" he growled as he began pacing. "So many lives have been lost to these *monsters*, and I refuse to let them take even more!"

It didn't slip my attention that the Krech had opened the eye facing us. Just a slit, but he was definitely intrigued by what was going on between me and Caspian.

"Caspian, *look*," I implored him as I strode up to the bars and gestured toward the Krech. "Look at the state he's in! Tortured and then left in a cold, empty cell."

"Aliya, back away." Caspian's voice had dropped to a hoarse whisper. He stood by the still-open door, but he looked nervous now, his crystal blue eyes open wide with concern.

I crouched and rested a hand against the cold metal separating us from the Krech. "He's probably hurt. He won't attack—"

There was a frantic rustle of cloth from inside the cell, and by pure reflex, I flung myself away from the bars, landing hard on my backside. With my heart pounding out of my chest, I looked back at the cell.

The Krech squatted on the opposite side of the bars, with one hand – his *normal* hand – reaching toward my throat.

If I'd been someone with normal speed, he would've caught me.

Up close, I was utterly *horrified* by what'd been done to the Krech. There were patches of missing scales all over his arms and neck, mixed with long, scabbed-over gashes. I imagined that his entire body bore similar wounds, and I couldn't fathom how much that must have hurt.

His eyes glittered with unchecked malice, and the longer I took in his appearance, the more his lips curled back into a haunting, razor-toothed grin.

Perhaps worst of all was the Krech's *other* arm. Pinned between the cell bars and the Krech's torso, his right arm ended in a stump at the wrist. Someone had *chopped the Krech's claw off*.

Logically, it made sense. A Krech's claws were tipped with some kind of poison, so anyone handling him would've been in grave danger from an errant swipe. But to cut the hand off completely?

I was shocked into complete silence while my heart raced like jackhammer within my chest.

"Aliya!" I nearly forgot that Caspian was still behind me.

"I'm… fine. I'm okay," I said in a shaky voice.

I turned my head to look at Caspian, whose face had paled. I probably should've felt embarrassed since he *had* warned me to get back, but I still wasn't past the trauma the Krech had endured. I shifted to stand up.

"Sssshow me," the Krech hissed.

I whipped my head back toward the cell. He'd retracted his hand, wrapping it around one of the bars, but remained pressed up against them.

"Show you what?" I snapped.

"The cccicruits."

Caspian shifted somewhere behind me but made no move to get closer. I was glad; he was giving me space to handle this. The Krech hadn't responded to him, and now it had decided to talk to me.

"How about we make a deal?" He cocked his head, scraping the scaly skin of his face against a bar. "You answer a few of my questions, and I'll show you my circuits."

I had to wait for two lazy blinks before the Krech replied. *"It'sss a deal."*

That was too easy. Was I missing something obvious here? I didn't know how much more time Caspian and I had down here before the guards outside changed or someone came down into the cells, so I figured I'd start asking questions.

"Why were you on Charra?"

I could've *sworn* that he glared at me before sitting back on his haunches. He tucked his handless arm against his chest. *"Exploring,"* he said, drawing out the 'x' sound as a hiss.

"Not good enough," I replied, shaking my head. I shifted and folded my legs beneath me. If he was going to drag out answers this way, I might as well sit comfortably.

The Krech's eyes narrowed. *"It'sss been many years… We needed to sssee how much hasss changed."*

"Why would us changing matter to you?"

"Sssso we would know where to attack." He graced me with another cruel smile.

I paused. I didn't want to continue with this line of questioning because I doubted he'd actually tell me where or when they were planning to attack.

"How did the cyborgs know about me?" I heard Caspian's sharp intake of breath behind me. He hadn't forgotten how one of the cyborgs on Vanthurium had tried to make it a contest to take down the "glowing Terran."

I'd never been able to figure it out. The only ones who had witnessed my abilities before Vanthurium had been half of my squad and the few Krech we'd encountered in the hangar. Yet somehow the cyborgs had known that I glowed *and* that I was from Terra.

The Krech didn't immediately reply. Instead, he held out the end of his stump and began unwinding a cloth from the end of it.

Although it wasn't freshly bleeding, the stump was still revolting to look at. I tried my best to keep my eyes on the Krech's face instead of the spot where his claws should have been.

"You're not the only one with wiressss," he said. There, at the end of his stump, was a thin, silvery wire. At least two inches protruded from the end of the scarred skin, held aloft by the Krech's remaining fingers.

How did a wire— I gasped as realization hit me. It must have been some kind of transmitter. I opened my mouth to ask more, but he cut me off.

"Enough! Your turn."

I wasn't sure that I'd gotten enough information out of him, but a deal was a deal. I held out my right hand and pinched the back of it, causing my circuits to light up.

The Krech leaned forward, gripping the bar once more as a low hiss escaped his lips. Once the golden glow faded, he sat back and watched me.

"We dessspissse you, cccircuit girl. Oh, yessss we do. But I, I do hope you ssssurvive what comesss," he said, grinning wickedly.

From far off down the hallway, the faint sound of footsteps reached my ears. "Caspian, someone's coming!"

Caspian swore quietly. He was probably hoping to get more out of the Krech as well.

He walked over and helped me get to my feet before scooping up his light from where it sat on the floor. With one last glare at the Krech, Caspian strode from the cell.

I slipped out behind Caspian and waited as he shut the door.

"I'm sorry that wasn't more helpful," I said.

He looked at me in surprise. "I'm willing to bet that you got more out of it than General Vinculus did. And," he continued as he walked back down the long hallway, "some of that *was* helpful."

We reached the stairs to find Roth waiting for us at the bottom. "Oh good," he sighed. "I was just about to come get you.

We're switching patrols soon." Roth paused and glanced at each of our faces. "Did it tell you anything?"

"Not a word," Caspian quickly lied. Roth grunted and started up the stairs.

I knew better than to question Caspian, but I was curious. Shouldn't we tell *someone* what the Krech said? He'd all but admitted that the Krech were going to attack again. At the very least, that information validated the king's travel restriction and reason to have more guards. It could help the citizens of the galaxy be more alert for something out of the ordinary – a rogue ship, a strange-looking person – that might indicate an attack.

Whatever his reasoning, I had to trust that Caspian knew best and would handle the information we'd received accordingly.

We stepped out of the prison into the warm night air, and Caspian thanked Roth before turning over the key. Setting his hand against the small of my back, he steered me toward the rows of bunkhouses.

"What does this mean for us?" I asked. Somehow, he understood without needing me to elaborate.

"It just means that we're going to have to *really* protect the king and his family. If the king falls… well, who knows what will happen to this galaxy."

I sighed, my mind pulling up thoughts of long guard patrols and intense combat training. It wasn't going to be fun or easy, but it's what I had signed up for.

At least, I hoped it was.

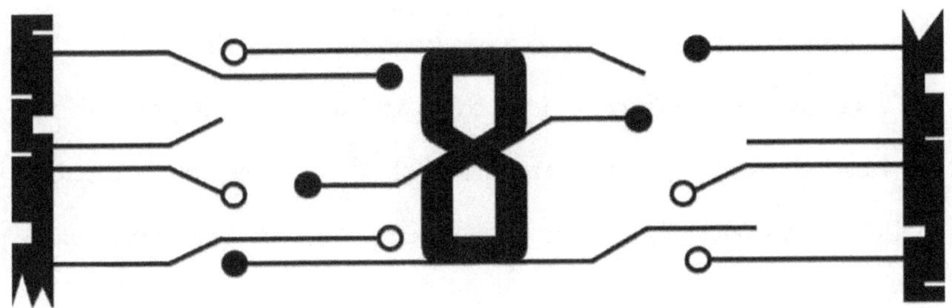

I was exhausted the next morning.

The interrogation had kept us up late into the night, and once we'd safely returned to the bunkhouse, I'd been unable to fall into a deep sleep.

My mind kept dredging up images of the abused Krech, his wild eyes, and the stump where his hand used to be.

And then, of course, there was the revelation that he'd been wired. Somehow he'd been set up with a transmitter of some kind that had relayed my actions on Charra to... someone. I wasn't entirely sure that the information had gone straight to the cyborgs; more than likely, the Krech had seen what I could do and tipped the cyborgs off before they launched their attack on Vanthurium.

I couldn't stop thinking about what I saw in that cell until I heard the sounds of others waking.

Caspian was the first one to rise. He dressed quickly and slipped out of the bunkhouse before anyone else was even up. I didn't think he had a meeting, so where was he off to?

I sat up, untangling my legs from my white sheets, and shook my head. A few sighs and grunts reached my ears, and I decided to hit the showers before everyone else was up and there was a line.

I couldn't bask in the shower as long as I wanted to, but I felt completely refreshed once I emerged. By then, almost everyone was up and preparing for the day.

Today. The end of the Nova squad as I'd come to know it.

My stomach sank as reality hit, but I plastered on a smile as I emerged from the bathroom. No need to have my sad mood rub off on the others when it was already a grim day.

As I passed through the doorway, the smells of a hot breakfast wafted to my nose, making my mouth water.

Caspian had returned, bringing a breakfast feast with him. He sat in the middle of the floor, and the beds around him had been pushed away to make space for everyone. Ever thoughtful, he even had everyone's favorite breakfast food.

Jorl, Lem, Ki'ran, the twins, and even Bragdan sat on the floor around the impromptu picnic. I watched as Bragdan accepted a glass of water from Lem, meeting her eyes and giving a small nod of his head. It seemed like he was having one of his better, more functional days, and I was incredibly glad to see it.

I tiptoed around the edge of the circle and made my way to

the open spot between Gunther and Jorl. Gunther held a plate which had a bit of everything mixed together on it, and Jorl's plate was piled high with breakfast sausages.

I crossed my legs and sat down, and Caspian immediately reached across the circle to offer me a steaming mug of coffee.

"Thanks!" I accepted it with a smile.

"We were all sharing our decisions before the king's guards come," Caspian said as he gestured to the others in the circle. "So far Ki'ran has agreed to come work for the king, but Lem will be returning to Vanthurium instead."

Lem's head dipped slightly, and I heard her mumble, "Sorry."

"Don't be sorry," Caspian said. "Your home needs you, and you're always welcome back if you wish to return."

Although I wasn't allowed to return, I almost felt guilty for lacking a potent desire to return to my home. I missed my family, my friends, and everything I had grown up with, but the sense of duty I felt to protect the King's Galaxy from the Krech was more important. After all, if the Krech conquered Callais, what would stop them for coming for every planet in the galaxy, including Terra?

"Aliya informed me yesterday that she would join the king's guards as well." Caspian paused and looked across the circle at me, so I nodded. "I look forward to having you with us. Has anyone else decided?"

Everyone was silent for a few moments, and the atmosphere of the room grew tense. No one felt awkward before I sat down, so why was there this tension now?

Then Bragdan cleared his throat. "I'm stayin' on the base. They have resources here… resources that can help me." He looked slightly embarrassed to be admitting that he needed the help, but I also realized that it was a huge step for him. Compared to days when he appeared comatose, today he almost seemed back to his normal self.

I wondered why he was so much better today. Perhaps the impending changes to the squad had shocked him out of his trauma?

Caspian, who was sitting to Bragdan's left, patted him on the back. "We all wish you a speedy recovery. And once you get past this, you're more than welcome to come join me, wherever I may be serving."

Bragdan beamed, his green eyes lighting up against the dark circles that surrounded them. "Thank you, Caspian. That… that'll definitely give me somethin' to work toward!"

I smiled down into my coffee and took another sip. Today might be hard on all of us, but this was a heartwarming moment that we'd remember for weeks.

Caspian turned his attention from Bragdan and focused on the three who hadn't yet voiced their opinions. Jorl, who scowled down at his plate, looked like he was still wrestling with his choice. But the twins didn't hesitate to speak up.

"We're—" Gráinne started.

"—in too," Gunther finished. Then he turned to his twin, and they shared such a vigorous nod that their red, untamed curls bounced wildly.

They offered no explanation for their choice, but that really wasn't abnormal. Gunther and Gráinne were always people of few words, but what little they said always counted. I'd be curious to see how King Locklyn would use them since they weren't fighters.

That left Jorl. He turned his fork over and over in his hand while his eyebrows knit together. Lem, sitting to Jorl's right, was still as a statue.

I had no idea why he was so conflicted. He was a great soldier – strong, brave, and loyal to his squad. I figured he'd continue on to serve King Locklyn, so what was holding him back?

Finally, Jorl let out a long sigh.

"I've been with Nova for quite a while. We've had our ups and downs," Jorl broke off to offer a sad smile to his friends, "but right now I need to follow a different path. I need to follow my heart." He gulped and turned to look at Lem, whose eyes shone with tears. "I'll be heading to Vanthurium with Lemaleion to help the recovery efforts and hopefully build something more with her as well."

My throat felt thick at his declaration of love, and it was all I could do to keep from tearing up as well. Lem had never been the most open and affectionate person during the brief time I knew her, but she clearly had been with Jorl. I wondered how long the two had been interested in each other.

I caught a brief flash of surprise on Caspian's face before he hid it with a smile. "I knew you were just a big softie, Jorl!" he said as everyone laughed. "But really, I wish you two luck. And as always, you can reach out to me if you need anything."

"Thank you." Jorl reached out to Caspian, and the two clasped forearms. "You've been an incredible captain and friend, and I know our time together hasn't ended. We'll all see each other again."

"I look forward to it," Caspian replied with a somber nod before addressing the group. "It's not easy to say goodbye, to change this squad after all we've been through together. You've all…" he paused and cleared his throat. "You've been a family to me, and it's been an honor serving beside you. Stand tall, burn bright."

We all chanted the phrase back at Caspian.

"Now let's go see what other troubles we can find!" Ki'ran bellowed, causing everyone to laugh.

Our departure came far too soon after cleaning up from breakfast. General Vinculus escorted King Locklyn's guards right up to our door before announcing it was time for us to leave. He'd been a bit surprised to see Lem, Bragdan, and Jorl remain behind but declared he would speak with them only after the rest of Nova squad had been sent 'on their way.'

Without ceremony or much of a goodbye from the general, we boarded the *Starfire* and lifted off as soon as the royal guards' ship did.

As we followed along behind the sleek, black-and-gold ship, Caspian's mood darkened. He sat stiffly in his captain's chair, one knee bouncing frantically.

"Is everything okay?" I sat at the station normally reserved for Adís. It felt strange, but since she wasn't here, it made sense for me to help with the controls.

"Of course," he tersely replied. Caspian's leg stopped bouncing, but his fingers picked up the rapid rhythm, drumming over and over on his armrest.

"Caspian…" I said, standing from my seat to approach him.

I felt like he was falling apart, and this probably wasn't a good time for it. The royal palace wasn't far, and Caspian needed to pull himself together before we met the king again.

"Hey," I said, "talk to me."

I felt a pang of worry as I took in his pinched expression and the dark circles under his eyes. My reaction must have been written all over my face because he quickly buried his face in his hands.

"I'm sorry," he mumbled around his fingers. "It's just… This isn't how I wanted things to go."

"What do you mean?" I dropped into a crouch and tugged his right hand away from his face. Caspian's eyes remained closed, but he shifted his hand to thread his fingers through mine.

"I thought we'd all stay together," he mumbled around his left hand.

"There was nothing you could do to make them come with us. In fact, letting them go was probably in their best interests. Lem would've been worried about her home, and it would have made her distracted. Jorl would've been worried for Lem. And Bragdan… he needs the help that the Protective Forces can provide. He wouldn't have been a functional guard, but maybe they can help him." It hurt to admit because I already missed them, but Caspian needed to hear the truth if he hadn't already thought of it.

"Are you sure? It was right to let them go?" Caspian dropped his hand and looked up at me with concern.

"Absolutely. You made the right call, captain," I said with a small smile. I remembered how he would correct me each time I used his title instead of his name. Hopefully it would cheer him up now.

"Caspian," he said and returned my smile.

A small *ding* sounded from where the twins were seated. "Descent," they announced in unison.

Giving our entwined hands a small squeeze, I released his fingers and stood so that I could stand to the side of his chair. What I really wanted was to stand right against the front window, so that I would have the best view. I'd never seen the Valley of the Crown before, and this would be my first chance to take it all in.

Just beyond the front window, the green valley stretched on for miles. The *Starfire* and the guards' escort ship weren't the only ones airborne in this region — several smaller white cruisers zipped through the air. I couldn't tell if they were for security or travel.

As we descended, I realized that half of the valley seemed to

serve some agricultural purpose. There were dozens of fields –
most had rows covered in different shades of green, one grew
something that was a coppery orange, and a few looked like they
were freshly-tilled dirt. The back half of the valley was framed by
towering, snow-capped mountains that stretched up, up, up into
the clouds, and a thin forest sat at their feet. Before it lay an
oblong, gleaming lake.

But the crown jewel of the Valley of the Crown was the palace
and its royal grounds.

The palace radiated brilliance – literally. All five stories of the
outer walls alternated between black or white blocks of gleaming
stone. It was like a vertical chessboard, but with much longer tiles.
Rectangular windows were cut into the blocks, and a long balcony
jutted out from the center of the third story.

At least one and a half stories tall, the doors leading into the
palace were wholly black and bore gleaming golden metalwork. A
long line of tall, gnarled trees – with emerald leaves and black
trunks – lined the walkway, and just beyond the lines of trees were
delicate gardens made up of low bushes and flowers. While mostly
green, spots of bright color popped from the manicured
landscaping. Although not ornamental by any means, the gardens
still were elegant.

The entire back side of the palace held a massive hedge maze,
and while the left side had what looked like training grounds, the
right had a large grassy pen – maybe for horses? I hadn't seen any
since I woke up on Callais, but I figured that galactic royals could

potentially possess horses. Or some similar animal.

We were headed toward a space across from the front of the palace where a large, open area was dotted with several other ships and cruisers sporting the royal black and gold colors.

Our escort ship touched down, and a few moments later, ours followed.

"Ready?" Caspian asked without looking at me. There was no going back now.

"As ready as I will be," I replied.

Ki'ran clomped into the bridge as the twins stood up from the ship's controls. They stood near the ladder, ready to face the welcoming party once we disembarked. Caspian, on the other hand, hesitated as if he were reluctant to head toward our new future.

Caspian released a deep breath and rocked upward onto his feet. "Let's go greet the king," he said before heading to the ladder.

Dutifully, we all followed him down into the storage level and toward the ramp. Not a single word passed between us as we exited the *Starfire*.

I felt my breath hitch with every step I took down the ramp. We were going to serve *the king*. A king who not only ruled a kingdom, but hundreds of planets.

Caspian gave my hand a little squeeze, pulling me from my thoughts. "Nervous?"

For a second I quietly marveled how such a simple touch could ground me. "A little," I admitted. I had been a soldier for only a few months, and now I was joining the king's guards. I didn't know the proper protocol for interacting with him, his family, and any guests they might receive, and I wasn't sure what would be expected of us.

Would we become part of King Locklyn's personal guards? Would we just become general guards around the palace? Or was there some other role intended for the former Nova squad?

I put an end to my questions as we approached the end of the short ramp.

The sunlight was blinding as we stepped out from the shade of the *Starfire*. I blinked as I waited for my pupils to adjust. Although there was no breeze, I could smell flowers in the air. It was pleasant and somehow served to relax me as we headed toward the welcoming party.

With Caspian and me in the lead, the five remaining Nova members marched toward the small retinue gathered before us. At the head of the party stood King Locklyn and his wife, Queen Estella. Both were resplendent in matching outfits of dark blue and silver – him in a high-collared, long-tailed coat and her in a strapless, glimmering gown with a plunging neckline. A single sapphire the size of a robin's egg hung from a slim silver chain around her neck, and the smaller gems set into her silver crown gleamed in the sunlight.

Queen Estella was stunning. Her round face held a small, button nose and full ruby red lips, and her eyes were a tawny yellow, with only a thin streak of black eyeliner to accentuate them.

She wore her midnight-black hair loose, hanging just below her shoulders.

Four stern-faced guards stood on either side of the king and queen, and although I found the guards intimidating, my gaze was drawn to the male standing – nearly hiding – behind the welcome party. For a moment I struggled to identify him, but the golden circlet sitting askew on the top of his head gave his identity away.

Prince Damien Talimore. The first male in eight generations of Talimore rulers to not receive the first name of Locklyn.

Dressed from head to toe in black, Prince Damien lacked the air of regality that his father seemed to ooze. The two males shared a strong jawline and hazel eyes, but that's where the similarities ended.

Prince Damien's hair hung just above his shoulders in a black, glossy curtain that had a hint of a curl at the ends. His pale skin seemed out of place for living on such a sunny planet, making him appear sickly. His nose was slightly pointed at the end, and, like his nose, Prince Damien was reedy, despite his tall frame and wide shoulders. Even his lips looked thin as they pressed together to form a scowl.

I couldn't take my eyes off him. There was something about this male that seemed off, and it wasn't the simple silver circlet that sat askew on top of his head.

As I continued to stare, I realized that Prince Damien's eyes were unfocused and glassy. He alternated between long blinks and squinting, as if he couldn't quite adjust to the sunlight. The direct light was harsh by my standards, but perhaps the prince *was* sick.

And then his face paled even further as he rocked back on his heels. The glassy eyes, the lack of balance…

Was Prince Damien Talimore *drunk?*

I was floored. A prince, drunk at the arrival ceremony for his father's new guards. Was this normal? Were the king and queen actually okay with him being in this state?

"Welcome!" King Locklyn exclaimed in his quiet way as he extended his hands toward us. *He is either oblivious to his son, or he doesn't care,* I realized.

"Your Majesties," Caspian addressed the royals as he bent at the waist. The four of us quickly followed suit. "We are honored to be here."

"And we are honored to have you," Queen Estella replied. Her voice was soft, but it held the same power as her husband's.

Prince Damien gave a soft snort, and I couldn't help staring at him once more. He swayed lightly as he met my gaze. The glassy look left his eyes as his scowl deepened. What was this guy's problem?

King Locklyn and Queen Estella went rigid at the improper noise. Perhaps they had tried to hide their son by having him stand behind them, but there was no way to conceal noises he made.

King Locklyn's eyes narrowed, but he cleared his throat and said, "No need to stand on ceremony, let us retreat inside so that you may get settled."

As one, the eight guards flanking the royals took a step back and performed a crisp about-face. King Locklyn turned on his heel and paused. I watched as Prince Damien's eyes flashed up to his father's.

I could only imagine the glare the prince likely received.

The king stormed away, roughly brushing up against his son's shoulder. Far more graceful, Queen Estella turned in a swirl of her skirts. Instead of chastising her son, she grasped his upper arm and tugged him alongside her as she retreated.

"Interesting," I murmured. Caspian didn't reply, but he nodded in agreement.

Turning to the group, he addressed us. "We'll come back later to retrieve our items. For now, let's just see to our new quarters and what the king has in store for us."

Receiving nods of assent, Caspian turned, flashed me a quick smile, and followed after the royal procession.

It was only day one at the royal palace, but I could already tell that we were completely unprepared for what we had gotten ourselves into.

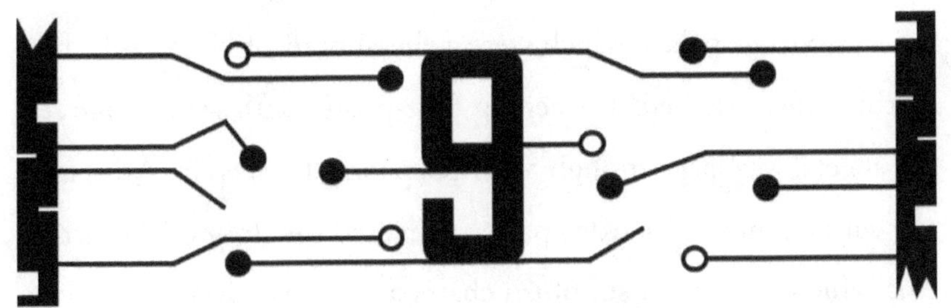

"I hope you found your rooms to your liking," the king said as we settled in around his massive, rectangular dining table.

With enough room to fit at least thirty people, the white marble table dominated the dining room. The seven of us – not counting the eight guards who stood like statues against the walls – were seated around the end of the table nearest the giant, black brick fireplace.

King Locklyn sat at the head of the table with his wife placed directly to his right. Ki'ran sat between the queen and the twins, and Caspian and I sat on the king's left with Caspian directly beside the king.

"Of course, Your Majesty. They're wonderful," Caspian answered.

Our rooms were magnificent, even for newly appointed palace

guards. Consisting of three rooms – a sitting area, bedroom, and bathroom – the floors matched the outer walls and floors throughout the palace which were a chessboard of black and white marbled tiles. My bed, a sweeping four-poster with sea foam green silk sheets, was large enough for three people to sleep in. An ornate rug with an intricate garden pattern covered the floor of the sitting area which contained six plush chairs as well as a low table made from a dark wood that I didn't recognize.

And the *bathroom!* It contained a pond-sized, white tiled tub built into the floor. Wide and deep enough to swim in, I couldn't believe that it was all for me. Did one person really need all this space?

I wasn't the only one shocked by the rooms provided for us.

Before I left for our first meeting, Caspian popped in to check on me. "Impressive, isn't it?" he'd asked. Leaning against the doorframe with his hands deep in the pockets of his black pants, he didn't nearly look as amazed as I felt.

"I couldn't have imagined a more perfect room if I tried," I replied, bubbling with excitement. "How is yours?"

"It's quite similar to your room," Caspian said. He hesitated and chewed the inside of his cheek for a moment. "They held on to my things… from before."

It took me a second to remember that he had been to the palace before. Back when he was being groomed to sit on the king's council.

"Oh… are you—"

"Okay?" he finished for me. He stared me down for a few moments before running a hand through his wavy hair with a sigh. "It's… not as bad as I thought it would be. Not as easy as I had hoped, either."

"I'm sorry." I wasn't sure there was anything I could do to help.

"It's alright," he said as his expression brightened. He pushed off the door frame, crossed the room, and placed his hands on my shoulders. "I couldn't avoid this place forever. Besides, it's an honor to serve the king directly."

But would that honor be worth Caspian having to face the place he ran from five years ago? The last time Caspian had been here, Leila had been sworn in as a council member, and immediately after the ceremony, Caspian left in order to make final preparations for a surprise – his proposal to her. But Leila and Caspian's parents, who had been escorting Leila home for the big moment, never made it. Their transport had exploded in an attack that Caspian blamed on the Krech.

Every year on the anniversary of the explosion, Caspian broke down with sadness. Every year the loss of his parents and Leila hit him so hard that he dropped his duties as a captain. Every year grief shattered the strong, successful male that Caspian outwardly projected.

And now we were back here, in the last place he saw his parents and Leila. Did their ghosts haunt these halls?

There were bigger things at hand – such as the now-tentative galactic peace – but I was concerned for Caspian. The Battle of Vanthurium had rattled us all, and I hoped that working for the king didn't upset Caspian further.

Whatever was in store for us, I hoped that we could all get through it together.

Now, seated with King Locklyn fifteen minutes after my conversation with Caspian, we were all eager to hear exactly what our new roles would be.

"I thought," King Locklyn continued, "it would be much more pleasant to talk over a meal." He clapped his hands twice.

The doors at the far end of the hall burst open, and in streamed servants carrying platters of food. After setting a dish in front of each of us, they quickly slipped away.

"Enjoy," King Locklyn said as he dug into the roasted fish before him.

Caspian and I shared a glance. King Locklyn wasn't immediately telling us what our duties were? It seemed like the group meal was intended to soften whatever he said next. Maybe this wasn't going to be the important assignment we thought it was going to be.

After a few moments filled with the clink of silverware and chewing, Ki'ran spoke up. "Your Majesty, what do you wish the Nova squad to do for you?"

The king took a long drink of the maroon liquid in his glass before answering. "After many meetings with my council I realized why, during the attack on Vanthurium, Lord Galven and Lady

Kalina were targeted by the cyborgs. By eliminating them, one has effectively topped Vanthurium's structure because they have no immediate heirs." Off to my right, Caspian stilled; he already figured out where this was going and wasn't pleased. "My personal guards have undergone years of training together to effectively protect me. I fear we may not have the time to incorporate you in the same manner."

We *weren't* protecting the king? Then why were we here?

Everyone but the twins had paused in the middle of their meal to listen to King Locklyn.

"But seeing how the three of you," he said indicating me, Caspian, and Ki'ran, "have worked well together on both Charra and Vanthurium, I have decided that you will be working with a different set of royal guards." He paused, the unnecessary suspense of the moment irritating me. "You will be protecting my son, Prince Damien."

I nearly snorted. Our job was to protect Prince Damien, the drunken brat from our welcome reception?

"But doesn't Prince Damien have his own retinue of guards?" Caspian asked.

"Ah," the king looked embarrassed, "yes, he does have guards of his own, but he… Well. He tires of them quickly."

Or maybe they tire of him, I thought. If he had been that visibly drunk at our reception, I could only imagine how bad his behavior could be at events requiring far less formality.

Perhaps, I tried to argue back, giving the prince the benefit of the doubt, *there was an event last night, and the prince simply got carried away*. He was a *prince* for crying out loud. There was no way a sloppy drunk would inherit the crown. Right?

"I see," Caspian replied. I heard a hint of irritation in his voice. "We're honored to protect your son."

"Excellent," King Locklyn beamed and reached for his wife's hand. "And you two," he spoke to the twins, "I think your talents for technology would be a wonderful asset to my personal technicians."

Gunther and Gráinne bobbed their heads excitedly in unison.

The Nova squad was getting split up after all. I was already sad to lose Lem, Jorl, and Bragdan. Hopefully the twins would still be at the palace, and I would get to see them from time to time.

"We thank you, Your Majesty." Caspian tried to sound grateful.

"Well then, now that that's settled, we can set you up with your new groups tomorrow. Today, we can familiarize you with the palace and grounds," King Locklyn said, ending the discussion on our new jobs.

"Your Majesty, I do have a question," I said. The king met my eyes and gave a slight incline of his head, indicating that I should continue. "We were told that Adís was already here…"

A quizzical look crossed the king's face, and he set his fork down slowly. "I had assumed…" he murmured and then continued in a slightly louder tone. "Yes, she has been here for some days now. Adjusting to her new circumstances, you see."

"Circumstances?"

"Well," King Locklyn looked genuinely uncomfortable with my line of questioning. "It's not my place to divulge that information if she hasn't already shared it with you. You've had no contact with her?"

"No," Caspian cut in. "We haven't heard from her since she was taken to a healing facility."

"I am truly sorry to hear that. She has been through a lot…" King Locklyn paused and took in our looks of concern. "I'm sure she just needed time to heal. I'll inform her of your arrival, and if she does not seek you out, you're sure to cross paths with her during your time here."

Caspian tapped my leg under the table, and I took it as a sign to end my questions. I had so many more, but it seemed like we weren't going to get any information out of the king.

The rest of the lunch passed quickly and pleasantly. Caspian and Ki'ran were polite; I kept my words to a minimum. After my questions about Adís, I didn't feel comfortable fully participating in the conversations about the king's health and the safety of the galaxy.

Eventually King Locklyn told us a bit about the palace's schedule and how many guards were on various rotations throughout the interior and grounds. We learned that Prince Damien currently had five personal guards who accompanied him in groups of two or three depending on the time of day and who was on duty. For the most part we would be his day-to-day guards, and when the palace hosted events such as a ball or conference, we would join the larger number of general guards doing security.

All in all, this didn't sound like a difficult job. The only unknown factor would be the prince. Would he be manageable or in the inebriated state he displayed earlier today?

I guessed we would find out once we officially became his guards tomorrow.

After lunch, we all returned to our rooms to freshen up before taking a tour of the palace and grounds. I didn't have much to do, so I quickly splashed water on my face and pulled my hair up into a ponytail.

I was nervous to serve as a personal guard for the prince. Aside from ground rules and learning his schedule, I was sure that protecting him wouldn't be so different from what I had done when protecting my Nova squad.

It was odd that he had been absent from lunch. Did he have other duties that he was attending to? Was he sleeping off his hangover? Or perhaps, I realized, King Locklyn could have forbade him from showing up. The tense moment between them before we all walked to the palace hadn't exactly been subtle.

Despite worrying about the prince, I was eager to study the inner workings of the galactic king's palace. The rules and regulations I had learned during my time with Doctor Givray and Captain Sansish had been few, and I had been too preoccupied with appearing unremarkable to ask for more information.

My brain went wild for a few minutes as it imagined countless new things that I could learn. I came up with so many questions about the king, his council, and how the galactic government functioned. I just hoped that my position as a guard would allow me to ask them.

There was a knock at my door. "Aliya?"

"Come in," I replied.

Caspian stepped into my room and slipped his hands into his pockets. "I'm... sorry," he said hesitantly.

"What for?" Had something gone wrong during the lunch that I'd missed?

"For getting you into this." He stared at the ground, rubbing the toe of his boot on one of the black tiles. "This isn't what I thought we were here for."

"Oh. Well it's not all bad. The food at lunch was pretty good," I joked.

He ignored it. "We saved the rulers of another *planet*, and now we have to babysit the king's son. I thought we'd become the royal strike force or emissaries or... anything other than this." He looked so upset.

"But this is an important job, Caspian." He looked up at me. "Prince Damien is Locklyn's heir. If the Krech organize another hit team and take out the king, the responsibility falls on Prince Damien. We're here because we need to keep him safe and alive."

Caspian huffed and rolled his eyes. "Clearly, you've never heard how bad Damien can be."

"I haven't," I said as I sunk into one of the chairs in my sitting room, patting the chair to my right. "How about you fill me in?"

Caspian reluctantly sat. He leaned forward, resting his elbows on his knees, and threaded his fingers together. "We rarely crossed paths when I was training to be a councilman, so I'm not sure what he was like when he was younger. But there was no shortage of reports on him and the latest scandal he'd caused once he started exercising his independence."

"Scandal?" Maybe the drunken state he'd been in this morning hadn't been an accident after all.

"You name it, he's probably done it. Joyriding in cruisers, public indecency, outrageous parties, breaking hearts…" He ticked each one off on his fingers. "And of course, King Locklyn can't name someone else as his heir, so Damien never learns."

"Has the king tried to punish him?"

"Oh, loads of times," Caspian said with a laugh. "He's even sent Damien to prison a few times, but it never makes him change his actions."

"*Prison?*"

"Well, a slap on the wrist wasn't enough to keep Damien from jacking ships and attending public events in an inebriated state. But, like I said, even prison didn't straighten him out."

I leaned back for a moment, letting it all sink in. Prince Damien seemed like an outrageously unruly playboy who was rebelling against his title. Adding that to what King Locklyn said earlier regarding the prince's previous guards…

"His old guards probably got tired of cleaning up after his messes, huh?"

Caspian nodded. "Either that or they left because they couldn't do their duty. On my way over here I questioned a guard about the last person to leave the prince's guards. Apparently, Damien would slip away so often that it looked like the guard couldn't do his job, so he decided to quit before he got in real trouble with the king. He was tired of being tasked with guarding someone who didn't want protection."

This job was starting to sound worse and worse.

"Wait a minute… you said Prince Damien was a heartbreaker? How many of his guards are female?"

"None." He grimaced. "This role will probably be the most difficult for you. We can try to keep you out of his immediate detail, but you're sure to cross paths eventually."

I groaned. I definitely *didn't* need a playboy prince hitting on me while I was trying to keep him safe.

Caspian reached over and grasped my hand. "We'll make it work, okay?"

I'd trusted Caspian when he first brought me onto the Nova squad. I'd trusted his orders when we were on Charra and Vanthurium. And now I just had to believe that he'd do all he could to keep us as stress-free as possible.

"Okay. We'll make it work."

"Alright," he said, standing and tugging on my hand for me to follow. "Now let's go join this royal tour."

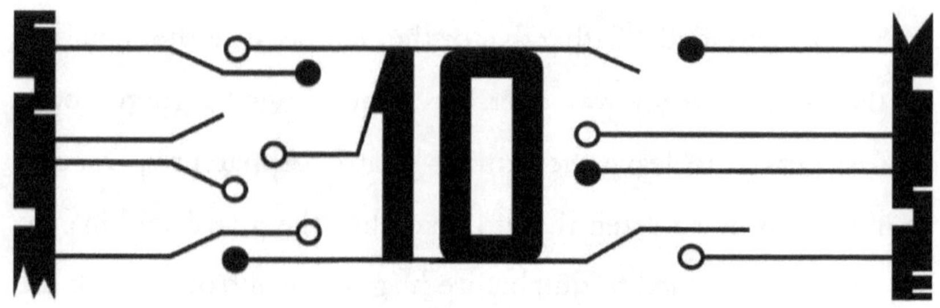

The tour of the palace and grounds was conducted by a guard named Gor. Towering at about seven feet, Gor looked like a six-limbed boulder that had been stuffed inside a navy tunic.

His wide body was covered in a slate gray, rock-like carapace that had lines like a cracked window, and each of his four arms were as thick as my torso, with legs even wider than that. Two red eyes, which were stacked vertically on his craggy face, glowed unblinkingly from within a web of cracks.

I was far too terrified of him to ask where he was from.

Fortunately, his tour was quick and to the point. Gor paraded us past the throne room, the reception hall where we'd eaten lunch, and a myriad of smaller rooms designated for private meetings. He didn't take us through the eastern wing of the palace since we'd been there to see our rooms, and he only gestured to the ballroom as we passed it to head outside.

Solar lighting was a prevalent decorative theme. While some light fixtures looked like sconces straight out of Terra's medieval ages, certain hallways flaunted elaborate chandeliers made from ornately twisted metals or colored glass. Within them flickered a pure white light, which really complemented the black and white marble floors.

What I wasn't prepared for was the wall decorations – or the lack thereof. I imagined that a palace would have pictures from centuries-old kings or historic moments… or, since this planet was technologically advanced, even some digitized imagery depicting royal histories. But there was nothing. No pictures, no screens. Just the occasional rectangular window or guard at his post.

For all its magnificence, the palace gave off the faint vibes of being a tomb. A plain, marbled tomb. How could anyone stand to live here?

At least the grounds were vibrant. Every walkway was lined with rectangular shrubs that had emerald, diamond-shaped leaves, and they were all manicured to the exact same shape and height. Garden plots boasted of flowers in every color, including some that I never imagined seeing on a flower's petals.

I felt like a tourist, oohing and aahing at everything I was shown, but I didn't understand how this immediately related to our new jobs as prince's guards. Shouldn't we have been learning his schedule and how to work with him?

"Trust me," Caspian said when I asked in a hushed whisper.

"You'll want to get comfortable with the layout of the palace as quickly as possible. It's a large place, and if Prince Damien really is the type to slip away from his guards, you'll want to scout out all the places he's likely to go."

It *was* good advice, but it was impossible to assume that I'd learn my way around in just one day. There were so many rooms and acres to cover, and what would happen if the prince was crafty enough to sneak onto one of the ships in the airfield? Thus far the prince seemed like the type who would laze around, but it was only day one.

The tour stretched late in to the afternoon, and once we were finished, Caspian suggested that the three of us have one last dinner together since the king hadn't requested our presence at his table.

Just like our breakfast this morning, Caspian ordered food sent to his chamber and cleared a space for us to sit on his floor.

It felt incredibly empty without Lem, Jorl, Bragdan, and the twins, but Caspian did his best to fill the conversation with stories from the Nova squad's adventures in years past.

The stories lightened the mood somewhat, but deep down I worried about my friends who were no longer by my side.

Would Lem be welcomed back to Vanthurium with open arms, especially by her family, or would they resent her for returning only after the attack on the palace? How would Jorl fit into the life that Lem would rebuild on her home planet? Would Bragdan eventually make a full recovery and return to us? What would Gunther and Gráinne create alongside the king's technicians and scientists?

And, finally, the most troubling of all: did Adís even *want* to see us again, or had she cut ties with her former squad for a reason?

I desperately tried to tamp down my concerns, but they swirled around my head throughout dinner and long into the night as I tried to sleep.

✳

My mind was foggy as I made my way down the marbled hallways, searching out the dining room where breakfast was being served.

I easily could've asked one of the numerous guards lining the hallway for directions, but I was too stubborn and not thinking clearly.

I'd tossed and turned all night fretting over problems that were out of my control. My friends, the irresponsible prince, the lingering threat of the Krech… The only thing I could do was tell myself that everything would work itself out, and I just had to take things one day at a time.

And today, that involved putting on my new uniform – navy combat boots with gold buckles, navy leggings, and a long navy tunic decorated with golden embroidery and buttons – and heading to breakfast so I could meet the other guards who were responsible for the prince's protection.

After getting lost once, I eventually found my way to the room with the elegant banquet table. I was surprised to see Ki'ran seated at the near side of the table while three guards were clustered together at the far side. Their hushed conversation paused for a moment as I entered, and then it picked up with renewed fervor, heads angled close together as they cast furtive glances my way. Had I already done something wrong?

I did my best to ignore them and slid into the chair across from Ki'ran.

"Morning," he rumbled around a large bite of toast slathered in an amber colored jelly.

"Have you been here long?" I asked as I reached for a large silver pitcher that had wisps of steam curling off the top. *Please be coffee*, I wished.

He shook his head while I filled my mug to the brim. "I have not seen Caspian either," he said as if anticipating my next question.

I didn't expect to see any of the royals this early in the morning, but I assumed that Caspian would be here to provide some direction for the day's events. We were meeting the rest of the prince's guards – the ones who weren't currently guarding him – and I had thought the three of us would arrive at the meeting as a group.

Maybe Caspian had gotten up earlier than either of us and had already eaten.

Ki'ran was silent as I helped myself to the spread set before me, but the other guards' whispering was becoming difficult to ignore.

"…doesn't look any different from us," one murmured to his comrades.

"She's *Terran*, but she fought Krech," another whispered back.

I turned to stare at them, catching them all watching me. They looked away quickly, but only one looked embarrassed to have been caught.

Why are they talking about me? I'd only been at the palace for one day, and my mind scrambled to think if I'd done anything to humiliate myself yesterday. I hadn't done anything abnormal, nor had I used my speed or strength. So why was I their object of fascination?

"They are curious about you," Ki'ran whispered to me. "One asked if you were really the one who killed the Krech on Charra."

"Why?" I wasn't surprised that they'd heard the report from Charra, but it was strange that my role in it was being questioned.

"Everyone knows your story now, so—"

"Everyone *what?*"

Ki'ran looked down at me, puzzlement written all over his face. "You did something no one else has: you fought Krech and lived. The story has been shared, your past dug into, and everyone knows who you are now."

I gulped and felt my pulse quicken. *Everyone knows everything?*

I felt like I'd been laid bare. My story was no longer that of a Protective Forces soldier blessed with heightened abilities. No, Ki'ran's explanation led me to believe that my Terran origins had been exposed as well.

I'd been naïve to assume that Doctor Givray, the Forces, King Locklyn, and the king's council were the only ones who would know where I'd come from. How often had a surprising hero emerged on Terra, and before long everything from that individual's past was brought to light? Of course, the same thing would happen out here.

I hadn't done anything terrible or scandalous during my twenty-four years on Terra, but I still felt uncomfortable by the thought of someone digging that far into my past.

"What did you tell them?"

"The truth — that you did kill the Krech, and the next time they have questions, that they should ask you." Ki'ran glanced down the table and caught the blonde Callaisan female on the very end watching us. "It seems they are too scared of you to come ask."

Why would they be scared of me? I was a soldier like them, not some dangerous mutant.

I'd scarcely touched my food, but I found that my appetite had fled. My unbelievable story had been passed around, setting some strange standards for who I was, and everyone who met me would want to validate what they'd heard. I wasn't used to scrutiny on such a large scale, and the thought of it happening now was daunting.

Ki'ran finally clued in to my discomfort. "Come, we need to meet our new team," he said, raising his voice for the whole hall to hear as he pushed his chair back with a loud scraping sound.

He led me down the hallways to the eastern wing to the door

that led to the training grounds. The day was bright but not nearly as warm as it had been the past two days, and I was grateful for the break from the oppressive heat.

I lagged behind Ki'ran as we strolled down the paved pathway leading to the grounds. As we got closer, I noticed Caspian standing with three male guards.

Caspian's shirt stretched tight across his shoulders as he crossed his arms, and I noticed dark circles under his eyes. He cut off his conversation and turned as Ki'ran and I approached. "Right on time," he said with a forced smile. I opened my mouth to ask where he'd been during breakfast, but Caspian continued, saying, "These are most of Prince Damien's remaining guards. Elgin Saxe, Ba'rin Wessex, and Omri Angefin." Each male inclined his head as he was introduced.

They were extremely different from each other. Elgin was clearly Callaisan – his humanoid form and pale skin were a testament to that – but his hair, which had been twisted into a bun on the back of his head, was dyed a dark shade of green. Elgin stood a few inches taller than Caspian, and the smile he gave me and Ki'ran was warm and welcoming.

Ba'rin looked startlingly similar to Ki'ran, and I wondered if they hailed from the same planet. Both males were imposing and stocky, with long, black hair, but unlike Ki'ran's braided mane, Ba'rin had one long pony tail tied with a leather strap. His face was long and angular, and his dark, almond-shaped eyes matched the chocolate brown of his skin.

And then there was Omri. I couldn't even begin to place where he was from. Omri's head reached my shoulders, and his uniform seemed to swallow up his thin frame. There wasn't a hair on Omri's nearly translucent skin, and his globular eyes reminded me of the eyes of a fish. A set of three dainty ridges marked where his ears should have been – gills, maybe?

I realized a second too late that I'd been staring for far too long, and I ripped my gaze away from the strange male as my cheeks heated.

I was surprised to see such diversity in the prince's guards since most of the king's guards had looked Callaisan. Perhaps that was due to the fact that the prince didn't have any curated guards, and the males standing before us were ones who had responded to the metaphorical "help wanted" ad. No doubt they were skilled, otherwise they wouldn't be near the royal family, but this was just another reminder of how little I knew of the universe. I thought I'd seen dozens of species while with the Protective Forces, but here I was, being proven wrong once more.

Caspian, continuing in his introductions, gestured to us. "This is Aliya and Ki'ran, formerly from my Nova squad."

My name sparked reactions of surprise from the three males. "Do you mean *the* Aliya? The Hero of Vanthurium?" Elgin asked in a hushed tone.

I resisted the urge to roll my eyes. Since when had I become "the Aliya?" I hadn't done anything that incredible on Vanthurium – I wasn't responsible for stopping all the cyborgs that had attacked. Yet these three males not only knew who I was but had also made me into a legend in their minds.

I was starting to miss the days of being plain old Aliya.

Caspian laughed. "Yes, this is the very same Aliya."

Omri turned to look at his comrades, and I heard his whispered, "Wow."

Feeling seriously embarrassed, I decided to speak up. "Really, what I did on Vanthurium was nothing. I was just doing my job as a soldier."

Elgin shook his head as Omri turned back to face me, but it was Ba'rin who spoke up first.

"What you do not understand," he started in a throaty voice as he stepped closer, looming over me, "is that you are singular. There is no other Terran skilled the way you are. No one has fought Krech and lived to tell the tale, and you were the one who saved your captain's life."

I shook my head. "I didn't ask for or learn these skills. They came as a consequence of me nearly dying. If I hadn't fought the Krech, my whole squad would have died. Yes, I saved Caspian, but anyone else who'd been in my position would've done the same!"

A mocking smile crept onto Ba'rin's full lips. "The reports didn't mention that you were blind."

Flames of anger simmered in my core. I was already embarrassed that they saw me as some kind of heroic figure, but now Ba'rin seemed to be mocking me. "I'm not—"

"Perhaps we can continue this another time?" Caspian interjected.

I wanted to demand that he explain himself, but I knew that I couldn't undermine Caspian's authority on our very first day as prince's guards. Reluctantly, I dipped my head and let him lead the conversation.

"I hoped," he said as he glanced at the five of us, "to hear a quick report on your strategy for handling guard shifts thus far. The sooner we can set up a new schedule, the sooner Aliya and Ki'ran can begin to get familiar with the prince's habits, and then the five of you can stop pulling such long hours."

"We've had ten-hour shifts when we can put two people on duty," Omri replied. His voice was nasally and much higher pitched than I had thought it would be. "That hasn't been ideal, since it leaves one person on a shift by himself, but we try to keep it shorter. On days when Prince Damien is being especially erratic, however, those shifts can become even longer since we're dragged wherever he wishes to go. With you three I think we should be able to do shifts of two for eight hours each."

It was clear that they'd planned this out beforehand because Omri looked hopeful after giving his report. I couldn't imagine how rough those "long" shifts covering the prince were, but Omri seemed fed up with it.

"That sounds reasonable," Caspian said with a nod. "When does the current shift end?"

"Half an hour, sir. It's supposed to be my shift."

"I'll gladly step in and take the next shift with you. Aliya and Ki'ran, you should speak to Elgin and Ba'rin to hear more about what guarding the prince entails."

Omri beamed at the announcement that he'd have company on his shift. "Excellent, sir. It'll be good to have you."

Sir? Caspian hadn't corrected Omri either time, so I wondered if Caspian was accepting a title once more. I knew he'd gladly step in as the new captain of the prince's guards, but I didn't think he'd go back to allowing us to call him "sir" or "captain." Once more I found myself worrying about Caspian's state of mind.

"Actually, would you mind meeting up with Seradon and Neygreen now? I'd like to hear how their shift went and if the prince has any plans for the rest of the day," Caspian asked.

"Yes, sir! Of course, sir. We can head back to the palace now. I'm sure Prince Damien is still asleep…"

Caspian gave us a curt nod and strode back to the palace, Omri half running to keep up with Caspian's longer-legged pace.

"That was… abrupt," Ki'ran noted.

I shrugged. "It sounds like they need the help, and you know Caspian is always eager to help others." I turned back to our new companions. "Did you two have plans today? You know, until your next shift?"

Elgin shared a glance with Ba'rin. "We usually train or sleep. Not a lot of time for much else," he said with a shrug.

"Then we will train, too," Ki'ran rumbled in his deep voice. I could tell that he was eager to be doing something – his hands, both metallic and flesh, clenched over and over at his sides.

"Fine with me," Elgin said. "Perhaps while we're working out, you two wouldn't mind telling us a little more about what happened on Charra and Vanthurium. Reports are usually filtered through a couple different sources by the time it reaches our ears. Just another downside of guarding the prince." He shrugged again.

I sighed. Was there nothing worth looking forward to in this new role? The prince was spoiled. The guards treated me differently – Ba'rin wasn't nearly as stealthy as he thought he was as he snuck glances at me as we walked. And, as if those two things weren't annoying enough, we would be the last to know things.

If this was why Caspian was in another bad mood, I couldn't blame him.

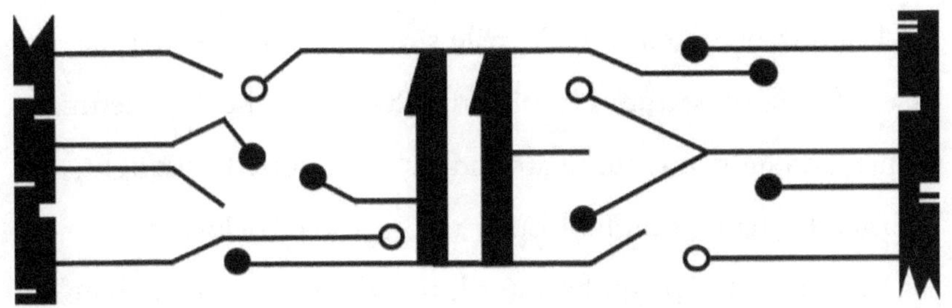

Elgin set a brisk pace as we headed toward the training grounds. Sticking to the paved walkways, our little group passed elegant statues, a few fountains, and tasteful landscaping. And, of course, guard patrols.

I wasn't sure how they knew who I was – part of me suspected that Elgin whispered it to every group we passed – but they would all pass me with wide eyes and intense stares.

The first group completely caught me off guard, but by the third patrol my face was bright red. It was made worse by the fact that Elgin would glance back shortly after we passed the other guards, and he'd laugh to himself as he faced forward once more.

Maybe I'd challenge him to a sparring match. That would teach him a lesson.

Not soon enough, the well-groomed shrubbery gave way to an

open and grassy area at the edge of the grounds which held shooting range targets in a variety of shapes.

Elgin strode up to a wide, pale stone box that looked like the base of a large statue. He placed a hand on the top, leftmost corner, and light gray stone around his hand pulsed with light, and he lifted his hand, simultaneously taking a step backward.

Silently, the top slid backward, revealing an internal chamber packed with blasters, swords, and other types of weapons.

"Lemaleion could use one of those," Ki'ran murmured as he sidled up beside me.

I nodded, not taking my eyes off Elgin as he leaned into the storage space beneath him, loose strands of his green hair tumbling free to hang in front of his face.

"What will it be," he announced, lifting a blaster in one hand and a thin dueling sword in the other, "fencing or shooting?"

A shiver rolled down my spine at the sight of the sword. A few of the cyborgs on Vanthurium had used them, and the sight of the fencing rapier sent my mind right back into the horror of that day.

We'd never practiced with swords during my time with the Protective Forces, and I was surprised that the royal guards could use them. Perhaps swords were reserved for those serving the king?

Fortunately, Ki'ran saved me from having to voice my displeasure. "Shooting. I am not in a fencing mood," he replied with a scowl. He approached Elgin and, flipping his long braid over his shoulder, leaned down to select a blaster.

A brief look of annoyance crossed Elgin's face, as if he hoped I would be the one to make the choice, but the moment quickly passed, his eager expression returning. "Excellent! We can have a one versus one shoot-off and really get a feel for each other's skills!"

Okay, *now* I was confused. Shouldn't he have known that I would out-shoot all of them? If he'd heard so much about me, there was no doubt he would have heard how well I could use a blaster.

I felt like there was a trick up his sleeve, but I couldn't imagine what it was.

"Alright," he drawled, strolling away from the weapons box, "what shall we play? Best successive shots across multiple targets, or best shot at a certain distance?" He glanced between me and Ki'ran.

Since Ki'ran picked the weapon, I figured that I'd choose the game. "Successive shots."

"Excellent." Elgin grinned and twirled the blaster around his hand.

While he and Ki'ran stepped up beside each other to decide which targets they would hit in order, my attention drifted to our surroundings.

I was already becoming fond of the palace grounds. They were clean and filled with vibrant plants, and the whole area just exuded a feeling of calmness, even peaceful security. It was *far* more welcoming than the Protective Forces grounds had been.

In the distance, to the north of the training grounds, I watched cruisers and ships dock and take off. It still amazed me that we could be on the ground so close to where these massive ships were. I thought back to how much space was needed for a Terran airport, and the contrast was striking.

People scuttled to and fro, unloading crates or passengers from recently-landed ships or loading up ones that took off shortly after. I found myself wishing for free time with Caspian so that we could go flying again. I'd love to soar above the Valley of the Crown.

The sounds of shooting shook me from my peaceful thoughts, and I turned back to the "competition" that was just starting.

Unsurprisingly, Elgin was the first one to shoot. His stance was too wide for my liking, and for some reason he held the blaster in a two-handed grip. With how minimal the kickback was from these weapons, I couldn't see a good reason for his strange form. However, I couldn't deny that he was still a decent shot.

A scorch mark sizzled inches from the innermost circle on the first target, roughly sixty feet away. His second shot – at a distance of around a hundred and twenty feet – was a little further off, hitting the target in the top half of the third ring. By his third and final target, a hundred and eighty feet away, Elgin's aim had gone wild. The blast clipped the bottom left corner of the square target, and he let out a groan.

"Moved a little too fast, I guess," he laughed, rubbing the back of his neck.

I rolled my eyes. For all his bravado and attempt to show off, he wasn't good at rapidly hitting targets at a distance. His embarrassment was obvious, but he tried to hide it under swagger as he moved so Ki'ran could take his place. "Okay big guy, you're up!" he cheered as he clapped Ki'ran on the back.

I could tell that Ki'ran was eager to knock some respect into Elgin. He took his time setting up and took a few long looks down his blaster at each of the targets. Then, after cracking his neck, Ki'ran started shooting.

His first shot matched Elgin's perfectly – the scorched spot was now a hole burned through the metal target. The second shot blazed into the opposite side of the target, but Ki'ran managed to keep this one inside the second-most ring. A smile crept onto Ki'ran's face. The third shot still proved tricky – although better than Elgin's, Ki'ran only managed to improve his placement by a few inches inward. Still, he'd beaten Elgin.

Now the smugness was gone from Elgin's face.

"Great shots!" I called.

Turning back to the group and fighting hide a full grin, Ki'ran gave us a shallow bow.

Ba'rin had no such hesitations when it came to displaying his emotions. "Ha-ha!" he bellowed at his friend. "And you thought you'd be able to out-shoot him!"

Elgin's face went red with embarrassment. "Yeah, well… this is all just for fun."

"Oh, no," Ba'rin said with a shake of his finger. "You are still paying up." And then he doubled over with laughter.

I tried to stifle my own laugher with my hand. They actually had a *bet* going over this? Hopefully they hadn't bet on my shooting.

Ki'ran flipped the blaster in his hand and offered it to me. "Uh, I'm fine, thanks. Ba'rin can go next."

With a shrug Ki'ran turned and offered the blaster to Ba'rin who was far more eager to take his turn. While he readied up, Ki'ran strolled over and took a place beside me.

"I like them," he said without preamble. "They will make this assignment more enjoyable, I think."

I watched Elgin and Ba'rin exchange a few teasing insults. We didn't have the best assignment here at the palace – and I hadn't even experienced the nonsense that the other prince's guards might have already endured – but somehow Elgin and Ba'rin were able to crack smiles and jokes.

At least, I reminded myself with a smile, *I don't have to deal with General Vinculus anymore.* That was definitely a bonus.

Ba'rin took his shots – one bullseye and two in the second-smallest ring. I couldn't help but smile as he turned to Elgin and proceeded to rub his success in his friend's face. To his credit, Elgin endured the teasing for a few minutes, as he'd clearly been in the wrong for taunting all of us at the start. But then he cut Ba'rin off with a wave of his hand.

"Okay, now it's Aliya's turn." He approached me with the blaster he'd used, a curious expression in his eyes.

I took a step back. "No, really, it's okay. I'm not really in the mood for a competition."

"Then don't think of it as a competition! Just you, some targets… and us watching excitedly from behind you." Elgin laughed.

Unfortunately, I knew that I couldn't get out of this. There was nowhere else for me to go, no one to come to my rescue. The other three had taken their turns, and I had been the one to suggest this type of shooting game.

Gripping the handle, I slid the blaster out from Elgin's loose grip. It was lighter than what I had used with the Forces and Nova squad, but not enough to really throw me off.

I took my time walking over to the spot where the other three had stood. I wasn't nervous to shoot – oh no, I knew how this would go. But I was nervous for their reactions afterward.

They knew who I was, had heard stories of what I had done on Charra and Vanthurium. Although I didn't know exactly what they were expecting to see, I knew that they wanted a show.

I am Aliya Rathburn. I fought Krech on Charra and survived the cyborg invasion on Vanthurium. I'd saved Caspian's life with a single shot. I can do this.

Settling into my casual shooting stance, I took aim and then released a deep breath.

"Double or nothing?" I heard Elgin whisper to Ba'rin.

"That would not be wise," Ki'ran interjected.

I heard a snort and then the smack of two palms sealing a deal.

What an idiot, I thought with a roll of my eyes. Well fine then. If he was ridiculous enough to bet on my skills, I'd show them exactly what I could do.

"Ready?" I called over my shoulder. "Don't blame me if you blink and miss everything."

"Dazzle us, dearie," Elgin called back.

I took another breath. Three shots. *Here we go.*

Zing! Bullseye.

Zing! Bullseye.

Zing! Bullseye.

All done within a heartbeat.

"Stars above," Elgin whispered.

I strolled back to the group, trying to ignore the looks of utter shock on Elgin's and Ba'rin's faces. Stopping in front of Elgin, I offered the blaster back to him.

He looked dumbfounded for a moment, and then he snatched it up, inspecting the nozzle and sides. "What'd you do to it? Is there a new auto-targeting mod that I don't know about?"

Ba'rin let out a low whistle. "The stories about you must be true." He glanced at the smoldering holes I'd left in centers of the three targets. "You fought four Krech at once?"

"I did."

He nodded, looking back at the targets thoughtfully. "I wonder why you are not in the king's guards then."

I opened my mouth to reply but then stopped. I understood that King Locklyn wanted to protect his heir, but it should have made more sense for me to protect the king. Maybe Caspian was always intended for the prince's service and had insisted on keeping me by his side? It was possible, but I still couldn't see the logic from the king's side.

Finished with his joking inspection of the blaster, Elgin stepped up to me. "Teach me."

"What?"

"You saw that." He gestured to the targets with the blaster. "I'm the worst shot out of the four of us. You've fought things that I haven't and came out alive, so clearly you know a few things about shooting and fighting that I don't. I'd like to learn from you." He paused and then turned to meet Ki'ran's eyes. "From both of you."

I'd never been the type of person who could say no when someone asked for help, and I was quite humbled that after all his bravado, Elgin was actually asking us for help. "Fine," I said with a nod as his face lit up. "Take your position. We'll take a closer look at your stance and hand position."

With a spring in his step, Elgin prepared to shoot once more. Ki'ran and I took turns adjusting his foot placement, his grip, and the height at which he held the blaster. By unspoken agreement we didn't have him shoot at the first or third targets we'd used in our "competition," instead, focusing on the second which seemed to be a more realistic distance for practice.

And of course, Ba'rin was always ready with a joke or teasing comment when Elgin's shot didn't go exactly where he wanted.

After half an hour my focus began to drift. Elgin was a quick learner, and there was only so much that Ki'ran and I could teach him in one day. The real test would be if he remembered all our new adjustments and suggestions when he tried again tomorrow.

My gaze was drawn back to the royal airfield. I marveled at the sheer number of small craft arriving and departing every few minutes. Who were these people, and where were they going? Would I be able to travel like that?

It was then that a sleek silver ship appeared on the far horizon. It truly seemed to glide through the air as it headed toward the palace. But this wasn't just any ship.

It was easily three or four stories high, and the double set of wings was a fascinating difference that I hadn't seen on any other ship, or cruiser, so far.

And then there was the massive set of double blasters on the front-most wings. The nozzle of the blasters had to be at least as wide as I was tall, and they extended back along the entire width of the wing.

This wasn't a ship that I'd want to run up against if I was an enemy.

The gleaming behemoth hovered to a stop and then gently lowered, touching the ground without the slightest bump. An incredible ship and a skilled pilot? I was immediately curious who owned the vessel.

It took a full minute before anyone departed through the rear gangway. Three tall individuals dressed head to toe in black prowled out, followed by a much smaller person who wore a silver jacket and black pants.

"I thought they weren't scheduled back until tomorrow," Elgin said, surprising me as he snuck up from behind.

"Who?" I asked, half paying attention to what he was saying because I was too intent on watching this latest arrival.

"The *Hellfire*. I thought their flight path would've put them away from Callais for another week, at least," he replied with a shrug.

I stopped listening when he said *Hellfire*. My breath caught, and my heart started to pound at the simple word. All of a sudden, my universe shrunk to the silver ship and the significantly smaller person who had emerged from that monstrous ship.

After all, there was only one person I knew who would name a spaceship *Hellfire*.

I took off, ignoring the shouts of surprise from my companions. My legs were a blur as I raced across the palace grounds, honing in on the one person I'd been missing.

As I drew closer, her telltale features came into view. Long blonde curls framed a sweet, round face, even as she carried herself with all the authority of a captain.

Dock and flight crews finally took notice of my rapid approach, rushing to grab blasters or scurry out of the way, so I slowed down, coming to a complete halt about a hundred or so feet from where the *Hellfire* had landed.

Her back was to me, but I noticed that her hands had balled

into fists and her shoulders were tense. Why wasn't she turning to greet me?

"Adís?" I tentatively asked.

She sighed and then half-turned toward me. Straightening her shoulders and lifting her chin she said, "Hey, Aliya."

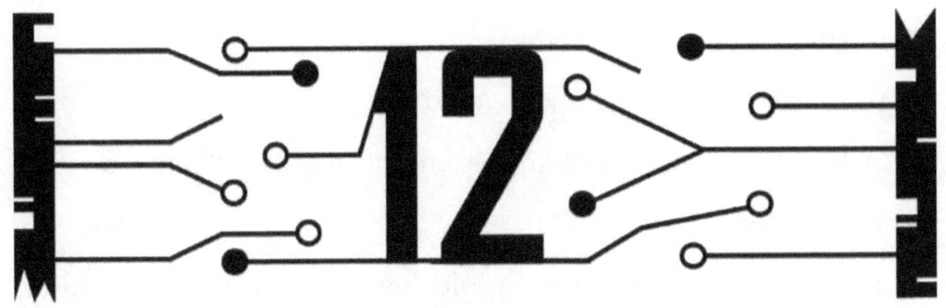

It was a cold greeting. There was none of the former cheer and friendliness that she'd shown me during our time on the Nova squad or that she'd shown her team just moments before my arrival.

A multitude of questions rose to my lips, but the one that won out was, "Where have you been?" It came out a little harsher than intended.

Adís seemed prepared for my question because she continued to hold my gaze with a cool stare. She turned back to her crew, all six of them waiting intently behind her, and waved them away. Without hesitation, they left and returned to their tasks.

With a curt nod of her head Adís motioned that we should move away from her ship, and she headed up the paved path toward the palace.

I couldn't help watching her walk ahead of me. *She could walk.* Her steps were even, and it looked like someone had been able to repair the damage to her spine.

Then why hadn't she come back to us?

Adís ground to a halt and spun to face me. "What do you want?" she demanded.

I was taken aback. This should have been a happy reunion, possibly with a hug and a few tears. Instead I found myself wondering how to handle the cold female before me.

"I wanted to see you. We've all been so worried…" I paused as I watched her roll her eyes. "Adís, I'm serious. Everyone was scared that you weren't coming back to us or that doctors couldn't help you."

"Because they couldn't," she snapped. "Doctors at three different facilities couldn't get the nerves in my spine to reattach completely, and they *couldn't figure out why.*"

"But you're walking…" Unless I was missing something major, Adís was clearly standing and walking around on her own two legs.

She snorted and turned away from me. Her breathing turned shaky, and I felt my stomach sink when I realized that she was crying.

"Yeah, they came up with a partial fix for me. A prototype they've dubbed 'mo-wear.' And I hate it." She wrapped her arms around her torso as if she was trying to hold herself together.

"Why?"

"Because it's not me! I'm *broken,* and now I have to constantly wear this…"

I couldn't handle staring at her back any longer, so I circled around and gripped her shoulders, forcing her to face me. "Adís, you're not broken! You can stand and move." I ignored the vigorous shaking of her head. "You're still you. We all missed you, and you should have at least let us know you were okay!"

"But I'm not okay!" She met my eyes as tears rolled down her face. "I'm not the same, and now I'm… limited."

I let go of her shoulders and stepped back. "What do you mean?"

Adís sat down on the ground and hugged her knees, and I took a spot beside her. "Mo-wear, or mobility wear, only partially fixes my injury. I have to wear this skin-tight set of nanotech pants that… sort of plug in, I guess, to a port set right above the injury in my spine. The port connects my live nerves to the mo-wear, like sending brain signals all the way down my legs. I can move, but I can't feel anything."

I sat in stunned silence for a moment. Her movements seemed so fluid and normal. You couldn't even guess that she had no feeling in her legs.

I must have turned the information over in my head for a few seconds too long because Adís turned her tear-streaked face toward me. "Well, say *something,*" she demanded.

"I—" I had no idea what to say to her. I'd never needed to console someone for a permanent injury before, and I was struggling to wrap my head around why she was limited when her full range of movement had been restored. "Why are you still limited?"

Her expression turned stony. "Because this is still a *prototype.*" She practically spat the word. "Every now and then there's a little hiccup that needs to be repaired, and obviously I can't do it because the port is in my back. And if I was running from enemies and had this system fail…"

Oh. I didn't realize that the mo-wear wasn't complete. To rely on something that didn't work one hundred percent of the time… I finally started to grasp Adís' frustration with her situation.

"They said I couldn't be in the field anymore, but that's who I *am*, that's who I've learned *to be.* I couldn't just… walk away from that. Stars, they wanted me to leave the Forces and military service altogether! *That* was really where I put my foot—" She cut off, realizing what she was unintentionally saying, and the tears started anew. "I saw so many doctors, heard 'no' or 'I'm sorry' so many times, and didn't get why this was happening to me. Why they couldn't just patch me up and send me on my way. It was just my back, not my whole body. You were nearly dead, *so why couldn't they heal me?*" she practically shouted at me.

And there it was, the true reason for avoiding the Nova squad and her cold attitude earlier.

My heart broke for Adís. I almost wished I'd seen this reason earlier.

It shouldn't have surprised me that after hearing about my

brush with death and how Doctor Givray had saved me, Adís would have hope that she would be healed. I'd nearly been a lost cause – and a final, wild hope brought me back to life.

Adís' injury should have been easier to fix than *that*. Shouldn't it?

Adís had curled in on herself, shaking from her sobs, and I couldn't help throwing my arms around her. She initially stiffened at the contact, but then she came alive, twisting in my embrace and wrapping her arms around my torso while she buried her head in my shoulder.

I let her cry. I let her release the burden that must have weighed her down ever since she met that first doctor. There was nothing I could've said to make things better anyway.

After several minutes of crying, Adís finally pulled back and swiped at her face with the sleeve of her shirt. "I'm sorry," she said with a sniffle. "This isn't your fault."

I shook my head. "I get it now. I'd be frustrated too."

"I just… I wanted to go back to normal. Every now and then there's some miracle surgery, and especially after knowing you, I kept thinking to myself, 'I'll be fine. This isn't a big deal.' But I guess it was." She brushed away a stray tear.

Her thoughts faintly echoed mine when I first woke up in the healing facility. I thought that since I'd been healed, I would be able to go home. My recovery would be called a 'miracle,' as Adís said, and everything would've gone back to normal.

But I'd never lost my ability to move or fight like Adís had.

"Well, have you had Gunther or Gráinne take a look at your port or mo-wear yet? Maybe they'd be able to fix the bugs in the prototype."

"They're here?" Her blue eyes sparked with hope.

"Yeah. The two of them, Caspian, Ki'ran, and I are here working for the king – well, I guess the prince."

Adís looked confused for a moment, but she gave a little shake of her head and continued. "Where are they? I guess I should say hi to Ki'ran and Caspian, but… I'd really like to see the twins first."

I laughed. "I don't blame you. They should be in the palace with the king's other technicians, uh, somewhere." I realized that I had no idea where the twins worked.

Adís must have known because she excitedly nodded her head. "Right. Okay, I'll go see them." She sprung to her feet and then looked back at the *Hellfire* and the crew awaiting her return. "Oh. I guess I should probably wrap things up over there first."

"That might be a good idea, *captain*," I said with a smile. "Congrats on getting your ship, by the way."

Adís squared her shoulders and beamed. "Fastest and deadliest ship in the King's Galaxy. You should've seen how much they laughed at me for naming it *Hellfire* before I had those cannons installed."

"No kidding." I crossed my arms and regarded Adís as she appraised her crew. She certainly wasn't her old self, but she'd regained something truly empowering when she became captain of the *Hellfire*. Feeling in her legs or no, Adís could stand and walk and give orders, and she was clearly proud of her ship and crew.

"Hey, Adís?"

She turned to look at me. "Yes?"

"Don't be a stranger anymore, okay? Come say hi whenever you're not busy flying that monster around and terrorizing the galaxy."

Adís swallowed once and then threw herself back into my arms. "Of *course*. I'm so sorry I stayed away."

I held her like I was afraid she'd disappear once she stepped out of my grasp. "It's okay. You're here now, and I'll do anything I can to support you."

We let go, and she took a step back. Adís looked completely different from the cold female who'd greeted me in the shadow of her ship. Now she appeared... happy. Hopeful.

And I could only hope that the twins would be able to help her further.

"I'll see you soon!" she called with a smile as she headed back to the *Hellfire*.

I really hoped so. I'd missed my friend.

Which reminded me...

I gave Adís one last wave and turned toward the training grounds. I thought that Ki'ran and the other two would have had more than enough time to catch up to me, despite how fast I ran.

Instead I was surprised to find all three males standing together, watching me approach. Ki'ran stood on the left with his chin raised a little, his arms linked behind his back. Elgin and

Ba'rin had slightly perplexed looks on their faces, as if they didn't know who Adís was or what she meant to me. Maybe they *hadn't* heard everything about me and the Nova squad. But then why hadn't they followed me?

"You didn't come over to say hi to her." I had to raise my voice a bit to reach Ki'ran, but I closed the distance quickly.

"She would have come herself if she had wanted to see me." It was a curious thing for him to say, and it took me a few more steps to see why.

In a rare display of emotion, Ki'ran's eyes glistened, just barely, with unshed tears. His dark face held color high in his cheeks, and a wistful smile was hesitantly perched on his lips, as if at any moment he might slip back into his typical and stoic self.

"Whatever she said, needed to be said to you, not to me or anyone else. She was weighed down by the gravity of many planets, and you just erased that burden." He refused to take his eyes off her distant form as he spoke, and the raw emotion in his voice sparked my own tears. "Adís was the first to understand you, and it looks like you were the first to understand this new version of her."

My throat was so thick with tears that it took me two tries to speak. "All I did was let her know that I'm still here for her, injury or not. She sees herself as changed, but I don't."

"You are good for seeing that." He finally shifted his gaze to me and offered a slow nod.

"I just hope that she eventually sees it too."

It took me a long time to come to terms with who I'd become and what my new limits were, but I'd faced those challenges alone. Well, alone until I'd joined Nova.

Perhaps Adís would realize that we – her eclectic, intergalactic family – were still here for her. And would be here for her every step of the way.

Ki'ran cleared his throat and clapped me on the shoulder with his metal hand. "Come," he said, pulling me back toward the shooting range. "Elgin still cannot hit the third target like me. We should return to teaching him."

"Hey!" Elgin cried in embarrassment.

I laughed, feeling much lighter than I had when this day began. Elgin and Ba'rin had proved to be fun and open to the three former Nova members joining them, and Adís was here and doing okay.

The only thing left was getting Caspian on board with this new situation, but that would be a problem for later.

After all, we still had to teach Elgin how to shoot.

We took turns shooting all morning until Elgin complained that his arm was going to fall off.

I was glad that he had finally called an end to our training. It was nearly midday, and the heat had become stifling once more as the sun beat down from overhead.

After everyone agreed that we needed a few minutes to freshen up before grabbing lunch, we parted ways at the palace's side door.

I made straight for my room, craving cool water to wash off my face and neck.

I had no idea how the other palace guards stood outside in the heat wearing long sleeves. We'd only been out in the morning, not even the hottest temperature of the day, and I was profusely sweating.

It was incredibly fortunate that I didn't have to guard the prince – or worse, the king – in this state of dishevelment.

Once in my room I rushed to the balcony doors and flung them open, hoping for a bit of a breeze up here on the third floor. I wasn't disappointed, and I couldn't hold back my sigh as a cool breeze kissed my damp neck.

I made my way to the bathroom and splashed cold water on my face and neck. *If only I had time for a bath…* Perhaps I'd indulge after lunch since I wasn't slated for guard duty.

After drying off I twisted my hair up into a bun – anything to keep it from sticking to my skin – and slipped back out of my room. I didn't want to keep the others waiting for too long.

The palace was quiet as I wound my way down to the bottom floor. I guessed the oppressive heat made everyone lethargic; I couldn't blame them. If I hadn't agreed to meet back up with Ki'ran, Elgin, and Ba'rin, I would've hung out on my balcony all day, soaking up that wonderful breeze.

Down in the lower floor's hallways the air was thick and still, yet it still managed to carry the voices of an approaching group who were down the hallway to my left.

"But King Locklyn… he's holding his meeting in the strategy room… uh, your highness?" a familiar voice said.

"My dearest father—" there was a hiccup "—would probably be happier if I was *not* part of that boring meeting." The deep, slow voice must have belonged to Prince Damien. There were no other highnesses in the palace – unless the queen could be called highness? Stars, I really had no grasp on royal etiquette.

My mind raced to think of an alternate route that I could take to the banquet hall so that I wouldn't have to pass the prince, but I couldn't come up with another way.

Groaning internally as I listened to him hiccup a second time – seriously, how was he drunk again? – I rounded the corner.

And ran smack into Prince Damien.

My quickened reflexes kicked in immediately. I stepped to the side and gripped the prince's slim shoulders, keeping him from falling over backward.

"I'm *so* sorry, your highness! I didn't realize you were there—" Prince Damien jerked out of my grip, stumbling a few steps before he regained his balance. Omri and Caspian, standing a few paces behind the prince, tensed as if preparing to catch him but made no move to get closer.

"You," he stated. It wasn't a question or an accusation but almost a bland recognition of who I was. At least, I hoped he knew who I was.

Prince Damien looked like an absolute mess. His hair was wild and partially plastered to his sweaty forehead, and his hazel eyes were completely glassy. He didn't sport the regal attire he'd worn yesterday. Instead the prince dressed in a loose, short-sleeved white shirt with a stretched-out neckline and a pair of incredibly wrinkled, olive-colored slacks. Even the tan boots he wore were half untied, the laces dragging along the pristine floors. His royal circlet was nowhere in sight.

Worse than his appearance was his *smell.* He absolutely reeked of some strong alcohol that I couldn't quite place, and it was nearly enough to make my eyes water. How had Caspian and Omri endured this appalling stench for so long? If it were me, I would've slipped off hours ago. In this state I doubted the prince would notice one less guard following him.

Unfortunately, the mess standing – well, more like gently swaying – in front of me was a prince, and I had to treat him with some respect. I offered a shallow bow and replied, "Yes, it's me, your highness." I straightened up and waited for what he'd do next.

Prince Damien said nothing for long enough that I became uncomfortable. His glazed eyes roamed my face and then down my body. I looked at the floor as an embarrassed blush rose to my cheeks.

There was a sharp intake of breath from either Caspian or Omri – I couldn't tell which one – and then a throat was cleared. But the prince spoke before either of his guards had the chance.

"I thought she'd been modified." It took a few seconds for me to realize that he wasn't speaking to me. Instead, he was speaking as if I wasn't in the room. "She looks rather normal to me. Even for a Terran."

Was he... *insulting* me? Worse than that was that he was insulting me in front of Caspian.

I don't think I'd been more embarrassed in my entire life.

My mouth opened, but I had no words to say. Rendered utterly speechless, I snapped my mouth closed again with an audible click of teeth.

But the prince was far from finished. "Although," he said as he started on a wobbly loop around where I stood, "the stories have to be true. Don't they? She—" *hiccup* "—I mean, you wouldn't be here if there wasn't a hint of truth to what we've heard." Prince Damien stopped directly behind me. I could feel his creeping gaze on my neck, down my back...

As I lifted my eyes, I saw unbridled rage in Caspian's face. I needed to get away *now* before this got weirder or Caspian did something that would get him in trouble.

"I would be curious, though," the prince stepped up behind me and trailed a single finger down the middle of my upper back, his foul breath wafting across my exposed neck, "to see. Where, exactly, you were modified, that is. Perhaps that could be counted as your... guard shift." He laughed once, his voice low and husky.

I was going to vomit. No, I was going to scream. No, I was going to punch him – at my full strength, too. Or maybe I'd do all three.

The insult was bad enough, but *this?* I didn't know what I

expected out of the prince, but being propositioned by him, in front of other guards, was not something I had anticipated.

Shock and revulsion and fury ripped through me like waves crashing on a beach. I'd never been in a situation like this before, and to make matters worse, this was a *prince*. Could I even do anything to show him how his words made me feel? As much as I wanted to, I couldn't hit him.

In front of me, Caspian had gone completely rigid. His hands were white-knuckled fists at his sides, and they twitched as if he, too, wanted to take a swing at the prince. "Aliya is your guard, Prince Damien. That's horribly inappropriate." Caspian's voice trembled with barely controlled rage, and his face was a mask of pure anger.

Prince Damien strolled around to my side; fortunately for me he removed his finger and created a few feet of space between us. "You're right. She's *my* guard and would do well to heed my orders."

My stomach plummeted, and I felt dizzy. Surely, he wasn't going to *order* me to do what he wanted?

That did it for Caspian. He took a short step forward but was quickly halted by Prince Damien's outstretched hand. "Just a joke, captain. I wouldn't want to offend my father's favorite hero." His voice turned acidic at the mention of his father. "Anyway, we had best be on our way. Things to do, people to see." The prince laughed but was cut short by another hiccup.

I had no idea what plans he had in store for his day, but I knew that I'd be doing everything within my power to stay far out of his way. Stars, I'd go beg Adís to take me on a trip if that's what it took.

Before Prince Damien walked away, he leaned close to my face. "Perhaps another time then," he whispered, lips a hairsbreadth from the shell of my ear. And then he was off, swaying down the hallway to terrorize some other poor guard or servant.

Caspian and Omri lurched into motion. While Omri shuffled past, Caspian stopped directly in front of me.

"Aliya, I'm so sorry. I'll make sure that never happens again." He kept his voice as low as possible, brushing his thumb over my cheek to wipe away a falling tear.

I didn't even know when I'd started crying, but I knew that I needed to get someplace private before the waterworks actually started.

"It's okay," I lied to Caspian. "He didn't hurt me." I was sure he didn't believe me.

Caspian frowned. "We'll talk and fix this later." Then he leaned in to plant a quick kiss on my forehead before heading after Omri and the prince.

I felt bad, knowing that Caspian still had a few more hours left on his shift before he could switch out and check on me. He'd likely fume over this interaction because he was unable to handle this situation the way he wanted.

I was worried he'd do something rash, but I had to trust that

Caspian wouldn't do something that would get him tossed in prison or somewhere similar.

In the meantime, I needed to speak with Ki'ran about switching guard shifts.

My feet refused to move at first. I was still too shocked, too disgusted by Prince Damien's actions.

Sure, I'd assumed that royals were entitled and self-important – I had seen so many movies and read so many books which played up that stereotype – but *never* had I anticipated *that* degree of horrible behavior.

He acted as if I was there to serve him instead of protect him. It was revolting.

The ghost of the prince's finger trickled down my spine, and this time I couldn't suppress the shudder that wracked my body. I needed several deep breaths before I could steady myself once more.

I felt sick knowing that Prince Damien would likely try to... proposition me again the next time our paths crossed. I could hear the palace gossip now: the playboy prince who made a move on one of his guards. The thought was revolting.

I wished that Caspian had been able to stand up for me more, but it was just an unfortunate circumstance. Caspian was a guard; what could he really say or do to stop the prince?

Moreover, I wished that *I* had said or done something to stop Prince Damien and let him know that his actions were unacceptable. I should've said something, should've walked away, should've done *something* other than stand there and endure his nonsense. Aliya Rathburn, the Hero of Vanthurium, should not have put up with that.

Where was that brave, let's run headlong into danger side of me now?

If only I hadn't agreed to come work for the king.

As soon as the thought occurred to me, I knew I didn't mean it. I could never abandon Caspian and Ki'ran and those who needed my protection. Because *that* – my drive to protect others with what I'd been given – was the real reason I'd agreed to come here.

Prince Damien was a mess and rude and horrible… but I wasn't going to let him scare me away.

However, that didn't mean I had to stand around and let him make passes at me.

The way I saw it, I had two options: face him and demand he never treat me like that again, or still do my job while finding ways to avoid him.

There was no universe where a guard would be able to stand up to a prince, especially one like Prince Damien, so the second option became my best course of action.

I balled my hands into fists and took one step forward. Then a second. And then I was walking down the hallway, finally headed to the banquet hall where lunch was being served.

My first guard shift was with Ba'rin and supposed to start later this afternoon, running through the evening, but I didn't want that anymore. I didn't want to spend time around Prince Damien, especially if he drank at dinner. The only time I'd want to be around the prince was when he was asleep.

My walk turned into a jog, and then I was sprinting through the hallways, ignoring the shouts of surprise from the few guards I passed.

I focused on the echoing thuds of my boots on the marble floor and my racing heart. Anything other than reliving the encounter in the hallway. The two beats nearly matched as I sped toward the banquet hall and its massive double doors.

I skidded to a halt and yanked open the black, metal door. Engraved down its length was a history of the first king of the King's Galaxy. On any other day I would've stopped to take in the majestic artwork and fascinating story, but not today.

Quickly scanning the hall for Ki'ran, I made my way down the center aisle. Yet again I ignored the many sets of eyes on me, the way I stopped conversations, and the whispers that started up after I had strode past.

But that didn't mean that I couldn't hear what was said about me.

"Is that her?"

"It's the Hero of Vanthurium."

"I heard that she can stop a whole *army* of Krech."

"Wonder why she's here at the palace."

The last comment resonated with some of my previous thoughts. If I was an asset in battle, why was I stuck at the palace?

And why did I have to deal with the prince?

Ki'ran sat on the far side of the table on my left. Across from him were Ba'rin and Elgin, and since their backs faced the aisle, they hadn't yet noticed me. Looking up from his nearly-empty plate, Ki'ran's brown eyes opened wide with surprise. *Did I really look* that *bad?*

He whispered something to them, and the three males turned to me. I must have had some wild expression on my face because they all looked concerned as they took in my appearance. While they made no move to stand, Elgin and Ba'rin's hands went to the blasters strapped to their sides.

"Aliya! Where have you been?" Ki'ran stood up quickly, knocking his chair over in the process.

I crossed my arms over my chest, hoping that I could keep myself together until we left the crowded hall. "Can we go somewhere private? To talk?"

Ki'ran's tanned brow wrinkled in concern. "Of course." He turned and took a step toward the door.

"All of you," I said shifting my weight from one foot to the other.

I didn't relish the idea of telling them what had occurred, but if I wanted to switch guard shifts, they needed to understand why.

I made my way back up the main aisle, Elgin and Ba'rin on my heels while Ki'ran walked parallel to us on the far side of the table.

All conversations died off as we passed. I was reminded of the first time I saw the Nova squad in the Protective Forces' dining hall. Everyone regarded them with awe while keeping their distance. They were elite, separate from the rest of us and considered an enigma.

I had no doubt that the four of us, broody and moving together, evoked those same feelings in the crowd that surrounded us.

Once the doors to the banquet hall thudded closed behind us, Elgin took over, leading us away from the east wing and into the west one.

"The second floor balcony of the ballroom is always empty unless there's a party," he explained over his shoulder. "We should be able to find an isolated corner where we can talk."

Neither Ki'ran nor I objected since Elgin knew the palace better than we did, so we simply followed in silence.

He led us to a hallway that ended with a set of golden, arched doors that stretched all the way up to the ceiling. Gemstones of all different colors were inlaid on the front in an artistic depiction of the King's Galaxy.

This time I was dying to stop and trace my fingers over the gems. I'd seen holographic models of the galaxy's planets while I was with the Protective Forces, but this felt like something wholly different. The two-dimensional display was beautiful in a way that a hologram could never be.

Elgin, however, barely paused as he eased one door open and slipped inside. I followed directly behind him, and a moment later, Ki'ran and Ba'rin passed through the doors as well.

"I'm sure you'll get better acquainted with this side of the palace and the rooms over here soon enough," he said. Elgin stretched his arms out and slowly turned in a circle. "The grand ballroom is reserved for royal celebrations… and Prince Damien's parties. It would do you well to spend a lot of time walking through here and finding all the little nooks and crannies that he and his guests love to get into."

I grimaced. Even if I was able to successfully avoid the prince during guard shifts, I wouldn't be able to completely keep away from him during a party. I hoped that his guests wouldn't be as bad as he was, but Elgin's comment made me think that they'd all have similar behaviors.

If they were that terrible, parties were going to be a nightmare, and that was downright unfortunate. I hadn't been to a party since leaving Terra, and the grand ballroom looked like it could host quite the party.

One could easily land two ships just on the main floor, which had been crafted from a cream-colored marble. The ceiling was easily one hundred feet, if not more, above our heads, and I saw not just one, but three wraparound balconies.

Gold and black paint mingled on the ceiling, mimicking the heavens once more. While I would've thought that a mostly black ceiling would darken a room of this size, it actually made the ceiling look as if it was farther away. At night the room might even feel like it didn't have a ceiling altogether.

Tall, rectangular windows were set into the walls on our right and directly across from us, and the long curtains covering them alternated between gold or black velvet. Two-thirds of the wall to our left displayed a massive bar, complete with seating, and the final section of that wall had a doorless archway. Because the lights were off, I couldn't tell where the hall led.

Between the four walls and the edges of the dance floor were rounded pillars made of white marble and wider than I could wrap my arms around which stretched twenty feet up to the underside of the first balcony.

This room was magical. I could easily imagine myself twirling around in a ball gown. With the lights down low and some candlelight, this room would accommodate any girl's dream of feeling like a princess.

Unfortunately, I wasn't here to live out my dreams of being royalty.

"This way." Elgin waved us toward the rounded archway on the left side of the ballroom.

The dim space held a twisting staircase which deposited us on the second floor. With only a few pillars supporting the ceiling, the entire floor was designed in an open concept. Groups of low, plush chairs were scattered here and there, and high tables made from a dark metal stood in the far corners.

It felt like a lounge. Strips of red and black velvet hung from the walls, and with only two thin windows set into each wall, the second floor was very dim. I couldn't imagine this space being used for dancing.

Elgin headed toward one corner of the lounge and then came to a stop, crossing his arms over his chest. "The curtains dampen sounds, so anyone walking across the floor below won't be able to hear us. Unless someone starts yelling, that is." He squared up in front of me. "So. What happened?"

My mouth went dry as everyone's eyes fell on me. I had no idea what Elgin and Ba'rin might have already experienced while working for the prince, and I worried that they might find my concerns ridiculous. They'd probably never experienced the type of humiliation and discomfort that I had, so would they be able to understand?

I decided I'd take a leap of faith. They'd all seen how freaked out I was, and Elgin had directed us to a quiet place where we wouldn't be overheard. It was a small yet initial gesture that they were taking this seriously.

"It was Prince Damien," I started. Ki'ran and the other two straightened up, giving me their full attention. That gesture gave me all the confidence I needed to share what had happened.

Words spilled from my lips as it all came out in a rush. How I'd bumped into him in the hallway. How, once again, he hadn't been sober. The awful things he'd said to me. And then how he'd shut down Caspian when he tried to defend me.

"It was *awful* and demeaning and…" I couldn't find the right words to describe how disgusted I felt. "I really can't believe that King Locklyn would allow his son to act like that. He's not princely at all, and he's a pig… Does he treat every female like that?" I directed my question to Elgin.

His jaw tensed as anger simmered in his eyes, and he heaved a deep sigh before replying. "Yeah, he does. *Prince* Damien," he said with a sneer, "thinks that his title allows him access to everything and everyone he desires. He thinks he's creation's gift to females, and he's broken many hearts with that horrible attitude."

"And his parents don't try to stop him?"

"Oh, believe me, they've tried. He offended a lord's daughter once while the lord and King Locklyn were negotiating a trade deal, and the deal was almost lost because of that." He rolled his eyes. "The king actually went so far as to lock Damien up for a few days. Thought it would teach him a lesson." He broke off with a shake of his head.

"Caspian mentioned something like that. I'm guessing it didn't teach him anything."

Elgin barked out a single laugh. "Nope. In fact, the prince's attitude got worse after his stint in a cell. That was the point when the king and queen really gave up on trying to change his ways.

Sure, they still step in from time to time to keep him from doing some really bad things, but he mostly goes around unchecked. At least he's not allowed around diplomats' or lords' daughters anymore."

I tried to imagine what it must be like for King Locklyn and Queen Estella. To have a son who was so out of control that they couldn't even act like parents to him… It was disheartening, to say the least. Even if my team took my concerns seriously and let me stick to shifts where I'd have minimal interaction with Prince Damien, no one would be able to curb his horrible behaviors.

"I am very surprised that King Locklyn made you a prince's guard, knowing how he acts. Perhaps he thought your reputation would prevent the prince from treating you poorly," Ba'rin chimed in.

There it was again. My 'reputation' making me stand out from everyone else. I looked normal. I acted no different from everyone else. Yet somehow because I could fight better than most individuals in this galaxy, it meant that I was special.

"Well, clearly my *reputation* doesn't matter to him," I snapped, crossing my arms over my chest.

Ba'rin's brow furrowed, surprised by my anger. "Maybe he will learn that he should treat you with respect."

"And maybe one day I'll become queen." I rolled my eyes. "Anyway, the point of me telling you all of this was because I need to switch guard shifts. Permanently. Preferably to something where I'll have minimal interaction with him."

Ba'rin glanced at Elgin, and the two shared a look. "That won't always be easy. As you can imagine, he doesn't exactly keep to a schedule…"

"Okay, but he has to sleep sometime. Right?" I was starting to panic. Was there no way for me to avoid another uncomfortable confrontation with the prince?

Elgin cleared his throat. "Ah. Well. As you're now aware, 'sleep' is a term used very loosely by the prince."

I held up my hand to stop him. "I get it. But if he's occupied with someone else, then he won't be bothering me. That's all I care about right now."

"I suppose that could work." Elgin shrugged. "Ki'ran, if you don't mind switching with Aliya, she and I can take the overnight shift today."

"Of course," Ki'ran replied with a slow nod. "I will join Ba'rin once Caspian and Omri are done."

A weight lifted from my shoulders. While we might have to adjust shifts from day to day, these three were going to help me keep away from Prince Damien. We'd just have to fill Caspian and Omri in on our plan when their shift ended. I had hope that they would also understand.

Elgin clapped his hands, drawing our attention back to him. "Now that that's settled, Aliya, you and I better get some sleep. We've got a long and boring shift ahead of us, and it's better if we don't doze off."

After providing directions to the prince's chambers where

we'd meet to switch with Ki'ran and Ba'rin, the four of us went separate ways.

I still had no appetite, so I decided I'd just return to my room. There was a bowl of fruit I could snack on if I got hungry again.

I felt relieved but also disappointed. My new team, whom I'd only met this morning, supported me and had acted on my concerns. I missed being around Lem, Adís, the twins… really, everyone from Nova, but at least Elgin and Ba'rin were funny and, most importantly, considerate.

At the same time, I found myself hating my new job. I finally understood why Caspian and Ki'ran were so upset when King Locklyn told us we'd be guards for his son. Never in a million years could I have predicted that Prince Damien would be so wretched.

How had no one been able to put the prince in his place? Did he not realize that he was going to inherit his father's throne one day? Surely, no one would respect a king with a reputation like Prince Damien's. So, what was he thinking?

It's not your problem to solve, I tried to tell myself. I wasn't Prince Damien's parent or even his friend. I had one role here, and it was to ensure that he was kept safe from the Krech or other enemies. That would be simple enough if he spent his time drunkenly stumbling around the halls or cooped up in his room.

But what was I supposed to do if the prince's greatest enemy was himself?

They royal wing of the palace was a marvel unto itself.

Honestly, at this point I shouldn't have been surprised by the magnificence and attention to detail that went into every aspect of the palace, but at every turn I still managed to find myself in awe at one thing or another.

Elgin's directions sent me down non-main hallways, and at first, I was skeptical of the small, tight back staircase near the kitchens, but now I could see why he'd sent me this way.

The entire history of the Valley of the Crown had been captured on the walls of the twisting stairwell.

This must have been one of the older parts of the palace because it didn't share the same design of the building. Instead of marble, the stairs and walls were made of rectangular stones, and on the walls were murals.

Intricate, hand-painted details stretched from floor to ceiling, telling a story that no book or storyteller would have been able to convey.

The first scenes were dark – whorls of black paint wrapped themselves around colored globes and strange, square spaceships. By my interpretation, it looked like a galaxy consumed by shadows – or maybe it just depicted how little the first travelers understood their universe. They could see other planets and travel, but couldn't comprehend the spaces in between.

From that first scene, the artist focused in on one globe in particular – Callais. The green planet was lush and detailed, all the continents and oceans captured perfectly. There were waves and shadowy creatures swimming in the ocean, and the landmasses had deserts, mountains, and forests.

I wish I knew how old these murals were because they nearly looked brand new. Some edges had chipped paint, but the primary focus of the images was crisp and bright. I'm sure there were artists who maintained the murals – after all, it would be a shame to lose a piece of history like this – but it was incredibly well-maintained.

For three steps up the walls were blank, and then there it was: the Valley of the Crown. I felt like I was seeing the valley from the *Starfire* all over again. A long green valley, the hills rising to form a mountain range in the back, the smooth lake, and even the forest were all shown in this scene. The only thing that was different was the middle of the valley.

Instead of fields growing crops around a palace, there was a small village. The buildings were small, brown or gray squares that filled the vast majority of the valley. Were these early Callaisans?

I picked up my pace, curious to see more of the first settlers.

A ship entered the next scene. Hovering high above the village, the ship cast a large shadow over the ground. For some reason the artist had drawn the village in less detail now that it was darker, and there were odd little shadows peeking around the sides of buildings.

The first Callaisans had visitors from another planet? If the colors of the buildings were any indication, these settlers were still in the sticks-and-stones phase. Some buildings showed one window set into an outer wall, so they must have all been one story tall. The simple structures really enforced the early settler vibes. However, someone was already technologically advanced enough to have a ship.

But the next image took my breath away.

It was the shadowy village again, but much closer this time. Angry splashes of red lined the streets – blood. Blood from pale-skinned figures that looked like slain Callaisans.

What the heck? I was incredibly disturbed. Yes, every history was fraught with bloody battles and cruel injustices, but this scene was so jarring from the other serene pictures before it that I was shocked. Was this a territory war? An early plague?

I leaned closer to the wall, running my fingers over the cool stone as I searched for answers.

And then I found the reason for all the destruction.

I shouldn't have been so surprised, but seeing *them* here in this early image of the Valley of the Crown shook me to my core.

The Krech.

While the depictions weren't great, it was still very obvious that the dark shadows skulking down the streets were Krech because the artist had captured their indicative clawed hand.

I now noticed several areas where three long scratches stretched across a door, the side of a house, or even the middle of the dirt street.

I stumbled back from the mural, my foot narrowly missing a stair.

The Krech had been to Callais before. They'd been here and slaughtered who knows how many poor souls.

Or, a horrible thought whispered in my head, *perhaps they were here first and Callaisans attacked* them.

Colonization wasn't an unfamiliar term to me, and if it could happen to beings living on the same planet, it wasn't a far stretch to assume it could happen across planets.

But it didn't make sense. Everything I'd learned about the Krech indicated that they lived in Kāäs. They lived on a dark, grim earth far from the shining civilized planets in the King's Galaxy. Unless someone had rewritten history.

No. These beings who built spaceships, wielded laser guns, and created medical miracles wouldn't have tried to wipe out a native species. It just didn't fit with what I had learned.

Too shocked to continue the story, I bounded up the last flight of stairs and strode down the hallway, keeping an eye out for Elgin who would've gotten to the prince's room first.

I found him leaning against the wall outside Prince Damien's room. "Ah, there you are, Aliya. I was worried you'd gotten lost."

"No, I… I just got sidetracked." I stood on the opposite side of the doorway from him.

"Ah, you saw it!" Elgin pushed off the wall with one booted foot and turned to face me. "What did you think?"

"I have no idea what to think," I admitted as I wrung my hands behind my back. "How old were those murals?"

Elgin exhaled and chewed on his lower lip. "I'm not exactly sure, but they were probably made when the palace was first built. So… at least eight or nine hundred years old."

That made sense. King Locklyn was the seventh of his name, assuming that the Talimores had been the ones to first establish the Valley of the Crown. "And the murals are all true?"

"As far as I know, they are." He shrugged and looked down at me. "But I think you're avoiding my question."

I wanted to pace. Pacing always helped me think when I had a lot on my mind, but because I was supposed to be on duty, I couldn't go walking off down the hallway. Plus making too much noise might cause Prince Damien to check out the commotion.

The truth was that I didn't know what to think of the murals. They were beautiful – a true work of art. The fact that they were hundreds of years old and painted on an old, stone staircase made the images all that more remarkable.

I couldn't, however, get past that one scene. It sparked too many questions to which I had no answers and wasn't even sure where to find said answers.

Elgin waited patiently while my thoughts spiraled. "They're fantastic, but…" I paused to search for the right words.

"But the first battle scene was unexpected?" Elgin suggested.

"Yeah. That's one way of putting it," I said with a nod. "I wish I knew more about what it was telling us."

Elgin crossed his arms and leaned back against the wall. "Everyone does. When I was new, my captain showed it to me, and I assume his captain showed it to him. I had the same reaction that you're having now, except I asked a ton of questions. Were Callaisans here first? Were the Krech? No one seems to know, and I can't figure out why no one knows."

"Maybe the mural is the only remaining piece of history from that time?"

"Maybe." Elgin shook his head. "But then why keep the murals at all knowing that someone will see it and come asking questions? It doesn't make sense."

It really didn't, and we both lapsed off into the silence of our thoughts.

After a few moments Elgin pushed back off the wall with a snap of his fingers. "Oh! I almost forgot to give this to you. Two crazy red-heads came by earlier with these and said we're all supposed to wear them." Elgin reached into the inner pocket of his uniform coat and pulled out a clear, plastic-looking cuff.

Elgin dropped it into my outstretched hands. Despite being an incomplete circle, I was surprised by the weight of the cuff – it looked lighter than it actually was. "What is it?" Knowing Gunther and Gráinne, it could be anything from an accessory to a portable bomb.

"Well, they didn't say much, but they said it's for communicating? I don't really know." I smiled as I examined the device. Leave it to the twins to develop something to help us but not explain exactly *what* it does. "What do you think? It could easily be seen as stylish, right?" Elgin asked as he brandished his wrist at me. The clear cuff had wrapped all the way around his wrist and wasn't all that noticeable – unless one showed it off the way Elgin currently was.

"It's interesting," I hedged as I slipped it onto my wrist. There was a slight tremor, and the two ends elongated, eventually joining to create one continuous circle.

"That's all? Interesting?"

I laughed. "Elgin, I'm from Terra. *Everything* outside of my home planet is interesting."

"Oh. Right."

He looked like he was about to ask questions, and while I was okay talking about Terra now, I was far more interested in my new accessory. "Um, can we take these off?"

Elgin's head snapped downward as he looked at the cuff, his green bun bobbing with the abrupt motion. "Oh no, I didn't even think about that when it fastened itself on me." His fingers hovered above the cuff like he wanted to rip it off. "I know we're supposed to wear them, but... oh man, now you have me worried that I'll have to wear it forever!"

I traced my finger over the smooth surface. It felt like plastic, but I had a feeling that wasn't a material used anywhere outside of Terra. "Trust me, even if it had accidentally sealed forever, I'm sure the twins could find a way to remove it." I just wished they'd explained how to *use* it.

"Those two are twins?" I looked up at Elgin's curious expression.

"You couldn't tell? Yes; their names are Gunther and Gráinne. They were on the Nova squad with myself, Caspian, and Ki'ran." I smiled as I recalled how bizarre they seemed when we first met. The interlocked pinky fingers, finishing each other's sentences, and jokes about telekinesis had certainly made a lasting first impression. I wished I'd been here to see Elgin interact with them for the first time.

"Huh." He chewed his lower lip again and turned his wrist, examining the cuff from all angles. "Well, if you trust them, then I will too. But... maybe you should be the one to ask them for instructions on how to work this thing."

Suddenly the click of heels on marble drew our attention down the hall.

A tall, slender female made her way toward us from the direction of the main staircase. I glanced over at Elgin, but he simply shrugged at me.

I was completely drawn in by her appearance. She had skin dark as midnight with wide eyes the color of a harvest moon. A short, button nose rested just above her full, bloodred lips. Although her limbs seemed more elongated than a normal being, they somehow added to the fluid grace with which she moved.

A fountain of black, silky curls flowed down to her waist – and between the two large bat wings protruding from her back. She didn't have her wings spread; instead they were tucked neatly, but I could still see the pointed ridges at the highest and lowest points of the appendages.

She wore… uncomfortably little clothing. An iridescent crop top wrapped itself snugly around the base of her neck while exposing her shoulders and stomach, and a matching skirt clung low on her hips and barely reached the midpoint of her thighs. And of course, she wore an obscenely tall pair of stilettos – complete with little bat wings protruding from each heel.

Based on her outfit and path, I assumed she was here for the prince.

"Who are you, and where are you headed?" Luckily Elgin had his wits about him to question the fierce-looking female as she stopped in front of us.

She shot a cold glare at him from those burnt-orange eyes, and out of the corner of my eye I saw Elgin wilt a little. "Xaxena, here for Prince Damien," she purred. "He's expecting me."

"Oh, right. Of course." Elgin plastered on a fake smile. "Go right on in," he said as he opened the door for her.

"Thank you, darling," she said as she flashed him a sultry grin and clicked her way into the prince's chambers.

Only after the door was firmly closed did I open my mouth. "Is that... is that normal?"

Elgin sighed and leaned heavily against the wall. "Unfortunately, yes. King Locklyn *highly* disapproves of the prince's... visitors, but much like his day-to-day behavior, there's not much anyone can do to stop him. Honestly, I'm surprised she came through the front of the palace. Usually he pays a guard to sneak his entertainment in the back."

"That's... horrible." I felt repulsed by the prince once more. Did he have any shred of respect for the title he carried?

"That's the prince," Elgin replied with a sad shake of his head. "Luckily for us, it means he won't leave his room tonight. All we've got to do is stay awake until the next shift arrives."

I grimaced. "Well we do have these nifty new cuff things to figure out. That should take up a good bit of time."

Elgin snorted, but he rolled up the sleeve on his right wrist to expose the clear band. "Alright, let's make these things work."

The hallways grew dark long before Elgin and I figured out how to activate our high-tech wristbands.

I'd done everything from tapping the surface with each of my fingers to rubbing them in different patterns. Eventually I got annoyed and wrapped my right hand around the band, intending to pull it off and chuck it down the hallway.

There was a slight vibration, and then the cuff lit up with a screen. On it was the time, a monitor for my pulse, and a box with three dots. Tapping on the box made the screen change to a list of my team's names.

Not wanting to accidentally disturb anyone else if they were sleeping, I selected Elgin's name. Once more the screen changed – it went blank, and a holographic keyboard materialized above the cuff.

"This is so cool!" I said while I single-handedly typed out a message for Elgin.

Once I hit the little arrow icon, which I hoped told the message to send, I anxiously looked over to Elgin's cuff to see what would happen next.

The entire cuff lit up with a pale blue light, and by wrapping his opposite hand around the cuff, Elgin was able to unlock the message. A short line of text appeared on the screen. *"You suck at figuring this stuff out,"* he read aloud. "Well ha-ha, Aliya. You're so funny."

We looked at each other and broke out into a peal of soft laughter. After spending so much time trying to figure out how these darn things worked, it was a relief to have worked out part of what these things could do. I was sure there were tons of other features to explore.

After that first message, Elgin and I passed the rest of the shift in a flurry of whispering, "did you see this?" and, "look what I found!"

If they'd been the ones to design these, Gunther and Gráinne had embedded a ton of useful elements into the cuffs. We could write messages and call each other, access news stories and videos, and even track other individuals who were wearing their bracelets.

All too soon Ki'ran and Ba'rin came lumbering down the hallway.

"How did it go?" Ba'rin asked.

"He has a visitor but has been quiet all night. Should be an easy shift for you as well," Elgin answered.

"Caspian wanted us to check in and let him know we'd switched," Ki'ran explained.

Someone must have shown Ki'ran and Ba'rin how to use their cuffs, because they quickly navigated to the screen where they could send a message. Ki'ran typed a short message while Elgin grumbled something about them getting the user's manual.

We exchanged goodbyes and wishes for an easy evening, and then Elgin and I made our way out of the royal wing. For several minutes we walked in silence, and then Elgin spoke up. "I'm very impressed by how you handled Prince Damien earlier. I didn't get a chance to say that when you called your impromptu meeting, but I mean it."

"Why?"

"I don't know." He came to a halt and tapped one booted foot. "I guess I was expecting you to want to quit or leave this team. The prince… he's tough to manage, and you really got the worst of it before you started your first shift."

I barked out a harsh laugh. "Oh, trust me. I wanted to destroy a few things and then take off running after he'd walked away. I don't think I've ever been so disgusted by someone in my entire life."

"But you didn't break things. You didn't run." Elgin caught my wrist, making me face him. "You're still here, and you're not trying to keep a few lightyears of distance between you and the prince. It's kind of impressive."

Not quitting the prince's guard had amazed Elgin? "That's just not who I am. My job is to protect everyone I can, and I can't exactly do that if I run off. Right?"

Elgin gave me a proud smile. "Oh, I know. It's just… you're not what I was expecting at all, Hero of Vanthurium."

I groaned. "Please don't call me that."

"But that's what you are?" He tilted his head, and a few green strands of hair tumbled down into his eyes.

"Well, yes, but I'm more than that. On Vanthurium… I was just doing what I could to help us survive. It wasn't a calculated attack or even an act of bravery. I—" I felt myself start to get choked up, and panic reared its ugly head. "I just didn't want anyone to die."

"And no one from Nova died. All because of you. I'd say you've more than earned your title, Aliya." Elgin released my wrist and stepped back. "You're a hero for a reason. Embrace it."

With one last nod and smile Elgin turned and left me in the darkened hallway leading to the east wing. I'd been fairly tired before Ki'ran and Ba'rin arrived, but after that conversation, I was wide awake.

Elgin thought I deserved to be a hero?

Sure, I'd accepted that I had physical limits that far exceeded what a normal being could do, but that was all thanks to luck. I was lucky that Doctor Givray had been part of the Terran doctor team who had tried to save me. I was lucky that Doctor Givray's procedure had worked on me. I was lucky that Caspian was different from all the other captains in the Protective Forces and had wanted me for his team.

Luck didn't make a hero – at least, not in my mind. I'd done what I needed to do, and anyone else in my position would've done the same. Well, I hoped they would have acted the same.

I started to feel anxious as I stood in the dark hallway. I'd been so good lately; not once since arriving here had I experienced a panic attack. Why had Elgin's praise triggered one now?

Painful thoughts and memories struck up a tempest inside my mind, battering against the tranquility I thought I'd firmly established.

This was all a mistake. I wasn't a hero and didn't deserve to be. I was just a lucky girl who had all the right pieces fall into place at the right times. And now… now I couldn't even maintain my composure.

My hands shook, and I wanted to bolt. I didn't know where, but I wanted to be far away from here and anyone who called me 'Hero.'

You're a hero for a reason. Elgin, someone who barely knew me but knew of my reputation, believed that I deserved the renown I'd received from my actions on Charra and Vanthurium. He believed in me.

Something inside my chest cracked, and I felt myself begin to relax.

No one was actually holding me to lofty standards. They weren't putting me through trials or sending me out to face the Krech head-on. They'd simply heard stories and wanted to see if I fit them. And now Elgin and Ba'rin, whom I'd gotten to know a little, could see that I wasn't some mythical figure sent to save the universe. I was powerful, yes, but I wasn't some fabled savior of the King's Galaxy.

I could still be Aliya *and* the Hero of Vanthurium, protector of the prince and soldier from the Protective Forces.

It wasn't about playing a part. It was purely stepping up to the challenges that came my way while using the many skills I now had.

And I could do that.

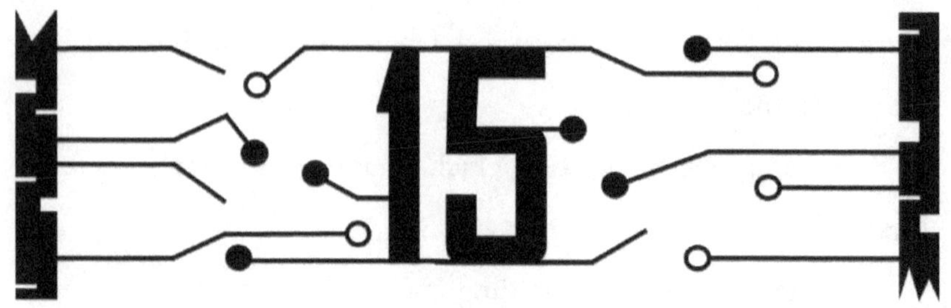

I woke up completely tangled in my sheets.

Staring through sleep-swollen eyes I realized that the sun hadn't even risen. *What woke me up?*

There. A series of short, soft knocks sounded at my door. I groaned at myself. If I could have Doctor Givray undo one thing from his life-saving surgery, it was my heightened hearing ability. Or at least I'd ask for a switch to turn it off at night.

Knock, knock, knock.

Rolling over onto my back, I sighed. If I ignored whomever it was, would they eventually give up? I knew that as soon as I got out of bed, my body would snap out of its current comfortable state, and I'd have trouble going back to sleep anytime soon.

"Aliya?" came a soft whisper from outside my door.

I bolted upright. Caspian. But… what was he doing up so late?

After I'd unwrapped my sheets from around my legs, I padded over to the door and pulled it open a sliver. "Caspian?" I asked, feigning surprise.

He wore a pair of black, loose cotton pants and a gray t-shirt. His hands were shoved into his pockets, and his wavy locks looked more tousled than usual. "Hey," he said. I couldn't quite make out his expression – something between a blush and chagrin? "Can I come in?"

"Oh. Um, yeah." I stepped back and tugged the door open wide. He strolled in and glanced about my room. His gaze settled on my bed for a few seconds before he turned to me.

"I'm sorry for waking you. I was trying to stay awake until the end of your shift, but…" He glanced down at his feet in a display of uncharacteristic shyness. What in the galaxy was going on here?

"Caspian, why are you awake? We would've seen each other tomorrow and been able to talk." I crossed my arms over my chest.

"I… I know. I really couldn't visit you on your shift, but I just—" Caspian ran both hands through his hair and locked them behind his neck. He looked more agitated than usual, and I was beginning to worry. "I wanted to make sure you were okay. What Damien did today was horrible, and I couldn't stop him, and then I had to go when you were clearly upset—" He rambled on for a few moments while shaking his head in frustration.

"Hey." I cut him off by stepping forward and putting a hand on his cheek. My touch seemed to thaw his anger because his shoulders relaxed, and his hands dropped to his sides. "You spoke up for me. You didn't just let him get away with that behavior unchecked. And," I said, bringing my other hand to his face to keep him from turning away, "I know you gladly would've done something more if he wasn't the prince. That really meant a lot to me."

A light smile touched his lips. "You're not mad that I couldn't make him stop completely?"

"Stars, Caspian! No, I was never mad. You did what you could, and it's not your fault that happened in the first place." I couldn't believe that he'd been beating himself up over this for hours.

"But you switched shifts and didn't let me know."

I laughed. "You were still on your shift. I wasn't going to walk up while the prince was there and say, 'hey I don't want to be around that guy while he's awake, so I'm switching to the overnight shift.' That wouldn't have gone well."

Caspian closed his eyes and leaned forward until his forehead touched mine. A few locks of his hair trickled down, tickling my face. "I thought you'd be upset with me." His whisper was filled with relief.

"How could I ever be upset with you? I was definitely mad at Prince Damien but not you." I dropped both of my hands from his face, feeling secure that he wasn't going to turn away. I'd assuaged his fears, and he no longer had any reason to feel embarrassed or worried that he couldn't completely protect me.

As soon as I let go of his face, however, Caspian's hands found mine.

Something small bloomed in my chest. With all the worrying over joining the royal guards, Caspian hadn't shown me much affection since my panic attack during our flying lesson. Him coming here in the middle of the night definitely wasn't ideal for either of our sleep schedules, but the gesture touched me deeply.

And then panic washed over me. Had anyone seen Caspian come into my room? Were royal guards even allowed to be together romantically?

I was sure that someone had put two and two together that Caspian and I were a package deal, but I didn't have the faintest clue as to what rules might govern our lives now. No one had explicitly said anything, but that didn't mean we were free to do... this.

Caspian must have felt my body tense because he pulled back with a look of concern. "What's wrong?"

I felt a blush rise to my cheeks and found that I couldn't meet Caspian's eyes anymore. Maybe I was overthinking the situation, but now that he'd taken notice, I couldn't brush off his question. "Is this—" I cleared my throat before trying again. "Is *this* allowed?"

Caspian didn't respond for a few seconds, and I started to panic. *Had* I misjudged his level of concern? Unless I was very mistaken, coming to my room before the sun rose and being this close to me wasn't something that just friends did. But... who knew? I was still learning how this galaxy worked, and perhaps affection manifested differently out here.

I needn't have worried. "Aliya, look at me." He released my hand and placed it behind my neck. Slowly, his thumb brushed my cheek, and now I couldn't resist looking up to see the emotion that swirled in his turquoise eyes. There was a tenderness to his gaze that made me want to trust him indefinitely, but then his lips quirked in a teasing smile. "What, exactly, do you mean by *this?*"

Oh, no. No, no, no. I enjoyed romantic feelings and would read a romance novel every now and then when I was on Terra, but I was *not* good at discussing those types of emotions with others. My blush deepened, and I stammered as I said, "N-never mind. It's not important."

I tried to step away, but his hand on the back of my neck kept me in place. "No, I think this is important," he said with a chuckle. "By this do you happen to mean... us?"

I wanted to kick myself. We'd been having a really nice moment, all worries smoothed over and an unspoken connection blooming, and I'd had to go and open my big mouth. If I could've crawled back under my sheets and disappeared, I would have in an instant. "Um, well, yeah. I mean, I guess so."

Caspian smiled again, his thumb continuing to brush back and forth along my jawline. "I've wanted time to talk about it too, but since arriving and jumping right into our shifts... Well, there hasn't exactly been a great window of time to talk about us."

Butterflies erupted in my stomach. There was an 'us' to discuss? My heart soared despite the little voice in the back of my head saying something about carts and horses.

"I meant every word I said in the tunnels on Vanthurium," Caspian continued, completely ignorant of the emotions battling inside my heart. "I've never met anyone like you, and the time that I've spent with you so far… Well, it's shown me things that I never would've realized."

"Such as?" I fought to keep the nervous tremble out of my voice.

Caspian leaned forward once more, closing the distance between us to mere centimeters. "That strength really does come in all shapes and sizes. Even in Terrans." He laughed, and then his tone became serious. "That tragedy and terrible change shouldn't keep us from moving forward. And that I have something right in front of me that's truly worth living for."

His eyes locked on mine as he said that last sentence, and I forgot how to breathe. "But you had your Nova squad." Once more I recalled Adís telling me how dedicated Caspian had become to his Nova 'family.' He'd brought them together, and then he'd done everything within his power as a captain to ensure they were happy and protected.

Surely, they had been worth living for?

But Caspian shook his head. "They kept me going, but how long can you keep a squad together? Someone would want to leave, and I always dreaded the day we'd get into a battle that we couldn't win…" He closed his eyes and steadied himself with a deep breath. "While I loved them like a family, they only motivated me to get through the next day, the next mission, or whatever goal the Forces had set for us. But with you… I find myself wanting much more than I'd ever hoped I could after—"

Caspian came to a full stop as a look of pain flashed across his face. I didn't know what to say or how to react. This was yet another side of Caspian that I hadn't seen before. I'd seen him happy and confident. I'd seen him as a leader. I'd even seen him emotionally broken.

What I was seeing now was someone wanting to let go and move on. I had no idea what type of person Caspian had been before Leila and his parents' deaths, but I knew without a doubt that it had changed him fundamentally. It altered the way he connected with others, keeping them close but not truly bonded with him.

And then I came along and shattered all of that.

Caspian recollected himself, and he opened his eyes once more. His gaze was so intense that I wanted to look away, but I refused to, knowing that this was a defining moment for us.

"I don't want to just get through each day hoping that nothing bad happens to the people I care about. I mean, obviously I *still* want that but—" I pressed my fingers to his lips.

"You showed me what it's like to live again, to not hide from the truth and hope for what was. Under Captain Sansish I couldn't look more than a day ahead because I was so scared of what I was doing at that exact moment. You were the first one to make me realize that I didn't have to spend each second planning the next few to come." I felt like I was doing a horrible job explaining how much his admission resonated with me, but honestly, most of this had been said before in the tunnels. He knew how I felt; I knew how he felt. This was just a reaffirmation that our hearts were both still in the same place. "I don't know what's coming next, and while I'm okay with that, I also know that I want you there beside me."

He trembled and breathed my name against my fingers. Unsure if he would speak again, I pulled my hand away and rested it upon his chest. When I felt his heart racing, just like mine, I couldn't hide my smile.

Caspian hesitated before asking, "Are you sure?"

I knew from the moment we were cornered in the hangar on Charra that I would go to any length just to protect Caspian. As I spent more time around him and he opened up to me, however, I realized that I didn't want to be his guard – I wanted to be *his*. I didn't even have to think before replying, "Of course."

Caspian's lips crashed into mine, and the fire that already burned in my cheeks raced down to the tips of my toes. The hand that I'd placed on his chest grabbed a fistful of his shirt, pulling him closer to me. I'd been dreaming of this moment for far too long, and now that it had finally come, I couldn't get enough.

It seemed that Caspian felt the same way. He dropped my hand and gripped my waist, while the hand on my neck twisted into my sleep-styled hair.

Caspian's lips were soft but insistent, and I felt myself melt into his embrace as he deepened the kiss.

For a few blissful moments it was just me and Caspian. There was no Prince Damien, no Krech, no concerns over losing sleep.

I'd lost a lot when Doctor Givray took me from Terra and saved my life, but what I hadn't expected was finding something out in this big galaxy that meant so much to me. I didn't mean that Caspian outweighed my family and friends I'd left behind, but having him made me feel like I belonged somewhere. Like I was meant to be here.

I lost myself in the kiss, drinking in every last drop of this incredible moment. It was like we were the only two people in the King's Galaxy, and I didn't want it to end.

Far too soon, Caspian broke the kiss, but he lingered only a hairsbreadth away as we caught our breaths.

"I'd follow you to the farthest star," Caspian murmured.

"Well, I'd never want to go alone."

He laughed softly, and then he pulled me against his chest as I nuzzled into the space between his neck and shoulder. I felt warm and secure, something I hadn't experienced in far too long.

Caspian's heart continued to race, and I felt his hands tremble. "I never want to lose you."

"You won't. I don't plan on going away any time soon." I laughed in an attempt to shift his mood back to our moment.

I completely understood how he felt. I'd watched Caspian put his life on the line twice now, and with the threat of the Krech hanging over everyone, I didn't want something terrible to happen once that hammer fell. I didn't know what I would do if I lost him.

And Caspian… He had every right to have concerns. In a time when there were no threats, the woman he loved had been killed. Without reason, without justice. If something like that ever happened to me, well, nowhere in the galaxy would be safe for the monster who broke my heart.

Perhaps my track record for saving our lives would help assuage his fears.

Caspian planted a kiss on the top of my head and replied, "Good."

We held each other as minutes trickled by, neither of us wanting to be the one who finally let go.

Eventually, Caspian leaned his head away, and all of a sudden, he started laughing.

"What?" *Had I done something wrong?* Maybe I'd accidentally spoken my thoughts aloud.

"Aliya, look at yourself."

Forcing myself to shift and create some space between us, I gasped at what I saw. Every inch of my exposed skin was glowing from my circuits.

It made no sense. I lit up when I was exerting myself, but right now? All I'd done was kiss Caspian.

My cheeks heated in embarrassment. "I—I'm sorry." *Of course my freakish self would ruin this!* "I don't know why this is happening."

"Hey." Caspian placed a finger under my chin and tilted my face back up to his. "I love your circuits. I think they're amazing and make you incredibly unique. And seeing how you've never lit up this much before, it has to be all for me." He gave me a devilish grin that made my stomach flip.

"I guess so." I tried not to stammer, but all I could think about was how I glowed like a lightbulb and how close Caspian's lips were.

"I love them," he repeated. Then he leaned in for another kiss.

This one was softer, more of a promise than raw passion. A promise that he loved all of me, no matter what odd things I could do. It was a kiss that made me arch into him, and my fingers curled into the back of his shirt.

This was worth living for. I'd cross the galaxy – heck, I'd even fight more Krech – just to make sure I could keep Caspian here in my arms, safe and happy.

There was little I *wouldn't* do to preserve what we'd started here tonight.

We ended the kiss and spent a few moments in silence, forehead to forehead.

"So, what now?" I finally asked.

Caspian laughed, his voice low and husky. "Whatever you want, Aliya." He pulled back to look into my eyes and patiently waited for my decision.

I didn't want him to go, but I knew I couldn't invite him to stay. This was just the beginning, our first real heart-to-heart with the promise of many more to come, and I didn't want things to move too fast. Yes, we'd been to hell and back on two separate planets, and yes, the Krech were still out there and most likely coming for us. But none of that meant we were out of time.

Also, I was sure it wouldn't look good if someone saw Caspian leaving my room in the morning. We *were* still guards, after all.

"This is good enough," I murmured. "We can take it day by day from here."

"I'm fine with that," Caspian said without hesitation. "We'll shift things around so that you and I can spend more time together, *while* keeping you away from the prince as much as possible. I know I definitely don't want to watch him do that to you again."

I smiled. The sweet, protective captain had resurfaced. "Okay. And who knows, maybe next time I will be able to stop him myself."

He kissed my forehead once more. "My fighter," he whispered.

Gently, I pushed him away. "You've been up for far too long. Go get some sleep. I'll still be here in the morning."

His arms tightened around me, and I felt my stomach flip. "Are you sure about that? You won't slip away as soon as I let go?"

"I promise, Caspian."

Reluctantly, he let me go. Hand in hand we walked toward the door, and I held it open while he slipped outside. "Until tomorrow, then," he said with a wink.

"I can't wait." My heart overflowed with joy as the door clicked shut.

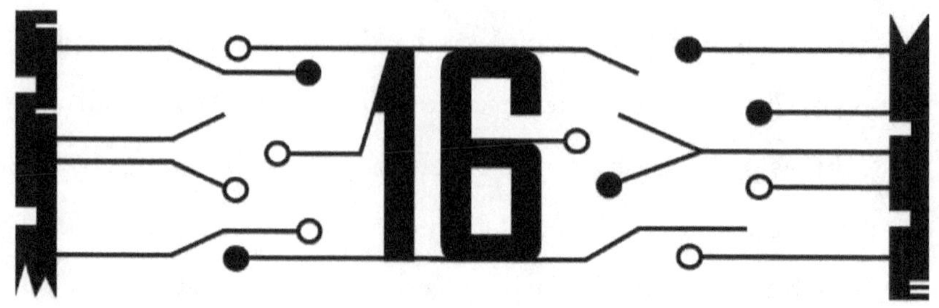

True to his word, Caspian shuffled everyone's schedules. In the week that followed, I spent every other night shift with him, staying completely out of the prince's daytime schedule.

Prince Damien had two more late night visitors, and the remainder evenings he spent in a drunken stupor. I still couldn't wrap my head around the reason behind his behavior, and I asked Caspian about it on several occasions.

"I know you've never asked Prince Damien a direct question before, but he will rarely answer anything," he'd told me, which hadn't come as a surprise, "but I'm sure he thinks that acting this way will somehow shift the burden of responsibility off his shoulders."

"Is that even possible?" King Locklyn didn't have another son, and while I wasn't entirely sure how succession worked in the

King's Galaxy, I didn't see the prince being let off the hook so easily.

"Well, he could give up his title if he wanted, and in that instance, the heir would become the next eligible relative in the Talimore line. King Locklyn has a brother. He's the lord of Petrolyese." I had no idea where that planet was, but I'd look it up later so I wouldn't be caught off guard if this came up again sometime.

"So why hasn't the prince given up his title? Seems like that would be the logical thing to do instead of acting like a spoiled brat."

Caspian shrugged. "Who knows how his mind works."

And because that statement was so true, that was the end of that conversation.

In the time I had between shifts, I tried to learn as much as possible about the Talimore family and the rules and responsibilities that King Locklyn had. Prince Damien might ignore every meeting he was invited to, but I wanted to understand what was going on. And there was so much to learn.

King Locklyn had his council — a small selection of planetary lords who governed things like trade, defense, currency, medicine, and so on. I probably could've learned a lot by sitting in on a council meeting, but I wasn't authorized to attend unless I was escorting the prince. Which wasn't going to happen any time soon.

When I wasn't researching, Caspian and I spent as much time together as possible. Whether it was training on the grounds, exploring the many rooms and hallways of the palace, or stealing kisses, we couldn't be parted.

I didn't want it any other way.

I couldn't get enough of Caspian. He made me feel so comfortable, and I loved how easy it was to be my true self around him. We joked and traded stories about our pasts, opening up more and more as the days flew by.

Before, I'd simply *wanted* to spend my future with Caspian. Now I could actually see it and desperately wanted it to happen – preferably sooner rather than later. But I didn't know how we could shift from guards to… something more.

Would one or both of us have to quit? Did we need to buy a house? How much money would we need to survive?

I knew the answers to those questions if we'd been on Terra, but I had no idea how to address them out here. Furthermore, I was too embarrassed to ask someone else.

For the time being, I let those worries go. I basked in Caspian's attention and the fun we had together, read and researched the king's history, and spent my night shifts learning more about Omri, Elgin, Neygreen, Seradon, and Ba'rin.

I learned that Neygreen Neonhes was from Vanthurium, and he was far more excited to meet me than I'd expected. The first time I was introduced to him was during one of our off-shifts, when I'd been out at the shooting range. Suddenly, an olive-skinned blur rushed up to me, snatched my hand, and began profusely exclaiming how honored he was to meet one of the soldiers who'd saved his planet and how incredible he'd heard I was.

I had to stop myself from batting him away because I didn't realize who he was. The thin, wide eyed male who vigorously shook my hand was completely unknown to me, and it took three tries before I got him to tell me his name.

It turned out that he was a prince's guard during the attack on his home planet, and thanks to the prince's aversion to duty, Neygreen hadn't found out about it until everything was already over. He'd felt immense guilt over being unable to help during the attack, and he only felt worse when Prince Damien forbade him from leaving to help rebuild after the battle.

I guess it made some sense that Neygreen, or Ney as he preferred to be called, would be so thankful when meeting someone who had been there and fought the cyborgs.

Since then, I'd grown fond of Ney's little quirks. He adored being outside and 'one with nature,' as he liked to say, and in his free time he liked to whittle wood. It took almost no prodding to get him to show me his collection of figurines which ranged from animals and plants on Vanthurium to creatures from places I'd never heard of.

Seradon Branable, on the other hand, was almost more mysterious than Gunther and Gráinne. When I first asked where he was from, he said that he was a descendant from a planet that no longer existed, and then he refused to explain further. I'd never heard of any planets in the King's Galaxy that had been destroyed, so I had no idea where he was referring to. The only thing he did tell me was that he'd been a guard for the prince for just over two years.

Truthfully, he was slightly terrifying. His seven-foot frame loomed over most people living in the palace, but it was his appearance that was the most shocking. Seradon had gray and white marbled skin, amber eyes, and a wide mouth full of pointed teeth. Even his white hair was cropped short and constantly spiked. He never appeared outright angry; instead it was impossible to guess his emotions by his expression. He was like a human-shark hybrid, without the fins and gills.

My overnight shifts with him were the ones I looked forward to the least.

As a team, we weren't as close as the Nova squad had been, but it definitely wasn't uncomfortable working with the new guards. They incorporated us into their ranks without question, even respecting Caspian as their captain although one of them probably deserved the title based on how long they'd served the prince.

Although we were still working out a few kinks with scheduling, the new team got along well. I'd be curious to see how we fared in a battle, should Prince Damien ever happen to wander into a dangerous situation, since these males were fierce and highly skilled. We were handling the prince and whatever he threw at us, but nothing prepared us for the bomb King Locklyn dropped at breakfast one morning.

I sat at the table between Caspian and Elgin while Ki'ran and Ney sat across from us. As usual, Seradon was absent since preferred to eat alone.

Caspian's and my fingers were wound together under the table – not that we were trying to hide our affection, but that it was easier to not throw the fact that we were together in everyone else's faces – while Elgin was telling yet another of his tall tales about something he 'did' before coming to work at the palace.

"So here I was, cramped under the floor panels of this rust bucket that hadn't been cleaned since the last war, and the smuggler is on his comm, talking about where he's dropping off his latest shipment! I mean, you think you'd scan your ship for drifters before launching into the detail I heard that day…"

"Okay, now hold on," Caspian jumped in, "you said you had to *pry* that floor panel up, unscrewing the bolts and all. How in all the worlds did you get the panel back into place without it being obvious that you'd opened it?"

Elgin leaned his elbow on the table, and, resting his chin on his hand, winked at Caspian. "That, my friend, is a secret I won't share."

Ki'ran groaned from across the table. "This is not possible. The smuggler would have seen! You… you are terrible at telling a story."

Our small group fell silent and then burst into raucous laughter. Ki'ran never outright insulted someone; he'd usually just give them his typical silence.

"Oh man, Elgin. You must have hit a new storytelling low to get *that* reaction from Ki'ran!" Ney bellowed.

Caspian slapped the table with his free hand. "Ki'ran, are you feeling okay today? Because, wow, that was harsh!"

Even Elgin joined in the laughter and had to swipe away a few tears from how hard he laughed. "Okay, okay. I *might* have stretched the truth there just a little bit."

There was more groaning and laughing until the great double doors at the front of the banquet hall boomed open, and King Locklyn, outfitted in his full kingly regalia, stomped down the aisle toward us.

The golden buckles on his shin-high boots jingled with every heavy step he took, and the long tails of his black jacket flapped in his wake. Two king's guards trailed behind him, bedecked in their black and gold armor – complete with a gold mask to hide their features.

King Locklyn never came to this hall because he would eat in his chambers or during a morning meeting, and I couldn't help wondering what occasion had brought him here.

Immediately, we all straightened up and wiped away any trace of amusement from our faces. I even pulled my hand from Caspian's grip, unsure if it was appropriate for the king to see us being affectionate.

A chorus of, "good morning, your Majesty," sounded as the king passed various groups of guards who had been eating their breakfasts.

King Locklyn pounded to a stop next to us. "Captain," he nodded his head toward Caspian, "and team."

"Majesty," we all said in reply.

"This is rather short notice, however, I need four of you to accompany Damien on a trip today." A trip? This was certainly unplanned. "I have a meeting with Lord Liseni on Aquillo, and Damien *will* attend it. See to it that he makes it onto the ship."

Caspian pressed a closed fist to his chest. "Of course, your Majesty. When are we departing?"

"Within the hour." And with that the king turned and strode out of the banquet hall.

Once the doors boomed shut, we shared a collective groan.

"As if it's not hard enough managing him here at the palace, now we have to contain him at someone else's," Elgin complained with his head in his hands.

"Perhaps we will be fortunate, and he will sleep through the whole meeting." Ki'ran laughed.

"Well," I said, standing up from the table, "we have to wake him first. An hour isn't a lot of time to make him presentable. You know how slow he is when he *doesn't* have appointments, and now that he's expected to go, I can only imagine how much longer he'll take."

"I'll contact Omri and Ba'rin to see if they can get him up," Caspian offered. He pushed his sleeve back and began tapping on his comm-cuff. "Since they are just finishing their shift, I won't ask them to accompany us. Neygreen, you and I are on for the night shift tonight, so stay as well and get some rest. As for the three of you, we need to be ready to go soon. Wear the full navy armor – we need to look unified and formidable."

"Meet at the airfield in thirty?" Elgin asked.

"Don't be late," Caspian said in reply.

✳

I stood in awe in front of my full-length mirror.

Yes, I was close to running late to meet back up with the rest of my team, but I couldn't tear myself away from my reflection.

I'd enjoyed the simple and comfortable training uniform that I'd worn with the Protective Forces. The black pants and shirt had been practical and unassuming.

Joining Nova had added a jacket to the ensemble. Once again, nothing flashy or uncomfortable to wear.

But now, decked out in my full regal armor, I was speechless.

Golden leather boots laced up to my shins, hiding the bottoms of my form-fitting, navy pants. Which weren't your average material, by the way. Despite how thin and flexible the material was, something about it felt as if it was reinforced with Kevlar. Although I'm sure they'd developed a better version of the Terran material.

I slipped on a navy, utilitarian long-sleeved shirt before strapping on the formidable breast plate. Once more, I was unsure of the material it was made from, but the shine and strength of it – because *of course* I pushed on it a little as a test – was impressive. Close-fitting and lightweight, the plating that covered my chest and shoulders proudly displayed the Talimore crest, a swirling galaxy set behind a three-pointed crown – all in gold filigree.

The gauntlets – gold as well – reached up to my elbows and, while made from the same material as the breast and shoulder plating, were comprised of diamond-shaped pieces all hooked together. The design was probably intended to allow for the greatest amount of movement in the wearer's fingers and wrists because I didn't feel limited in the slightest.

With my hair braded back and my usual blasters strapped around my hips, I looked formidable. I truly felt like a warrior prepared for battle.

It's just for show, I had to remind myself. We weren't in danger by visiting Aquillo today; this was a purely diplomatic meeting. The regalia was simply a show of status and power.

So why did I still feel like I was heading off into a fight?

Ignoring my unfounded concerns, I finally pulled away from the galactic warrior in the mirror. Although I could've been lost in that powerful image for hours, I couldn't be late.

Heads turned as I strolled through the castle and out onto the grounds. Perhaps this wasn't the best image for me because it reinforced my 'hero' status, but I felt a swell of pride and confidence.

Maybe, like Elgin had suggested, it wasn't so bad to have a bit of renown.

It was another hot day on Callais, and while the armor definitely didn't help, it wasn't as stifling as I thought it would be.

Whomever the manufacturers were, they knew how to create awesome armor that didn't turn someone into a walking furnace.

Elgin and Ki'ran had already arrived, looking every bit as magnificent as I felt. "Well aren't we the most stylish team in the palace?" I joked.

Elgin flipped his hair, which he'd pulled back into a high ponytail. "You know it!"

I laughed. "Any word from Caspian yet?"

"Yes. He said he loves you and can't wait to spend some more alone time with you," Elgin replied with a scandalous wink.

My cheeks heated. "You know that's not what I meant," I mumbled, wishing I could sink into the ground to hide my embarrassment.

"I know, I know! I just couldn't let that opportunity pass!" Elgin continued to laugh and slap his knee. Wiping away a fake tear he said, "But to answer what you *really* meant, he should be here any minute with our guest of honor."

Sure enough, I heard gravel crunching from the path leading back to the palace. Two sets of feet approached, and surprisingly, both sounded like they had a steady gait. Maybe the prince hadn't had enough time to down a few drinks before being ushered to the ship.

"Showtime," Elgin stage-whispered, and the three of us stepped into our formal greeting pose.

I felt unnaturally tense, and it had nothing to do with standing up straight to greet the prince. This was the first time in a week that I'd be face-to-face with him since he'd solicited me in the hallway. I cringed as I imagined him trying again once we had boarded the ship. *Please just ignore me*, I prayed as Caspian and Prince Damien drew near.

By some small miracle, Prince Damien was dressed and presentable. His collared white shirt and navy vest were unwrinkled and tucked in nicely, and even the laces on his boots were done up correctly. I wondered if he'd had an assistant dress him or if he'd managed to accomplish all that himself.

For once, his eyes looked clear, but the scowl on his face was worrisome. It was no surprise that he didn't want to come on this trip, and I desperately hoped that he wouldn't try to cause trouble. Would it be our fault or the prince's if something happened that offended the Lord of Aquillo?

The prince ignored all of us as he stomped up the gangway and into the massive belly of his father's ship. I glanced at Caspian who just rolled his eyes. The prince was unhappy, but he was here. It was far better to have Prince Damien annoyed instead of King Locklyn.

Walking in two rows of two, we filed after the prince.

Still acting as if none of us existed, Prince Damien wound through the wide, utilitarian hallways. Right, left, and right again until he reached a room that looked like a lounge. It had a long glass window set along the wall, and the middle of the room contained several plush couches, a rectangular coffee table, and a well-stocked bar.

A bar. Prince Damien would head straight to the room with a bar.

If he'd been sober when he woke up, he certainly wouldn't be once we arrived on Aquillo. I cringed watching him pour a large glass of some dark brown liquid before he plopped down onto one of the couches.

"I don't need all four of you staring at me for the next half hour. Two of you, go stand guard outside the door. Whoever stays, don't bother lecturing me," he snapped before downing the glass in one gulp.

I practically jogged for the door. There was no way I was spending this trip stuck in the lounge while Prince Damien drank. I felt bad for the two who would have to stay and keep watch over him, but they all knew what he'd said to me and would understand why I needed to be outside the door.

I knew I was just avoiding this problem, and it was bound to resurface at some point. But I was still just a guard, and Damien was a prince.

No matter how I looked at it, there was nothing I could do except stay away from him.

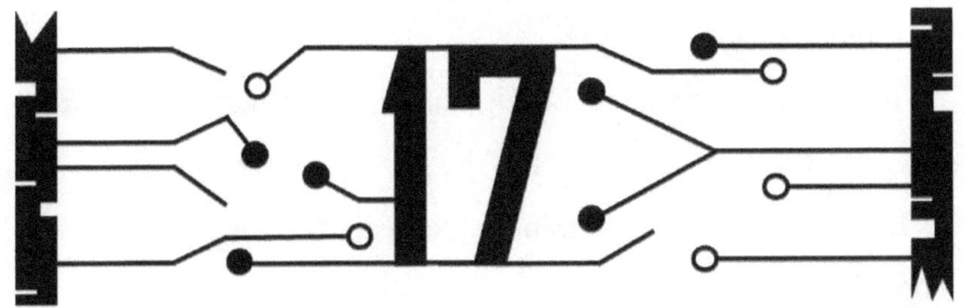

I didn't know how much Prince Damien was able to drink in the half hour flight to Aquillo, but when Caspian emerged from the lounge after we landed, he didn't look pleased.

The prince, on the other hand, looked much happier than when he boarded.

"You both missed a good time," he slurred to me and Elgin as he walked through the doorway.

Despite the short timeframe, he already walked on unsteady legs. I couldn't understand how he'd managed to get so drunk in so little time, unless he hadn't been entirely sober when he boarded. I sincerely hoped that we could get Prince Damien to wherever we were meeting and a seat before he fell.

We headed toward the rear of the ship, and I was too focused on watching the prince's steps to take in much of my surroundings other than the gray metal floors. Not that there was much to see, anyway. For how grand the palace was, it surprised me how simple the interior of this ship was.

King Locklyn waited beside the raised gangway with four guards of his own. "About time," he growled at his son. He shook his head, and I couldn't help noticing just how worn and tired the king seemed around the prince.

Prince Damien gave him a mocking smile that turned the king's face purple. "Late, but here. As you so adamantly requested."

Surprising us all, King Locklyn took a step forward and grabbed a fistful of the prince's shirt. Prince Damien's eyes flew open as his father hauled him closer. "This is an important meeting for us and, hopefully, for your eventual rule. Do *not* misbehave and ruin this alliance," King Locklyn hissed before shoving the prince backward.

Prince Damien stumbled a few steps before regaining his footing. "Maybe I don't care!" he shouted back.

If looks could kill, the prince certainly would have died from the glare his father now wore. "Then don't care, keep your useless mouth shut, and don't ruin this for *me*." Turning away from the prince he snapped, "Lower the gangway!"

Guards snapped into motion, pressing a button on the wall and then forming a group around their king. We followed suit, Caspian and I slightly ahead of Prince Damien while Elgin and Ki'ran took spots behind the prince.

The gangway lowered, and a blast of salty air raced into the ship. *Where were we?* I didn't have time to look at what kind of planet Aquillo was before we left, and I didn't like feeling surprised now.

Without a second glance at his son, King Locklyn proceeded down the gangway. After a few seconds we followed them, and my breath was taken away by the sight that greeted us.

The king's ship had landed on a sprawling, sandy dune. Tall grasses swayed in the mild, salty breeze. I saw no other ships parked around us and wondered if this was a reserved location or if ships didn't remain on land for long because it wasn't safe.

Because, stretching around us for miles and miles was a turquoise, open ocean. Every now and then a tall, jagged rock structure broke forth from the massive waves, dripping with seaweed and other plant life. But the majority of area around us was water.

It was incredible – an ocean-lover's dream. The soft sand crunched underfoot as we followed the king and his guards, and I noticed small pink and blue crabs scuttling out of our way.

The sun broke through the scattered clouds, and a smile stretched across my face. "I love it here," I whispered to Caspian, completely not caring if Prince Damien overheard.

"This is just the surface, love. Wait until we descend."

Descend? As in, go *under* the water?

Before I could ask what he meant, King Locklyn stopped at the end of a long wooden dock. At the far end were a group of six males – the lord and his guards. Behind the lord, a large metal object bobbed in the waves. A submarine of some sort? The water off the end of the dock must have been deep for so much of the submarine to be submerged.

"Lord Liseni, it is a pleasure to return to Aquillo and your company once more," King Locklyn said as he touched his index and middle fingers to his forehead.

The lord returned the gesture before waving us forward. "It is always an honor to have you, my king."

As we drew nearer, I took in the features of Lord Liseni and his guards which resembled various types of sea creatures.

Lord Liseni looked like a crab. His coral-colored skin appeared rough, as if covered by carapace, and a raised ridge about an inch tall ran down each of his forearms. An extremely short and thick neck supported his oval face, in the middle of which sat two slits for his nose. Wide, black pupils danced inside his too-large and lidless eyes, but as I watched, a white inner lid slid laterally across his eyes in a lazy blink.

The rest of his guards resembled different kinds of fish, complete with gills or short fins on the sides of their necks. If I had to guess, I would've said that the spears they carried were made from coral or shell.

"Omri is half Aqui," Caspian whispered to me. That made sense; he *did* have webbed fingers, after all.

"I see you've brought the prince as well," Lord Liseni continued. All traces of friendliness vanished from his face as he regarded the approaching prince.

"My lord," Prince Damien purred as he touched two fingers to his forehead and bowed.

It was at that exact moment that a wave broke over the surface of the dock. There wasn't enough water to knock someone over, but it did soak the boards.

As Prince Damien stepped forward into his little bow, however, he lost his footing and slipped to the side. Completely taken by surprise, I didn't turn fast enough to catch him before he hit his head on the dock, his circlet tumbling off with a soft clang, and tumbled into the water, where he sunk beneath the aquamarine waves. For a second I thought he would kick back to the surface, but then I realized that his eyes were closed.

There were shouts of alarm from the guards, but I drowned them out as I moved, dropping the blasters from my hips and diving into the ocean.

The water was *cold*. My knee-jerk reaction was to resurface and get the heck out of the water, but I knew I couldn't do that without the prince.

My armor weighed me down as I kicked down to the prince's limp, outstretched hand, and I was grateful for the extra weight. I hadn't tried swimming since I woke up in Doctor Givray's healing facility, so I didn't know what I could and couldn't do. But I *was* fast enough to reach the prince before my lungs started burning from air depravation.

I grasped his wrist and pulled, hauling him up so that we were face to face. Prince Damien's head lolled back, completely weightless under the waves, and his hair fanned out around his face like a black halo.

I'm so *going to kick your butt once we get out of this mess*, I promised.

A school of tiny neon fish broke around us as I wrapped an arm around Prince Damien's waist. Glancing up toward the light, I was startled to realize how far down we'd sunk. And were still sinking. *Time to go!*

Weighed down and swimming with one arm, I fought to get us back to the surface. My legs felt like tree trunks had been tied to them, and I panicked that I wasn't getting any closer. If I knew that I could recover my armor from the bottom of this sea, I would have removed it all, but I also didn't have a change of clothes waiting for me at the surface.

I had to do this myself.

With burning muscles and black spots beginning to swim across my vision, I propelled us to within a few feet of the underside of the dock. My body had been pushed to its limit, and I didn't think I had any strength left to lift Prince Damien back onto the dock.

Fortunately, the guards who had remained on the dock were ready for us.

I grasped the first submerged hand that I could reach, and others followed, wrapping around my wrist and then Prince Damien as I pushed him closer to the surface. He disappeared from my grip as another set of hands reached down to grab my now-freed arm.

I dug my fingers into the arms of my savior – or saviors since I couldn't tell if one person was hauling me up or more than one – as my face finally broke above the waves. I spat salty sea water from my mouth as I struggled to take a full breath of air.

With a thump I landed on the dock as a soggy, gasping mess. "Aliya! Aliya, can you hear me? Are you okay?" Caspian demanded as he knelt and cupped my face.

I pushed him away. "Damien – is he…?" I panted as I struggled to see around Caspian.

The sunlight made me squint, but what I could make out around my shuttered lashes wasn't encouraging. Prince Damien lay on his back as two guards hovered over him performing CPR.

"No… I wasn't—" I coughed, my throat raspy from swallowing half the sea, "—fast enough!" With shaking arms, I dragged myself closer to the prone prince. A gentle hand came to rest on my shoulder, and I knew without looking that it was Caspian's.

A sea breeze blew across the dock, and I shivered. I should've worried about catching a cold from being soaked to the bone, but all I could think about was how the one person I was supposed to protect was possibly dead because I couldn't reach him in time.

Suddenly Prince Damien's back arched, and he began coughing up water. Elgin knelt and turned him on his side.

A sigh of relief reached my ears. Over the noise from the prince's coughing, it was likely that no one else heard the small sound. But I knew exactly who it came from.

With tears streaming down his face, King Locklyn pressed a fist to his mouth as his eyes refused to leave his only child's soaked form. His normally light skin had gone paler than usual, but it was clear to see that relief was slowly erasing the fear he'd felt at seeing his son nearly drown.

This was but a small crack in the terrible façade that the king had to put up each and every single day – hatred and disgust for his son's disregard for his title, all the while loving him deeply.

For a moment King Locklyn glanced my way. I expected him to press a finger to his lips or do something indicating that I shouldn't mention his reaction to anyone, but instead he gave me a small, curt nod before wiping away his tears.

I didn't mind the brevity of the gesture because it was all the thanks I needed. *This* was my job, and I did it.

"Oh, thank all the stars. Aliya, you're incredible," Caspian said as he pressed a kiss to the top of my dripping head.

Now I'd really received all the praise I needed.

Prince Damien hacked up water for another minute while Ki'ran called for a few towels. Unfortunately, people didn't fall off the dock every day, so there were none to be had.

"Once the prince can stand, we'll be on our way. I'll have an attendant waiting who will direct them to a place where they can dry off," Lord Liseni promised.

Elgin helped Prince Damien to his feet. With Ki'ran under one arm and Elgin under the other, the prince looked like a soggy puppet. Content that Prince Damien would make it to the submarine this time, King Locklyn and Lord Liseni walked down the last stretch of the dock and stepped down into the submarine's hatch.

As I got to my feet, the prince and I locked stares. "And here I'd hoped that *you* would have been the first one to go for my lips," he said with a mocking grin.

Elgin, Ki'ran, and the king's guards all froze. Caspian sucked in a sharp breath, but I held out a hand to stop him. Violence or harsh words from the captain of the prince's guard would do nothing except get him fired. Or worse depending on the prince's reaction.

I couldn't believe the nerve of Prince Damien. He'd made an utter fool out of himself and nearly drowned, and while I was the one to save him, he couldn't find it within himself to be thankful. Oh no, he had to try and make me uncomfortable.

Well, I was done with his games.

"I wouldn't have touched them even if you paid me all the units in the galaxy," I snapped back and was pleased to see a look of disbelief on the prince's face. Pointedly looking at Ki'ran and Elgin I said, "Let's follow our king. Oh, and make sure the prince doesn't try to take another swim."

Prince Damien made a choking sound, but I ignored it. Making sure that the prince was totally supported by their arms, Ki'ran and Elgin hauled him to the end of the dock and into the gaping maw of the submarine. Hopefully there weren't too many stairs that Prince Damien would have to take on his own to get aboard.

A warm arm slipped around my waist. "Who was that captivatingly assertive soldier?" Caspian purred into my ear.

I shivered from his warm breath on my skin. "I just don't want to deal with his nonsense anymore." I shrugged. "It helped that Ki'ran and Elgin were completely holding him and could drag him away."

Caspian's laugh rumbled against my back. "Sometimes you truly amaze me. You know that?" He pressed a kiss to my temple, making me shiver once more. "Now let's get going so you can dry off."

The ride down to the underwater capital of Aquillo was incredible. I'd never been snorkeling or in a submarine on Terra, but I couldn't imagine that either of those experiences would've come close to the things I saw in the Aqui sea.

What I saw was more than coral formations and strange fish. It was architectural masterpieces made from coral and rock and ocean plants to create the most stunning city I'd ever seen.

Twisting spires in vibrant reds, greens, and oranges rose from the sandy ocean floor. They had outward-facing windows and doors, but they seemed to have a rippling, translucent material covering them. I watched a silvery, bipedal creature kick through the water and pass through the barrier, and once through, the weightlessness of the water appeared to leave them. Past the barrier and inside the spire, the creature walked around on two legs until it disappeared from view.

It must have been some type of force field that kept water out of the buildings. How odd. An underwater society that recreated land conditions in their homes.

Fields of plants resembling seaweed swayed in the current while small fish that blinked yellow and purple darted between the leaves. Just outside the city wall a rotund, brown creature resembling a horse with the legs of a crab made its way through the sand, pulling a wide sled covered in crates.

And then all around us was the city, sprawling farther and deeper than I realized. With each passing second as we descended, more coral buildings became visible. I couldn't fathom just how far the city stretched, and I wondered just how many creatures called this place their home.

Although I'd already had my dip in the sea, I found myself longing to exit the submarine and explore this underwater world.

The submarine propelled us down toward a massive building that resembled a conch shell on its head. As we came to a stop on the sandy ground, a bubble-barrier rose around us, draining the water from our area and connecting to the large building.

Lord Liseni, King Locklyn, and both groups of their guards exited the submarine. After a moment Prince Damien exited as well, grumbling about being cold. I longed to ask whose fault it was that he was cold, but I held my tongue. One snappy comment today was already pushing my luck.

The air inside the bubble was surprisingly warm and held the faint, salty tang of the sea. As we approached the great shell building, I almost lost my footing in the soft sand as I tried to guess just how tall the structure was. Skyscrapers on Terra had nothing on this.

As promised, a frog-like attendant waited for us just inside the strange building and eagerly escorted me and Prince Damien to a set of rectangular, empty rooms.

"What is this?" I asked as the prince stepped unevenly into the first chamber.

The walls had been smoothed perfectly, lacking any of the curve from the shell building. Oddly, there was nothing inside the room. No tub for bathing, no bench with fresh clothes, and not even a chair to sit in.

"This is a drying chamber. Quick and effective for incidents such as this," the short, carp-like attendant replied. "The door will seal, and you'll feel a hot breeze. Breathe normally, and this will be over in a few seconds."

I entered the second chamber, and as a solid door made of shall slid shut, I tried not to panic. *It's just a drying chamber. I'm not trapped.*

Indeed, a burst of hot air filled the room, causing my hair to whip around my face. The heat managed to permeate my armor, and when the gust died down, I was miraculously dry. Windblown, but dry.

"That was incredible!" I exclaimed as the door opened.

The attendant bowed. "Thank you, Hero of Vanthurium. I'm pleased you find our invention so exciting."

I immediately felt uncomfortable. How did he know who I was? "Um, yeah," I awkwardly replied.

Offering me a strange, thin lipped smile, the attendant held out an alabaster comb and pointed a webbed finger down the hallway. "The next door leads into a bathing chamber with a mirror. You can freshen up in there, and when you're ready, another attendant will be waiting to bring you to the main hall."

"Thanks." I headed to the room he'd indicated, and behind me I heard him guide Prince Damien away.

After I finally tamed my wind-blown hair, the new servant – a brown, scaled creature with whiskers like a catfish – led me down several hallways before gesturing to a rounded doorway. Through it I could see the Callaisan and Aqui parties seated at a long table made from driftwood.

For being in a conch shell, the room I walked into was massive – easily five or six stories tall. The orange and white walls curved inward just slightly, and every few feet there was a clear bubble, fixed slightly above head height, that contained bioluminescent algae. A spiraling, multi-tiered chandelier hung from the ceiling, also covered with smaller algae bubbles to illuminate the cavernous room.

Heads rose from the table as I drew close, and Ki'ran, seated at the end of the table, patted an unoccupied wooden chair on his left side. Unfortunately, the spot was also next to Prince Damien.

That was the last place I wanted to be right now, but I couldn't refuse since everyone was waiting for me to be seated. Perhaps

Prince Damien's previous embarrassments would prevent him from doing anything else stupid.

Caspian, on the prince's far side, offered me an apologetic smile. Once again, this was a situation in which he had no say. I attempted to give him an encouraging smile as I drew the chair back from the table.

I sat in the creaky driftwood chair, and immediately a servant materialized over my shoulder, offering me a small ceramic cup filled with a steaming liquid.

"Uh, thanks," I said as I accepted it. The white cup contained a clear, scentless liquid, and I hesitated to raise it to my lips.

"Tea," Ki'ran whispered to me. "It is very bitter, but the custom is to consume it all in one sip."

I wasn't the biggest fan of tea, especially unsweetened, but when I noticed Lord Liseni watching me from the head of the table with his unblinking eyes, I knew I couldn't refuse the drink. I raised the cup to him and then tipped the whole thing back into my mouth.

The tangy liquid spread over my tongue, and I rushed to swallow it before I felt compelled to spit it out. It was just as bitter as Ki'ran had warned, and I hoped that was the last time I'd have to drink Aqui tea.

"Excellent," Lord Liseni said with a nod of approval as he folded his hands atop the table. "Now that we're all present, shall we begin?"

King Locklyn nodded, and a long discussion about supplies and armies ensued.

Although Lord Liseni would often use words that I couldn't understand, the gist of the meeting was this: the Aqui people believed they were safe under the ocean of their planet, despite the increase in attacks throughout the King's Galaxy, and Lord Liseni didn't want to risk his soldiers' lives by sending the king military support.

I kept my mouth shut as the king negotiated with his lord, but I was troubled by Lord Liseni's decision. How could he not want to help prevent attacks since he had soldiers to spare? Did he really believe that the Krech would simply leave Aquillo alone because its people lived underwater?

I squirmed in my chair, uncomfortable from the seat and the

discussion. The negotiation between the two rulers was tense, and every now and then I noticed King Locklyn look down the table at his son. A look of disapproval followed each time when he realized that Prince Damien wasn't even paying attention.

Instead the prince snacked on the trays of ocean delicacies provided for us and downed cup after cup of a ruby liquid that the servants provided. He wasn't contributing to the conversation, but since he wasn't detracting from it in any way, no one thought it necessary to scold him.

At one point I noticed Prince Damien nodding off, and I didn't hesitate to kick the leg of his chair, jolting him back awake.

His head snapped up, and he adjusted the circlet sitting on his black locks, creating the appearance that he was simply grooming instead of falling asleep. But under his breath he hissed, "Rude," followed by a glare that could've curdled milk.

"Pay attention," I snapped back in a low voice. "This meeting affects you, *prince*."

He turned away, signaling a servant for another drink, but at least he remained awake for the duration of the meeting.

In the end, a small deal was struck with Lord Liseni providing two hundred of his soldiers in exchange for their weight in Callaisan fruits and vegetables. I wasn't sure if that was a detrimental number to Callais's supplies, but King Locklyn seemed pleased when they finally stood and shook hands.

And with that, the meeting was over. All the chaos of this morning, settled over a few thousand pounds of produce. It didn't make sense to me, but I was happy to see the matter settled on what appeared to be agreeable terms.

We stood for formal goodbyes and then made our way back to the submarine. This time, Lord Liseni and his guards wouldn't accompany us on the trip up to the surface.

Before I boarded, however, Lord Liseni called for me to wait. He gestured to one of his guards, who stepped forward with a shell-encrusted box. "I had hoped to present you with this before the meeting, but in all the… excitement I didn't have the time." Lifting the lid, he reached inside and pulled out a small object. Raising his voice, Lord Liseni continued, "I present this gift to you, Aliya Rathburn of Terra, Hero of Vanthurium, as a sign of respect and friendship. What you did on Charra and Vanthurium has not gone unnoticed, and I am grateful. It is my sincerest hope that in times of need, you may call upon the Aqui or we may call upon you for help."

In his rough palms lay a gorgeous glass pin in the shape of a half clam shell. The translucent glass contained a multitude of tiny shells, and in the very center was a silver pearl the size of my thumb nail.

Simultaneously chaotic and delicate in its design, it was a magnificent gift. I wanted to scoop it up and proudly display it, but I hesitated, unsure if accepting the pin was a safe move. Would I be required to answer any and every call for aid from Lord Liseni? Or was this more of a gesture of friendship instead of an agreement?

"Lord Liseni," I started but found myself at a loss for words. "Thank you for this kind gesture, but I really can't accept this."

He hesitated, and for a moment I worried that I'd offended him by refusing. "Other lords have offered you similar tokens, no?"

"Um. No, sir. I haven't… no one has given me anything." Was I supposed to have received other gifts?

A look of understanding crossed Lord Liseni's face and he laughed. "Ah. I understand your hesitation now. I present this pin to you out of respect for your skills and as a token of friendship. You shall not be in my debt for accepting this, but in the times that may come, we will never know when powerful allies are needed."

It still sounded like he wanted to call on me if he had a problem, but I could also see the benefit in accepting this token. Essentially, it was thanks and recognition for being a hero, and a show of alliance between myself and him.

I mulled over my response, not wanting to offend but also wishing to convey my stance to this lord. "Then I thank you for your kindness. While I offer my protection first to my king and his family, I will gladly assist you should you need it."

"That is all I ask," Lord Liseni replied with a smile, passing me the pin. I couldn't fasten it on while in my armor, and I prayed that I wouldn't drop it before we returned to the palace.

With one last bow of thanks, I boarded the submarine, and we began our trip back to the surface.

"Well, that was unexpected," Caspian remarked as I settled into the seat beside him.

"Why?"

Caspian laughed. "If you couldn't tell from the negotiations, the Aqui are rather… self-contained. They don't like making deals or friends with 'landers,' as they call us behind our backs, so it was strange to see Lord Liseni make that connection with you. Especially in front of King Locklyn."

I had no idea the Aqui thought of us in the *us versus them* mindset. They were part of the King's Galaxy, after all, so I'd assumed that they participated in the galaxy's politics like other planets did. "Did I do the wrong thing by accepting?" I cradled the pin in my hand, watching as light reflected off the pearl.

"Absolutely not! I'd say that was the best political arrangement of the day." Caspian rested his hand on my knee, pulling my attention back to him. "You heard how much debating King Locklyn had to do just to get a few hundred soldiers from Lord Liseni. Now, because of your arrangement, we'll have better leverage to ask for things from Lord Liseni in the future."

I felt like a pawn. I'd made the right move, but knowing there was a future cost made me concerned. Hopefully it wasn't something I couldn't complete or something that would go against my values, but I couldn't control that until the favor was called in.

The submarine jolted as it reached the surface, and we stepped back out onto the dock. "By the way," Caspian said, "I told Ki'ran and Elgin that we'd cover the afternoon shift." I rolled my eyes.

Great, more time with the prince. "I know, I know, but they did have to carry him after you fished him out of the ocean."

I laughed. "You're right. They definitely deserve time to clean up and rest after that."

We returned to the palace with far fewer incidents than when we left. Prince Damien actually chose to nap on the flight back instead of drinking. That didn't make him any less irritable when we woke him after landing, but at least he could walk on his own two feet.

Caspian pinged Omri and Ney before we'd arrived, asking if they were available to briefly guard the prince while we changed out of our armor.

Back in my room, I pinned the gift from Lord Liseni to my old Nova jacket. I didn't have many chances to wear it now that I had to wear a royal uniform, but I knew the pin was safe on the jacket because I'd never lose it.

Tapping on my cuff, I sent Caspian a quick message asking where the prince was so I could rejoin my shift. Surprisingly, he replied that Prince Damien was in the grand ballroom.

I was thankful Elgin had brought us to that room after my first altercation with Prince Damien because now I didn't need to ask for directions.

What business did the prince have in the ballroom? Then, with a sinking stomach, I remembered Elgin's comment from that same day about how the prince liked to throw parties in that space. *Please let this not be happening…*

But of course, it was. When I arrived, an army of servants had surrounded the prince, and he turned in circles on the center of the ballroom floor, pointing to certain areas as he gave them orders. "I want another bar set up against this wall on each floor, and don't forget the top floor like you did last time. Make sure the lighting is synced up to the music unlike last time. And I want a full menu ready for my review by tomorrow."

I glanced over at Caspian who gave his head a shake of disgust. "I don't know how he managed to get everyone assembled so fast, but apparently he wants to throw a party. Next week."

"Is that bad?"

"Yes. It means a week of chaos for us and the servants as he rushes to get everything ready. This will be yet another distraction keeping him from meetings or royal duties. If our fellow guards' stories are to be believed, the prince likes to throw parties on a massive scale," Caspian explained with a scowl.

"You'd think that he would take it easy after nearly drowning," I replied. "Or maybe that's the reason behind this sudden celebration."

Caspian scoffed. "He never needs a reason to throw a party. If the prince wants a party, he gets one."

It was then that Prince Damien realized I'd arrived. "Ah, our dutiful Hero. Be a dear and fetch me something to eat from the kitchens?" he asked before turning back to his hoard of servants.

I had to take a few breaths in order to keep the bite out of my voice when I said, "With all due respect, your highness, no."

Still keeping his back to me, Prince Damien froze and cocked his head to the side. "What did you say?" he threatened in a low voice.

I'd pulled his sorry butt from the ocean, and this was how he saw fit to treat me? Like another servant? With more force in my voice I replied, "I said no. I'm your guard, and it's not my duty to bring you food. You can ask one of the other individuals in this room."

He slowly turned, and I could see the raw malice in his hazel eyes. I kept my face blank as I gave him a cool stare. "You think you're special just because you survived two battles? Because everyone you meet calls you the Hero of Vanthurium? Well, you work for me, and you'll do as I say."

I should've been afraid of angering him. I should've been concerned that he was a prince with the power to make my life a living hell. But I couldn't find it within myself to care because all I saw was a lonely, spoiled brat. "I don't care what anyone calls me, but at your father's request, I'm here to keep you safe. Not fed. If I'm not here and you fall again, who will save you?"

His face turned purple, and I laughed inwardly, imagining that it must be a hereditary trait. I expected to receive the full force of his anger, but instead, he turned and unleashed it upon a small Callaisan female who was standing beside him. "Send my usual up to my chambers, now! And the rest of you," he turned and shouted at the larger group, "I want the layout plans and menu ready for my approval by tomorrow. Now go!"

The servants scattered, and the female sprinted out of the ballroom toward the kitchens. Prince Damien fixed his glare on me and Caspian and stomped over to where we stood. "The two of you will stay out of my way," he snapped pointing a finger at each of our chests. Then he drew up close to me, close enough that I could hear his racing heart. "I don't care what my father thinks of you. You're nothing."

With that, Prince Damien stormed from the ballroom, Caspian and I trailing in his wake.

While the prince shouted for servants and guards to get out of his way, Caspian and I lagged behind. Neither of us wanted to get close and put the prince in a worse mood, but we couldn't leave him completely alone either.

"Why would you challenge him like that?" Caspian asked as he caught my wrist.

"Because I'm not a servant. We protect, not coddle." I certainly wasn't going to apologize for standing up to Prince Damien. Now that I was in King Locklyn's and Lord Liseni's good graces, I had no concerns over potentially losing my job. At the very worst, I'd just get moved from the prince's guards to the king's.

Caspian sighed and waited a few moments before replying. "I understand, but I'm not sure that was smart. He was in a bad enough mood, and he's already going to make this week a mess with this party. We don't need him taking out additional frustrations on us."

I hadn't thought about that. If the prince was hard on the rest of us, it would be my fault. "I'm sorry."

"It's okay," Caspian replied as we came to a halt outside the prince's room. "Maybe I'm just imaging the worst, and he'll actually stop bothering us now that he knows you'll stand up to him."

I chuckled. "We can certainly hope so."

Caspian and I took up our posts outside the door. I started to feel a smidge of regret for embarrassing Prince Damien in front of all the servants, but he was being unreasonable. I truly didn't care what he thought of me, so long as he accepted the fact that I was only here to protect him.

I did hope that Caspian was right about him backing off now that he knew I wasn't going to roll over and take his verbal abuse. That certainly didn't keep the prince from arguing with his father, but that was a different situation entirely.

After a few moments of silence, Caspian spoke up again. "Dinner tonight?"

I couldn't hold back my laugh. "Don't we always get dinner together when we don't have shifts?"

"I don't mean inside the palace, silly," Caspian said with a roll of his eyes. If we weren't eating in the palace, where would we go? He turned and gave me a lopsided grin. "Meet me on the far side of the hedge maze, on the lake side, around eight?"

"Um, okay." He had something planned, and I resisted asking for more information. If he wanted to surprise me, then he could.

"Excellent." And then Caspian leaned across the doorway and gave me a kiss that made my toes curl.

✳

It never occurred to me that Caspian might pull a prank.

I stood in the dark, just outside the hedge maze, watching the moonlight shimmer off the lake. It was a very peaceful night, and I would've enjoyed it a lot more if I knew that Caspian would eventually appear.

For what felt like the twentieth time, I checked the time on my cuff. He was half an hour late.

I was sorely tempted to send a message demanding an update on his whereabouts, but yet again, I stopped myself. Caspian was the captain of the prince's guards – maybe something had come up.

But he could've sent me a message.

I paced for a few minutes more, jumping at every rustle from the forest and every crunch of gravel as guards performed their nightly patrols.

Caspian, where are you? I'd give him five more minutes, and then I'd send him a message.

Just as I was beginning to give up hope, I heard the sound of running feet on the path behind me. Sure enough, Caspian jogged around the side of the hedge maze with a basket on his arm.

"I'm. So sorry. Aliya," he panted as he approached. Drawing up alongside me, Caspian placed the wicker basket on the ground and pulled me into a hug.

"Hey, it's okay. Sit and catch your breath. What happened?" His heart raced, and his breathing was erratic. I didn't need him passing out on me after running here from… wherever he'd been.

Refusing to sit, Caspian pulled back a bit to look into my eyes. "I didn't mean to be late. As I was about to head over here, King Locklyn called for me," he explained with a sigh. He looked so worried, as if he'd stood me up completely instead of having a legitimate reason for being late for our dinner.

"Caspian," I murmured as I cupped his face, "it really is okay. You report to the king. If King Locklyn needed you, you didn't have a choice but to go to him."

Relief washed over his face. He really thought I'd be that upset? "Thank you… for understanding. I thought—well, that doesn't really matter now, does it? Either way, I have dinner, as promised, and a little more to make it up to you!"

His smile was so cheerful it bordered on comedic, and I couldn't help the laughter that it drew from me. "Okay, let's eat."

With a quick kiss on the cheek, Caspian released me and stooped to open the basket. Immediately the smells of fresh bread, grilled meat, and something sweet wafted out. My stomach growled in response.

A brief look of chagrin crossed Caspian's face. "I'm sorry for making you wait." He pulled out a navy and gold blanket and then proceeded to unload covered dishes from the basket.

"Stop it." I playfully swatted at him. "You have nothing to apologize for."

We settled next to each other on the blanket and ate under the stars. He'd somehow brought all the dishes that I really enjoyed here at the palace, and it touched my heart realizing just how much he noticed those things. Caspian had even brought a large slice of chocolate cake for us to share.

"What did the king want?" I asked around a bite of cake.

"Oh, the usual." Caspian leaned back on his hands, staring up at the stars and two moons that were out tonight. "He wanted a report on how shifts have been, how difficult it's been to manage Prince Damien, and how you are after today's events."

"Me?" I'd done my duty and saved the prince from drowning. It's not like I'd been attacked or injured in the rescue, so it surprised me that the king had questioned Caspian.

"Of course. He's… well aware just how difficult the prince can be with his guards and, ah, females." Oh. Apparently, King Locklyn was more concerned about what Prince Damien had said after he'd been revived instead of me pulling the prince out of the ocean. "He was mostly worried that Prince Damien would eventually push you so much that you'd want to leave the palace altogether."

Well, he wasn't wrong there. I certainly didn't feel comfortable around the spoiled prince, but he wasn't going to be the reason I left. If I ever did leave. "And what did you tell him?"

"I told him that you can manage the prince on your own," Caspian replied with a chuckle. He sat up to look at me as I set the empty plate on the blanket. "You're amazing, Aliya."

I was thankful for how dark the evening had become so that Caspian couldn't see how deeply I blushed. "I'm not *that* special…"

Saving Prince Damien had, once again, been another situation where I acted to protect someone else. I hadn't gone above and beyond my role when I dove into that ocean, and I barely needed to tap into my abilities to pull him out.

Caspian leaned closer and huffed out a short laugh. "You'll never see yourself the way we all do, will you?"

"The way who sees me?" As far as I knew, King Locklyn liked me because I was a hero and had the potential to keep his heir alive in the face of danger, and Caspian… liked me, for some reason.

He shook his head as a playful smile spread across his lips. Which I really wanted to kiss. "Everyone. Every single guard and servant in the palace know who you are and what you've already done for this galaxy. Lord Liseni knows it too, and that's why he gave you that pin today. The way you are… you could become anything, do anything, yet you're here. You're a soldier keeping the least respectful and appreciative being in the King's Galaxy alive. When we were first debriefed that a biologically altered Terran was entering the Protective Forces, I'd imagined some mindless weapon who took orders and destroyed things. But that all changed as soon as I watched you walk off that cruiser with Doctor Givray."

It was strange to hear those same fears that held me back during my initial training coming from Caspian now. I'd explained to him how I hadn't wanted to be used as a super soldier, but he'd never told me that he had been worried for the same thing before we'd met.

"Strength aside, everyone's now seen how kind and honest you are. You worked with Elgin and Ba'rin on their shooting during our second day at the palace. Quite a few people saw your emotional reunion with Adís. And after how awful Prince Damien has been to you, you were still the first person to jump into that water to save him today." Caspian tapped my knee with a single finger. "There's so much to you that people can finally see. You're a hero but you're also—" He stopped as he sought out the right word.

"On Terra we would call that 'being human.' I'm not sure what you call it out here."

"Human." He let the word linger between us for a moment before nodding. "That sounds about right. Everyone can see how human you are toward others."

I looked away, uncomfortable with receiving so much praise. I hadn't thought about how much my actions would be seen by others – and how much those actions meant. All I had wanted was to keep the people I cared about safe, and it had earned me the title of hero and a reputation larger than I could have anticipated. At least people were seeing that I could be just as normal as them.

"I'm glad they don't think I'm a freak."

"Aliya, no one ever thought that – except you. You're so amazing," he said again, leaning in close. "One day I hope you see it too." Closing the distance between us, Caspian pressed his lips to mine.

It was hesitant, as if he thought I'd pull away because I disagreed with what he'd said. Sure, I didn't think I'd earned some great status, but Caspian's compliments comforted me in ways he probably didn't know.

The one thing I'd wanted since waking up in the healing facility and learning that I'd been changed was to feel like I fit in. I'd started to accept myself when we were part of the Nova squad, but hearing just how much Caspian thought of me hit me in a whole new way.

Caspian was never scared of or repulsed by me. Instead, he liked how I was different. He wanted all of me, the way I was. And I wanted him.

So I kissed him back without abandon. Let the other guards on patrol see if they wanted.

Butterflies erupted in my stomach as I wrapped my arms around Caspian's neck, and he pulled me close against his strong body as I ran my fingers through the soft waves of his hair. Our pulses skyrocketed as we gave each other everything we had, and I found myself wishing for this moment to never end.

I wanted Caspian now and forever, and I could tell that he felt the same.

He pulled back and stared deeply into my eyes. "I love you, Aliya Rathburn."

My breath hitched at those three words. *He actually said it!* I was overjoyed and surprised, but I must have paused for a moment too long because Caspian started to look worried. "I love you, too," I blurted before he could regret his declaration.

The night fell silent around us as those two admissions were voiced into the evening air. Caspian and I stared at each other for what could have been seconds or years – I didn't know, and I didn't care.

Finally, Caspian broke the silence. "You really love me?" he asked in a shaky voice. "As incredible as you are, you don't want someone more like you?"

"*Stars*, Caspian! Yes, I love you just the way you are!"

His grin was bright enough to illuminate the valley as he leaned in for another kiss. "You've made me the happiest male in the galaxy," he said when he pulled away again.

"And you've made me the happiest female," I replied, brushing the tip of my nose against his. "I love you. Always and forever."

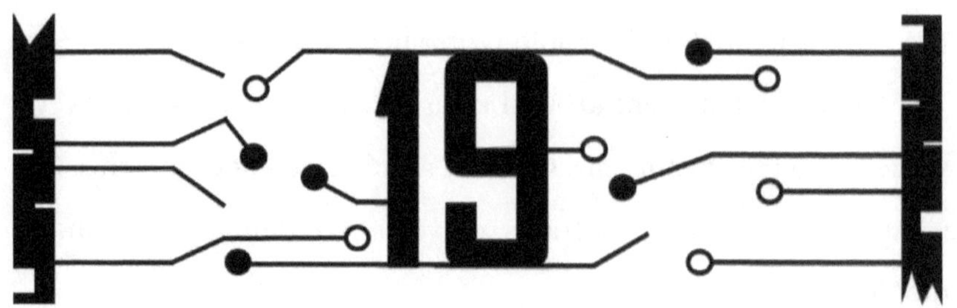

Caspian had been right. The week was a flurry of constant activity as the servants and guards prepared for one of Prince Damien's legendary parties.

We maintained our usual two-guard shifts since the prince was less frantic than everyone else who had to clean the palace, prepare food for the guests, and decorate the ballroom. For the most part, he sat in his room sending invitations to guests through his personal dataport.

Neither the king nor us guards were allowed to see 'the list,' and slowly it became a point of contention.

"How are we supposed to prepare for this stupid event if we have no idea how many people are even attending?" Caspian shouted one night.

We knew we couldn't stray too far on the grounds since they'd been manicured and were under constant patrol, so Caspian had come to my room after dinner to chat.

"Is that really our problem? I doubt Prince Damien is inviting criminals." I sprawled on my bed watching as Caspian paced in frustration.

"What do you mean?" He stopped midstride to look over at me.

"Well," I sat up and crossed my legs, "these guests are probably people who already know him, so do they pose him a threat? I don't see why we need to rework our shifts that much if he's going to be around his friends."

Caspian groaned and sank into one of the plush chairs in my sitting room. "Aliya, there are going to be hundreds of guests, if not more since we can't see the list, in two days," he said while directing a glare at my door. "With that many individuals milling around, who knows if someone uninvited will be able to slip in? *That's* when we would have a serious issue."

I rolled my eyes. As if I hadn't imagined this scenario already. "Right, but Prince Damien will already have two guards following him to prevent that kind of thing from happening."

This time Caspian sighed. "And you think the prince will just *allow* us to follow him around during this party? I'd imagine he'd take every opportunity to lose us and create some space. You remember how he is around females." As if I needed a reminder. "Well, I doubt he'd want to get that close to others while we're standing over his shoulder. He doesn't care, but I'm sure *they* will."

He had a point there. Two guards in full uniform would be a bit of a mood killer in the middle of a party, like having your parents at a school dance. "What are we going to do?"

Caspian's eyes flicked down to his arm band and then back up to me. "I've been asking King Locklyn what he suggests, but he's been too busy with far more pressing issues."

I perked up. As far as I knew, the Krech's attacks on trade ships and other vessels had slowed if not ceased altogether. "What happened?"

For a few moments Caspian was quiet. He chewed his bottom lip as he weighed what he could and couldn't tell me. But I knew Caspian – if I waited patiently enough, he'd tell me everything because I wouldn't run down the hallways shouting the news to everyone within earshot. "Krech were spotted on Charra again."

"What!" There was no reason for them to be there since Charra's inhabitants were mostly criminals, and their goods primarily consisted of scrap metal and other useless oddities. "What happened?"

"They blew up the entire oil district."

I gasped. Oil was barely used since most of the galaxy harnessed solar or atomic energy, but some older machines still needed oil. Losing the entire oil district must have cost a fortune. "Casualties?" Caspian set his jaw and looked away. "Caspian, please tell me."

"Roughly a million," Caspian mumbled, still refusing to look at me.

A million lives lost. Sure, no one *really* liked Charra, but losing a million people... That was still a million lives. It was a blow to society, and I couldn't even imagine the chaos that must have caused on the miserable little planet.

"Adís is somewhere out there, isn't she?" I hadn't seen her all week. She'd sent me a message in the afternoon before we were supposed to have dinner and catch up, but her message had been brief. *Can't make it, called away for duty.*

Caspian's expression sank even further, his fingers digging into his knees. His reply was a curt nod.

"Gunther and Gráinne were moved out of the palace, too," I whispered.

I felt like the worst friend in the universe. I'd only found out that they left when I'd gone searching for them the other day. Ney had wanted to remove his cuff, and after several unsuccessful attempts by him to smash it off, I'd offered to find the two geniuses who'd made the cuffs.

When I finally made it to their design rooms, the space was empty. Since then, I'd sent them several messages but hadn't received a reply.

"I know," Caspian said as he raked his hands through his hair.

"You knew? Caspian, you knew and didn't tell me?" I slid off the end of the bed and went to stand before him.

"They asked me not to."

Why on Callais would they have told him not to tell me? "Why?" I demanded.

"They didn't give me details, but it was something to do with Doctor Givray."

My anger immediately dissipated. Doctor Givray needed them? Or had they signed up as subjects for his work? Again, I felt like a bad friend since I hadn't once checked in on the doctor and his new project. His work was massively important to the future of warfare for this galaxy, but since I hadn't heard from him, I assumed he hadn't succeeded in making any monsters. But that also meant he hadn't succeeded for the council.

I frowned. I should've been called before them by now.

I decided to put that out of my mind since it wasn't an issue. I hadn't been summoned, and now the twins were likely helping with Doctor Givray's work. Everything would be fine. Right?

"Well, this has become quite the mess. Hasn't it?" I sank to the floor and pulled my knees to my chest.

Caspian gave a dry laugh. "Yes, it has. And we still have that party to deal with." I groaned, but he continued before I could cut in. "Let me work with King Locklyn on the best plan of action. I'm sure between him and the other previous guards, they'll know what to expect and how we should handle it."

I gave Caspian a tight-lipped smile. "Yes, captain."

Now he really laughed. "You know I hate hearing that."

"Oh, I know. But you're being such a captain here, calling all the shots."

He sank to his knees before me, a playful smile on his lips. "Am I supposed to be doing something else?"

I tapped my chin and pretended to think. "Well, you could kiss me," I said with a sly smile.

"I can do that," he replied, leaning forward to oblige me.

✳

I trusted that Caspian would come up with a plan.

But here it was, roughly a day before the party, and we hadn't heard anything.

A quiet *ping* sounded from my cuff – a message from Elgin. *Any news?* Somehow the rest of them thought that I would hear about our strategy first because Caspian spent so much time with me.

Well, that certainly wasn't the case here. *Nothing yet. Caspian is on a shift. When he has a plan, he'll let us all know.* I hoped that would keep him off my back for a few more hours.

Elgin's reply *pinged* immediately. *Yeah, yeah. You let us know when you* hear.

Typical. Sighing, I closed the message and resumed my reading.

It had taken me long enough, but I'd finally found the palace library. Luckily it wasn't all converted to digital reading, and now there were several tomes stacked on my bedside table.

Unbeknownst to Caspian and the others, I was researching the history of the murals in the palace stairwell that Elgin had shown me. Two history books mentioned them – mostly as a study of art in the galaxy – but none offered an explanation as to who had created the beautiful and haunting images.

A few sharp knocks sounded from my door.

Putting the book aside, I stood up from my bed. Since I was off shift, I'd dressed casually, and today I wore blue jeans and a long-sleeve black shirt – comfortable but sturdy enough to do my job if there was a surprise attack on the palace.

I smoothed the front of my shirt as I crossed the room to my door. Caspian was on a shift right now, so unless he'd 'taken a detour' far from the prince's room, I had no idea who was calling on me.

"Your majesty," I said with a hint of surprise. I quickly moved to the side as I pulled the door open wide. King Locklyn strode into my room as if it were his own, glancing at the stack of books on my side table before returning his gaze to me.

"Aliya, good afternoon. I apologize for calling upon you without prior notice, but we need to discuss security plans for tomorrow night." He stood in the center of my room while Tormic, one of his personal guards, remained dutifully in his shadow.

"Of course, your majesty. What do you need me to do?"

"Because you and Caspian have been my son's personal guards since you arrived, and because he finally seems to have accepted *your* presence, I will need you both to dress as guests for the party, keeping an eye on him and the people with whom he interacts."

I froze. I expected to be on some kind of patrol during the party, but now I had to dress up and socialize with his guests? I didn't even have anything acceptable to wear.

The king stared at me, and I could see in his eyes that he dared me to object.

"Of course, your majesty," I said with a bow of my head. "And the rest of the prince's guards? What should they do?"

"Ah, yes." King Locklyn paused as if he hadn't thought about the rest of his son's guards. "Have them stationed around the perimeter of the ballroom. Most people will remain on the bottom floor, and I'm sure Damien will flock to the biggest crowd. Their formal armor will suffice."

He wasn't wrong about that; the prince would want to be the center of attention. "That sounds like a good idea. I will let the others know, majesty."

"Good," he replied as he moved back toward my door. "Tomorrow I'll send a few maids who will help you get prepared. You'll be armed, but you will look like another one of Damien's guests. When you're dressed and ready, assume Damien will have already begun his nonsense, so you should head immediately to the ballroom."

"Yes, your majesty," I mumbled as he left the room, Tormic shutting the door behind them.

I was confused. I was a soldier, then a personal guard, and now… a party guest? Keeping an eye on Prince Damien wouldn't be too hard now that I could move about the party without attracting too much attention, but I was worried about the other guests. How would I keep close enough to Prince Damien so that I could be there should someone try to attack him?

I groaned in frustration as I ran my hands through my hair. Since joining the prince's guards, Prince Damien had done a number of annoying things. Creating so much chaos over a stupid party *and* inadvertently making me join that party certainly topped that list.

Turning to my cuff, I opened a message to everyone. *Received orders from King Locklyn. Caspian and I will pose as guests. The rest of you will be stationed in the ballroom.*

Replies flooded in immediately.

Guests? You mean that you two have to participate in that madness? Elgin said.

The ballroom is going to be a madhouse, Ney sent to everyone.

In hindsight, I probably should have called a meeting to prevent this flood of messages from happening. Luckily Caspian stepped in, putting a stop to all the replies. *We will all meet to discuss this tomorrow morning after Ba'rin and Seradon finish their overnight shift.*

I might have been imagining things, but Caspian's message seemed tense. At least these orders weren't only annoying me.

I checked the shift schedule and groaned when I saw how early Ba'rin and Seradon would end their shift. The sun wouldn't even be up yet. It would probably be a good idea to turn in early since I had to wake up so early for the meeting. And then I'd be up late for the party.

It seemed silly that I wasn't looking forward to attending my first galactic party, but I had a good reason. The other guards' stories about how wild Prince Damien's past parties were worried me, and now that I was going to be a guest, I didn't know how I was supposed to act.

Hopefully, I'd be able to hang around Caspian, and we could pose as a couple.

With a sigh, I drew the curtains in my room. I'd *definitely* need a lot of sleep in order to make it through tomorrow.

Curling up in the bed that was far too large for one person, I drifted off to sleep while thoughts of dresses and music filled my head.

The sun had barely risen, but we'd all managed to wake up in time. The prince's guards, assembled for the pre-party strategy meeting, waited in the second floor hallway of the royal wing for Caspian to discuss his plans.

We'd left Prince Damien alone while he slept just so we could have this meeting in peace. It wasn't like he was going to get into trouble. Apparently, he liked to sleep all day before a party just so he could stay up throughout the madness.

I hated that I now had to be a part of it.

"Okay, Aliya. Would you mind going over what King Locklyn said once more?" Caspian said, drawing me out from the irritated thoughts swirling around my head.

I sighed. It was the third time I'd relayed the king's message — the first time in a message yesterday, again when I'd arrived at this powwow, and now in front of the whole group. "He said that he wants me and Caspian to dress as guests and sort of mingle with everyone while keeping an eye on Prince Damien. He also wants us to keep tabs on the people the prince interacts with. The rest of you will be in formal uniform and stationed around the edge of the ballroom."

Ki'ran scratched his chin. "Why would King Locklyn have you and Caspian dress as guests? Perhaps we all should be guests at this ridiculous party."

I shrugged. "I don't know. Perhaps he will have other guards posing as guests, but the king only asked for me and Caspian."

Caspian nodded and took a step into the center of our circle. Everyone looked slightly haggard and sleep deprived. I didn't blame them. It was ungodly early, and this week had been pure madness as we rushed around assisting the palace servants with preparations. Tomorrow, hopefully, would be a well-deserved change of pace.

"While it might be better to have everyone mingling with guests, we'll follow King Locklyn's plans. I trust you all know where you should be stationed in the ballroom?" Caspian asked. Nods followed from everyone except Ki'ran. "Can someone help Ki'ran get into position once you take up your spots? I trust you know the layout and flow for these events a bit better than I would."

It was odd to hear Caspian deferring judgment to the other guards since he was our captain, but after a moment I understood why. He was nervous. Attending this party as an undercover guard had him more anxious than I'd seen him in a while.

But why? There was no guarantee of danger, just a massive throng of people who would be drinking and dancing and… who knows what else.

Omri leaned forward, catching Caspian's eye. "I will show him."

"Great. Thank you, Omri." Caspian glanced at the guards gathered around him. "I figure Aliya and I will arrive once the party has begun, so prepare however you need to and get into the ballroom early. If anything does come up during the party, don't hesitate to ping me."

There was more nodding and a few affirmations of, "yes, sir."

This would be the first time the entire prince's guard was present for an occasion, and I was curious to see how we'd work in tandem. Sure, we'd taken shifts together at some point, but working as a team would push us to reach new levels of communication and coordination.

Truthfully, I naïvely hoped that this party would be incredibly boring. I didn't want to fight someone in a crowded ballroom, dressed in whatever I had to wear tonight. That wasn't my definition of a good time.

Caspian stuffed his hands in his pockets and nodded once more. "Good. Until then, you can all do as you please. Aliya and I will take this next shift. Then Ney and Elgin will take over and escort him into the ballroom."

"And then we party!" Elgin crowed. His attempt to lighten the mood fell flat, and I couldn't resist offering him a small smile in apology.

No one was looking forward to tonight. It would be hours and hours of constantly monitoring everyone and everything. Fortunately, most of them knew what to expect. Caspian, Ki'ran, and I, however, were going into this party blind.

Caspian dismissed the group and asked me to walk with him to the prince's chambers. Our footsteps echoed down the silent hallway. The only other sign of life was a guard, someone I'd seen a few times before but didn't know, stationed behind us at the top of the stairs.

The next few hours would be the calm before the storm — although it would hopefully be contained to the ballroom.

"Nervous?" Caspian was the first one to break the silence.

"I just… I don't know what to expect."

"Me either," Caspian said with a grunt. "I've heard plenty of stories about how wild Prince Damien's parties can be, but I don't think I heard anything too ridiculous in the orders he gave the servants."

I snorted. "Seriously? What about the flying drink-drone things? Or the light-changing bubbles?" I had *zero* idea what either of them were, but Prince Damien insisted that both be present.

"They're just techie toys," Caspian said with a shrug. "I'm not too worried about *what* he has there as opposed to *who* he has there." He caught my puzzled expression and continued. "There will be so many people that it'll be a nightmare keeping track of him and questionable guests. Okay, yes, if they know the prince, they're likely questionable to begin with, but you know what I'm trying to say." Caspian playfully elbowed me in the ribs.

"Sure, that sounds annoying, but it's not our job to watch over everyone. All you and I have to do is keep reasonably close to the prince." I poked Caspian in the shoulder as we walked along. "See? It won't be *that* hard."

Caspian roared with laughter. "Oh, you innocent Terran. You have no idea what you're getting yourself into."

For the next six hours, Caspian and I discussed bizarre foods and items that Prince Damien had ordered for the party. We made guesses about the total number of guests who'd arrive tonight. Then I asked him what people usually wore at these events. I recalled Xaxena's outfit when she came to visit the prince during my first overnight shift and shuddered, hoping clothing like that wasn't the norm.

"Well," Caspian hedged, "it definitely won't be what you expect. Male clothing is usually quite standard – nothing too wild or revealing. Most of the time. But for females…"

I groaned. "Do you think I'll have any say in my clothes tonight?"

Caspian chewed his bottom lip for a few moments. If I wasn't so concerned about attending tonight's party half-dressed, I would've stopped him with a kiss. "Probably not. But," Caspian's expression brightened, "King Locklyn or Queen Estella likely would have selected your outfit for tonight, and I doubt either would have chosen something that they normally see on the females who hang around the prince."

Well, that was a good start. Hopefully they knew more about respectable fashion on Callais than I did. Otherwise I'd be attending tonight's party in my full armor.

Far too soon, Elgin and Ney arrived to start their shift.

"Good luck," Elgin teased with a wink as Caspian and I walked away.

Being the mature person that I was, I stuck my tongue out at him. His and Ney's laughter followed us down the hallway until we were completely out of earshot.

Caspian walked me all the way to my door before pulling me in for a kiss. "I'll be with you all night. We'll be fine," he murmured.

My head swirled from the kiss – I'd never get used to the rush I felt whenever his lips touched mine – but I managed to nod. "We'll be fine," I agreed.

"Meet by the stairs when you're ready?"

"Of course." I beamed as I thought about walking into a party on Caspian's arm.

Caspian left after one final kiss, and then I slipped into my room and began removing pieces of my guard uniform. Blasters, off. Heavy boots, off.

I paused when I reached the comm cuff, unsure if I could even take it off now that Gunther and Gráinne were no longer at the palace. I hoped that I wouldn't be asked to remove it since the design was simple enough to pass as a regular bracelet.

A couple light taps were all the warning I received before three Callaisan maids rushed into my room.

The tall, limber blonde had a wicker basket over one arm that overflowed with bottles and brushes of all sizes and colors. The tiny brunette carried a stack of silver cases that rattled with the sound of jewelry. And then the final female – of medium height and with raven-black hair – carried dozens of bags containing dresses.

So. Many. Dresses. Surely I wouldn't have to try on *that* many?

"Ohmygoodnessitsreallyyou!" the blonde gushed as she came to an abrupt halt in front of me. "I've heard so much about the Hero of Vanthurium, but I never thought I'd actually get to meet you! And being asked to dress you for this party? It's such an honor!"

"Um, hi. Yeah… thanks?" I felt incredibly awkward as I stood in front of the tall female. She ogled as she looked me over, and it took a few seconds before I realized she must have been looking for my circuits. "Who are you?"

"Oh, I'm so sorry! I'm Anita," the blonde said, "and this is Mira and Ciena. We're here to get you ready!" Anita cheered as the other two females began setting their items down all over my room. Mira nodded my way as she set the silver cases on my vanity table, but Ciena only met my eyes before dumping the dresses on the bed.

"Lovely," I grumbled which elicited a giggle from Mira. "I'm surprised you showed up so soon. I wasn't expecting all of you for another few hours." I'd *really* wanted a nap before I had to get ready, but that didn't seem to be in my cards this afternoon. Instead I'd be plucked and primed… for the next *four hours*. I resisted the desire to let out another groan.

"No, no! Then we'd never have time to get you all dressed and pretty," Mira replied as she set out ribbons and necklaces and pins all over my dresser. She turned to face me with bright red cheeks. "I didn't mean that! You're already pretty! We just… well, we need to—"

"There's a lot to do," Anita said, cutting Mira off.

Ciena spread the dress bags out across my bed and hummed excitedly at all the options in front of her. If it was possible, I gladly would have let her take my place tonight.

I sighed. I wasn't excited for the party, and I definitely didn't have enough enthusiasm to keep up with these three. I debated ordering them to leave so that I could take even a short nap, but I didn't get the chance.

"Time to get you cleaned up!" Anita proclaimed as she marched into my bathroom, her arms laden with bottles.

I am a soldier, and I have been through much worse than this, I reminded myself as I shuffled after her. *Let the fun begin.*

✻

Anita insisted on helping me bathe with the million products she had brought, and at the end of it, I was more irritated than I should have been. There was a different product for *everything* — hands, feet, face, body, and even multiple shampoo-like substances for my hair.

Normally, I loved a relaxing bath, but I'd never been so happy to step out of this one.

Thoroughly scrubbed and smelling of flowers, I stood in the middle of my room wearing a robe while Ciena unveiled the dresses.

"You have got to be kidding me!" I shouted at the fifth option she presented.

They had all been insanely tight and far more revealing than I was comfortable with. Plunging necklines, backless options, and even ones that looked like two pieces of fabric held together by strings on either side. This neon green and black option was by far the worst — sleeveless and sparkling, the sad excuse for a dress had a plunging neckline, no back, and triangular cutouts above my hips. If this was standard party attire, I wasn't sure I wanted to go. King's orders or not.

Ciena sulked as she and Anita stuffed the dress back into its bag. At the beginning, Ciena had gushed over each and every dress she revealed, but my resistance was beginning to wear on her mood. Mira smartly stood out of the way, waiting for her chance to do my hair and makeup.

"Isn't there something a bit more modest? Or at least a more subtle color?" If I was being forced to look like a guest, I didn't want to look like a walking neon sign.

"But these are all so gorgeous!" Ciena whined as she pawed through the remaining dresses. There were so many more options remaining that I couldn't understand why she seemed so put out. I was the one wearing the dress, not her, and I wanted to feel somewhat comfortable in it.

"Oh! What about this one?" Anita asked as she dug a dress bag out from the bottom of the pile.

She held the bag up while Ciena unzipped it, and out spilled an odd combination of black chiffon and… peacock feathers? The plumage seemed an odd touch, but it appeared far more modest than the others that Ciena had previously suggested. I gestured for Anita and Ciena to continue.

Gently removing the dress, Ciena giggled as she saw my star-struck expression. The dress was incredible.

The top was a simple sweetheart neckline – strapless but not revealing in the slightest. The simple design ended at the waist, and beyond that the dress really *popped*. Embroidery in vibrant gold, teal, and purple swirled down the shortened front of the skirt in the shape of long feathers. Each one was intricate and realistic, and they didn't make the dress look garish. Upon closer inspection, the dress even had tiny, shimmering gems sewn into gaps around the feather pattern. They sparkled in shades of ruby, turquoise, and amber as Ciena turned the dress to display the back.

The embroidery wasn't all the dress had going for itself. The entire back, which started just below where my shoulder blades would be, was covered with layer upon layer of long, glittering peacock feathers that trailed all the way down to the floor. Their colors matched the embroidery on the front, and although I thought the feathers would be odd addition to the outfit, these actually complemented the overall appearance quite well.

I couldn't resist running my fingers over one because I didn't believe they were real. Incredibly soft and glittery, the feathers were the perfect accent for this dress. I actually found myself looking forward to wearing this to the party.

"I think we found our winner!" Anita squealed.

Mira began sorting through the items on the dresser while Ciena and Anita unzipped the dress and held it out toward me.

No one had taken my measurements since I arrived at the palace, but all of my guard clothes fit perfectly. I was eager to see how this dress would fit, so I cooperated as they slid the dress on and zipped it up.

It was as if the dress had been made for me – a perfect, slightly snug fit through the torso, and the feathery back was just long enough that it wouldn't get caught under my feet.

I twirled and let the high-low skirt swirl around my legs. "I don't think I've been this happy to wear a dress in… well, in a long time," I announced with a laugh.

Anita clapped her hands. "It looks amazing on you! Everyone, and I mean *everyone,* will have their eyes on you tonight."

And just like that, my bubble of happiness popped. I didn't want undue attention, especially if it came from Prince Damien. I halted my twirling and brushed my hands down the front as the dress settled. I really enjoyed this dress and didn't want to change, but I couldn't make myself the center of attention tonight. "Um, perhaps we should choose another one then…"

Ciena looked shocked. "But this one is *perfect!* And if you feel good in it, then it's the right one." She propped her hands on her hips and gave me a stern look.

I couldn't deny the fact that this dress was gorgeous and exactly my size. It seemed exotic enough to fit in with tonight's festivities without making me look weird. And it certainly wasn't as skin tight and revealing as the previous dresses that Ciena had shown me.

Perhaps, if this party really was the wild event that everyone expected it to be, I wouldn't draw so much attention. "Okay, fine," I said, giving in because I really didn't want to spend more time looking through the other dresses. "What's next?"

Anita steered me toward the vanity table. "Hair and makeup!"

I winced. "Please don't go too crazy on the makeup, okay? I'd like to look somewhat like myself tonight." That probably sounded like an odd request, but since I had no idea what fashion was like for Callaisan parties, I didn't want the girls going overboard on me.

Mira twirled one of her long chestnut locks around her finger as she mused. "Hm. I think we can make that work," she said with a smile.

I zoned out and lost track of time as Mira, with Anita's help, brushed and tugged my hair in various directions, hemming and hawing as she tried several different styles.

At some point I closed my eyes as boredom and fatigue washed over me. How in the worlds would I be able to stay up for the entire party?

Finally, I felt the girls stop tugging on my hair. It was entirely off my shoulders, and I was curious how they'd styled it.

"Keep your eyes closed!" Mira chirped. "It'll be a surprise once I'm all done."

"Okay. Makeup next?"

"You bet," she replied. I felt her rub a smooth cream onto my cheeks and forehead, followed by a soft brush. She traced something over my lips once, twice, and then she started applying eyeliner.

I was dying to fidget and rub away the tickle that plagued my nose, but I dutifully held still, not wanting to mess up her work. I trusted that Mira knew what she was doing, but I still couldn't wait to see the final product.

Minutes ticked by, and then I felt her hang something around my neck. The metal was cold and slightly heavy, fitting more like a choker than a necklace. "Earrings next," Mira hummed as she slipped them onto my ears. And then her touch was completely gone.

"I think you've outdone yourself this time, Mira," Anita whispered from behind me.

"I know, right?" she bubbled. "Okay, Aliya, now you can look!"

Slowly, I cracked my eyes open to observe the damage.

I didn't know the female in the mirror before me.

Whomever she was, she looked fierce, and her features were accentuated so well that she was stunning.

Black lipstick with flecks of gold covered her lips. A golden, shimmering powder was spread across her cheekbones but didn't obscure her dusting of freckles. Her eyes had been lined with black eyeliner that fanned out into replicas of peacock feathers at her temples.

And instead of a complicated design, her hair had been pulled back into a bun. Several real feathers had been threaded into the top half of it, and it looked like a peacock's tail on full display.

It was a wild look. But it also seemed… right?

"Wow," I breathed. I didn't know what more to say. The dress, the hairstyle, the makeup – they all looked amazing. "Thank you so much!"

Over my shoulder, the three females beamed.

Anita stepped forward and rested a hand on my bare shoulder. "All you need now are shoes—"

"And a weapon!" Ciena cut in.

"—and then you're all set."

Mira stepped forward with a silver box and lifted the lid. Inside was a pair of golden shoes, which looked like an odd combination of high-heeled boots, but the heel contained a triangular cutout. I was thankful that they weren't stilettos.

I slid the shoes on and stood, now several inches taller than Anita, before I took a few test steps. The bottoms of the shoes were flat enough that I wouldn't be teetering around all night, and they were surprisingly comfortable.

Mira stepped back, and Ciena took her place. In her hands was a palm-sized blaster and what I assumed was its holster.

"Um, where am I supposed to hide that?" I couldn't very well wear the blaster on my hip.

Ciena giggled. "It goes around your thigh. It's lucky that you chose a dress with a shorter front because it'll be easier for you to reach."

My cheeks heated at the idea of reaching under my skirt to get the blaster, but it was necessary since I was an undercover guard. I felt awkward sliding the stretchy holster up my leg, but it wasn't uncomfortable or too obvious once the blaster was in place.

"Perfect," Mira crooned. "Oh! You should probably get going now. I'm sure the party has already started."

"Right." I wrote a quick message to Caspian, letting him know that I was finally ready. I hoped he hadn't been waiting too long. "Thank you again. For all of this."

Anita stepped forward and gave me a quick hug. "It was our pleasure. Now we can say that we've styled the Hero of Vanthurium!"

I rolled my eyes but couldn't hold back a laugh. If they felt honored to have interacted with me, I wasn't going to ruin their excitement.

They began packing up as I headed to the door. "Thank you. I hope we see each other again sometime!"

"Of course!" they said in unison.

With one last glance at the trio, I left my room. I needed to meet up with Caspian and then make my way down to the party. And then the real fun would start.

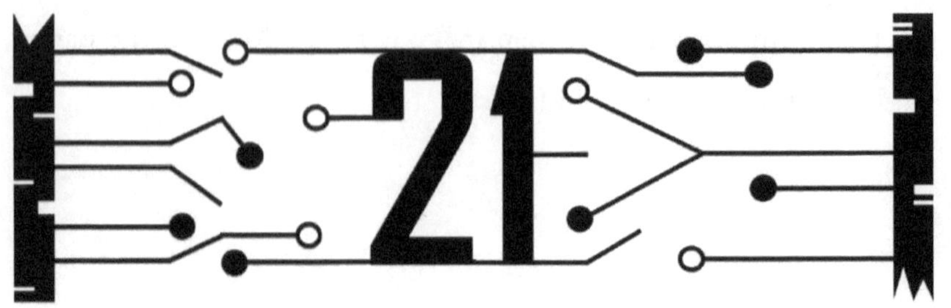

The door clicked shut behind me, and my heart leapt into my throat.

Why was this party making me so nervous? I wasn't on a date. I wasn't responsible for any messes made tonight. I was just going to guard the prince. Like usual.

Deep breaths, Aliya.

My shoes clicked on the marble floors, and the feathers on my dress rustled softly as I made my way to the stairs. It was impossible not to feel regal in this outfit. Already, my back was straighter, and I walked with my shoulders thrown back. With some new clothes and careful styling, I felt like a completely new person.

Apparently, I looked like a new person too.

Caspian stood at the top of the stairs, oblivious to my approach for a few moments. He looked incredibly handsome in a snug, black suit jacket and matching pants. His normally loose locks had been slicked back, highlighting his face and turquoise eyes. The collar on the jacket was tall enough to brush the bottoms of his earlobes, especially since his shoulders were hunched – probably from being stressed.

It was simple, but something about the clean lines on the suit jacket seriously enhanced Caspian's overall appeal tonight. Probably the most striking part of the ensemble were the stripes of gold that ran from the top of the collar down to the bottom hem. And they pulsed.

I would've asked about the lights on his jacket if not for Caspian's expression as soon as he turned and saw me.

Caspian's jaw hit the floor as all the tension seeped out of his frame. He stood there, staring up and down and up and down… I worried that his eyes would roll right out of his head.

After far too many seconds of being stared at, I mustered up the courage to ask, "Well? Do I look okay?"

His gaze locked onto mine as he finally clicked his mouth shut. "Okay?" Caspian approached me slowly, looking between my face and my dress a few times. "Just okay? Aliya, you look absolutely *incredible.*"

My mouth automatically quirked up into a shy smile. "Thank you. I… I had help." *I had help? Really, Aliya, that's all you can say when you already know that he likes you?*

Caspian looked me over for a few more seconds, shaking his head in disbelief. He reached a hand out toward me but stopped a few inches away.

"You're not going to break me," I said with a laugh.

It was all the encouragement he needed. In two quick steps he closed the distance between us, and his lips crashed into mine.

My body tingled as I lost myself in the kiss, not even caring if my circuits were glowing. I couldn't care less if my makeup got smudged or if I left lipstick on Caspian. As my arms wound around his neck and his circled my waist, I realized that this was exactly where I wanted to be.

Caspian's wrist cuff pinged, but he showed no signs of breaking the kiss. Instead, one of his hands snaked up to the middle of my back, grazing the exposed skin there and pressing me closer to him. I shivered at the contact.

And then the cuff pinged with a second message.

"You should probably get that," I mumbled around his demanding lips. I would've been happy to let this moment last all night, but we really were expected elsewhere.

Reluctantly, he groaned and broke our embrace. "It's Omri. He's asking when we'll be down."

I sighed. "I guess we should go do our jobs then, right?"

"Or we could run away." Caspian raised his eyebrows and gave me a wicked grin.

Laughing, I playfully pushed him away. I needed to create more distance between us before I caved and let him kiss me a second time. "You know we can't do that. Besides, it would be wrong. We're needed here."

"Always so loyal," Caspian commented with a chuckle. "Fine then. Let's…" He paused and seemed to remember something. Reaching into an inner pocket of his jacket, Caspian said, "Here, you need to take this."

In his palm was a tiny, white pill. I regarded it with a healthy amount of skepticism. "What is it?"

"According to King Locklyn, it's a little trick that guards at parties use to keep from getting drunk. This way we can drink and blend in without being affected."

Where's the fun in that? I was tempted to joke, but I knew the pill was a good idea.

"Okay." I plucked it off his outstretched palm and placed it on my tongue. Wincing at the bitter taste, I swallowed quickly before the pill could fully dissolve. I wondered how quickly it would start to kick in or if I would need to avoid drinking anything for a certain amount of time.

"Now we're ready." Caspian gave me a thousand-watt smile that made my stomach flip, and then he offered me his silk-clad arm.

I laughed. "This is like some crazy fairy tale." When Caspian looked confused, I continued by saying, "I'm dressed like an exotic princess and am on the arm of my prince."

Caspian's brilliant smile returned as I looped my arm through his. "Well it's quite the honor to walk in with you, my lady."

Together we descended the stairs. His jacket pulsed and my peacock feathers rustled, but together we made quite the fashionable pair. Unsurprisingly, we drew stares from the guards and servants we passed, but I didn't mind. Everyone knew me as a soldier. Now they would know me as a woman.

We didn't come across any other guests as we made our way through the palace and down the hallway where the doors to the grand ballroom were. The jeweled planets shimmered in the early evening light, but I couldn't stare at them for long.

Two guards were stationed outside the doors, and upon seeing us, they sprung into motion and heaved the two doors open. Through the gap I could see an opaque, filmy substance, and blurred figures moved beyond it.

"What's that?" I hadn't noticed this shifting barrier the first time I visited the ballroom with Elgin and the rest of the team, and I didn't see it during Prince Damien's planning session.

"A sound bubble. Notice how quiet it is in the hallway?" I hadn't, but now the silence was shocking. "The party is already in full swing, but you can't hear it outside of the bubble. I'm sure King Locklyn had it installed shortly after Prince Damien threw his first party."

"That's so cool!" I couldn't believe that a somewhat-transparent sound-proof barrier existed. I loved the inventions out here.

We drew close to the opening between the doors, and Caspian paused before the sound bubble. "Are you ready?"

I knew I probably wasn't prepared for what I'd see on the other side, but I still nodded.

Leading us forward, Caspian passed through the sound bubble. It made my skin tingle as I entered. The sensation was like a faint mist or electrical current.

The sensation was over in an instant, and then we were inside.

The party was *nothing* like I'd imagined. There was something happening in every inch of the ballroom – from the main floor, to the balconies above us, and even in the air above the dance floor.

Music with a heavy bass beat thundered from an unknown source, and I could feel it reverberate inside my chest. It was an odd combination which I could only describe as electric, rock and roll, and pop. I wasn't sure if I liked the sound, but apparently everyone else did.

Bodies bobbed and swayed on the dance floor, somehow keeping tempo with the erratic beats. Males, females, and other beings I couldn't immediately identify clustered together as they danced, sang, and celebrated.

As I scanned the crowd, I was simultaneously relieved and startled to see that my outfit was far more... conservative than most. Some males strutted around shirtless while female styles revealed large patches of skin, if not most of their bodies.

There was everything from leather to lace, scales to feathers. And *everywhere* outfits flashed, sparkled, or changed colors.

Servants skillfully wove through the crush of bodies while they balanced large trays of multicolored drinks in champagne flutes.

They, at least, were easy to identify in their all white outfits — females wore nondescript dresses that stopped just above the knee while males wore pants and a collared shirt.

My gaze was drawn into the space above us. Bubble-like objects which were roughly the size of a basketball drifted up and down while they flashed in shades of neon in time with the music. I lifted my hand in an attempt to touch one that floated down toward me, but it changed direction just before it landed in my palm.

Even the pillars in the room acted like neon strobe lights. Perhaps they weren't meant to be pillars at all, but instead they were additional lights for events like this one.

"It's a lot to take in, isn't it?" Caspian had to shout over the music in order to be heard.

My eyes darted around the room, desperately trying to drink in each of the quick and chaotic details before me. The people, the outfits, the drinks… I could even smell food somewhere in this room. It was vastly overwhelming, and I felt myself beginning to panic.

Luckily, Caspian knew me well. He slipped behind me, wrapping his arms around my waist, and pulled me close. "I'm right here, Aliya. I won't leave your side."

"It's just so *much,*" I said, tilting my head back onto his shoulder so he could better hear me.

"I think this is actually tamer than the prince wanted. I heard King Locklyn denied his request for animals to be brought in."

Animals? In a packed room in the palace? Prince Damien was seriously crazy if he thought mixing all that together would be a good thing. "Speaking of, let's go find the prince."

Caspian's hands took a long time to leave my waist, but when they did, he took my hand and led us around the outer edge of the dance floor where the density of bodies was lighter. We wove around individuals and groups, discussions and toasts. I still couldn't wrap my head around how many people managed to fit in here.

We had to stop as a large group merged and began dancing in front of us. It was either wait for them to break up, or try to navigate the dance floor. Because we had a little bubble of space around us, we decided to wait.

Caspian looked back at me and then beckoned me to come closer. "What?"

"Could you try to look like you're here enjoying the party? You look absolutely petrified." He laughed before pressing a kiss to my temple.

I shook my head and gazed off at the sea of dancers. This was probably as far out of my element as I'd ever been, and considering all I'd been through since my accident, that was really saying something.

I didn't like crowds or chaos, but here I was in the middle of both. I knew no one except Caspian, and the thought of getting separated from him in this mess made me anxious. We'd only just arrived, but I was already dying to leave.

Caspian snared my free hand and tugged so that I was facing him. *Everything is going to be okay*, he mouthed before leaning in for a kiss.

He was really good at distracting me. The sounds of the room faded away as my eyes drifted closed, and I finally felt my body relax. I should've felt self-conscious, making out in public like this, but the chances of someone actually paying attention to us and caring were slim to none.

Besides, I thoroughly enjoyed kissing Caspian.

When he finally pulled away, Caspian leaned close to my ear. "Better?"

"Much." I received a devilish grin in return.

"Good. Now trust me." He tugged me forward, heading toward the dancers who blocked our way. The sea of bodies caved in around us as Caspian and I fought for each step. Still facing me, Caspian pulled me close, and as we wove through the guests, I found that our movements began to match those of the dancers'. We swayed when they swayed, stepped when they stepped, and jumped when they jumped.

It would've been fun if I didn't feel so claustrophobic.

The fear I thought I had conquered resurfaced, and my brain automatically told my body to find a way out and *fast*. People were too close and constantly bumping into me. There was nowhere to go for a bit of space. Any of these people could be dangerous. Those thoughts and more tumbled around in my panicked brain as I started to tremble.

Did the male in the yellow leather with spiked hair glare at me? Or what about the female with pale blue angel wings – was that something in her hand?

"Aliya!" My eyes snapped up to the ice blue ones inches from my face. "Look at me. I'm right here. Don't look away," Caspian repeated over and over. He continued to lead me through the waves of people, but I stared at his face, letting all the other distractions fade away.

Twenty-seven shuffling steps later, Caspian and I finally broke free of the crowd. There were still people around us, but they weren't pressing in like the dancers had. I felt exhausted as the tense muscles in my arms and torso loosened.

Caspian pulled me in for a hug. "I've got you, Aliya. I'll always be here."

I hoped he knew just how much those words soothed me.

Over Caspian's shoulder I noticed a smaller knot of people. Four males and three females stood in a loose circle near the outer wall, several of them with drinks in their hands.

The males were far more clothed than other individuals in the room, and I wish I could've said the same for the females. One of them – a Schlee with long, red curls – wore a bikini as she clung to a Vanthuri male in a torn, orange t-shirt.

Prince Damien stood with them.

For once, he was actually dressed very well. His red pants were unwrinkled, the black vest he wore over a white collared shirt was properly buttoned, and the long, half white, half red suit jacket he wore over it all was clean. Upon closer inspection, the red half of his jacket was actually white, massive swirls and lines of red silk embroidery decorating his right side.

He'd even found a crown to match his ensemble, and the rubies embedded in the golden peaks flickered with the flashing lights.

"I see him," I said to Caspian. "What should we do now?"

Caspian took a step backward but didn't turn to look at the prince and his entourage. "We just play it cool. Talk for a bit. Wander around the outside of their circle. Follow if they start to move." He shrugged.

"You don't think he'll notice us?"

He didn't answer right away because he was too busy grabbing drinks from a server. "Then he notices us. We're not the first undercover guards at a party, so he should know not to draw attention to us. But if he does, then we no longer have a reason to stay so far away." Caspian handed me one of the two glasses he'd plucked from the silver serving tray.

The bubbling liquid in the tall champagne flute was a brilliant shade of blue. Was it soda? Champagne? Perhaps something even stronger?

"You're safe to drink it, remember? Besides, this is the least potent concoction circulating tonight." Caspian raised his glass and waited.

I was *so* skeptical. What if the pill didn't prevent us from becoming drunk? What if this tasted terrible? What if—

I cut the thought off. I was seriously overanalyzing everything. Here I was, wearing a gorgeous dress while at a party with the male I loved. There was no reason to worry this much.

So I smiled and clinked my glass to Caspian's before taking a sip. Bubbles burst against my tongue as the taste of raspberries and mint filled my mouth. This was delicious! How had I never tried this before now? I tipped the remnants of the drink into my mouth.

"Can I try others?" I eyed a server who passed by with a tray of glasses that contained either a lime green or violet liquid.

"Of course, but I'd suggest sticking to the lighter colors. The darker the color, the more... exotic the flavors tend to get." Caspian rolled his eyes. "Trust me, there are flavor combinations that you do not want to try."

We'll see about that. I swapped my empty glass for one filled with a pink drink as another server passed us along the outer wall of the ballroom.

Caspian laughed as I took a sip and scrunched up my face in confusion. Pink was not the flavor I expected it to be. This drink was spicy, like a liquid chili pepper.

It was at that moment that a male stumbled off the dance floor and straight into my side. I spilled half of the contents of my glass on my shoes, but neither of us fell to the floor.

"Oh my stars, I'm *so* sorry!" The male straightened up, brushing off his gray suede vest although I didn't spill a drop on him. Clearly Callaisan, his skin was exceptionally pale, and he had a long, sharp nose where a pair of thick cat-eye glasses rested. Beyond the frames was a pair of tawny eyes. His orange hair, parted down the middle, had been combed into two wings that pointed sharply away from his head.

The rest of his outfit looked far more normal than his hair – if a mobster-style suit in gray suede was considered normal. Even his black wing tip shoes looked plain in comparison to the rest of the styles in the ballroom.

I realized that he was waiting for me to say something. "It's okay! No harm, no foul!" *Well, except for my shoes.*

The expression confused him for a second, and then he flashed me a huge, pearly white smile. I gasped when I saw his elongated canines. "Fabulous! It would've been a shame to ruin your *stunning* outfit!"

I blinked a few times, completely taken aback by the compliment, and before I could fashion a reasonable response, he had melted back into the crowd.

Caspian guffawed from my right. "I was ready to toss him away from you, but seeing the look on your face after the compliment was absolutely worth it!"

I playfully – and very lightly – punched his shoulder. "Thanks for coming to my rescue! What if he'd knocked me over?"

I received an eye roll in reply. "Like someone could knock you over. Your reflexes would kick in well before you could come close to being unbalanced."

Well, he was right. Not that I'd admit it.

Movement from the corner of my eye caught my attention. A tall, muscular male approached Prince Damien's group. Sure, he was probably six and a half feet tall and built like a linebacker, but if he threatened the prince, we had to act.

He strolled up to the group and gave a low bow. The four cords – in white, navy, yellow, and red – that he wore around his neck in the absence of a shirt skimmed the ground.

"What?" Caspian wasn't facing the group, so he hadn't noticed the newcomer.

"Prince Damien has company." I longed to drift closer so that we could hear what they were saying, but I worried that would give us away.

For a few tense moments the two talked, and then the stranger departed after a second bow.

"He's gone."

I just picked up Caspian's sigh over the booming music. "Here." He pressed a cold glass into my free hand and then removed the almost empty glass of the spicy pink drink. "Now switch with me."

"Why?" I looked down to see that Caspian had given me another glass of the blue liquid.

"Because, Aliya, you need to relax a little," Caspian chided me. "Everyone isn't running up to stab the prince. The overwhelming majority of these people really are just here for a party. I'm sure they could care less who was hosting it."

We rotated spots so that Caspian could see the prince and his companions, and I looked out on the dance floor. I wanted to be the one watching over the prince, but I had to admit that this was the better view. I could watch the goings-on of the party and see if there were potential threats on the floors above us.

"I'm sorry," I said as I dipped my head. "This is really overwhelming, and I don't even know where to look for someone who might try to hurt Prince Damien."

"That's why you don't need to worry so much." Caspian laughed and took my hand. "There are far more guards here than you realize, and with all these people, someone will have to get very close to the prince before they can successfully harm him."

"If you say so." Once more, I had to trust Caspian's judgment.

"I know so." Caspian clinked his glass to mine, and then we took another sip.

I smiled at his confidence and tried to relax as I scanned the room. Even if I'd been invited as a regular guest, I don't think I would've wanted to be here. There was just *so much* going on and so many people. I didn't like how frequently I was getting bumped, and I worried that someone was going to snag the back of my dress. The last thing I needed tonight was a wardrobe malfunction.

Caspian and I stood together for a while. I watched the room and relayed funny outfits or interactions that I saw, and he provided updates on the prince and his companions. Prince Damien received several female visitors, but aside from that, he didn't do much.

"I was expecting more from him," I admitted.

"So was I." Caspian's eyebrows drew together for a moment before they relaxed. "But that's good because it makes our job easier."

I smiled. "That's very true."

Suddenly my attention was drawn to the third floor balcony where a group of people had pressed up against the railing.

A female in a green and gold tulle dress awkwardly clambered onto the railing. Her gold curls tumbled around her shoulders as she sought her balance, and then she stood up straight and threw her arms out to her sides. The crowd behind her cheered as she looked back over her shoulder.

Every muscle in my body tensed. What was she thinking? Had she been dared to stand up there?

Many eyes on the ballroom floor had drifted upward, and we all watched the female on the railing. *Please, please, please just get down,* I prayed. I didn't see anyone moving to pull her back.

And then she stepped forward and plummeted toward the ground.

She willingly stepped off the railing.

My mind went into panic mode as I watched the small female flip head over heels once, twice… all while falling toward the packed dance floor.

The skirt of her dress ruffled in the wind as her outstretched arms flailed. Wind whipped her hair across her face, so I couldn't read her expression. Her shrill scream rang in my ears.

Onlookers shrieked and pointed at her, but none of them rushed to help. None of them seemed to think this was a tragedy in the making.

I concocted several plans for how to catch her safely, but none of them would prevent me from barreling through the crowd and possibly causing harm to the bystanders. It wasn't going to be pretty, but I could do it.

Just when I decided that a messy rescue was worth it, a calloused hand closed around my bicep.

"Let me—" I started to snap until I realized that it was Caspian who was holding me back.

His expression was tired as he said, "Just wait. Watch."

Just wait? Is he crazy? I wanted to snap at him, but I turned my attention back to the female who was now ten feet from hitting the floor.

All of a sudden, the bottoms of her shoes, which I hadn't previously noticed, lit up. I thought she was wearing a regular pair of gray boots, but now I saw that they were oddly shaped and made from metal. Metal boots that lit up. And made her fly.

She ground to an awkward halt in midair where she remained hovering above the crowd. Holding her arms out to each side, she wobbled as she found her balance, and then she cheered. The reply from every individual in the ballroom was nearly deafening. They applauded and waved, jumping up and down as the music picked up louder than before. The lighting, which had paused during the female's dramatic drop, flashed and resumed its erratic pulsing.

With a large, theatrical twirl the female flew upward and completed a loop. *What the heck is going on here?* I felt like the only sane person in the building.

Dozens of people began to jump off the balconies, plunging to the floor before their strange shoes kicked in to save them.

I felt relieved that no one was actually in danger as they jumped from the upper levels. And then I felt frustrated that everything here was so bizarre. Finally, I felt incredibly overwhelmed by everything.

The constant noise, the lights, the smells... all of it was beginning to give me a massive headache.

I turned back to Caspian who had patiently waited during that entire episode. "You were right." I didn't bother raising my voice because he was close enough to hear.

"I'm sorry." His brow was furrowed with concern, and I felt bad for being the cause of that expression. "I should've warned you that many people here have grav boots. They've become a staple at parties everywhere."

I didn't bother asking how he would know that since he'd been in the Protective Forces for years. I simply accepted that he was right, and yet again I had no idea what this universe held. Everything was so far beyond my imagination and comprehension, and right now I wanted nothing to do with it.

"Do you think I could get outside for a few minutes? I really need some air." We'd only been here for maybe an hour, and I was already about to scream.

"Um, sure," Caspian said, although he didn't look very sure. "Want me to get Elgin or Omri to go with you?" He started to reach for his cuff.

"No! I just... I only need a few minutes. I'll come back. I promise," I replied as I tried my best to look reassuring.

Caspian scrutinized me for a few moments as goosebumps rose over my skin from the intensity of his gaze. I had no idea what he was thinking, but I'm sure he wondered if I was going to run screaming into the night. "Fine," he finally said. He pointed to the back left corner of the ballroom. "There's a hallway down there that runs along the side of the palace. It'll take you out and into the gardens."

"Thank you, thank you, thank you!" I rose up onto my toes to give him a quick kiss.

Fighting my way through the crowd wasn't as easy as I'd hoped, but at least no one tried to pull me onto the dance floor or trap me in a conversation. I didn't even bother looking Prince Damien's way to see if he'd spotted me. All I wanted was a break from this madness.

The hallway was easy enough to find and surprisingly empty. I was expecting to find a few couples cocooned in the shadows, but I was blissfully alone in the darkened passage.

Relieved, I rolled my neck, stretching out the stiff muscles as I listened to the click of my shoes. There wasn't a good spot on my dress for me to wipe off my clammy hands, but I tried anyway. Anything to fully de-stress.

I walked around the curving path, and the party disappeared behind me. Because I hadn't left the sound bubble, I could still hear the music and shouting, but I wasn't caught up in the middle of it anymore.

Just a few minutes outside, and then I'll be okay. Hopefully it's a cooler evening.

I was so caught up in my own thoughts and trying to ignore

the sounds from the party that I completely missed the sound of footsteps jogging up from behind me.

What I *did* notice, however, was the arm that slipped around my waist.

I was so startled by the sudden contact that I nearly tripped. Cursing myself for lowering my guard, I regained my balance and assessed the situation.

The way I saw it, there were two options. The person holding me was either a guest looking for an intimate moment, or it was Caspian who'd decided that I shouldn't go off alone. Because I figured all the guests would be too enraptured by the party, I went with my second guess.

"I told you I didn't need company…" As I turned to face Caspian, my words died in my throat.

It wasn't Caspian.

It wasn't even a random party guest.

It was Prince Damien.

He stared at me with the glassiest, heavily lidded eyes I'd ever seen. Honestly, it was a miracle that he could even keep them open. His dark locks were seriously messy, as if someone had run their hands through his hair repeatedly – and not in a styling-his-hair kind of way. As he leaned toward me a thick clump of hair fell over one eye, and he didn't even bother brushing it away.

The scent of the darker liquor that had been circulating around the party wafted off him in nauseating waves, and as I tried to lean away, his arm tightened around my back.

My mind was absolutely blank from shock and panic. What was I supposed to do? How could I possibly get away from him?

And then I had another thought: *why did he follow me?*

"You ssshouldn't be goin' off alone, love," Prince Damien said through a very heavy slur. He leaned his face closer to mine, and a very poor attempt at a sultry smile slid onto his thin lips.

If the prince had been sober, this encounter would've just been annoying. But because he was drunk, I didn't know how to handle the situation. Caspian and I were supposed to be protecting him, so running off wasn't the logical thing to do while he was in this state. I couldn't lecture him because he never listened to anyone. And the last thing I wanted was to drag him back to the party from this dark corridor. I absolutely *did not* need rumors being spread about the prince and his guard.

So I remained frozen, like an idiot. Fortunately, I did muster up the courage to sternly say, "Let me go."

Prince Damien lazily shook his head from side to side a few times, that stray lock of hair flopping back and forth in front of his eyes. "Ssshouldn't be alone," he repeated. And then he wrinkled his brow with a concerned look in his eyes. "You don' like meee."

I wonder why. "I'm your guard, your highness. I'm not supposed to like you." Maybe that was a bit harsh, but I wanted to get out of this horrible embrace as soon as possible.

"But I like you." He tried to focus on my face, but his eyes kept dancing back and forth.

This was quickly becoming a dangerous situation for both of us. Yes, he was drunk, but I was sure that he believed what he was saying to a certain degree. "Prince Damien, please… I need to go—"

There was no warning. One second he was staring at me, and in the next second his lips were against mine.

With his left arm still circling my waist, his right hand came up to cradle my cheek. His lips felt slightly chapped, and now I could taste that awful liquor I'd smelled on him.

I was utterly repulsed and knew this would take more than a few baths to wash off, but this was also my breaking point.

I quickly snaked my left arm between us and knocked away the hand touching my face. Then, keeping his now-free hand in my line of vision, I twisted my hips slightly and stepped my right leg around both of his and ducked under his right arm.

Spinning so that I now faced his back, I snagged his right wrist and pinned his arm behind his back before shoving him face-first against the white marble wall. And it all happened before he'd managed to reopen his eyes from the kiss.

Blood thundered in my ears, and I felt like every nerve in my body was firing at full capacity. This was *definitely* the wrong thing to do to a prince, but I didn't care anymore. He'd insulted me, came on to me, and kissed me without my permission. I'd had enough.

Prince Damien groaned as I continued to push him into the wall, and I leaned in close to his ear. "Listen here, you spoiled brat.

I don't care who you or your parents are, but *no one* should treat females the way you do. You're repulsive and rude and lazy, and it's no wonder that you're always alone." I was probably going *way* overboard, but once I'd started, I couldn't stop. "You're a disgrace of a prince, and that's coming from a Terran. We've had tons of awful royalty, but somehow you take the cake. Maybe if you gave a damn about your role in this galaxy you would be respected, but right now? No one, and I mean absolutely no one, cares who you are."

I released his hand and took a few steps back. He didn't bother to move from where he stood. Instead he seemed to lean more heavily against the wall.

Whatever. He was still breathing, so I hadn't hurt him with my quick escape. If I'd hurt his feelings… well, I'm sure I could get a new job somewhere else. If I was allowed to.

Turning on my heel, I marched back into the party. I didn't want to go outside anymore. I wanted Caspian.

This time I didn't bother looking at details as I rudely pushed my way through the oblivious revelers. I received a few comments for shoving someone out of my way, but I didn't care. Let them try to fight me if I'd actually slighted them.

I did have to give a larger male who looked similar to Ki'ran and Ba'rin a harsh stare down, but whatever fire burned in my eyes must have warned him not to mess with me. After that, making my way through everyone was a piece of cake.

Caspian didn't see me approaching because he was too busy

tapping away on his cuff. It wasn't until I came to a screeching halt in front of him that he finally noticed me.

"Aliya! Thank the stars. I was just about to send you a message – we've lost track of the prince." Caspian seemed frantic with worry and completely missed my irritated expression.

"Oh, don't worry," I drawled. "I know where to find him if you really need."

My tone finally tipped him off because he grasped each of my shoulders and leaned in to examine me. "Where is he? What happened?"

"He followed me. I thought he was you, and then he wrapped his arms around me and tried to kiss me." I shuddered as I recalled the feeling of Prince Damien's lips against mine.

"He *what?*" I thought Caspian's eyes were going to bulge out of his skull. I watched his jaw tense and his cheeks flush with anger. Caspian's fingers tightened around my shoulders a smidge, but it wasn't enough to hurt me. If I hadn't been so upset by the prince's actions, I would've found the protective response very hot. "Where is he now?"

I pointed a thumb in the direction of the hallway. "Probably where I left him."

And then it dawned on me. *I just assaulted a prince.* If I was simply dismissed from my position as a prince's guard, I'd be lucky. I didn't know what actions earned galactic punishments… or what those punishments could be.

The blood drained from my face as all manner of horrible

deaths crossed my mind. *What had I done? How could I have been so careless?*

I looked up at Caspian as a tear slipped down my cheek. "Aliya, what's wrong?" he asked as both of his hands cupped my face.

"I'm dead. I'm so dead," I whispered. Would my actions tonight affect Caspian too?

"Aliya, darling, talk to me. What happened?"

"I pushed him into the wall." I spoke in a horrified monotone. "I broke his hold on me and then pushed him into the wall. I said… I said horrible things about how awful he is."

Caspian pulled me into a bear hug, and I practically melted against the soft silk of his jacket. I was still in shock that I'd manhandled Prince Damien, but being in Caspian's arms lessened my panic. Well, a little bit.

"You're not the first one to lecture Prince Damien, and I'm sure you won't be the last. King Locklyn already loves you for what you did on Charra and Vanthurium. As long as the prince wasn't actually hurt, I'm sure you'll be fine," he murmured into my ear.

I back leaned so that I could watch his face as I said, "But what if—"

Caspian silenced me with a deep kiss. "There are no ifs," he said when he finally pulled away. "If he really intends to dismiss you, I'll do everything in my power to keep you here. Or maybe I'll just leave with you so we can finally have our own adventures."

My heart soared from the pits it previously wallowed in. Caspian said I'd given him a reason to keep living when he finally professed his feelings for me, and hearing that he would give up his status in order to be with me... There was no amount of happiness that captured how I currently felt.

Then I noticed Caspian watching something over my head.

"There he goes," he remarked followed by a small sound of surprise.

I felt like I knew exactly who Caspian was referring to, but I still had to ask. "Who?"

Caspian's eyes hadn't left the prince's retreating form. "Prince Damien. I can't believe he's leaving so early." He finally looked down at me with a curious expression. "Just what, exactly, did you say to him?"

I gulped. "That he was disgusting and lazy and no one cares about him?"

For a moment Caspian looked shocked. My heart dropped, and I panicked, thinking that this could be the end for us.

And then he laughed. Caspian laughed so hard that he let go of me and doubled over. He laughed hard enough to draw attention and make me seriously embarrassed.

When he finally straightened up and wiped tears from his eyes, Caspian embraced me once more. "You are, without a doubt, the best thing that's come into my life. I never would've imagined saying all that to Prince Damien and walking away, but you...!" He laughed again.

I scowled and tried to twist out of his arms. I could have broken free if I wanted to use more force, but I wasn't sure if

Caspian was being serious. "Caspian, I could get in trouble for this!"

He snorted and shook his head. "Like I said before, if anything happens to you, they'll have to deal with me too."

Suddenly Omri appeared out of the crowd behind Caspian. He lithely stepped his way over to where we were entwined and tapped Caspian on the shoulder. "Captain, Elgin and I are heading out with the prince. I think you two are free to go if you wish."

Caspian nodded and wished Omri a good evening before he slipped back into the crowd, heading for the doors. "Well," he said as he looked down at me, "it seems that our evening has just been freed up. What would you like to do, my razor-tongued warrior?"

I rolled my eyes and gazed at Caspian. I wasn't sure if I would be banished from the palace – or worse – in the morning, but I definitely didn't want to spend my evening in a panic or alone. "Could we stay?"

His eyebrows shot up in surprise. "You want to stay here at the party?" I nodded. "I'd like that. A lot," he said with a smile that took my breath away.

How in all the worlds did I get so lucky? I thought as Caspian tugged me onto the dance floor.

I woke with a smile on my face.

My feet hurt, I wanted to sleep more, and I had no idea what time it was — but last night ended up being one of the best in my life.

Caspian managed to sweep away all the panic and fear I felt in the wake of my confrontation with Prince Damien. He kept me on the dance floor, jumping and shouting and twirling me until I begged for a reprieve.

While the music was unfamiliar and I worried about being noticed by the people around us, Caspian seemed to throw caution to the wind. He sang along with songs that he knew, and he laughed — a full-bodied, genuinely cheerful sound that I'd only heard a few times before — when I was unsure of my footing or bumped into another dancer.

After a while, I stopped caring about my missteps and focused purely on Caspian. His eyes sparkled from the pulsing and multicolored lights, and he didn't seem embarrassed when his face became flushed from exertion and beads of sweat rolled down his brow.

I loved Captain Caspian, the serious and strategic leader. I loved vulnerable Caspian who wasn't afraid to reveal his feelings. And last night I fell in love with the fun side of Caspian.

If only we could have more nights like that.

A small laugh escaped my lips as I thanked my lucky stars for the anti-drunkenness pill. Who knew how many glasses of that sweet, bubbly liquid I polished off last night? I certainly stopped keeping track long before the night was over.

And then, as the euphoria began to wear off, my nerves kicked back in.

I'd slammed Prince Damien into a wall and told him that no one cared who he was.

Yes, the wall-slamming was partially an act of self-defense against his unwarranted kiss, *and* I didn't use my full abilities so that he wouldn't get hurt.

But I still technically raised a hand against the crown prince.

I dragged myself out of bed, groaning as I stretched the stiff muscles in my shoulders and legs. *What I wouldn't give for a long, hot bath right now.*

Luckily it was just about afternoon, so I hadn't slept the entire day away. Caspian had mentioned something about changing up the guard shifts before he kissed me goodnight, and I assumed that I hadn't drawn the early morning shift.

As much as I didn't want to jump right into another guard shift for Prince Damien, I felt bad that the others had probably stayed up late with the prince – wherever he'd gone off to. Hopefully he wasn't too difficult for them to handle.

I slipped in to my daily uniform and padded out into the hall. I wasn't sure when the current shift ended, and I really wanted to grab something to eat in case I was on duty next.

When I reached the first floor, a stern voice caught my attention.

"I need to see the king *now*." With a commanding yet sweet tone like that, there was no one else it could possibly be.

"Adís?" I spun around to see her marching through the grand front doors. Two of her crew walked in her wake.

"Aliya!" She jogged up and embraced me. "I'm glad to see you in one piece! I heard that the prince had a party last night. How was your first space spectacular?"

I laughed along with her. "Overwhelming. There were so many people and so many things going on! But in the end… I think I enjoyed it," I said with a shrug.

She feigned surprise. "If you enjoyed it, the party wasn't wild enough," she joked with an elbow to my ribs.

"Trust me, that was plenty wild enough." I wanted to tell her about the prince, but I didn't know her companions and couldn't risk one of them telling the king. If Prince Damien hadn't already.

"What are you here for? I heard that you needed to see King Locklyn."

Her cheerful demeanor came crashing down and was replaced by the blackest scowl I'd ever seen. "I was helping escort cargo from Charra to another planet – just a routine thing, no big deal. And then we were ambushed by two Krech ships."

My mouth dropped open. Adís had a run-in with the Krech and was, fortunately, here to talk about it. "What happened? How did you get away?"

She lifted her chin as her shoulders rolled back. "I'm the captain of the *Hellfire* for a reason, Aliya. The cargo ship took some damage, but once I opened up our guns, the Krech focused on us, and the cargo ship got away safely." She bit her lip for a few moments, and I felt something big coming next. "Then the two ships played dirty – they split up and went on either side of us. We couldn't fight both at once, so we had to make a split-second decision as to which was more dangerous."

Adís paused again, and my impatience got the best of me. "Then what happened?"

"Well, I didn't necessarily choose wrong, but I don't think I chose correctly either. They… they were both equally dangerous. Although my crew and I managed to take down the one ship, the other got away. We couldn't give chase because of the damage we sustained." She looked pissed. It made sense – I would've wanted to go after the other ship too if I had been in her position.

I pulled her into a hug and was rewarded with her deep sigh as she relaxed. "I'm so glad you're okay. That's… that's absolutely terrifying."

Stepping out of my hug, she nodded gravely. "It is. I feel like everything we knew about the Krech was wrong. The ones we found on Charra proved that they weren't gone or solitary. The cyborg attack revealed that they have dark connections in this galaxy. And now… Now they're demonstrating that they have strategy," she murmured. "We don't know our enemy *at all.*"

It was a terrifying thought. I wondered who the original person was to come forward with those now-false 'facts' about the Krech. Ultimately it didn't matter because the reality crept closer every day: the Krech were out there, and they were coming for us. All of us.

"You're here to give a full report to the king." It wasn't a question. Adís most likely already relayed a message about what had happened, but now she was here to answer any additional questions the king had.

"Exactly." She studied my face for a few moments. "You're still training, right? Not getting lazy following the prince around day and night?"

"Yes, I am," I nearly snapped at her. And then it hit me. Adís wasn't making fun of my role here in the palace and how I served the most pathetic royal of all time. She was genuinely asking if I would be prepared to fight more Krech if it came down to it. "Oh. I hope it doesn't come to that, but yes, I'll be ready."

Adís gave me a curt nod and then tilted her head toward the

doors of the throne room. "I should probably get going. King Locklyn needs to hear my news sooner rather than later."

"Right. Of course." She started to walk around me, but I pulled her into another tight hug. Adís' body went taut with surprise. "I'm really glad that you made it back okay."

I felt her shoulders droop – from comfort or fatigue, I couldn't tell – as she wrapped her small arms around me. "Me too, Aliya. Me too."

✻

I mulled over Adís' news as I munched through my second piece of toast. Since it was so late, regular lunch had been taken out of the banquet hall. Luckily, I was able to smooth talk the kitchen staff into putting together a plate for me.

So now, as I sat at the far end of the table in a mostly empty hall, I considered what it meant that the Krech were launching attacks on cargo ships. And that they were using strategic attacking maneuvers.

How many Protective Forces' squads had been deployed to protect the citizens of the galaxy? I hadn't thought about her since I'd returned to the base with the Nova squad after our mission on Vanthurium, but Maeve popped into my mind.

Powerful and driven, she'd been in charge of her own squad in no time – according to Thun. She hadn't been the kindest to me, but I still hoped that if she was out fighting Krech, that she would be safe.

Unrealistic as the thought was, I hoped that everyone was safe.

I slowly tapped my fingers on the table as I tried to put all the pieces together. Why were the Krech just attacking planets and ships in the Outer Rim? Why were they going after cargo ships? And what was on those cargo ships? Something important was missing, but I didn't have enough information to determine exactly what it was.

One thing that seemed obvious was that a majority of the attacks were happening on or near Charra. That left a few possibilities: there was something valuable on Charra that the Krech wanted or it was close enough to their mysterious origins that they could keep hitting the area over and over.

Had anyone else figured that out?

I sent Caspian a flurry of messages, after wishing him a good afternoon and thanking him again for making last night so much fun. But I relayed my interactions with Adís in detail along with the questions and realization I'd come to over my meal. I wasn't sure if he could do much of anything with the information, as we worked with the prince and not the king, but knowing Caspian, he'd find a way to get that information to someone with influence or answers.

Just as I got up to leave, my cuff pinged with a message. *You're on duty with me in fifteen — Ney.* I groaned. I didn't want a day shift, but Caspian had warned me that we'd have to change things up so that everyone could rest after last night.

A few maids entered the hall as I left. I panicked, imagining that they'd heard about me and Prince Damien from last night. I crept around them as quickly as possible, offering a nod and a forced smile when they said hello.

My fears were ridiculous. Prince Damien was a mess and rude – or inappropriate – to everyone. They'd all probably be happy to know that I finally told him off.

My cuff pinged, and I jumped. Placing a hand over my racing heart, I read the new message. *That's quite the wakeup call, love. Thanks for last night and the deep thinking. I'll let King Locklyn know when we meet in a bit to report on last night. Don't worry – I'll leave that bit out.*

I heaved a sigh of relief. If he didn't already know, Caspian wouldn't rat me out. Although I was slightly curious to know if the king would secretly approve, I didn't want to risk facing his anger.

I sent off a quick thank you to Caspian, and then I asked Neygreen where he was. Unsurprisingly, Ney was currently stationed outside of the prince's room.

Please let him sleep all day, I chanted over and over as I headed to the royal wing of the palace.

Ney smiled and waved as I approached. "I'm surprised you're up this early. I heard that you and Caspian got to enjoy the party after we left with Prince Damien."

His bright smile naturally pulled one from me in return. "We did have a good time. After I got over how loud and busy it was, I actually had fun. But what happened after the prince left?"

He shrugged his shoulders. "He just came back to his room. Didn't say a word to Elgin, Omri, or myself as we trailed after him. Just went into his room and hasn't come out."

My stomach sank. "No visitors either?"

"Not one."

"And you're positive that he hasn't left through the window or anything like that?"

Ney paused. "Well, I haven't exactly gone in to check…" He turned his head to stare at the closed door. "Do you think we should?"

I crossed my arms. "If he's missing, that could be a big problem, Ney." *A problem that I, most likely, caused.*

He sighed and smoothed his already impeccable shirt. "Let's hope he doesn't get mad and try to throw something at me," he mumbled under his breath.

Ney took a deep breath as he placed his hand on the silver doorknob and then slowly twisted it. He peeked through the crack before he opened the door halfway and took a step inside.

Never having seen the inside of the prince's chambers before, I couldn't resist peeking inside as well. The prince's room was dark, which wasn't a surprise since Elgin mentioned that he rarely bothered to open the drapes over the massive windows, but that meant I couldn't see much past the light which shone in from the open door. What was shocking, however, was the pile of bottles – some empty and others with varying levels of fullness – which Ney stumbled into as he moved into the room. I heard him curse quietly as he scrambled to stop a few rolling bottles.

Still in the hallway, I held my breath, waiting for a reprimand or some kind of commotion.

"Neygreen, what are you doing?" The prince's voice sounded from deep within the room. His words were neither sleepy nor slurred, and I couldn't believe that he'd addressed Ney by his full name. It was the most concise sentence that I'd ever heard him speak.

"Um, Prince Damien – I mean, your highness. I was just checking to see if you were okay, sir. You've been quiet for, um, for a long time now." Ney's voice shook as he rushed to piece together an answer. Clearly, he wasn't expecting the prince to be conscious or clear-minded enough to ask a direct question.

"You assumed I was drunk or asleep, perhaps?" The prince didn't even wait for Ney to respond. "I'm quite all right, I assure you. I was just about to call for some servants, but since you're here, would you mind removing all those bottles you kicked? Dispose of them however you wish, but I want them gone." Despite the question, his tone implied that he'd given an order.

"Y-yes, your highness," Ney stuttered. I heard more clinking, and then hasty footsteps as he retreated.

A look of pure shock covered Ney's thin face as he emerged from the prince's chambers. *Take these*, he mouthed as he nodded down at the bottles in his arms.

I wasn't sure what to do with them since most were nearly full, but I plucked all six from him before setting them on the decorative table across the hall. I recognized several of the liquids from the drinks that were served last night – unsurprisingly, they were the potent kinds that Caspian warned me about.

I turned to ask Ney what we should do with them, but he ducked back into the prince's room once more before returning with a second armful.

"Would you like some help?" I felt bad that he was doing all the work.

Ney shook his head. "Stay out here. Maybe you should ping one of the kitchen staff to see if they want any of the full bottles returned to the cellar."

"Okay." I knew Ney was trying to keep me away from the prince, completely unaware of the fact that he no longer scared me. Well, not in the way he used to. So I sent off a message to the head of the kitchen staff and continued relieving Ney of the bottles he brought me.

When all was said and done, forty-three bottles of alcohol sat on the table. Short and tall, round and skinny, the bottles covered the entire top of the table, and a few even rested on the floor. Half were completely empty, but the rest ranged from half-full to unopened.

Despite knowing how little the king cared for his son's doings, I was still floored that the prince managed to hoard that much booze in his room. Did no one notice a lack of liquor in the cellar, or did they simply not care?

Furthermore, I was shocked that he *didn't* want it anymore. What changed his mind? An uneasy feeling in the pit of my stomach told me I knew the answer to that. But why?

Ney and I weren't the only ones who didn't expect this turn of events. When Brigeeta, the head cook, arrived to assess the situation, she gasped. "Stars and comets! Were these all from…?" she trailed off, glancing over at the prince's closed door.

"Yes, ma'am," Ney replied. "Do you see anything there that you'd like to store again?"

She turned to the bottles, running her hands over them as she read labels. After a few moments she said, "Anything still sealed can be stored and reused. I guess I should have brought more hands with me." She laughed in disbelief as she propped her hands on her wide hips.

After checking with Ney, I offered to help her bring everything she wanted back down to the cellar. Between the two of us, we managed to carry all but four bottles.

Brigeeta promised to send other kitchen staff up to help dispose of the rest of the unfinished or empty bottles. Ney looked relieved that he wouldn't have to carry all of them down to the kitchens.

Still shaking my head in disbelief at the prince's change of heart, I hurried along behind Brigeeta, wondering how long this would last.

After one full day of staying in his room, Prince Damien emerged. It was noon, and he joined his parents for a long lunch. He returned to his room afterward, but that evening, he joined them for dinner too.

On the second day, he joined them for all three meals. He even ordered Elgin, who was on the morning shift, to have a charged dataport sent to his room.

The third day, which was perhaps the craziest of all, he dined with his parents and attended a meeting on current galactic affairs.

And so it went.

Having grown accustomed to the prince's lack of interest in his family and responsibilities, it took the prince's guards a while to adapt to efficiently moving about the palace with Prince Damien. No longer did we need to stand outside his room for hours on end and find ways to curb our boredom. Now we accompanied the prince to his parents' chambers for meals, to the council room for meetings, and over the grounds as he met with guards, pilots, and engineers in an attempt to reacquaint himself with those who worked for the royal family.

There were no more late night guests, orders to prepare for a spontaneous party, or drinks consumed in large quantities. In fact, Prince Damien avoided alcohol altogether.

It was bizarre.

After one week, we thought that the prince had hit his head or the male we followed around was some sort of imposter.

At two weeks, guards and servants alike began to whisper that this was a permanent change to the prince that they finally felt like they could respect.

I don't think I took a deep breath during that strange time.

Each time the prince had a meal or meeting with his father, I worried that he would say something about my harsh treatment and insults during the party. But after each day without an incident, I wondered if the prince was going to tell anyone. Ever.

Prince Damien ignored me when I was on shifts, instead asking the other guard questions he had. I tried many times to catch his eye, but he always turned away or found something more interesting with which to occupy his time.

And he refused to be left with me as his only guard.

The one time that Seradon offered to fetch a meal for the prince – because, of course, the prince was reading a report of recent attacks carried out by ships we assumed to hold Krech – he nearly knocked over his chair.

"No," he said with more force than I'd ever heard out of him. "Others can go, but I order you to stay, Seradon."

Since Prince Damien had only spoken to Seradon, it took me a few moments to figure out that by 'others' he meant me. When I finally pieced it together, I let out an angry huff and immediately marched out of the small meeting room.

I'd been so irritated and offended at the time, but as I returned with Prince Damien's lunch, I realized that he might be afraid to be alone with me. Surely he didn't think I'd go off on him again…?

It was then that my anxiety over being reprimanded faded into embarrassment. Should I apologize to Prince Damien? I certainly didn't feel sorry if my words brought on this total change of behavior. This new, responsible prince was better for the King's Galaxy – right? King Locklyn had definitely become less irritable and stressed over the past two weeks as his son took part in meetings and embraced his princely responsibilities.

In the end, I let the whole matter go. With how hard he tried to ignore and avoid me, Prince Damien would never apologize for his inappropriate treatment when I first started or at the party, so I felt validated that I didn't need to apologize for setting him straight.

The only thing that kept me up at night was *why* my confrontation had changed him so much.

Caspian's presence, thankfully, kept that question off my mind when I wasn't on shift. Today we were sparring in the outdoor arena and enjoying the warm weather.

In a full council meeting yesterday, Corvius Lontarre, King Locklyn's Master of Defense, mentioned that the king needed to strike back at the Krech. Having guards patrolling the Outer Rim was helpful, but the frequency of attacks hadn't decreased as much as the council hoped.

With the Callaisan branch of the Protective Forces already spread thin and not many other large forces left in the galaxy to deploy, the royal guards would likely be used next. At least, that's how Caspian interpreted Corvius' suggestion.

The King's Galaxy was at a tipping point. Everyone was so scared of being attacked that travel had ground to a near-complete stop. The only ships that moved between planets were ones under heavy military protection, and even then, those trips occurred only when completely necessary.

With no clear lead on where the Krech came from and where they'd attack next, I thought an organized assault was unlikely to happen. It wouldn't make sense to send a sizeable portion of the galaxy's defenses off into the unknown when the enemy could easily slip around them and head straight for Callais.

So, while we waited for the order to assemble – which may or may not be given anytime soon – Caspian and I trained in our downtime and tried to accommodate other guards who wanted to freshen up their combat skills.

Luckily, today it was just me and Caspian.

I raised my left forearm across my body to block a jab aimed at my face, and in anticipation of Caspian's punch aimed at my ribs, I snagged his left wrist and tugged hard. His hand skimmed the front of my shirt as I spun him around, pulling his left arm behind his back and flush against my body.

Wrapping my left arm around his neck, I leaned in close to his ear and whispered, "I win. Again."

Caspian sighed in frustration, and I placed a kiss against the side of his damp neck. Even at greatly reduced speed and strength, I still beat Caspian every time.

"How are you still that good?" he complained at I released him.

"I learned moves from Captain Sansish and you." I shrugged. "And even though I'm purposely moving slower, I can't dampen my senses."

Caspian snorted and reached for my left hand. His fingers traced the circuits in my arm as they faded, as did the sting from his jab. "And here I imagined that I'd be the one saving a damsel in distress. Not that I'd be the damsel." He laughed before pressing a kiss to my knuckles.

"Oh, stop that! If I was anyone else, you'd be winning." I slipped my hand out from under his insistent lips.

His eyes flicked up from where my hand had been and into my eyes. The serious look in his eyes had me glancing away, but I only got as far as the scar on his chin.

Gentle fingers on my cheek guided my gaze upward and back

into the path of that dangerous stare. "But you're not anyone else. That, I think, is a greater prize than winning a sparring match." Caspian gave me a devilish grin before leaning in to press his lips to mine.

Kissing Caspian never failed to take my breath away. My heart raced, my stomach filled with butterflies, and I always wanted *more*. More of Caspian. More kisses from those soft, insistent lips. More time for us to be together.

While our shifts only lasted eight hours, I felt like I didn't have enough time with Caspian outside of being guards. He was often called away to sit in on private meetings that King Locklyn held – ones that Prince Damien, now that he was acting like a prince, couldn't even join – or to help train soldiers who hadn't come up through the Protective Forces or servants who wanted to learn to protect themselves.

I joined those sessions whenever I could, but I was never much help. I moved too fast and hit too hard to be a real asset when teaching someone new fighting techniques, so I watched and offered advice.

But it was still time spent with Caspian as we demonstrated techniques in slow motion and offered critiques as individuals practiced on their own. I felt like Caspian and I had truly become a team – not the Nova squad or prince's guards, but an unbreakable team of two.

Caspian leaned away and then gave my braid a playful tug. "And what about you? Do you enjoy your wins, or is there something more that you're enjoying?" He teasingly brushed his lips against mine but didn't go for a full kiss.

"Well," I said as I looped my arms up and around his neck, "I definitely enjoy how sparring gets me so close to you."

"Is that so?" Caspian asked with a dark chuckle. His arms wrapped around my waist and pulled me against his warm, toned body. "And how's this?"

"It's perfect," I whispered before initiating another kiss.

"And what would you call that move, Captain?"

I'd been so lost in Caspian's flirting that I missed the sound of soft footsteps on the grass.

Prince Damien, flanked by Seradon and Ba'rin, approached the dirt circle where Caspian and I were sparring.

His eyes were slightly squinted from the bright sunlight, and a smirk pulled at the left corner of his mouth. Dressed in a snug, black collared shirt and equally dark pants, the prince actually looked somewhat formidable. Especially when followed by Seradon and Ba'rin.

I practically jumped out of Caspian's arms, incredibly embarrassed to have been caught making out on the job. Well, technically we were off duty, but I still felt like a kid who was caught with her hand in the cookie jar. Fortunately, Caspian wasn't as mortified by the situation as I was.

"Apologies, my prince. I often find that I can't help myself when around Aliya," he said smoothly with a bow. "Is there something that you need from us?" Caspian's tone was calm, but the sharp look that he gave Prince Damien revealed his irritation at the prince's interruption.

"Yes, actually." He cleaned some imaginary dirt from under his fingernails. "Since you two have the most recent combat experience and some of the best skills I've seen, I request to be trained," Prince Damien paused and looked from Caspian to me, "by both of you."

He had to be kidding. After doing everything in his power to avoid me, Prince Damien now wanted to *train* with me and Caspian? What was wrong with this guy?

I could practically feel my hackles rising as a horde of harsh words stormed to the tip of my tongue. But out of the corner of my eye, I watched Caspian take a step forward. "It would be our pleasure, your highness."

My jaw snapped shut with a click, and I pasted what I hoped was a pleased smile on my face. I didn't trust myself to say anything kind, so I offered the prince a shallow bow.

Prince Damien clapped his hands with an excited gleam in his eyes. "Marvelous. Where do we begin?"

Caspian cleared his throat. "Well, my prince, how much training have you received before?"

"Ah." Some of the prince's excitement died off. "What I know was taught to me years ago, and I haven't practiced since then."

"Better late than never, hm? That's just fine. We can start with the basics." If he'd been surprised by Prince Damien's admission, Caspian worked quickly to hide it.

While Caspian walked Prince Damien through the proper stances for fighting off an attacker, I kept my distance. I wanted nothing to do with the prince, and getting close enough to adjust his footing or his hand positioning was the last thing I wanted to do today.

Irritation set in as I realized that this would now occupy the rest of my day. All I'd wanted was more time with Caspian, and of course Prince Damien had appeared and requested our attention. There were dozens of guards here at the palace, and yet he wanted the two of us.

To his credit, the prince was a quick learner, absorbing Caspian's direction without a fuss or eye-rolling. While it was strange to watch Caspian order his prince around the sparring ring, it was much odder that the prince sought us out of his own volition.

I suppose he really had changed for the better. Finally.

A chime brought my attention back to the action happening in the ring, and a sinking feeling filled my stomach as Caspian read the message that had arrived on his cuff.

He read it once and then twice as his surprised expression faded into a small scowl. "The king has requested my presence at a private meeting. I apologize, Prince Damien, but I have to go."

Prince Damien dismissed Caspian's apology with a wave of his hand. "I completely understand, captain. I appreciate what you've taught me to get started, but I'm also sure that Aliya will be able to continue the lesson." He turned to me with a quirked brow.

"Of course," I said with forced enthusiasm. "We'll be fine, Caspian."

Caspian looked skeptical, but he nodded to the prince and then crossed the sparring grounds to where I stood with my arms crossed. After pressing a kiss to my cheek, he lingered by my ear for a moment. "Take it easy on him. He's trying to be better," he whispered before walking away.

I took a deep breath and approached the prince. But before I could say anything, Prince Damien spoke up.

"He loves you." It wasn't a question, and his eyes still hadn't left Caspian's retreating form.

I wasn't sure why this seemed to matter, but I also couldn't let the prince think that Caspian's feelings were one-sided. "He does. And I love him."

Prince Damien turned his hazel-eyed stare to me and didn't speak for a few moments. I shifted on my feet, uncomfortable because I didn't know what thoughts might be churning in his mind.

After a few moments he nodded and said, "Right." He cleared his throat twice and glanced down at his open palms before meeting my stare. "What should we do next? Will I be sparring against you?"

I snorted. "You're just learning, and you think that I'm going to spar with you? I don't train at my full abilities with Caspian, let alone with you. You definitely won't be able to keep up with me, so I suggest asking Seradon or Ba'rin." I shouldn't have sounded so harsh and dismissive, but I truly couldn't train with him more than demonstrating moves and techniques.

Prince Damien blinked in surprise. "But I'd like to learn from you. What are you able to teach me?"

It was my turn to be shocked. My retort hadn't phased him, and I couldn't fathom why he wanted to learn from me specifically, especially in light of our… history together.

"Well. I… I suppose we could do some target practice." I'd taught Elgin how to improve his aim, and this way I wouldn't have to touch the prince as much as I would have to if we were doing combat training.

"I would like that," Prince Damien replied with a smile.

What game are you playing, prince? Something seemed off about his willingness to be taught by me and the enthusiasm he oozed when I suggested shooting. Perhaps he really did want to learn, but I didn't quite believe that.

We strolled over to the shooting range, and I offered Prince Damien one of my blasters. The ones used for practice usually weren't fully charged, or they'd been used so much that the trigger was tougher to pull. As much as I hated this situation, I didn't want Prince Damien having difficulty practicing.

"Alright, focus on that first target. The traditional stance is to have your feet shoulder-width apart and knees slightly bent, but some people find it easier to place one foot slightly forward." I waited while he tried out both stances, finally settling on one with his right foot ahead of his left. "Good. Now lift the blaster to about chin height – you want to be able to see over the top of it without craning your neck."

Once more I was stunned by his willingness to take direction. How was this the same prince who ran rampant throughout the castle, drinking all the booze he could get his hands on and disobeying every order his father gave? I shook my head, unable to reconcile the two males.

I watched as he settled into the stance, and after holding it for a handful of seconds, he grimaced. "What's wrong?"

"I fear I'm more out of shape than I realized. Holding my arms like this is already making me shoulders ache." Prince Damien laughed as he shook out his arms. "There certainly is a lot for me to catch up on."

"You'll get stronger and that position will become more natural with practice. Go ahead and try a few shots." I took a few steps back in case his weaker frame was more susceptible to recoil. The last thing I needed today was to be glanced by a shot if the prince's form broke.

Prince Damien wet his lips and took a breath. As he exhaled, tension faded from his shoulders and his stance looked a bit more natural. "Okay," he murmured, and then he pulled the trigger.

I was right. The force of the shot made Prince Damien wobble backward, and he needed to take a step to regain his balance. His eyes flew open wide – as did his shot. Off to my right, I heard Ba'rin snicker, but I couldn't join in his amusement without potentially offending the prince.

Still recovering his footing, he mouthed a quick *wow* as he turned to gauge my reaction.

"Again. Remember, this takes practice." I felt like a hypocrite saying that, but for everyone who hadn't been physically reconstructed, lots of practice to improve one's aim was necessary.

Prince Damien got back into position and repeated the shot. Once more he was knocked off balance and missed the target completely. Then he did it again. And again.

After his sixth shot, I realized that I couldn't let him flounder around any longer. He wasn't changing his stance or grip. It was like he truly expected to improve by doing the same thing over and over.

"Wait," I called as he set up for yet another shot. "Let me take a look."

His knees were bent just enough to keep him balanced, but his elbows were straight as an arrow. On top of that, his knuckles were white from how tightly he gripped the blaster. After pointing out the small changes he needed to make, I set Prince Damien loose once more.

This time he hit the second ring on the left side.

I could see a difference in his attitude immediately. His chin lifted, and the smile on his face became natural, reflecting the pride he now felt.

"Thank you." He turned from the target and offered my blaster back to me. "I'll practice more in the days to come."

"Good. You'll get there, and if you need more help along the way, don't hesitate to ask." The words were out of my mouth before they registered in my brain. I definitely *didn't* want him coming to me for more advice, but the kinder side of me had stepped in before I thought through my offer.

Assuming that I was being dismissed, I turned and began to walk back to the palace.

"Aliya, wait."

It certainly hadn't skipped my attention that he used my name while calling Caspian 'captain' earlier, and I bristled at hearing my name on his tongue once more. But, being the good guard that I was, I turned back to him and replied, "Yes, your highness?"

Prince Damien's mouth opened and closed, and then he took a few steps to close the distance between us. "I wanted to apologize. I know that my behavior has been… far less than desirable for one of my status, but I was also terrible to you. I was inappropriate and highly offensive, and I'd like to offer you my sincerest apologies as well as a promise to never do that again."

My mouth dropped open in shock. *He* was apologizing to *me?* As if his change in behavior wasn't enough, now he was actually humbling himself to admit old faults. "Why did you act that way in the first place?"

He hadn't been expecting that question, and it took him a moment to form a response. "I… I didn't want to be a prince. I didn't want the responsibility of making sure that trillions of lives were protected, that trades were upheld, and that lords and ladies followed the rules set down by my predecessors. So, I thought that acting up would pass the burden onto someone else. I should've known that my father would never do such a thing.

"I acted in every way that a prince shouldn't. I broke treaties and friendships, and most of all I shattered all respect my parents had for me. They gave up on me, everyone did. Until you came along." He laughed. "I was utterly floored by the way you spoke to me at the party. How could a guard get away with saying that no one cared about me? But the more I considered it, the more I understood that you were right. People came to my parties or to my chambers, but that all meant nothing to them. I meant nothing to them except a fleeting, good time. *I* was the reason no one respected me, and it was a foolish thing to do. And I realized that no matter how poorly I acted, no matter what horrendous thing I did, I would still be the prince. My parents have no other children, and I didn't want to be the first Talimore king who was an utter failure."

Utterly speechless, all I could do was watch Prince Damien. There was no way this was actually happening. Even Seradon and Ba'rin looked as shell-shocked as I felt.

Prince Damien's cheeks were faintly pink with emotion as he wrung his hands and looked at me shyly. "You didn't give up on me, and you've helped me see that I can do much better — as a son, as a Callaisan, and as a prince. So once more I apologize for my past self, and I thank you for setting me straight."

He motioned to his two guards, and then Prince Damien marched back to the palace.

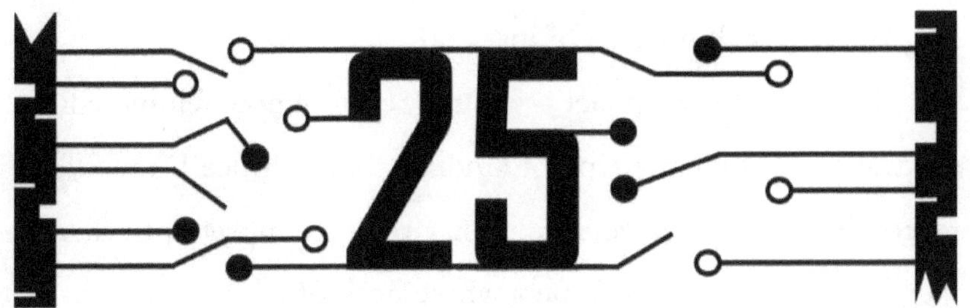

I flopped facedown onto my bed after what might have been one of the most awkward guard shifts of my entire life.

The ones where Prince Damien had ignored me were frustrating, but now that he was accepting my presence and talking to me, I wanted nothing to do with him.

Sure, it was lovely to finally have a prince who took his role seriously and actively participated in royal duties. The entire mood in the palace shifted once everyone realized that this new Prince Damien was here to stay.

Female servants didn't rush by with their heads down when he passed, nor did they solicit themselves to him for extra attention – the prince had also issued many apologies since turning his attitude around.

His drinking stopped completely unless there was a special

toast at a meal, but even then, he would only take a few sips from his glass and then send it away.

And it was all because of me.

That – that singular fact – was the reason I now felt incredibly awkward receiving any type of kindness from Prince Damien. I'd forced him to change, and he wasn't remotely upset with me. In fact, he seemed to respect me a whole heck of a lot more now.

For example, even though he'd been invited to a meeting on the agricultural status of the Valley of the Crown and whether or not there was enough food stored up to support Callais should a war begin, Prince Damien declined the meeting and asked if we could continue the shooting lesson I'd started yesterday. I couldn't very well say no.

In the end, all three of us – Prince Damien, Omri, and myself – traipsed back out to the shooting range for another lesson. This time I pitted the prince against Omri in accuracy shots which was amusing until Prince Damien finally got the hang of shooting a blaster.

He was still far from perfect, but at least he hit the closest and second-closest targets every time.

"Why me?" I moaned into my sheets. I never wanted Prince Damien's attention or kindness; all I had wanted was for him to pull himself together and actually act like a prince. *Well, you got more than you asked for, Aliya.*

At least I wouldn't have to see him again until tomorrow afternoon. There was another council meeting on next steps to combat the Krech, and although I wasn't technically supposed to go back on guard duty until the evening, my presence had been requested.

I didn't like the sound of that, but I was grateful for being included.

Rolling onto my back, I typed out a quick message to Doctor Givray. This would be my third in a week – all without a response. Neither Caspian nor I had heard a word about him and his work since the twins left the palace to assist him, and I was starting to worry.

Had he finally succeeded in replicating the surgery that gave me my speed and strength? I was inclined to think yes since I hadn't been dragged before the council for an examination, and I hadn't been called to the healing facility to clean up a potential mess.

But why wasn't he replying to me?

Exhaustion and frustration swirled around my brain, giving me a headache. Prince Damien and Doctor Givray were things I couldn't control, and worrying about them would only make me feel worse.

I was about to give in and take a nap when my cuff pinged with a new message. Bounding upright, I felt my hopes soar that the notification was a message from the good doctor. But it wasn't.

Aliya, the message read, *I know that I promised to spend the afternoon with you, but something came up. I'm so, so sorry. My evening, however, is still yours for the taking if you are still free.*

I felt my mood darken from Caspian's message. I'd wanted to spend the afternoon and evening with him, and I was curious what had come up to alter his plans. But an evening together was better than nothing. *Afternoon, evening. It doesn't matter so long as I get to see you.*

I felt incredibly corny after I hit send, but falling in love with Caspian had brought out the worst – as far as mushy romance went. It *didn't* matter when I got to see him because we'd be together again. Eventually.

And a few more hours were a small price to pay for an evening of bliss.

Another message arrived. *Excellent. Let's meet in the middle of the hedge maze once the sun sets?*

The hedge maze? I hadn't explored it much since arriving here, and I'd never wanted to go alone in case I got turned around. But if I was able to get a look at it from above before this evening, I'd be able to chart a path to the center and reach it in no time once darkness arrived.

I'll be there. I can't wait to see you.

I can't wait too.

With a smile on my face and butterflies in my stomach, I decided it was worth taking that nap. Who knew, it could be a long night, and I didn't want to pass out too early.

□

A light vibration on my wrist woke me from a far deeper nap than I'd expected to take. With heavy limbs and eyes, I rolled onto my back with a groan. *Why had I bothered to set an alarm in the first place?*

And then I remembered – Caspian. Hedge maze. Nightfall.

With renewed vigor, I bounded out of bed. Somehow pre-nap me thought I'd be able to get ready in an insanely short time, but I wasn't so sure about that since darkness was nearly upon the valley.

I was all thumbs and left feet as I rushed to look presentable, settling for combing my fingers through my wavy hair instead of pulling it all back. With a fresh black shirt and a pair of gray slacks, I almost looked like I had been prepared to see Caspian. Even with my rapid pace, I still managed to leave my room just as the sun was setting.

With only a short stop at the southern-facing windows to take a good look at the maze, I jogged down the stairs and out the back door. Caspian wasn't likely to mind if I was a few minutes late, but those were minutes I didn't want to miss since we'd lost the afternoon together.

The hedge maze was a behemoth and certainly intimidating if one didn't know what path to take. I was glad I'd cheated by looking out over the top of it because now that I stood before the towering foliage, I could see the true challenge it presented to those adventurous enough to go inside.

No person in their right mind would attempt this alone during the day, let alone at night. But if Caspian was waiting in the middle, I had to make my way there too.

The evening air was crisp on my face as I wound my way around and around the walls of the maze. The path switched from soft grass to dry, packed dirt several times, as if someone had traversed these corridors many times. However, there were no additional signs of use – lush and full, the walls didn't appear to have a leaf out of place.

Nocturnal insects made their presence inside the shrubbery known with soft clicks and chirps. I hadn't encountered many bugs during my shifts, and this was certainly the least preferable time for me to discover what kind of nightlife existed on the grounds. Aside from them, the air was totally silent – the sheer height of the walls having blocked out the sounds of life coming from the palace. Trapped in these verdant walls, the silence created the illusion that the entire valley was at peace.

A smile crept onto my face as I rounded the last few turns that would take me to the center, and I couldn't help picking up my pace.

I knew I was nearly there as my ears picked up the soft sounds of boots on grass. Back and forth they paced just beyond the wall in front of me, and I came to a full halt to listen. There was no doubt that it was Caspian because I'd grown so accustomed to his stride, but it seemed odd that he was pacing. Had something gone wrong this afternoon?

I rounded the corner and took in the scene before me. A three-tiered stone fountain softly gurgled in the middle of a circular, grassy courtyard. Well-worn and far too simple to match the

palace's architecture, the middle level even had a hairline crack running down the part facing me. It must have been installed back when the maze was initially constructed.

In front of the fountain was Caspian. As always, he looked handsome in his black pants and boots, and tonight he'd paired them with a long-sleeved, red collared shirt.

His hands weren't in his pockets, which was a far too common occurrence when Caspian was thoughtful or annoyed. Instead, he wrung them in front of him as he paced – ten steps to the left, ten to the right, and then he restarted his loop.

I could've watched him forever, but he was the one who asked me to meet him here.

"Caspian?" He was so focused on whatever was occupying his thoughts that he didn't notice me approaching.

Caspian's face broke out into a smile that put the sun to shame. "Aliya. I missed you." And then he was crossing the small courtyard to pull me close for a kiss.

For once I didn't get lost in his touch. Something about this meeting and his behavior seemed off. Even his heartbeat, which I could hear clearly now that we were touching, thumped at a quicker pace than normal.

I tried to shake off my worries and live in the moment. I'd wanted to see Caspian all day, and here I was acting suspicious when there was likely nothing wrong. Caspian wouldn't wait this long to tell me if something was amiss. Right?

He brushed the tip of his nose across mine after we both came up for a breath. "How was your day?" Despite his earlier pacing and racing pulse, everything about his tone seemed normal. *This is just another night spent together, Aliya. Relax.*

So, lingering in the circle of his warm and sturdy arms, I relayed my day. Everything from Prince Damien's new attentive nature to his second shooting lesson. I did, however, leave out the part where I napped almost until I was late for our meeting.

"And how about you? Today seemed busier than normal for you."

I watched a flicker of annoyance cross his face before it disappeared. "The king keeps asking me for battle tactics and numbers of available soldiers. I'm honored to be part of these conversations, but I feel like he's directing them at the wrong person. General Vinculus would be able to give him better advice than I can."

I scowled as that name pulled up a slew of unpleasant memories. "Do you think King Locklyn is going to start a war with the Krech?"

Caspian sighed and lowered his forehead to mine. "I don't know. It wouldn't make sense to since we have no idea where to actually fight the Krech, but we're losing the galaxy's trust by sitting back and losing lives to their attacks." He sounded frustrated, and I didn't blame him. There was no clear path that would help us defeat the Krech, but like Caspian said, the King's Galaxy was at the point where it couldn't tolerate further destruction.

"Well," I said, tapping my finger against his chest, "we can save that problem for another day. For now, let's just be us." Sliding my arms up and around his neck, I nuzzled into the space below his chin and shoulder.

Oddly, I heard his heart skip a beat on my last sentence.

We remained wrapped up like that for several long minutes. Time melted away as we listened to each other's breathing, the water splashing merrily in the fountain behind us, and the insects going about their nightly adventures.

Caspian was warm and firm as he held me to his chest, and I sighed as the day's stresses melted out of my body. All the irritation and confusion… simply gone now that I was where I wanted to be.

"I love you," Caspian murmured over my head.

He couldn't see it, but I smiled at his words. "I love you too," I replied, meaning every single syllable.

"This just feels right, doesn't it? It's like we were meant to find each other and end up here." Caspian's voice took on a wistful tone, and I found myself pulling away so I could see his expression.

His sapphire eyes were guarded, but a soft smile played on his full lips. There was a flicker of emotion as he studied the obvious concern written all over my face.

I couldn't ignore my worries any longer. "What's going on, Caspian? Something just seems… off."

He chuckled and bit the corner of his lip. Releasing me from his grip, Caspian's fingers trailed down my arms until he reached my hands. Once there, he threaded our fingers together. Keeping his eyes on our interlocked hands, Caspian said, "For a long time I thought I was going to be alone. I thought I had everything, knew where I wanted to go with my life, and then it was all taken from me. Nothing could have prepared me for the loss and confusion I felt. I even wondered if I'd been wrong to think that I'd found my path back then. Perhaps that *was* meant to be my path."

"Caspian, what are you talking about?" He'd already told me how he felt lost after his parents' and Leila's deaths, and I couldn't fathom why he was bringing them back up now.

His eyes snapped up to mine, and they absolutely smoldered with raw emotion. "I'm talking about *you*, Aliya, and how being with you just feels *right*. Like this was all meant to be. *You* were the one who saved us on Charra and then again on Vanthurium. You saved *my life* in the tunnels under the palace." My stomach flipped as I recalled the sight of Caspian with a blade held to his throat. "Somehow, despite your galactic renown, you were asked to babysit the prince who didn't deserve our protection. And I suspect that you played a large part in changing his attitude."

I shook my head. "Caspian, I was just doing what I needed to do. I couldn't sit by and let you die! And as for Damien... I didn't *try* to change him. I was just fed up with his attitude. He's the one who took my words to heart."

"Intentional or not, *you* did those things and *you* caused that change. Whether it's fate or luck, you're right where you need to be."

He was correct that I had a hand in each and every one of those scenarios, but someone else certainly played a part in getting me to where I needed to be.

I untangled one of my hands and lifted it to cup his smooth cheek. "It does feel right, and I consider myself lucky every day that you were on the Protective Forces base the day I arrived. You were the first one who saw me as a person, not just a physically modified weapon. You believed in me and encouraged me to embrace who I am. Without your intervention, I don't know where I'd be."

"And what about the future? Where would you like to be then?"

I laughed. "I don't know, but I know I want to be by your side through it all."

"I want to be with you too, Aliya," Caspian replied in a rough voice. I was so caught up in his intense gaze and the love I felt for him that I almost missed Caspian's hand snaking into the pocket of his pants. "I—I wanted to do this right. For you, I mean. You won't believe how hard it is to find detailed histories of Terran customs, but I finally found what I needed." He laughed, just once, nervously.

He'd lost me again, but something about the serious edge that crept into his tone put me on high alert. "Caspian, what's going on?"

Without breaking eye contact, Caspian sank down onto one knee.

My stomach fell right out of my body as realization hit.

My mouth dropped open, but every muscle and fiber in my body locked into place. Was Caspian actually doing this? With our roles as guards and the approaching threat of the Krech, how could he *possibly* be thinking about proposing right now?

I'd never dreamt of this moment – since leaving Terra my life had become unpredictable, and settling down with someone was the last thing on my mind. But in this moment, I'd never wanted anything more than the male kneeling before me.

"I want to spend each moment of the rest of my life with you. I want to hear your jokes and sarcasm, cheer for every feat you accomplish, and support you when you're upset. I want every second of now and the future with you. So, Aliya Rathburn of Terra, will you marry me?" Caspian extended his right fist between us, and then he opened his hand.

In his hand was a ring. At first glance it looked like *the ring*, the one I'd plucked off the floor when I found Caspian drunk and devastated in his cabin upon the *Starfire*. The ring he carried with him every single day as a reminder of the tragedy he suffered in his past.

But this wasn't the ring he'd hoped to use when he proposed to Leila. It was similar, but this was unique.

The double silver band ended at a circle covered with navigational directions, and within it was a stunning, golden compass rose. The twelve-pointed star supported a single, shimmering diamond that reflected the weak moonlight.

That star – the mark of the Nova squad – meant so much to me. It symbolized the family I'd found with the Nova squad. It was the strength I'd embraced when protecting them. And it guided me toward Caspian.

Toward where I was always meant to be.

Tears streamed down my face, and my breaths came in gasps. "Yes! Yes, yes, a billion times yes!"

Caspian beamed as he slid the ring onto my finger and stood. "I love you so much," he said as his own happy tears started to fall.

With one hand he brushed away a few of my tears, and his other wrapped around my hips, pulling me as close to him as possible. My hands came to rest atop his chest as I replied, "I love you now and forever, Caspian Tassarion."

And as his lips claimed mine, I could've sworn that the stars overhead shone just a bit brighter.

This time I followed Caspian back to his room where we spent the night kissing, talking about our dreams for the future, and basking in the incredible moment.

My heart had never been so full of love as it was that night.

When I came to in the morning, the first sight that greeted me was my sparkling ring as my hand rested atop Caspian's chest. Thin rays of golden sunlight snuck around the thick curtains covering the windows in his room and added to the shimmering, bubbly feeling that threatened to burst out of my chest.

Every morning from here forward can be like this, I realized with a smile. Caspian could be the last thing I'd see at night and the first in the morning. It sounded like heaven.

His breathing stuttered, and Caspian sighed before shifting to wrap his arms around me. With a start, his eyes flew open. My name on his tongue was the only warning I received before his lips joined mine for a toe-curling kiss.

"Good morning to you too," I said with a laugh after we'd had our fill of each other.

In reply, Caspian snuggled closer to me, taking a long and shaky breath before saying, "I was worried that it was just an incredible dream. But you're here, and you said yes…"

He looked down at me, and I was touched by the amount of adoration I saw in his crystalline gaze. While it was silly for him to think that last night had been a dream, I wanted to pinch myself to make sure that this was really happening.

"You're sure you mean it? You want to spend forever with me?" Caspian had the audacity to look concerned.

"Are you kidding?" I playfully smacked his arm. "I'd gladly spend forever and then some with you."

"Good." And then he kissed me once more.

Some time later we decided that it wasn't entirely professional to skip our guard shifts, and propelled by growling stomachs, we reluctantly untangled ourselves from the bedsheets and prepared for the day.

While I braided back the tangled mess that was supposed to be my hair, Caspian went to his closet and put on a fresh shirt. Now *that* was a sight I wouldn't mind seeing every day.

I sat on the edge of the bed as he prowled back toward me with a hooded stare that made my cheeks hot.

"Keep looking at me like that, and I just might quit my guard job on the spot," I teased.

"I wouldn't mind that," he purred. "Then I'd get more time with you."

I sighed. "If only." Caspian and I were driven to protect others, and neither of us could turn away from the danger that now threatened the King's Galaxy without feeling some degree of guilt.

Caspian held out a hand, and once I was standing, he pulled me in close. "We'll find a way to stop the attacks, and then you and I will find a peaceful planet where we can spend the rest of our lives together. How does that sound?"

I tucked my head against his chest. "That sounds perfect."

He kissed the top of my head. "Aliya, I—" Caspian cleared his throat. "I want to tell King Locklyn and Queen Estella about our engagement. It's not that we have to seek their approval, but I don't want it coming as a surprise to them when we both eventually resign."

"Okay." It did make sense since we technically worked for the king, but I wondered if there was a possibility that King Locklyn would disapprove. "Is there anything I need to do?"

Caspian was quiet for a few moments as he thought. "I'm not sure. I don't want to go right to him with the announcement, but I'm not sure when the best time will be. We might have to keep this a secret for a little while until I can have a few moments alone with the king."

I nodded. "Maybe I shouldn't wear the ring out in the open like this." It certainly was the fastest way for people to see that I'd become engaged overnight.

A flicker of sadness passed over Caspian's face as he pressed a kiss to the knuckles of my left hand. "I love seeing it on you, but I think you're right. Here," he said as he walked over to his desk. "I used to keep it on a small chain. Perhaps you could use this."

Caspian held up a silver necklace chain – the perfect size for the ring and for me to wear. I accepted it from him and slipped the ring on before closing the clasp around my neck. "It's perfect." I held it up for him to see before tucking the ring beneath my shirt. "And now only we know it's there," I said as I smiled up at him.

He beamed. "Thank you, Aliya. We'll get it back on your finger in no time."

"I can't wait."

Caspian and I got breakfast together and encountered Ki'ran, Elgin, and Seradon along the way. They chatted about their latest shifts and the tension present throughout the palace. Last night two separate reports came in: there had been another, smaller, attack on Charra, and Vanthurium had successfully shot down a Krech ship attempting to enter the planet's atmosphere.

"It seems like the king's meeting today couldn't come soon enough," Caspian remarked. "I only hope we can come up with good countermeasures. What we've been doing isn't working."

There were murmurs of agreement and then the sounds of breakfast being eaten.

Of course, the first thing we'd hear this morning is more bad news. The blows against the King's Galaxy just kept coming, one after another after another, and all the soldiers — not just us prince's guards — were chomping at the bit to take action.

In this moment, last night really seemed like a wonderful dream. How could Caspian and I be so blissfully happy when panic and fear were running rampant throughout the galaxy?

I felt selfish for wishing that the conflict would simply dissolve or that Caspian and I wouldn't have to play a role in it. Maybe it was foolish for becoming engaged right when our services were likely needed for battle, but if something went wrong…

No. I stopped the thought before it could go further. We'd been in danger together before, and we'd survived each time. If we were sent to fight the Krech, I knew that we'd both make it out and could return to the happiness we'd just started.

I could feel the ring, a small but pleasant weight, as it sat right above my heart. I was dying to prance about and shout to everyone how I was Caspian's and Caspian was *mine*, but I'd made a promise. For now, we'd keep quiet. The time for the joyous announcement would come later.

Caspian must have noticed how deep in thought I was because he bumped my leg under the table. The playful touch brought a smile to my face, but I kept my head down so that my reaction wasn't too obvious to the others.

I should've known better.

"Aliya," Ki'ran said in his deep voice, "you look as if you are in a better mood than normal today."

"Oh, did something *happen* last night?" Elgin teased and waggled his eyebrows.

"No!" Caspian and I blurted at the same time. We turned to look at each other, and I blushed while Caspian cleared his throat.

"It wasn't like that," he clarified, directing his attention back to Elgin.

"Really," I added when Elgin continued to look amused and skeptical. "The night was… really lovely last night, and um, we both had a good time watching it." *The night was lovely? Really, Aliya? He definitely won't buy that*, I mentally scolded myself.

Fortunately, he seemed to drop the issue. "Fine, keep your secrets. But you do seem more cheerful than normal, Al."

"Al?"

He shrugged. "Just trying a new nickname. Sometimes Aliya can be a mouthful."

I hesitated, unsure if he was making a joke or not, before attempting to back up my previous, lame explanation. "I mean it. Caspian and I just had a good time searching for the center of the hedge maze yesterday evening."

That earned another mischievous grin from Elgin. I groaned and let my head sink into my hands. There was nothing I could say that he wouldn't attempt to twist.

Before I could put my foot further into my mouth, I was saved by the bell. Well, chime.

Our cuffs went off at the same time, a chorus of high-pitched pings which drew the attention of the other guards sitting around us.

"Prince Damien needs us already?" Caspian asked. It was more to himself than to any of us.

"Earlier meeting, go figure," Seradon announced, having read the message faster than the rest of us.

Grabbing one last quick bite of breakfast, I stood with the others and followed them out of the banquet hall.

King Locklyn's council room wasn't too far, but with his new commitment to staying on schedule, Prince Damien had likely already taken his seat.

I felt far more anxious for this meeting than I had for any of the ones I'd attended in the past few weeks. It wasn't just that the entire council would be present; no, it was that this gathering was to determine what action we would take against our enemies.

Action that would undoubtedly put lives in danger.

I tried to shake off the dread I felt when imagining myself heading off into battle once more, but I couldn't get it to budge.

Being ambushed on Charra had been just that – a blindside. The Nova squad had been summoned to inspect suspicious activity at Master Yornuk's request, and we certainly hadn't anticipated running into those four Krech. The only reason we'd survived that encounter was because I finally decided to accept the version of me that Doctor Givray created.

And on Vanthurium… we'd been surprised. While we knew that they'd been threatened, no one knew when the Krech were going to attack and if they were going to attack. In the end, it hadn't even been them — they'd sent murderous cyborgs to terrorize Lord Galven and Lady Kalina's home. Being backed into a corner, literally, had forced us all to fight to the best of our abilities, and even then, we'd been lucky to walk away from it. Well, almost all of us.

Heading off to fight the Krech this time would be extremely different. There would be no surprise attack, no unclear plan of escape. We'd be bringing the fight to them, knowing full well how dangerous they were.

It was starting to seem, however, that there wasn't another option that would end their unprovoked attacks. Too many lives had been lost for King Locklyn's guards and armies to sit back on their heels any longer.

If only we knew just *where* to take the fight.

As usual, the council room was lit by natural light streaming through the wide, ceiling-to-floor windows. They offered a wonderful view out onto the airfield, but today it was empty, with only a few ships and cruisers still grounded and awaiting orders.

Walking beside Caspian, we circled the half-moon table to sit in the row of chairs along the back wall of the room. Each wall held chairs for the councilmembers' and king's guards, but we sat along the back because Prince Damien decided to sit directly in the middle of the curved table.

Omri and Ney nodded to us as we took our seats.

As we settled in, Prince Damien turned to look at us. "Captain.

Team. Thank you for coming quickly. I'm not sure why my father moved this meeting up, but I, for one, am glad that we can decide on our course of action before we get word of another attack." Prince Damien scowled and then pointed to the three former Nova members. "You've seen and fought Krech before. If there's anything that comes to mind which you might deem important or helpful, do not hesitate to share it with the council."

"Of course, my prince," Caspian replied. He looked like he was about to say more, but the council had finally arrived.

The first one into the chamber was Garath Brut. The Callaisan Master of Currency was short and rotund without a single hair on the top of his egg-shaped head. His bushy eyebrows nearly concealed two dark, beady eyes that raked over us guards as we stood to greet him. With a swish of his formal, deep blue council robes, he selected the high-backed chair at the far end of the table and stood while he waited for the arrival of his companions.

Next one through the door was Silene Essa, Master of Medicine. Although I probably should have formally met the graceful Schlee female before now, we'd only ever been around each other at meetings like this one. However, I was afraid that if I introduced myself, she'd say something about my history with Doctor Givray. And the last thing I wanted was to call unnecessary attention to myself.

She glided into the room, dressed in the same style robe as Garath Brut save for it being yellow, and claimed the seat next to Prince Damien, leaving a chair between her and the Master of

Currency. It was far closer to me than she'd sat in previous meetings, and I resisted the urge to dip my head and avoid eye contact. After all, there was no doubt that she, too, knew my name.

Fallon Vo-Qi, the Master of Trade who bore a shocking resemblance to Gunther and Gráinne, and Corvius Lontarre, the stern and rugged Master of Defense, arrived next and were deep in conversation.

After the first council meeting Prince Damien attended, I questioned Caspian about Yornuk, the quirky 'Master of Trade,' on Charra.

"Self-proclaimed," Caspian had replied with a laugh. "He's managed to wriggle his way to the top of Charran society by controlling all avenues of trade onto and off Charra."

It barely made sense to me, but then again, so did Yornuk.

Fallon's olive robes were heavily wrinkled, as if he hadn't cleaned them since the last council meeting and had donned them in a hurry today, and his short reddish-brown hair stuck up in odd tufts. I pitied the Master of Trade. His industry had largely been the focus of the Krech's attacks, and I could only imagine the amount of stress he must be under to maintain and protect his remaining trade partnerships.

It came as no surprise when he took the seat next to Corvius on the far side of the table and continued their hushed discussion. The Master of Defense looked severe in his black robes which, in direct contrast to Fallon, were pristine. Everything about the male exuded the feeling of control – from the clean lines of his blonde buzz cut to his tidy and trimmed fingernails. I couldn't quite place where he was from; Corvius looked like a combination of Ki'ran's bulk and brunt nature with a Callaisan's pale skin.

He'd lead today's meeting and give advice that held the most weight. I knew very little about the male, so I hoped that his logic was sensible.

The final councilmember, Acacius Urgo, Master of Law, glided into the room wearing gray robes. The rail-thin male resembled a specter more than any other species I knew. Long, black hair hung to his shoulders in limp locks. His pallid skin seemed as if it were stretched thin over sharp cheekbones, and the deep shadows around his dark eyes never seemed to fade.

He was the one person whom I'd never want to encounter outside of these chambers, and unfortunately, he took the seat between Silene and Garath. It was far too close for my liking, but he didn't seem like the talkative type as he sat down without acknowledging the prince or his guards.

Greetings were quiet as the council settled in and observed us. Despite accepting Prince Damien back into the council chambers after his miraculous attitude shift, none of the council were overly pleasant to him.

That behavior carried into today – Prince Damien received a few nods but wasn't drawn into the smaller conversations that the elite individuals initiated with each other. Fortunately, the awkward exclusion didn't last for long.

King Locklyn marched into the council chamber, a shining

crown atop his graying locks and no less than five guards in tow. While we were able to wear our everyday guard uniform, the king's guards sported head to toe navy armor, complete with a helmet.

"They're wearing the new blastgear," Caspian leaned over and whispered to me.

"What's that?"

"Some new combination of metals and fibers that is supposed to repel blaster shots. It's lighter than our usual armor, and rumor has it that it's able to withstand insane levels of heat. I hope they have enough for all of us."

My shoulder ached with the memory of being hit on Vanthurium. The pain and smell of burning flesh had been horrible, and I hoped that this new armor would hold up to its hype.

Claiming the final chair which sat across from the Master of Currency, King Locklyn took a moment to pass his keen eyes over every individual in the room.

His crow's feet and the creases at the corners of his mouth seemed more prominent today. It was as if he was completely engulfed in an air of exhaustion. The dire reports and concern over where the next attack would strike were truly beginning to wear on the king.

Resting his elbows atop the wooden table, King Locklyn rested his chin atop folded hands before closing his eyes. The room was silent enough to hear a pin drop for several long seconds while we waited for our king to speak.

When he reopened his eyes, there was a fierce determination burning within their hazel core. I could feel the air in the room shift, and several individuals sat up straighter.

"This has gone on long enough," King Locklyn announced, authority oozing from every syllable. "How do we stop the Krech?"

"We are *not* sending soldiers off into that… that void! We've already lost too many as it is!"

After two hours of updates and debates, the council was no closer to deciding on a course of action than they were when we began.

King Locklyn had opened the meeting with several updates: various sightings of Krech ships darting about the Outer Rim, another attack – this time on a Protective Forces ship – that occurred on the close side of the Outer Rim, and the proposed defensive strategies for planets located near the Rim and where previous attacks occurred.

All in all, the outlook was grim.

Two-thirds of the galaxy's standing military had already been deployed to run patrols and form a defensive line between the

King's Galaxy and where Kāäs potentially was. Of those units, six ships had been destroyed in Krech-related attacks, losing nearly one thousand soldiers. The losses that civilians faced, however, were far higher.

King Locklyn even described the attempts to draw information out of the Krech prisoner. I was surprised to hear him mention it since the monster had practically been snuck onto the Protective Forces base and hidden from all soldiers, but of course the council would have known. He neglected to mention the torture the creature had experienced, but Caspian and I played dumb, acting like this was all new information.

Once the reports had been delivered, the three former Nova squad members were put in the spotlight.

King Locklyn asked each of us in turn to describe our encounter with the Krech on Charra. What had their ship looked like? Had we seen the blasters they used? How did they move when they attacked – as individual opponents or as a group?

I was especially nervous to recount my time actually fighting them. The council nodded as I spoke, indicating that they'd heard the same story previously, but I didn't miss the gleam in a few of their eyes – Silene, Corvius, and Acacius regarded me as if I were a weapon at their disposal.

It was like the Protective Forces all over again.

Once every detail had been wrung from Caspian, Ki'ran, and myself, the debates began.

The Masters of Currency and Trade were loudly arguing for a

full-scale assault – all available soldiers should be sent into Kāäs to locate the Krech home planet and "destroy the root of this evil," as Fallon Vo-Qi had stated. His industry was suffering greatly because the multitude of Krech attacks had been on trade ships, and now very few interplanetary deals were being struck or fulfilled.

Since the two industries were related, it came as no surprise when Garath Brut, the Master of Currency, sided with the anxious redhead.

Silene Essa, Master of Medicine, advocated against such action, citing how many soldiers would likely be lost in such an attack. Her soft voice carried around the room as she brought up the current death toll and the limited number of resources available for healing in the field. With no easy way to transport soldiers back out of Kāäs and to a healing facility, she argued that it would be a reckless waste of soldiers' lives.

Acacius Urgo was a surprisingly neutral party. As Master of Laws, Acacius supported both sides by quoting laws and precedents that the council swore to uphold. He also reminded everyone how *a threat to even a single planet is a threat to all* but that *the cost of a victory should not be measured in lives lost.*

I almost wished the specter-like male wouldn't speak. Every time he opened his mouth to quote a law or philosophy, the debates became more heated.

The loudest opponent to Garath and Fallon, however, was Corvius Lontarre. He trusted his soldiers and vouched for their skills, but he vehemently refused to send them into Kāās in search of a planet that no one knew even existed.

I wondered if Fallon regretted choosing the seat next to the Master of Defense.

"But the longer we wait, the more men and resources we lose! We will have defeated ourselves before the full Krech armada arrives, if it even does!" Garath slammed his fist on the table in emphasis.

"We send all our trained soldiers into Kāās. Then what? Say they never find that damn planet – we'll have left ourselves nearly defenseless," Corvius shouted back.

Prince Damien nodded. "I agree with Master Corvius on this point. Our defenses are spread thin enough as is. Sending any number of soldiers into that darkness severely cripples our ability to keep our people safe."

"Is that true, Corvius?" King Locklyn finally stepped into the debate. "Are we unable to afford even a few ships?"

Corvius opened his mouth then snapped it shut. He brushed a large hand down his face with an aggravated sigh. "Statistically, we can afford a few." He looked up at his king and held his hands out wide. "But for what purpose? We have no idea where to begin searching! It's impossible—"

"We do have a theory," Fallon cut in. "The majority of planetary and ship-focused attacks have occurred around Charra. I'd say it's more than reasonable to send a scouting party out from that sector. After all," here Fallon turned to King Locklyn, "we haven't detected an armada lingering on the fringe of the Rim. We wouldn't be sending those soldiers into a trap."

Silene shook her head and spoke up before the king could reply. "We've failed to detect the few Krech ships that have entered the Outer Rim. Who's to say that they haven't developed a way to cloak their ships?"

Her suggestion brought a halt to the debates. It was widely accepted that no one knew much about the Krech. When I and the rest of the Nova squad saw them on Charra for the first time, the previous assumption that they were solitary creatures had been shattered.

Although… The Krech had launched attacks in the devastating war over one hundred years ago. Surely they hadn't been singular threats back then. I wondered how the assumption about their nature began.

"If only we had stronger weapons of our own," Silene continued in a quieter voice. I didn't miss the way her golden eyes skipped over to me for a second.

My hands balled into fists in my lap. I *was not* the solution to this problem. It was a far larger threat than I could ever defeat. Even if Silene was referencing Doctor Givray's work – recreating my physical alterations with other beings – there was no guarantee that those individuals would be prepared for a battle against the deadliest enemy known to the King's Galaxy.

Unless one side conceded or King Locklyn decreed a definitive course of action, this argument was going to end in a stalemate.

We all agreed that *something* should be done, but the potential loss of life wasn't worth a blind attack.

It seemed that King Locklyn had reached the same conclusion. Rising slowly from his seat, he placed his hands palm-down on the table and took a deep breath. "I have greatly appreciated hearing from all of you. This is certainly not a matter to take lightly. I respect and value all members of this galaxy, and the loss of one life is a blow to everything I and my forefathers built. And we've lost too many thus far." He paused and met the stare of every single person in the room, ensuring that they were giving his words their full attention. "I have not come to this decision easily, but if we maintain our current course of discussion, we will reach an impasse. We cannot afford to waste more time. Therefore, I have decided that we shall—"

The door to the council chamber flew open and slammed against the wall. In the doorway stood a red-faced messenger. The golden buttons of his navy jacket were mismatched, as if he'd hastily thrown it on before running here.

What stood out the most, however, was how deathly pale his face was.

"Your majesty," the young male panted, "we received—a distress signal. It came from—Aquillo." He doubled over and gasped for breath.

The councilmembers and soldiers leapt to their feet in an explosion of noise. Fallon shouted how they should've taken action sooner while Corvius demanded additional details.

In the midst of the chaos, Caspian's hand found mine. I was grateful for his touch, but this time it didn't manage to soothe the panic that gripped my body.

"Silence!" King Locklyn thundered. The room acquiesced but remained standing, and the solemn king turned to the messenger who had finally recovered. "When, exactly, did you receive this message?"

"Only moments ago, sire. I ran here as fast as I could once we decoded the signal."

"And what exactly did it say?"

The boy gulped. "A fleet of unknown ships was headed their way. They couldn't make contact, so they assume…"

"They assume it's the Krech," King Locklyn finished. "Did the message say how many ships there were?"

"Three or four, majesty. But they appear to be small, like cruisers."

King Locklyn abruptly turned away from the messenger and faced Corvius. "Have three warships prepared for immediate deployment. Is the *Hellfire* still grounded?" The Master of Defense nodded in reply. "Include them in the three. Schedule takeoff in half an hour, or less."

Corvius bowed to his king and jogged from the room.

Then King Locklyn turned to his son. "I would like to borrow some of your guards, if you would allow it."

Prince Damien bowed deeply. "Of course, father. They are at your disposal." The prince glanced back at where Caspian, Ki'ran, and I stood, and I could've sworn there was a flicker of sadness in his eyes.

The king turned to the three former Nova squad soldiers. "I ask that you accompany these soldiers. While you have only fought the Krech once, your experience is invaluable, and I would like you to instruct your peers. Keep them safe."

We couldn't refuse our king, not that any of us even wanted to, so we bowed deeply. "It would be our honor," Caspian solemnly replied.

"Good. Then get ready for immediate departure. I have new armor for each of you; wear it today." Good; I'd feel a lot more comfortable heading into this mess while wearing the new blastgear.

Without another word, we left the room to prepare for battle.

"Engines working at full capacity. We should be within range in approximately fifteen minutes," Adís' first in command announced.

With three ships sent to intercept the Krech fleet, Caspian decided that it was best if the three of us split up. I ended up on the *Hellfire* with Adís.

"How come we didn't get new, fancy gear?" she teased as she rapped the plating that covered me from head to toe.

"I'm not sure. Maybe there isn't enough to go around yet." It felt wrong that I was in sturdier armor than Adís, especially since she still needed the mo-wear in order to walk. I even offered to give it to her, but she declined, insisting that my suit had likely been made specifically for me.

It certainly felt that way. The blastgear looked like overlapping, octagonal scales that responded incredibly well to every movement. Form-fitting and flexible, I was also pleasantly surprised at how light it was.

Initially open in the back, the suit had responded to my body the moment I stepped in by closing around me and adjusting to my size. The scales over my cuff had even gone translucent so that I could see and use my communication bracelet.

I just hoped that I didn't need to test the blastgear's durability so soon.

In a more serious tone Adís asked, "Are you ready?"

I let out a short, harsh laugh. "No. I knew it was inevitable, but I'd hoped that I wouldn't have to head into another battle ever again."

Adís was quiet at my side for a few moments. "I get what you mean. When I was being shuffled from healing facility to healing facility, doctor to doctor, I swore to myself that I'd never fight again. I didn't want to go through that again." Her voice hitched, and I looked down to see her wipe away a single tear. "When the king asked me to captain the greatest warship he'd ever owned, I accepted without hesitation. I've always been a pilot, and even losing the use of my legs didn't keep me from choosing that path all over again. I certainly don't regret it," she said as she looked up at me.

"I get that. Battles are horrible, but it's also where I need to be. No one can do what I do, and that's why I needed to be here."

"Right," Adís replied. Then she elbowed me in the ribs. "No need to fret! The *Hellfire* is the strongest ship in the galaxy. We'll end this before the fighting even has the chance to get dirty."

I smiled at her enthusiasm. "I sure hope so."

My thoughts drifted to Caspian aboard one of the other ships. He'd gone with a large number of the king's personal guard on what Adís declared was the second-best ship in the galaxy. While I believed that he would do everything to keep himself out of harm's way, the possibility of losing him and not even being by his side weighed on me.

Our goodbye had been brief yet passionate – hungry, devouring kisses in the midst of desperate hands that held each other close. It wasn't nearly enough time, and something within me felt empty when Caspian unwillingly pulled away.

I prayed that it wouldn't be the last time I'd be with him.

"Sixty seconds." The pilot's voice was amplified throughout the bridge and the rest of the ship.

There wouldn't be much I could do from the interior of the *Hellfire*, but if the Krech somehow managed to breach her hull, I was supposed to dispatch them.

Adís settled into her captain's chair while I gripped the railing that circled behind her. I could feel the ship's engines slow as we dropped out of lightspeed.

"Standby for initial contact. In five, four, three, two, one…"

The *Hellfire* rocked as we reached our destination. We held our position as we waited for the other two ships to drop out of lightspeed and assessed the situation.

Just as the report indicated, four smaller ships lingered just outside Aquillo's atmosphere. They were an odd group, all differing slightly from the others in terms of size and shape. And just like on Charra, these ships appeared as if they'd been constructed in a piecemeal fashion — scraps of metal in different sizes and colors had been welded together.

I had no doubt that each of the four vessels carried Krech. Although there was no way to tell how many beings occupied each ship, I considered us to be at an advantage. Our warships were larger and had more blasters, including several with long range capabilities. We were trained soldiers prepared to fight to the death to protect our galaxy. And once the other two ships arrived, we would have the upper hand.

Or so we thought.

Yes, the Krech ships waited outside of Aquillo's firing range, but they weren't even facing the aqueous planet. The four ships were facing us.

Adís swore and punched the radio button that would allow her to contact the king's other ships. "*Talimore* and *Renegade*, come in. It's a trap. I repeat, it's a trap! Disengage from the arrival point. Over," she shouted.

Lifting her finger from the button, she waited for the reply.

There was only static.

"What the… Did we damage our comms?" Adís snapped at the nearest crew member.

The tall female with a lizard-like snout conferred with a monitor near her before addressing her captain. "No, ma'am. All systems functional."

"What's going on then?" Adís punched the button once more. "*Talimore* and *Renegade*, come in! I repeat, come in!"

Once more the bridge filled with the sound of radio static.

"They're jamming us," I whispered in horror.

"What?" Adís whipped around to look at me.

"There's no other explanation. They're jamming your radio signal. We need to get out of here!"

It took only a second for Adís to spring into motion. "Evasive maneuvers, *now!* We must draw their attention away from this spot before the other ships arrive!" she barked to her crew. "Aliya, you might want to strap in."

I nodded and retreated to one of the crew seats several paces behind me. The leathery seat was plush beneath my back as I scrabbled to fasten the x-shaped harness across my chest. Right after I got it locked into place, the *Hellfire* rolled to the right before plunging downward.

A second later, and we would've been blown to bits. Through the front window we watched four streaks of red light race for the space we'd previously occupied.

"Get them to chase us!" Adís shouted.

The *Hellfire* rolled again, righting itself before racing away from the Krech ships and Aquillo. I tried to ignore the sick feeling in my stomach as the g-forces acted upon my body. I didn't need to get sick on the bridge while we were running for our lives.

"Three in pursuit," Adís' second announced.

"Stars and supernovas, how did they know we were coming?" Adís asked aloud. When no one answered her, she pounded the armrest of her seat with a fist. "Circle back. That last ship is waiting on our backup which will be arriving at any moment."

We'd taken off first, and because the *Hellfire* was so powerful, we'd traveled the distance from Callais to Aquillo in a much shorter time than our companions. Undoubtedly, Adís regretted that decision now.

Our warship whipped around again, executing a double roll as it dodged blasts from the ships behind us, and we flew directly at the last Krech ship lying in wait outside Aquillo.

"Rear path clear, no chance of hitting backup. Fire at will!"

We opened fire upon the enemies behind us. I couldn't see the shots, but I felt each *boom* from the blasters in my chest.

"They're here!" Adís shouted.

Indeed, the *Talimore* and *Renegade* had finally reached Aquillo. No doubt they'd be in shock to see us already engaged with the enemy when only a few minutes had passed since we dropped out of lightspeed.

They split, the *Talimore* coming behind us to help pick off the three ships while the *Renegade* looped away and circled around the final Krech ship.

"Direct hit! One target destroyed!" Adís' co-pilot announced. I wanted to cheer, but we hadn't secured a victory just yet.

The sharp motions of the ship were making me nauseous, and I looked down to discover that my fingers had ripped into the padding on my seat's armrests. The metal beneath was slightly bent from my grip, but I didn't let up as the ship plunged to avoid a shot from behind.

"*Talimore* has taken out another!"

"Yes! Let's finish this!" Adís cheered. It was two against three, the advantage finally on our side.

But it was then that everything went wrong.

The Krech ship that *Renegade* had previously been engaging flipped nose over tail into a downward dive. Its small size gave it an advantage in changing direction faster than *Renegade*, and it streaked downward. Toward the *Hellfire*.

"Evade! Evade!" Adís screamed as we became sandwiched between two enemy ships.

They fired on us.

The impact was bone-shaking as the *Hellfire* took damage. The entire ship shuddered, and I was thrown forward into my harness. Adís hadn't been strapped in and wasn't so lucky. She flew forward, smacking against the back of the co-pilot's chair in front of her.

"Adís!" I screamed.

She groaned weakly as the downward gravity kept her flat against the back of the chair.

I unbuckled myself and slid across the floor. "Adís, hey. Look at me. Open your eyes, please," I begged. *Don't let this happen again!*

"I'm… fine," she finally managed to say. "Status?"

"Rear engines gone. Several significant punctures. And we're dropping," the co-pilot read from the cracked screen in front of her.

I looked around the bridge, not liking what I saw. Adís had been lucky that there was another chair to break her fall. A few members of her crew hadn't been so lucky.

Another blast rocked the ship, and I wrapped my arms around Adís, holding the both of us against the back of the chair. Now the *Hellfire* was seriously dropping.

"Entering atmosphere. Shields holding at sixty-three percent," the co-pilot announced. "Brace for potential impact!"

The speed of our descent pulled at my body, threatening to rip me away from Adís. I held on for dear life, praying that the *Hellfire's* shields would lessen the impact enough that we'd make it through this.

I cried as the fear of dying – again – took hold. I'd always been so worried about losing Caspian, that I hadn't even imagined that I could be the one to go first. I cried for myself. For him. For more lives lost in this horrible war.

Beneath me, the blastgear began to shift. The scales parted, and I pulled Adís against me as the armor closed around us. Once we were sealed inside the strange gear, I felt it thicken, as if it knew what was coming.

The roar of re-entry drowned out all other sounds as we raced toward Aquillo's surface. Inside the armor I could hear my breathing and Adís', and then I heard a small chime. My cuff had received a message.

In another oddly intuitive move, the blastgear displayed the note I'd just received on a screen inside the scales covering my face.

We've had a breakthrough! You're no longer alone. GG.

Despite the horror and sadness I felt, I somehow managed to be shocked by Doctor Givray's message. They did it? He and the twins managed to replicate my abilities? How? On whom? And what about—

At that moment, the *Hellfire* slammed into one of Aquillo's sandy islands, and my world went black.

My entire body hurt.

From the tips of my toes all the way up to the hair follicles on my scalp, I ached. I kept my eyes closed as my body took a mental inventory of my agony.

This is what that car crash should have *felt like*, a little voice inside my head said.

But no, I survived the car crash – Doctor Givray saved me. I didn't feel any of that pain, so this must be… Memories, blurred with pain, flashed through my mind.

The four Krech ships.

A wild chase in the airspace above Aquillo.

The *Hellfire* crashing.

Adís!

I struggled to open my eyes. If I was thinking and feeling pain, then somehow I had survived the crash landing on Aquillo. And if I survived, hopefully Adís did too.

Slowly, my eyes cracked open to reveal the dimmest light I'd ever seen. Yet through the shadows I could see gray, porous stone. Similar to a honeycomb but with far less symmetry and organization, the rock in front of my eyes was lumpy and misshapen, with holes ranging from a pinprick to ones that could swallow me whole.

Is this what lies beneath Aquillo's sandy islands?

I groaned aloud as I sat up, the muscles in my arms and back protesting loudly as I pushed into a seated position.

I was in… a cave?

The odd rock ceiling hadn't been an anomaly – the irregular holes trickled down the curved walls to my left and right, and they continued down the tunnel in front of me. Oddly, the ground beneath my feet was solid. Brushing my fingers against its surface, I mentally confirmed that it was, indeed, stone without a layer of dust or dirt on its surface.

"What is this place?" I asked aloud. My ears strained to pick up another sound as my question echoed off the cave walls.

My first instinct was to panic, but I knew that wouldn't help me think through this situation clearly.

I was alone, in an unfamiliar place, and terribly sore. This place was also really, really cold. A shiver wracked my body as I went to wrap my arms around my torso.

And then I did panic.

The blastgear, which had presumably saved my life during the *Hellfire's* crash, was completely gone. There wasn't a scale left covering my body, and I was left in the skin tight black suit I'd been instructed to wear under the armor.

At least I'd ignored the recommendation to not wear boots under the blastgear. The floor immediately around me felt smooth enough, but there was no telling what I could encounter in this tunnel.

Someone had to have removed the blastgear… after the crash? Unless it had been destroyed upon impact – a highly unlikely option since I was alive.

I patted my neck and chest, frantic as I searched for the small lump that should have been present under the suit. When I finally found the necklace with Caspian's ring, which had twisted around to my back, I sobbed in relief.

Despite the protection that the armor provided, Caspian's ring was the one thing I couldn't stand to lose.

I shivered again and decided that I couldn't remain sitting upon the cold ground any longer. If I could walk, I was going to find out exactly where I was.

Brushing my hands down my legs, I found a few sore spots but no broken bones, so I decided to test my luck on two legs. Again, it took a good deal of effort to make my muscles move the way I wanted, but I eventually managed to stand on my two, wobbly legs.

But now where would I go?

It was like I'd literally been left in the middle of a cavernous hallway. Each side of the tunnel faded into impenetrable darkness, so I couldn't immediately detect a clear path that would take me back to the surface.

My chest began to constrict. I was lost, most likely trapped. I was separated from everyone else on the warship, and I hadn't even heard from Caspian since we'd arrived outside Aquillo.

I attempted to activate my cuff and was further disheartened when it failed to even light up. I didn't think it was broken because it was still wrapped around my wrist, but something wasn't right. I assumed that if it ever truly died, it would simply fall off. But what did I know?

At this moment, nothing.

My eyes filled with tears as I looked back and forth between my two possible paths. What if one way led further into the cave? What if I picked a direction but fell into some hole that I couldn't see?

In a burst of anger, I cursed Doctor Givray for not altering my eyes so that they could see in the dark.

But getting into this situation wasn't his fault. It wasn't necessarily mine either, but right now I was the only one who could get myself out of it.

"Left it is, then," I mumbled as I shuffled down the path I'd laid eyes on when I first woke.

I took a few clumsy steps into the void before I realized that I did, in fact, have a light. Myself. Pinching the backs of my hands to get my circuits to light up, I started forward once more, this time slightly more confident with my choice of direction.

I traveled no more than ten steps when a faint echo sounded from behind me.

My heart leapt into my throat as I imagined various monsters slinking through the darkness toward me. Mutant spiders, or rock monsters, or things with long, sharp claws…

Aliya, stop it, I snapped at myself. *You can handle anything that tries to pick a fight with you.*

Unless, of course, they could see me before I saw them. My circuit-lights helped a little, but anything living down here would undoubtedly have the advantage of being able to see in the dark.

A shiver ran down my spine as I stopped walking. If something *was* coming toward me, I wanted to hear its approach.

There wasn't a single sound for several long seconds, but I waited patiently even as the cold began to seep into my bones. And then I was rewarded with a single word.

"Hello?"

Someone else was down here! Because of the echo, it was too hard to make out whom the voice possibly belonged to. But I knew one thing for certain: my companion in these tunnels wasn't Krech. The shout I heard was nothing like their low, hissing voices.

I changed direction and slowly made my way down the opposite hallway, sweeping my arms back and forth in front of me so that I wouldn't run into any walls or objects. The backs of my hands began to ache from the frequent pinches, but it was far more necessary to see, even a little bit, than worry about bruising my skin. It was agonizing enough that I needed to move slowly while someone was calling for help, but I couldn't take any chances in this unknown and mostly invisible terrain.

"Hello?" The voice was closer now that I was moving in the right direction, and this time I could tell that it was a female.

"Hello? Who's down here?" I called back.

"I was on the ship the *Hellfire*. We crashed... I can't walk..."

"Adís? It's Aliya! I'm coming!" I picked up my pace. "I can barely see. Keep making noise so I can find you."

I searched and searched, following the sounds of fingers tapping on rock. I was still terrified that I'd accidentally find myself tumbling down a hole in the floor, but knowing that Adís was so close made me bold.

Eventually her outline appeared in the dim light cast by my circuits. She sat flat on the floor with both legs stretched out in front of her. It didn't look like she was wearing my blastgear, so I assumed it was truly gone.

"Aliya?" she whispered as I drew close.

"Adís! I'm here, and I'm so glad I found you!" I held a hand out toward her seated form, and she grasped it with cold fingers. I fell to my knees and pulled her into a hug. "Stars, Adís. I thought we were going to die, and then I thought I was alone... I have no idea where we are," I rambled in a shaky voice. This time I didn't care as the tears spilled over.

"I know," she replied in a quiet voice. "I thought the same things too."

We stayed like that for a few moments, holding each other close and listening to every heartbeat and breath that signaled we were still alive.

Somehow, we'd both escaped death twice.

"Your legs?" I remembered she'd said she couldn't walk.

She sighed. "Something's damaged, and I'm guessing it's the connection between the port in my spine and the mo-wear. It almost feels like… I don't know, like something cracked the port."

"Do you think it was damaged in the crash?"

"No. I can feel some sharp pieces," she said, letting go with one arm so that she could touch the mechanism that had allowed her to walk, "as if something was stabbed into it."

I felt a chill, but this time it wasn't from the low temperature. "Adís, my blastgear is completely gone. I don't think it was destroyed in the crash either."

"You think it was… them?" Her voice dropped to a whisper.

"I don't know. Maybe? Right now, it's the only thing that makes sense."

Adís gulped, but she didn't reply again.

My armor was missing, and the one thing that allowed Adís to walk had been damaged. It wasn't a stretch to think it was all because of the *Hellfire* crashing, but considering that we'd been moved away from the site of the crash… I shuddered at the thought of the Krech touching me.

"They left us defenseless and immobilized. Why do you think that is?" Adís asked.

"I don't have a single clue. They told the cyborgs about me, and even the prisoner tried to attack me—"

"You saw the Krech prisoner?" Adís yelped and finally drew back. "How in all the systems did you manage that?"

"Um," I hesitated, not wanting to drag Caspian into this, "long story?" Adís huffed but didn't push me for details, so I continued with my previous train of thought. "They were waiting for us to arrive near Aquillo, and I'm assuming they had something to do with leaving us here. But how are we still alive?"

My question was met with silence. I didn't expect Adís to have an answer anyway, but it was troubling to imagine why the Krech would've gone through all the trouble of attacking Vanthurium if they were going to leave us – especially me – alive now.

"We need to find a way out of here." A sharp edge slipped into Adís' voice, the voice of a captain giving orders.

"How are we going to do that? We can't exactly see in this darkness, and you can't walk." I certainly didn't mind carrying her, but with my arms supporting her, I wouldn't be able to use them to keep from bumping into walls or other unseen obstacles.

"I don't know, but we have to try. Right? Besides, if we can reach the surface, someone will be able to find us."

"How?"

Adís rubbed at her unresponsive legs. "The mo-wear was built with a tracker. That way, if the gear failed and I was left without the use of my legs, someone could come to my rescue. I'm sure the tracker is active, but if we're deep beneath the surface of a planet, no one will be able to follow it."

"Okay." That was assuming the tracker hadn't been destroyed, but I didn't want to voice my concerns and shatter what little hope we had left.

We settled on me carrying Adís in my arms. I felt silly as I scooped her up princess-style, but she assured me it was for the best because she could be on guard for things in our path. I gave her permission to activate the circuits in my arms, and although she was hesitant at first, Adís caved when she realized it was the only way to create some illumination.

Something in my gut told me to continue in the direction where I'd found Adís, so we set off into the unknown.

✳

"Up… ahead – do you see… that?"

After what felt like hours of walking, the tunnel ahead was finally beginning to brighten.

The temperature had dropped considerably, and I clutched Adís to my chest as if she was a heated blanket. But even that did little to stop our shivering.

Strange as well was how much all this walking was impacting me. I'd never had trouble running with my modified body, but now I was wheezing and starting to gasp for breath.

"Stop here," Adís rasped.

"But we're so close!"

The light far before us was decent enough that she stopped pinching my arms, and I watched her shake her head. "Not safe. I think… I know where we are. Kind of."

"Where?"

"An asteroid."

"How… how is that even possible?"

She shook her head again, signaling that she didn't know. "Think about it. All stone. So cold. And hard to breathe."

I had no experiences to compare this to, but I couldn't imagine that being right. If we were in space, shouldn't we be completely unable to breathe? It was impossible – unless this asteroid was big enough to have developed its own atmosphere.

But wouldn't breathable air would require plants and other life forms?

I couldn't make sense of the situation, but I trusted Adís' judgment. She knew far more about space and the things in it than I did, and I couldn't deny that there was shift in the temperature and air quality.

"So now what?" Trekking further would possibly make our situation more unbearable, but we needed to get out of this place so that Adís' tracker could work.

"I think we need to wait," she murmured.

"Wait? Here, in the cold? With no protection? No food or water? What if no one comes for us?" My questions poured out in an angry and terrified stream because the thought of waiting here indefinitely seemed like a death sentence.

One of her hands found mine where it was wrapped around her legs. Curling her fingers around mine, she said, "Yes. That's all we can do."

I wanted to scream and cry, but instead I gently set Adís down upon the cold, hard ground and helped maneuver her so that she could sit and pull her knees to her chest. I knew it would be a waste of energy to pace, but I couldn't sit still as worried thoughts bounced around the inside of my skull.

After three passes I'd finally calmed down enough to realize that Adís was sitting in the cold – alone. Reluctantly, I quit my angered march and settled down beside her, wrapping my arms around her smaller frame.

"I don't want to give up," I whispered against her shoulder.

"They'll come for us. Just wait," she replied.

So, we waited.

And waited.

And waited.

At some point we'd given up on sitting upright and had curled together on the ground. Adís kept her arms around her shaking body while I tried to hold her together.

"C-C-Caspian. W-will. Find. Us," I managed to say through chattering teeth.

I wasn't sure if Adís nodded or shivered harder. "He is. S-s-so lucky. T-to have you."

"I. L-love. Him." She made a small sound in her throat in reply. "He p-p-proposed."

"He'll. Come."

After that we lapsed back into silence.

I must have drifted asleep because the next thing I knew, I could feel vibrations in the floor, like the pounding of feet. Something – or someone – was coming.

"Adís." My lips were too numb to say more than her name.

She grunted, and that was the only confirmation I needed that she was still alive.

Too cold and exhausted to move, we waited for the footsteps to reach us.

"I found them! They're over here. Hurry!" The voice was muffled as if it was coming through a thick mask.

Hands pulled at my arms as Adís was pried away from me. I tried to protest but my mouth wouldn't respond.

A beeping sound filled the air, and then it sounded a second time from right above me.

"They're both alive. Just barely. They need warmth and oxygen, stat!"

Someone maneuvered my unresponsive body into what felt like a thick sleeping bag. Only when the zipper closed it around me did I finally feel a speck of heat. For a moment my head was exposed, and then a helmet was placed over it. There was a click as it connected to the top of my cocoon and then a *whoosh* as oxygen finally filled my lungs.

"Aliya! Where is Aliya? Get out of my way!" I heard Caspian's desperate voice amid the cacophony of noise, but I couldn't muster the strength to open my eyes, even when a pair of strong arms wrapped around me. "Aliya, baby, can you hear me? Please look at me," he begged.

I'm here! I wanted to shout. But all I could manage was a weak, "Caspian." I wasn't even sure he could hear me through the helmet.

He fiercely clutched me to his chest. "I'm here, love. I'm here. I've got you, and I'm never letting go."

Reassured by the feel of his arms around me and the raw passion in his voice, I finally let myself slip back into a deep, dreamless sleep.

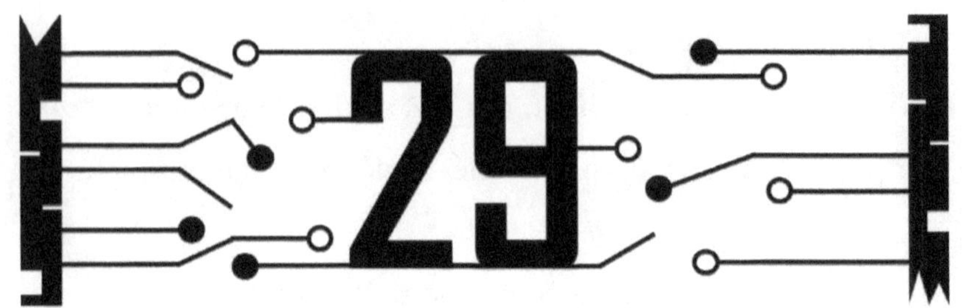

Thump, thump thump, thump.

There was a pause and then a soft scrape of a booted heel on metal.

Thump, thump thump, thump.

Over and over the thumps and scrapes went. And then I realized I could wake up.

My heavy eyelids fluttered as I fought for consciousness. *This whole waking up and having no clue where I am is becoming way too common.* The last thing I remembered was being so cold...

There was a sharp intake of breath. "Aliya?" The steps came closer and the surface I was on – definitely a bed – tilted. "Stars above, Aliya. I was so scared that I'd lost you forever," Caspian's voice trailed off into a whisper.

"I'm here," I mumbled as I finally came to.

A smooth, metal ceiling with canned lighting greeted me before Caspian's face came into focus. He looked horrible, as if he hadn't slept in days. Dark shadows circled his eyes, and his forehead was creased in worry.

But the relief in his sapphire eyes was what pushed me over the edge.

"Caspian," I sobbed as he pulled me close. "I thought I was going to die again! It was terrifying! Everything was going fine, we were winning, and then we were falling… Adís got hurt—oh no, Adís!" How could I forget that she'd been with me in that cold and horrible place? "Is she okay?"

"Shh, it's all right. You're both just fine. Somehow." I didn't miss the edge that slipped into his voice on that last word.

"What happened? Where are we now?" I pulled back so I could look him in the face.

"We're in the Scadian asteroid belt in the Outer Rim, maybe two days' travel from Charra. I can't believe we found you." Caspian's voice shook as he nestled into the spot between my neck and shoulder.

I relaxed, fully leaning into him. My body still ached, presumably from the crash and the excessive shivering, but I was finally warm. And safe.

"How *did* you find us?"

A tremor wracked Caspian's body as I clung to him, and my fingers began to trace idly up and down his back. "Right after *Hellfire* took its first hit, *Renegade* got targeted. Those two, tiny ships somehow managed to dodge us long enough to blow a hole in *Renegade's* side, and by then you were falling into Aquillo's atmosphere. There was no way for either of us to contact you or stop your descent, so we all watched in horror as you plummeted to the ground. We didn't even care about the Krech ships at that point." Caspian pressed a kiss to the side of my neck and straightened up, his hands sliding from my shoulders so that we could hold hands, and his eyes went glassy as he recalled the crash. "It was horrible. I thought… I thought I'd lost you, like— Once *Renegade* was stable, we went down to look for survivors. And then we saw the smallest of the Krech ships dart away from the wreckage."

"They came for us." My voice was hollow, and my stomach flipped in revulsion. "Were there any other survivors?"

Caspian slowly nodded. "All the crew was accounted for – except you two. We'd lost track of the Krech and had no idea what to do, so we contacted King Locklyn. He and Prince Damien urged us to return to Callais. We couldn't travel at lightspeed since *Renegade* was so damaged, so by the time we arrived, they had the whole fleet ready for takeoff."

"What? They sent the rest of the royal fleet after us?" *No way.*

"As many as they could afford, but yes. We're currently aboard the *Estella* and have about twenty other craft surrounding us."

The *Estella* was King Locklyn's personal warship. While *Talimore* and *Renegade* were deadly, nothing outclassed *Estella*. The story goes that each galactic king had a grand warship created at the beginning of their rule, and these ships were only used for ceremonial purposes… and war.

I gulped. "And we're headed back to Callais, right?"

Caspian's lips drew into a thin line as his eyes hardened. "Unfortunately, no. Following Adís' tracker this far made the king realize that we're exactly where we need to be to launch a counter-attack. This is exactly where we've been seeing the most Krech ships, so they think we can either search for their home planet starting from our current location or personally handle any that come our way."

"But we have no idea where to look! Wasn't that the point of the council meeting? That we *have no clue* where to find the planet that the Krech come from?"

"That's not how King Locklyn sees it. Apparently he was going to order the counter strike before we got the message from Aquillo."

I was floored. I thought our rational king wouldn't try to pull something like this when we'd already lost so many lives to the Krech, but I was wrong. Even with twenty-plus ships, sitting here in the Outer Rim was like painting a target on our back and closing our eyes. There was no way to tell when or where they'd strike again.

"And it's not just the fleet that's come out here," Caspian continued. "King Locklyn and Prince Damien are onboard as well." I felt my blood boil and opened my mouth to complain, but Caspian cut me off. "I know, I know. Believe me when I say that

I told them both how reckless of an idea that was. To lose one of them right now would be bad enough, but both…"

Caspian didn't need to continue. I could imagine the chaos that would engulf the King's Galaxy if they lost both their king and their prince. The two of them were taking a massive gamble, and I only hoped that we wouldn't be tested.

"Idiots," I mumbled under my breath.

Caspian laughed and then tilted my chin up. "You keep defying death. It scares me more than I've ever been scared before, but I thank the universe that you're alive."

"I promise that'll be the last time," I said with a chuckle.

He smiled in return. "I'm *very* happy to hear that."

And before he could make the move, I leaned in and kissed him with every last ounce of energy I possessed. I savored the moment – the feeling of being close to him, the raw passion with which he returned the kiss, and the ferocity as he tangled his fingers into my hair.

Unbidden, tears rolled down my face as we drank every drop of passion that the other could give. I thought I was going to lose Caspian in that pointless fight. All that we'd worked toward could have been lost in those awful moments, and for being newly engaged, this certainly wasn't a great start.

I didn't want to be away from him ever again because I wanted this moment, and all the ones to come, to be spent at his side. I'd travelled across the stars and faced death multiple times just to get here, and it was time for the danger to back off.

It was a pointless hope, given the current situation, but it was what I clung to as Caspian kissed my tears away and my heart became his once more.

✳

A wailing alarm broke the silence.

"What is that?" Over the sound of the alarm, I could hear running footsteps outside the door as if a mass of people were running away from something.

After I'd finally stopped crying and we'd both calmed down, Caspian had urged me to eat and get more rest, claiming that the cold and oxygen deprivation I'd experienced on the asteroid would take a toll on my body.

I'd only agreed once he promised to lay with me. I didn't want to sleep alone and wake to find myself in yet another new location.

It seemed as if Caspian had fallen asleep while holding me. His arms were wrapped around my torso while his chin rested on my shoulder. It had been the most comfortable nap I'd ever had – and now, of course, something was wrong.

"I'm not sure, but... I think we're under attack," Caspian whispered in a hollow voice. He jumped up and began donning his own set of blastgear and weapons. Captain Caspian, ready to serve once more. But this time I could see his fingers shaking. "There's another set of blastgear for you to wear." He gestured to a large, black metal box which sat next to the door.

I didn't reply as I rose from the bed and padded over to my new armor.

Even being aboard the *Estella* and with a few dozen backup ships, we weren't prepared for another fight. We'd lost the *Hellfire* and its entire crew. We'd lost many more ships and soldiers in the past month. I didn't know what kind of firepower and supplies we had now, but it was dangerous to be here in the Outer Rim, far away from anyone who could help us.

"This is a shell formation, right?" It was the most common ship-shielding technique. The "pearl," or the ship that was being protected, was supposed to be completely surrounded by its escort ships. They'd engage enemies first, should they appear.

"Yes," Caspian replied. Strapping his set of blasters to his hips, he looked formidable in the scaled blastgear.

I reluctantly stepped into my own gear. While I was grateful for my last suit saving my life, being encased in armor once more made me nervous. I didn't want to fight more Krech.

The siren continued to wail as the blastgear sealed around me. I didn't engage my helmet just yet because I didn't think we'd be in danger that fast.

Caspian took one look at my face and rushed to close the distance between us. Taking my face in his calloused hands he said, "Aliya, everything is going to be okay. Someone probably just spotted a few enemy ships and sounded the alarm. It's not a big deal. We'll be fine."

If everything was fine, why were we both wearing our blastgear?

I wanted to believe him. I wanted to believe that it was a false alarm or just a single Krech ship. I even started to tell him that he was right—

And then the explosions started.

I broke out of Caspian's grip and stumbled over to the rectangular window. "Oh no..." The scene outside made my knees weak, and I had to clutch the sill for support.

Around us floated the flaming hulls of several escort ships. Our first line of defense had already been severely crippled.

I watched in mute horror as a yellow cannon blast screamed through the darkness and tore into another escort ship on our side of the *Estella*. The fiery explosion momentarily blinded me, but it was far worse to see the wreckage once my sight returned.

Caspian swore violently from behind me and caused me to jump. He quickly murmured an apology and pressed something into my back – the belt with my blasters.

Without taking my eyes off the window I fastened the belt around my hips.

This can't be happening again so soon.

My very first battle aboard a spaceship hadn't gone so well, and now I was experiencing a second round. I certainly didn't feel as strong as I normally did – I internally grumbled about how Caspian had been right – but I knew that if it came down to it, I'd fight however I could. With my strength and speed, I was still the only person who could take on a Krech soldier.

The fear of being involved in another battle warred with a fiery rage that sprung up inside me. How could we have been taken by surprise when the whole reason we were still in the Scadian belt was so that the king's precious warship could destroy Krech ships?

I wanted to destroy whoever had started this. It had gone on for far too long, claiming too many lives and causing too much fear. *Let them come.*

At that moment a teardrop-shaped ship, not even half the size of the destroyed escort ships, zipped through the wreckage. It had been very quick, and its black hull nearly blended into the darkness surrounding us.

For a moment I wasn't sure that Caspian had even seen it, but then I heard his breath hitch. "Tell me you saw that, too," he whispered.

"I did."

"Describe it." He knew that my sight was better than his and probably hoped that I had picked up more details.

"Small, maybe thirty meters long. Too dark to see into the front window. And it was," I paused as I mulled over what I had seen, "it was another patchwork ship. Just like—"

"Like the one we saw on Charra," Caspian finished for me. He swore once, then twice as he paced away from me. "We need to evacuate this ship. Now. I don't know if anyone else saw that or if the *Estella's* radar even picked up something that small. With our backup getting blown up left and right, we won't stand a chance fighting the Krech here and now."

"How are we going to evacuate?" I turned and challenged him. "If any of the escape pods leave, they'll just get picked off."

He paused, probably having not realized just how trapped we were. "I don't know. Maybe King Locklyn or Prince Damien will have an idea."

Suddenly the *Estella* rocked. I was able to keep my grip on the windowsill, and I was able to catch Caspian's hand before he fell.

The Krech were either attacking us directly and ignoring the rest of the fleet, or they were trying to board. Both realities were equally horrible.

"Aliya." Caspian rapidly closed the distance between us until he stood inches away. "You need to get to Prince Damien." I started to protest but he cut me off. "No, listen. You're the only one who has fought the Krech and lived. The royal heir must live so that the King's Galaxy doesn't dissolve into chaos. If anyone can protect the prince, it's you."

"No, Caspian I can't..." My hand flew up to the chain hanging around my neck. Suddenly the ring hanging on the slim chain felt too heavy.

I didn't want to leave him. Being separated after the *Hellfire* crashed had been difficult enough, but this... this somehow felt worse.

In all the battles Caspian and I had fought, we had always been on a planet. And when you're on a planet, there was always somewhere you could potentially run away to.

But now... Now we were on a warship in the middle of the Outer Rim. Surrounded by asteroids and possibly Krech, there was only so far we could run. And if they didn't want us running...

I turned away from Caspian's earnest stare to look back out the window at the burning escort ships. How long would it be until the Krech did that to the *Estella?*

"Aliya." Caspian cupped my cheek in his hand and turned my face back to his. "You need to protect Prince Damien. I'll go to the king if they're not already together, and we'll get them to an escape pod. By the time we meet back up, someone will have figured a way out of this situation."

"No," I murmured as I began to cry. "Please don't make me leave you."

Caspian's hand grazed down the side of my neck and slipped behind my shoulder as he pulled me to his chest. I closed my eyes as I wrapped my arms around him and listened to his heartbeat. It was faster than usual, either from his own fear or from me being close, but the beats were steady and even.

He pressed his lips to the top of my head once, twice. "We have to do our job, love. Once we're back on Callais, I'll never leave your side. I promise."

The warship rocked again, and I knew that we had to go. We were soldiers, and we had a duty to protect the royal family. But this felt like a goodbye, and I hated it.

Caspian pulled back slightly, and when I looked up at him, his lips fell on mine. They were soft but urgent, as if he, too, could feel the weight of this moment.

I hoped this wasn't our last kiss.

Far too soon, he pulled away. "Protect them, but most of all, protect yourself," he ordered. "I love you, and I'll see you again soon. I promise."

"I love you too."

Taking me by the hand, he led us toward his door. We stepped outside, dodging a couple crew members as they raced down the hallway.

I would have to go left toward the bridge – the most logical place for Prince Damien to be at this time. Caspian was going right toward King Locklyn's rooms since they were nearby.

With one last squeeze of my hand Caspian whispered, "Soon." And then he sprinted away.

My hand rested over the middle of my chest, and I could feel his ring through my blastgear. Our story was far from over. It had only just begun, and there was no way it would end here.

As I ran toward the bridge, one thought played through my mind over and over like a prayer. *Please don't break your promise, Caspian. Please don't break your promise.*

My heart thundered in my chest as I pushed through the tide of crew members fleeing to the landing bays. I wanted to stop each and every one of them and tell them how futile it was to flee in escape pods at this time. With the Krech surrounding the *Estella*, any escape pod could easily be targeted and eliminated.

But I didn't have time.

I raced to the bridge, dodging as many individuals as I could possibly manage, and skidded to a halt just outside the double metal doors. My fingers anxiously drummed against my legs as I waited for the facial scanner to recognize me. The red beam of light seemed to take forever, scanning up and down my face twice as it verified my identity. *Come on, come on,* I chanted until it clicked off with a little beep. The doors slid open, and I darted through before they had fully parted.

The scene inside was madness. Several of the warship's sensors wailed indicating damage to various areas, and the bridge crew raced back and forth reading off status reports and locations of enemy ships.

In the middle of it all stood Prince Damien. He stood with his arms folded neatly behind his stiff back as he took in the destruction occurring outside the front window. Dressed in a black, high collared coat and his gold circlet sitting atop his black locks, he truly and finally looked like the prince he was supposed to be.

Hopefully he would be able to survive this and eventually become king.

I wove through the panicked crew and their blaring monitors until I drew up alongside the prince.

"Prince Damien," I huffed, "we need leave the *Estella*, now."

Prince Damien didn't immediately react. In fact, during the time that I'd entered the bridge, he hadn't shouted or paced as other ship captains might have when under attack. Instead he stood rigidly, watching the fiery hulls of his escort ships in a manner that seemed... calm? Accepting? I couldn't get a good read on his outward demeanor, but I assumed he was trying to remain collected in front of the crew.

But I knew that he was far from calm. Behind his back, one fist was clenched so tight that his knuckles were white, and I could hear his shaky breathing.

He was panicking.

"Your Highness…?" I tried again.

Slowly the prince turned to face me. A slow grin spread over his face, but it didn't quite reach his eyes. "Ah, Aliya, excellent timing. Where has Captain Caspian gotten off to?"

"He went to collect your father. I mean King Locklyn," I replied. Prince Damien's face remained expressionless, so I continued, "You know, so we can escape? We can't stay here any longer. The Krech will either breach the *Estella's* hull or cripple her further."

"Yes, yes. Of course," he said distractedly as one hand snaked out from behind his back to brush off the front of his immaculate coat. "We will make our escape. But only when the timing is right."

"Excuse me?" He was drunk again; he had to be. Nothing about him suggested that he was in a rush to leave the *Estella*, which was pure madness. We had to leave *now* before the Krech turned the full force of their blasters on us.

For a moment I was utterly disappointed in him. Prince Damien had turned his life around so much in the past few weeks. But now it appeared that he had relapsed.

Sure, there was a very, very high probability that we were going to get blown up in space should we leave in an escape pod, but I thought he had sworn off alcohol.

"You think I'm crazy, but I have a plan," he said in a defeated tone as he turned back to the window.

"And what might that be?" My tone was much harsher than I'd intended, but the prince wasn't making sense. Any type of plan should involve fleeing or some type of action… not staring out into space.

"Do you trust me?" he suddenly asked.

"What?"

He turned and closed the distance between us until he stood no more than a foot away from me. At this distance I could hear his heart pounding in his chest, see the wild look in his eyes, and smell… nothing out of the ordinary. I blinked in shock a few times. Unless he had found some type of liquor that didn't taint his breath, Prince Damien was completely sober.

Shame flooded through me at the disappointment I had felt for him only a few moments ago. He really *had* changed and was sticking to it, even in this dire situation.

Which meant… that Prince Damien really had come up with some sort of semi-rational plan. At least, I hoped it held some degree of rationality.

His hands came around and landed on the tops of my shoulders. Slowly, they slid down my arms, not stopping at the edges of my shirt sleeves, until he reached my hands. I couldn't stop the goosebumps that rose from my skin at his touch.

I'd hated every fiber of this male since first arriving at the palace, but since my confrontation at his party, I'd slowly discovered a newfound respect for him. He was no longer a rude, drunken womanizer. Instead, before me stood a prince who'd taken serious steps to change his life and ease into the ruler he was supposed to become.

But something about this gesture felt wrong. I was Prince Damien's guard, and he knew what Caspian and I felt for each other. He'd made no more passes at me in the past few weeks, and I'd assumed those actions were spurred by the copious amounts of alcohol that the prince used to consume. So why was he touching me this way now?

With painstaking gentleness, Prince Damien curled his fingers around mine. "When I received word about the crash on Aquillo, I'd worried that we had lost you forever. You're an incredible soldier – strong, brave, and collected in the face of danger. And those qualities extend to who you are outside of wearing a uniform. We would've lost much more than the Hero of Vanthurium if you'd died," he said quietly. My mind had gone completely blank as I tried to figure out where this was going. "When we picked up Adís' tracking signal, I just knew you'd be there with her. I demanded this rescue mission. I begged my father to deploy the *Estella*, but it was his idea to send more of the fleet. I wanted you back, and now that you're here and alive, I'll make sure to get us back to Callais."

"What… what does that even mean?"

Prince Damien cleared his throat. "I've seen the way you and the captain look at each other, so I'm not a big enough fool to think I can come between you two. But you've become someone important to me, to my life, and right now I'll do whatever it takes to get you to safety. I have a plan to get us out of this mess. The question is, do you trust me?"

So it was true. He had feelings for me. I felt blindsided by the information, not that I'd do anything with it anyway since I was Caspian's, but hearing the truth from his lips was surprising.

Part of me wanted to care for him. He'd been lost and then written off by everyone – although that had been entirely his fault. And even after realizing how horrible he'd been to me, Prince Damien had humbled himself to ask me for shooting lessons. He'd also apologized for his past self.

Perhaps, if I hadn't met Caspian first, I could've fallen for this reformed prince. He'd shown himself to be a strong, thoughtful leader, and he saw beyond my skills as a soldier.

However, I loved Caspian, and once we'd escaped this mess, I would marry him. But we needed to survive this attack first.

I pulled my hands out of the prince's grip and took a slow step backward. I certainly didn't miss the pang of hurt that flashed in Prince Damien's eyes. "I trust that you know this warship and her crew far better than I do, so yes. Whatever plan you've come up with, I trust that it'll work."

Another blast from the Krech rocked the *Estella*, and we struggled to remain upright. More sensors wailed behind us, and I wondered how Caspian was faring with the king.

"Good," Damien said, exhaling as his eyes closed. "It's… well, it's a terrible plan but also the only thing I can think of for getting us out of here." He ended with a short, shaky laugh.

"I've already cheated death a few times; what's one more?" I tried to joke but it fell flat.

"Hopefully it won't be as close this time," Prince Damien said with a sad smile. Stepping further away from me, he twisted his hands behind his back once more.

"Your Highness," a reedy voice huffed from behind me. I turned and was surprised to see a short, round creature dressed in stained overalls with his taloned hands on his knees as he gasped for breath. "Everything… is in position."

"Excellent work, Chauffin. Now, get yourself, and everyone else you can, onto a pod. Wait for my signal." The prince bowed to dismiss the exhausted creature.

"What did you need him for?" Their exchange didn't make any sense to me, and because I didn't know Chauffin, I had no idea what he'd put in place for the prince.

"A distraction and our means of escape. Now, everyone," Prince Damien raised his voice to address the few crew members who remained at their positions on the bridge, "calmly evacuate to your assigned pods. Bring anyone you pass along the way. We'll be departing the *Estella* shortly."

The crew bowed and scrambled out the doors, leaving just myself and Damien standing on the bridge.

"Prince Damien, what's going on?" His calm demeanor was beginning to make me anxious. I was supposed to get him to an escape pod, and I prayed that his plan somehow didn't involve him being a sacrifice.

"Come on." He motioned toward the doors as he directed the both of us out of the bridge. "I'll explain along the way."

As we exited the bridge, Prince Damien motioned for the guards stationed outside the doors to follow us. They followed behind as the prince led the way to the closest elevator.

"I'm going to blow up the *Estella*," he stated matter-of-factly.

"*What!*" I screeched as I skidded to a halt.

Prince Damien gripped my arm and hauled me forward. "Aliya, we can't stop now, and if you'd let me fully *explain*..."

"Fine," I grunted.

We reached the elevator, and the doors opened immediately after the prince punched in a six-digit code. The four of us piled in. "Fourth level," he ordered as the guard pressed the corresponding button. "It's the only way to make sure we can all get away," Damien continued. "The Krech *are* going to board. It's only a matter of time. Seeing how unprepared we were, they could have easily blown us to bits from the beginning, but they didn't. I can't exactly fathom why, but I figure it's because they might want to capture one of us." He turned to me so I could see the anger in his eyes. "Myself and my father are the most obvious targets, but you... They could have killed you after the crash on Aquillo, but instead they stripped you of your armor and left you out here. It's clear that they're toying with you. Perhaps leaving you and Adís on that asteroid was a trap because they assumed we'd come for you. But I can't shake the feeling that they've been ordered to keep you alive."

My stomach sank as I saw the logic in his theory. The cyborgs on Vanthurium had been warned about me. Maybe I was just a threat they wanted to eliminate back then, but I felt that the prince was right. The Krech had outright destroyed countless ships and even parts of Charra before today. They were vicious monsters, but so far they'd left the *Estella* intact. There was a good chance they were coming for me, and I didn't want to imagine what might happen if I got caught.

"You're going to blow up the ship once they board." It was dangerous, insane really, but I could see how it might work. Everyone on board the *Estella* would be loaded onto their pods, and when the detonations began, we would all take off, meeting fewer enemy ships in space since they would be aboard the exploding ship.

"Exactly," he replied grimly. The elevator came to a halt, and the doors slid open to reveal an empty corridor.

"But what about the guards? The entire crew?" Surely there weren't enough pods for *everyone*.

"Landing bay Seven-E," he said to the guards who set off immediately. We all took up a brisk pace as we headed to the bay Prince Damien had indicated. "I contacted the rest of my guards when the first blast from the Krech hit. I've told them of my plan, and they'll meet us down here. Captain Caspian too, if he's managed to find my father in the chaos." Damien sighed. "But… yes, not everyone will make it, and for that I am truly sorry. I wish we'd had more of a warning before the Krech appeared on our radar, but then, where would the pods have gone? It's not like we're flying through safe space…"

Sacrificing some so that the majority might live. It was a terrible decision to have to make, and I pitied the weight it would likely leave on Prince Damien's shoulders. If we lived.

I hadn't paid much attention to our path as we walked through the fourth level of the ship, but I paused to take in our surroundings.

"Prince Damien, what's in bay Seven-E?" Pods could only fit ten passengers, and with the four of us, not all the other guards would be able to fit – especially if Caspian and King Locklyn arrived. Either Prince Damien was choosing to sacrifice more of us or...

"An I-Wing."

"An *I-Wing*? How is the *Estella* even able to store an I-Wing? Does everyone know it's here?" An I-Wing was the fastest deep-space cruiser money could buy. At least triple the size of a pod, the I-Wing would easily get all of us away from the Krech and the explosion *fast*.

"The more people who knew about it, the more who would be down here, begging to be let aboard." Prince Damien shrugged. "This half of the floor is completely blocked off from most of the crew."

Okay, his plan was making a lot more sense now. Even though it wasn't the best idea to put both royals on the same escape ship, the speed advantage would most likely make the risk pay off.

We marched down the corridor, and after making a left turn, I saw the rectangular door for bay Seven-E. Waiting outside were

Elgin, Ki'ran, Ney, a few guards I didn't recognize… and Joss.

His blue skin paled when we made eye contact. Like the rest of the group, his clothes were slightly singed, and his left arm hung limply at his side.

"It looks like you made it." Oblivious to the stare down happening between me and Joss, Prince Damien marched up to Ki'ran and shook his hand. "Any word on the others?" he asked as he looked them over.

"No, your highness," Elgin immediately replied. "We only just made it onto the *Estella* before the shots began in earnest. As you can see our bay was targeted, along with several others, so you're down more pods than planned."

I only took in half of Elgin's report. Instead my eyes flicked back and forth between Ki'ran and Joss, until Ki'ran finally met my gaze. "How did he get here?" I said with an angry wave at where Joss stood. Ki'ran knew exactly who Joss was to me, but instead of answering, he only shook his head, his long braid swaying behind his back.

"Aliya? What's wrong?" Prince Damien looked between me and Joss. "Do you know him?"

"Yes," I ground out between clenched teeth. It took all my effort not to snatch the front of Joss' uniform and shake him. "From my time in the Protective Forces."

"Ah," the prince replied. "That makes sense. General Vinculus lent us several of his better squads for this mission."

Joss still wore the plain black uniform of the Protective Forces.

He didn't wear any sort of patch or button to signify that he'd become a captain, which I was happy to see, but I didn't like that he was here.

"Fine." I didn't back off the glare that I gave him.

Prince Damien turned back to the others, ignoring the anger that rolled off me in waves. "Have any of you contacted the other guards or Captain Caspian yet?"

"No, my prince, but I can now," Ney offered. He typed a quick message on his cuff and looked back up once he was done.

"Thank you, Neygreen. Shall we head in then?" Prince Damien walked over to the keypad and punched in another code that opened the doors. The two guards who'd accompanied us from the bridge entered first, checking to make sure the bay was safe, and then we all followed them.

Something felt wrong. Caspian was only retrieving King Locklyn, and if Prince Damien had reached out and let him know to meet us here, he should've been here by now.

Where are you? I sent my own message to Caspian, hoping he'd reply to me before Ney.

He promised that we'd see each other again soon. Caspian was a man of his word, and if something had gotten in his way, then I'd just have to go and find Caspian.

I hated waiting.

The minutes that ticked by were silent and tense as we waited for the rest of the prince's guards and King Locklyn to arrive.

While everyone else boarded the massive and beautiful I-Wing, I couldn't bring myself to sit inside the ship's cabin. I needed space to pace, to breathe, to worry.

Unsurprisingly, Prince Damien had been the first one to offer to wait outside the I-Wing with me. He sat at the bottom of the I-Wing's ramp, his fingers steepled under his chin while Ki'ran stood watch over him. The prince was still as his eyes followed my path back and forth in front of him, but Ki'ran stood still as stone with his arms crossed over his chest.

I paced the length of the ship's bay, from wall to wall, as I argued with myself over what I should do.

The *Estella* was huge, and I'd barely seen any of it since being brought on board. If I went off looking for Caspian, I'd be more likely to find trouble before I'd found him. And, since we sat in the Scadian asteroid belt being blown to pieces while Krech boarded, that trouble would undoubtedly be something I couldn't handle alone.

But I was miserable waiting here, hoping Caspian would arrive. Too much time had passed since Caspian and I first parted ways, and my mind was already jumping to the worst possible conclusions. The Krech had boarded and found Caspian. A blast had hit an area Caspian was walking through or needed to get past to reach us.

It was a blessing that I'd been given space to worry, but I felt like those who hadn't boarded the I-Wing were here to keep an eye on me. In case I did something rash.

I'd finally quit my pacing, my mind completely made up, when Prince Damien spoke up from behind me. "We need to prepare for takeoff soon. There are only twenty more minutes until the first of the explosions will start, and we need to be well away from the *Estella* by then."

"No." This wasn't what I wanted, and prince or not, I wasn't going to let him tell me what to do. I couldn't bring myself to depart the *Estella* without knowing where Caspian was. "Can't we delay them?"

"Aliya," I heard Prince Damien stand and walk up behind me. "Caspian will be fine. He's a seasoned soldier and knows where to find us. Maybe his path was blocked and he needed to board another escape pod."

"He would have let us know," I said as my gaze drifted to my wrist. The clear cuff revealed nothing new, no message from Caspian that he was on his way.

A hand rested on my shoulder. "Come on. We need to get ready so that we—"

There was a commotion in the hallway just outside the landing bay. I heard many running feet, but through the wall, it was difficult to gauge how many individuals were outside the door.

Friend or foe? Caspian or Krech? A small kernel of hope bloomed in my chest.

Behind us, I heard Ki'ran draw his blaster, and two other guards came down the I-Wing's ramp.

We waited, and then the door opened into the hallway. King Locklyn spilled through first, looking anxious and haggard, followed by Omri, Ba'rin, Seradon, and Adís.

No Caspian.

My stomach sank even as my friends ran toward me. I should've been happier to see them alive, should've said *something* to show I was glad to see them safe… But instead I stood in mute despair, even as Adís slammed into me with a monster hug. Someone had repaired her mo-wear, and I faintly registered the fact that she smelled like smoke and grease.

"I'm so glad you're safe! We didn't think we were going to make it in time! Whole floors are a mess, and anyone not boarding a pod is frantic. Oh, and I think comms are down again because I was trying to reach you but couldn't…" She rambled on for a while before realizing that I didn't even react. "Aliya?"

My horror had increased tenfold. Deep down I knew that Caspian wouldn't ignore a message from me, and now I knew why. Just like in the brief battle above Aquillo, he couldn't reach us, and we couldn't reach him.

Adís tapped my cheek with two fingers. "Aliya? Is she okay?" she asked someone behind me.

"What happened?" I finally found my voice, and it rasped as I tried to form words. "I thought Caspian was getting King Locklyn…" My gaze drifted to where the king embraced his son. I watched as they shared a few quiet words before joining the larger group.

"Caspian did reach the king first. We all crossed paths on the second floor when we received Prince Damien's message about rendezvousing here," Adís explained. King Locklyn nodded in confirmation.

"So where is Caspian now?"

"He. Well, he—"

I fixed her with a hard stare as her words faltered. Adís had pulled away from me and stood staring at the floor.

"We were crossing the third floor when we ran into a group of Krech." Fatigue seeping into his voice, King Locklyn stepped in to continue the story. "It was difficult to tell just how many there were, and they were blocking the elevator we needed to reach in order to get down here. Captain Caspian created a diversion and drew them away from us."

"No!" My hands covered my mouth in despair. Why would he do that? Caspian *promised* that he'd come back to me.

"Aliya, relax! The Krech were practically tripping over themselves to get to him. It wasn't hard for him to get away, and he knows to meet us here. I'm sure he'll arrive any minute now." Adís tried to reassure me, but all I could think of was when Caspian tried to create a diversion on Charra. It wouldn't have ended well if I hadn't turned the tables on our enemies, and I had a horrible feeling this time wasn't going to work out either. Unless I saved him.

"I'm going to find him." I jerked out of Adís' grip and made my way toward the door. I didn't care if they all left without me, but I wasn't letting Caspian remain behind.

Even if he was already injured, I'd find a way to drag him to a pod so we could escape.

My head spun and I saw red as I marched toward the door.

"Aliya, stop!" The authority in Prince Damien's voice actually caused me to halt. "Look at me." I took back every kind thought I'd had about the prince on the bridge. He was controlling and insensitive, and my body trembled in anger as I slowly turned around. "You are not—I repeat, you are not going after Captain Caspian, especially alone. The *Estella* will begin to detonate in fifteen minutes. That's not enough time to locate Caspian and return here. You'd put the rest of our lives in jeopardy."

"Then don't wait for me," I snapped and spun on my heel. Royalty be damned, he had no idea how scared I was to lose Caspian right now.

"Aliya! Get back here or—"

Another explosion rocked the warship. It was bigger than the blasts before, and I worried that someone had triggered the detonations before they were scheduled to start.

I sprinted across the bay and frantically mashed the button to open the door. Behind me, I could hear rushed footsteps of guards trying to catch me.

I'm coming, Caspian. I'll find you.

I slipped out the door and paused as I debated which way to run.

And then, around the corner of the right hallway, a door crashed open.

At least, I *think* it was a door. The boom and commotion that followed it was deafening, and I could smell smoke.

My senses went on high alert, and I held a hand up to everyone in the bay with the I-Wing. "Stay back! Something's coming."

Indeed, it was. I could now hear the pounding of many booted feet. It was accompanied by the sound of scraping – as if someone was dragging hundreds of forks, tines down, on the metal floors.

A chill went down my spine as I raised my blaster.

There was a single shot of green light. It briefly illuminated the corridor, and in that moment, I saw a wild wave of shadows spilling over one another as they headed my way.

I was so transfixed by the horrors approaching that when the blast hit the wall at the end of the hallway, I jumped.

"Get back in here!" a guard behind me hissed.

I wasn't going anywhere. What had Adís said? That the Krech were tripping over themselves to get to Caspian?

I knew what was coming, and I was more than ready, even excited, to face it.

Planting my feet, I braced for the storm to hit.

Caspian rounded the corner first. There was significant crack in the breastplate of his blastgear, but he didn't seem hurt from whatever had managed to wreck his armor. His forehead, however, sported a shallow gash right above his left eye that dripped blood down his temple.

Cheeks red with exertion, Caspian dashed down the long hallway toward me. I stumbled a few steps forward, desperate to reach him, before I remembered that he wasn't alone.

Krech after Krech after Krech came after him. It was a sea of scaly, green faces while their clawed hands flailed and reached for the male ahead of them.

Finally, guards spilled out from the I-Wing's bay. I didn't bother to look at who they were as they stood behind me. One swore under his breath.

Another green blast raced out from the herd of Krech. It missed Caspian easily, but a few people behind me had to move to avoid being hit.

"Should we fire back?" someone asked.

"No!" I snapped. "If you hit Caspian, this will all be for nothing. Let him get a bit closer."

Arms and legs pumping, Caspian outran certain death. *Faster, faster!* I wanted to scream.

When enough Krech had rounded the corner that I could no longer see the end of the hallway, they let out unearthly shrieks. Worse than nails on a chalkboard or an explosion in a small space, the ear-piercing noise made my ears ring.

Whether it was seeing me or more survivors, the Krech somehow put on a surprising burst of speed. Their thick, awkwardly bent legs pounded across the floor as they closed in on us.

And then, Caspian's steps faltered.

I must have missed it, but one second Caspian was doing fine, and then he was stumbling, slowing to a complete stop.

He cried out in pain, and that's when I saw the blackened tips of a Krech's claws poking through the crack in his blastgear. I was no doctor, but it looked like the claws had gone through Caspian's back and came out of his stomach.

As spots of red began to drip off the claws, Caspian's head lolled to the side, and I could see the monster standing behind him. A wicked grin that revealed all of the Krech's sharp teeth leered at me.

"No!" I shrieked. *"Caspian!"*

The rest of the Krech swarmed around Caspian and his attacker, ignoring them both.

My vision began to blur, but I frantically fired shot after shot into the oncoming mob. I screamed, not with any words, but with the pain and anger that coursed through my body. As always, I was deadly and accurate, and the lizard-like bodies began to pile up in the hallway.

Even as one Krech fell, another took its place. And another. And another.

Finally blasts came from the guards behind me, and I was able to turn my attention back to Caspian and his attacker.

Aliya, I saw Caspian mouth to me.

"Caspian, hold on!"

I took one shaky step forward, and then another.

I'm coming for you. Hold on, Caspian, I'm coming. Why, oh why hadn't I left to find him sooner?

I was numb as I stumbled forward, oblivious to the blasts careening down the hallway and around me. There was so much discordant noise happening around me that I couldn't tell if Caspian was calling my name or someone else was.

Suddenly strong arms wrapped around my waist.

"Aliya, no! You have to come back to the I-Wing immediately! We need to leave now." It was the same guard who'd tried to call me back before the Krech arrived.

I struggled to escape his grasp, and then a second pair of arms wrapped around me.

"Caspian!" My voice broke as I fought to break away. "Let me go!"

I was practically dragging the two guards, their feet sliding across the floor as I trudged forward.

"Stop! It's not safe!"

"Release me!" I screamed.

"You can't save him!"

It was then that I fully snapped. I screamed and thrashed, alternating between calling for Caspian and demanding that the guards let me go. I was the only one who could possibly get to Caspian and bring him back.

"Hold her still!" Prince Damien had joined the fray, and while I worried about hitting him, my desire to break free was more pressing.

I *had* to get to Caspian. He promised he'd come back to me and that we'd have a future together...

His beautiful blue eyes began to drift closed.

"Caspian! No, Caspian, please look at me!"

Something pricked the side of my neck, and I began to feel cold and numb.

"I'm sorry," I heard someone murmur.

What's happening? My mind was getting foggy, and my attempts to fight back were becoming more and more feeble. I could feel myself being dragged backward – the opposite direction that I wanted to go.

My blaster tumbled from my grip as black spots swarmed my vision. "Caspian, Caspian..." I continued to cry even as my words began to slur.

I felt helpless and devastated and weak. Someone had intentionally drugged me, and now I was going to lose the male I loved.

There was a roar from ship's engines. It was louder than the cries from the Krech, and I knew that I'd been dragged back to the I-Wing.

My world went dark, and in my last seconds of consciousness I felt two warm hands envelop one of mine as someone whispered, "Aliya, I'm so, so sorry."

I woke up in my bed.

Not Caspian's bed on the *Estella*. No, I was laying in the bed I'd had at the palace. On Callais.

And it was strange because I didn't remember how I'd gotten here.

The gears of my mind turned sluggishly as I lay on my back, desperate to uncover a memory of how I got into this very bed.

I felt completely fine. I wasn't in pain. I wasn't restrained, or bandaged, or… anything, really.

I just felt numb and heavy.

What happened?

My thoughts were blurry, like objects under a pool of water. There was something I needed to do… or to get to… But what was it?

And then I finally got something.

Two words and a voice. *His* voice – Prince Damien's. *"I'm sorry."*

He was sorry… for…? *Stars, what happened to me?* No, not me… something happened to…

Like a shattering dam, the memories flooded back all at once.

Being left with Adís on the asteroid.

The royal fleet coming to our rescue.

The surprise attack from the Krech.

Racing for the I-Wing with Prince Damien.

And then Caspian…

I bolted upright, my hands poorly muffling my scream.

Caspian…!

No, no, no!

Caspian had been just down the hallway, fleeing for his life. The Krech were on his heels, but he was almost there, almost to me, and then—

Tears cascaded down my cheeks as the horrific scene played again and again in my mind.

A great hollowness yawned open inside my chest, rapidly expanding at a rate that was sure to consume me within seconds.

You're in shock, a small, detached part of my mind noted.

I paid it no attention.

Instead I kept seeing the blood dripping out of Caspian's blastgear, his shout of pain, the way his body went limp while speared on the Krech's claws.

Caspian.

My Caspian.

He was gone.

My hands, still pressed to my open mouth, were soaked from the tears streaming down my face. In another flash of panic, they raced to my neck. Reaching the collar of my shirt, my hands began searching and searching.

As they grasped the delicate chain that still circled my neck, my sobs began anew. I might have been drugged and dragged away from the battle, but I hadn't lost the one thing – the only thing left – in this universe that mattered to me: Caspian's ring.

My trembling fingers traced the metal circle once, twice. As my mind spun and I cried from the depths of my very soul, I lost track of how many times I turned the ring over and over between my fingers.

The ring was still there.

But Caspian, my fiancé, wasn't.

I howled in grief again, not caring if anyone heard. I was sure they all knew what had happened anyway.

Caspian wasn't just dead – he was *gone*, lost to space in the explosion that Prince Damien had ordered to secure our escape from the Krech.

And I could've reached him.

The thought was like a fist to my stomach, making me nauseous and dizzy all at once.

I could have reached Caspian.

It wouldn't have been easy because there were so many Krech streaming down the hallway around him, but I knew I could have done it.

I could have brought him back and given him a chance at being saved.

But Prince Damien stopped me.

The prince!

My body jerked into motion, completely on autopilot, as I leapt out of my bed and raced over to where my boots – neatly lined up beside the door – sat. I didn't even bother with the laces as I stuffed my feet inside and reached for the door.

The emptiness within me was shifting. As if a spark had been lit, I now burned with rage.

Prince Damien had most likely ordered the guards to hold me back.

Prince Damien had drugged me. He'd even apologized for doing so.

And, ultimately, Prince Damien had let the love of my life die.

With my hand on the doorknob, I paused. I was shaking from head to toe, my circuits glowing as I'd never seen them before, completely out of control.

Yes, I was utterly devastated. Yes, I was enraged – and rightly so. But I had to be careful with my actions. I couldn't go around causing damage and risk being ruled a threat to the royal family.

Getting locked up, or worse, would definitely be a setback in getting retribution for Caspian's death.

With painstaking gentleness, I opened the door and looked around for the closest guard. Despite this being the wing of the palace where the prince's and king's guards resided, someone was always supposed to be on watch.

Oddly, the hallway was completely empty. There wasn't a soul in sight, and the usual decorative tables and vases were absent as well.

Were they anticipating some sort of destructive rage from me? Considering how I felt just moments ago, that assumption wasn't entirely unrealistic.

Still hyperaware of my movements, I strolled with agonizing slowness down the hall as I searched for someone, anyone. There was a heavy silence lingering throughout the palace, and it made me uneasy.

I made my way down the stairs, heading to the king's council chamber. Perhaps everyone would be gathered there, discussing the aftermath of the most recent battles.

Only once I padded past the throne room, I noticed more guards than normal. They stood at closer intervals throughout the hallway, and, looking through the windows, I noticed larger groups of them moving together across the grounds. Maybe King Locklyn had finally called in all of his reserves, not wanting to risk a gap in security that could threaten him or his family.

Hopefully the added security wasn't because of me...

I kept my eyes down, refusing to meet the stares of the males and females I passed. I didn't want to see pity or distrust in their eyes, but I could certainly feel the weight of their stares. When I passed a guard who gave a quiet gasp, I decided I couldn't keep walking any longer.

"Excuse me." The amber-eyed Callaisan wasn't one I was familiar with, but it was obvious from his look of surprise that he knew *exactly* who I was. Hopefully I would be able to use that to my advantage. "Where's Prince Damien?"

"Uh, miss—I mean Hero—I mean, Aliya…"

He was terrified of me, I realized as I watched a few beads of sweat roll down his pale temple.

"Please," I said in a softened tone. "I need to know what happened. And what my new orders are." There, maybe that would make him believe that I wasn't a danger to the prince.

"Oh, well then. The king ordered a council meeting. I can have someone let you know—"

"Thank you!" I called over my shoulder as I dashed away. Now that I knew for certain where the king and the prince would be, I didn't bother to move slowly. Thankfully, the guard didn't try to follow me.

Council meetings could take forever, especially when discussing the Krech and war, but I knew that Prince Damien or even King Locklyn would allow me into the room. After all, I was still the prince's guard; I probably should've been invited to this meeting to begin with.

But when I drew close to the council room, I realized that getting an audience would be difficult.

No less than ten guards stood outside the doors, some of them more familiar than others, but they were all armed. Their hands rested on their blasters, as if they were expecting me.

Singling out one of my friends, I slowed my approach and made my way over to him. Ney looked wary, and Ba'rin, who stood next to Ney, moved a step closer. Even Elgin, who'd been lounging against the wall, squared his shoulders and faced me.

A pang of sadness struck my chest. *Are they truly afraid of me?*

"Aliya," Elgin said by way of greeting.

"Elgin," I replied with a curt nod. When they realized I wasn't stopping on my way to the doors, the three of them shuffled together so that they were shoulder to shoulder.

I didn't have to look to know that the other guards had shifted, forming a loose semicircle around me.

"We have orders to keep you out," Ba'rin warned. His expression was unreadable, but something from his tone told me that he meant every word. When I didn't back away, his eyes narrowed, and he tightened the grip on his blaster.

I didn't want to start a fight with my friends. No, that would be reserved for someone else — if I was able to get to him.

I raised my hands in a gesture of peace. "I'm not going to hurt anyone. I just need to talk to Prince Damien so I can figure out what happened." Still, none of them moved to let me pass. *Well, at least I tried being nice first.* "Fine. This can go one of two ways," I threatened as I lowered my voice. "You can let me in, or we can cause a scene."

The mood in the hallway immediately became tense. A brief look of shock crossed Ney's face before his expression became stony. Although I didn't check, I was sure that Elgin wore the same look.

Without looking, I knew that every guard around me had drawn their blaster. I didn't think they'd been given orders to kill me, but with this many weapons in the tight hallway, I knew my chances of walking away without a scratch were slim.

I should've been scared. Instead, I felt nothing.

My life didn't matter anymore. I wanted answers from the prince, and then I wanted nothing more to do with the royal family, this palace, or even this planet.

I was getting to Prince Damien one way or another. Clenching my fists at my sides, I prepared to make the first move.

Surprisingly, Ba'rin acted before I could. He took a single step to the side, breaking contact with his fellow guards. Dropping his eyes to the ground, he gave me a single nod. "Let her go. She won't hurt him."

"Ba'rin, are you serious?" Elgin yelped. "We all know what she can do, and if—" He was immediately silenced by Ba'rin's upheld hand.

Elgin's mouth hung open in shock, but I paid him no attention as I slipped between them and walked the last few steps to the council room's door.

"Thank you," I murmured over my shoulder. And then I opened the door.

The inside of the chamber was quiet, but every seat was filled. With my head held high, I met the eyes of every councilmember. Some of them regarded me with confusion, others with a mixture of fear and distrust. Silene's eyes brimmed with tears, and I had to look away before my own began.

I realized that someone was missing. King Locklyn and the chair in which he usually sat were notably absent. It didn't make sense since the guard in the hallway told me the king was the one who called the meeting, but as my eyes glanced around the crescent table once more, my concerns for the king disappeared because I found the person I'd come looking for.

Prince Damien sat in the middle of the table with his hands resting atop it. His thin shoulders were slumped, and dark circles rested under his eyes. A simple gold crown, larger than the circlets he used to wear, rested atop his head. Once more he was dressed from head to toe in black, but unlike his previous dark outfits, this once didn't have a single trace of gold on it.

He was wearing mourning clothes.

The realization threw me, and before I could ask what was going on, Prince Damien stood and addressed me. "Aliya. I was hoping you'd be awake soon. Can we talk?"

I nodded, and he rounded the table to where I stood. Taking me by the arm, Prince Damien led me from the council room and back into the hallway.

The guards outside snapped to attention at the sight of their prince but were quick to back away when he asked for space.

When the door clicked closed and we had a little bubble of space, Prince Damien met my stare.

"I'm so sorry, Aliya," he said as his voice broke. Heartbreaking agony was written on every square inch of his face.

But little did he know, those were the last words I wanted to hear.

"How dare you!" I shrieked, grabbing him by the lapels of his jacket and roughly pushing him up against the wall. The crown tumbled from his head, hitting the floor with a metallic clang. Tears streamed down my face, and my breaths rattled as I tried to contain my sobs.

The click of ten blasters sounded behind my head.

"No," Prince Damien gasped. He raised a hand and looked at the guards behind me. "Stand down."

There was silence and then some shuffling as the guards moved away.

"You let him *die*," I hissed between clenched teeth.

"Aliya, let go," he replied in a calm voice. When I made no move to release my grip on his jacket, Prince Damien sighed and continued. "If he wasn't going to die from being stabbed, the poison in the Krech's claws would have killed him. There was *nothing* we could do."

"No," I sobbed. "No, I could have saved him."

"And if you couldn't? There were so many Krech! Even if you'd reached Caspian, one of them surely would have gotten you too."

"I could've made it." My voice cracked, and I finally backed away from the prince. I angrily swiped at my face, trying to clear the tears that blurred my vision, but they wouldn't stop.

"I'm sorry," he said again as he wrapped his arms around my shoulders.

I jerked away from his touch. "Don't touch me! You *drugged* me, Damien! You made them hold me back, and then you put me to sleep! How could you?"

"Would you have given up?" Prince Damien raised his voice. "You weren't listening, and you were going to get yourself killed. Are you so selfish to think that you're the only one who lost someone in that mess?"

"But he was going to marry me!" I screamed. I fished under my collar and pulled out Caspian's ring. The diamond atop the compass rose sparkled as I held it up between my fingers, and I focused on it instead of the prince's face.

There were several gasps from behind me. The engagement was supposed to be a secret until Caspian and I could get the king's blessing, but that didn't matter now.

Finally, everyone could see why Caspian's death hit me so hard.

"Aliya... I'm truly sorry for your loss. I... I had no idea." The anguish in the prince's voice was so sincere that it took me by surprise. Indeed, a quick glance at him confirmed that he wore an incredibly devastated expression as he looked between the ring and my tearful face.

"I could've saved him," I whispered.

I quickly tucked the ring back under my shirt, and Prince Damien caught my hands before they could fall down to my sides.

I felt too many conflicting emotions as we stood a foot apart, my hands cocooned between the prince's. I hated him for what he caused me to lose. I felt sad and lost. And I wanted to feel comforted by the male who recently revealed that he cared for me, but my desire for connection wasn't outweighed by the simmering resentment that refused to fade.

I couldn't, however, pull my hands away from his.

This was all a mess, but I was in no shape to sort it all out.

"You could have saved him," he said gently, "but we could've lost you too. And we lost more than enough in that explosion."

There was an edge to his voice that I didn't understand, and my mind spun as I tried to figure out who else we'd lost.

All the prince's guards were here except for Seradon and Ki'ran, and I hadn't seen Adís since waking up. "Who? Who else did we lose?" I croaked.

Prince Damien dropped my hands and leaned heavily against the wall. He stared at me for a second, his hazel eyes sharp yet unreadable, before bending to pick his crown off the ground. Rubbing at an imaginary spot of dirt on the golden circle, the prince kept his eyes down as he said, "We lost my father."

"What?" How was that possible? King Locklyn had been on board the I-Wing before the Krech arrived, so there was no way he should've been involved in the battle.

The guard's words echoed in my head once more: *the king ordered a council meeting.* The heavy silence, the increased guard presence… it all made sense now.

"After I knocked you out—" *Well at least he was taking full responsibility for that,* I thought. "—the tide started to turn. It was difficult to get everyone back inside the bay while keeping the Krech as far away as possible. My father…" Prince Damien paused and cleared his throat. "My father took a blaster and joined the guards. But they kept coming. And coming. One… one got too close and slashed at his chest. I got him onto the ship, and we were able to take off before the *Estella* blew. But…"

Prince Damien stopped and wiped his eyes. He didn't need to finish explaining what happened. The poison in the Krech's claws would've finished King Locklyn long before we could've returned to Callais.

"So you're the king now." I stepped away and watched as Prince—no, King Damien replaced the crown on top of his head.

"Yes. We broadcasted the short ceremony yesterday, and tomorrow we'll have a memorial for him and everyone else who was lost in the attack." He gave me a measured look, waiting for my reaction.

I wanted nothing to do with a memorial. Even if it was just the new king remembering those we lost, I didn't want to hear King Damien talk about Caspian making a sacrifice or some nonsense like that.

I wanted to leave, to disappear forever and pretend like this was all some horrendous nightmare. The kind where you'd pinch yourself and wake up.

But that wasn't going to happen. Just like I wouldn't be able to avoid the service tomorrow.

Knowing that I was far more likely to snap at the king instead of saying something sensible, I kept my mouth shut. He must have realized that he wasn't going to get anything else from me because he straightened the lapels on his long coat and moved back toward the council room.

Pausing on the threshold, he said over his shoulder, "You're relieved of all guard duties for the time being. Take some time for yourself, within the grounds of the palace, and then we'll figure out what to do next."

The door clicking shut was the only sound in the hallway.

The guards were likely focused on me, anticipating some type of backlash, but I couldn't find it within myself to move.

Without realizing it, King Damien had taken away yet another piece of who I'd been.

I'd lost Terra, my old home.

I'd lost the Nova squad.

I'd lost Caspian.

And now I'd lost my position as a guard.

Even if it was temporary, that last one hit me the hardest. I needed the structured guard routine. Being a guard was what I'd come to know since leaving Terra, and I had no idea what I'd do with myself if I wasn't taking guard shifts.

Spending time on the training grounds probably wasn't what he had in mind for 'taking time for myself,' but I wasn't the type to take up sewing or walks in the garden.

I wasn't Aliya the soldier or Aliya the Hero.

I was just Aliya Rathburn, the girl lost amongst the stars.

"As many of you know, three days ago the royal fleet was involved in a battle near the Scadian asteroid belt. We thought we'd be retrieving hostages, but instead we found ourselves ambushed by the Krech."

Guards and servants had set up a platform in front of the palace yesterday afternoon. After my conversation with the new king, I'd returned to my room and cried, but I'd heard the construction outside. And now, here I stood, on top of the platform, listening to King Damien's memorial for his father, Caspian, and all those lost in the attack.

When Anita, Mira, and Ciena had barged into my room this morning – horrified to find me curled up on the floor with red, swollen eyes – I'd shouted at them to leave, insisting that I wasn't going anywhere near the king's ridiculous ceremony. But they'd been given orders, and there was no way for me to get out of attending.

This wasn't guard duty, they'd said. I needed to be there so the people knew I'd survived.

"Many lives were lost in the attack — parents, brothers and sisters, friends... Their sacrifices were heartbreaking, but they have my utmost respect for allowing me to stand here today. Because today... Today is a new beginning for us all!"

I stood with my companions behind the king. We'd all been given a fresh set of black blastgear — to be worn as a set of formal mourning clothes and as protection in case the Krech caught wind of this memorial and tried to attack. It felt wrong to be here, and it was even worse that his speech was being broadcasted to all citizens of the galaxy.

I had no doubt that my face was being scrutinized on billions of dataports and display screens.

"We lost countless lives that can never be replaced; my father was one of them. But I say that ends here! We will fight back to stop further bloodshed and destruction. And we will secure the freedom of our galaxy!"

The crowd gathered in front of the palace roared. Surely, they all didn't buy into this nonsense, right? We tried fighting back by patrolling the Outer Rim and sending the royal fleet into the Scadian asteroid belt. Clearly, neither of those actions worked.

Surely, King Damien wasn't suggesting that he'd follow his father's belief that soldiers should go into Kāās to *find* the Krech?

"For my father and Captain Caspian Tassarion, who both gave their lives so that my guards and I could escape and return to Callais; for the brave soldiers who fought the Krech and destroyed dozens of their ships; for the brave males and females who stood up to fight and protect this galaxy – we will be brave. We will fight. And we will rip out the root of this evil and bring peace back to our galaxy!"

Thousands of beings roared in support of their new king. It was odd to see such a turnout when roughly a month ago, most of the galaxy had written off their former prince as a failure. But it was clear that he'd changed, and this rousing speech was doing wonders to garner further support.

I wanted to scream and cry. I wanted them to know about the depths of my loss and what more fighting would do to this galaxy. We'd lost so many already…

I wobbled and my breath caught in my throat. Just as I was searching for the best place to bolt to, a large hand wrapped around mine.

I looked up into Ki'ran's face, shocked to see a few tears running down it. He nodded once before turning back to the cameras and crowd. He'd always been a male of few words, but this time he really hadn't needed any. Ki'ran was still here for me.

And when Elgin gently took my other hand, I let myself cry.

✳

It rained after the memorial and pep rally ended because… Well, because of course it would rain. I didn't jog to get out of it like others did. Instead, I plodded along, letting my thoughts consume me.

I didn't want to be here anymore. The people, the palace… It all reminded me of what I'd lost.

I passed the training grounds where I'd spent so much time with Caspian.

Walking down the main hallway, I could imagine Caspian's footsteps beside me as if we were going to the banquet hall or following the prince around.

The hallway before my room was by far the hardest spot. There I recalled the night before the prince's party – how charming Caspian had looked, how stunned he'd been to see me, and how he'd pulled me out of my shell that night and showed me an amazing evening.

Worst of all, I couldn't bear to look out the windows onto the hedge maze.

Back in my room, I slumped against the foot of my bed, feeling the weight of the universe settle on my shoulders.

I knew why King Damien had me suit up and stand with the other guards today. My presence was a visual reminder of the battles I'd fought and won. He wanted to send a message to the galaxy – and presumably to the Krech as well – that I was still alive and able to fight.

Little did he know that I didn't want to.

I was tired of the fear. Tired of suffering losses. But most of all, I was tired of feeling like I *had to* fight.

I'd been made into a weapon without my permission, hating the uncertainty of whom I'd become, but I'd embraced my incredible abilities when I needed to protect others.

Right now, I didn't want to protect anyone, not even myself.

But what was I supposed to do? I still lived in this galaxy with billions of other beings, and our collective safety was seriously being threatened. There was nowhere I could run to avoid the Krech and their destruction.

Terra, defenseless and naïve as it was, was the last place I should go.

But I couldn't stay here. That much I knew for certain.

Caspian was everywhere I looked, and I could feel his presence like a blanket around my shoulders. Or perhaps it was a noose around my neck.

I wish I could've saved you, I thought. After hours and hours of sobbing, I still had tears left to shed.

Tucking my head between my bent knees, I let my grief consume me once more.

It could have been minutes, hours, or even days before someone finally stepped into my room.

There was no gasp of surprise when they discovered me in my miserable state, nor was there an order to stand up and pull myself together.

My quiet visitor simply stood with their back to the closed door and waited as the minutes trickled by. After an eternity, they spoke.

"I think you should go."

King Damien's voice wasn't harsh or pitying. Instead, it was even, as if he'd spent a lot of time coming to this decision. But there was still a hint of sadness to it.

"Go where? And why?" I croaked, my mouth beyond parched.

"Anywhere that's not here." I heard the groan of wood as he leaned against the door. "This place reminds you of him, and I can't have you as a guard if you're distracted. It's... it's certainly not my first choice, and I know the council will disagree with my decision. But for once I can't think about myself."

I peeked up at him, not bothering to dry my eyes. "I thought you needed every guard you could get right now."

He didn't look away as he took in my expression and gave me a nod. "You're right. We need strong and brave soldiers more than anything right now. While we'd be losing more than that if you left, I can't have you here, broken and resenting my choice to save you." I opened my mouth to disagree, but the king continued, saying, "I meant what I said about you taking time and finding some space. Any planet would be glad to have you right now, should you reveal who you are, but somehow I don't think you want to work under any leader for the time being."

It was eerie how well he could read me. We'd barely spoken since he righted his path, but he knew exactly what I needed right now.

"I don't even know where I'd go," I said. "It's not like it's safe to travel right now."

"I know, but I also know that you're more than capable of taking care of yourself." He stood up from the door and slowly tugged it open. "There is a small ship waiting on the airfield. It's stocked and fully fueled, and it's completely yours. Do with it as you wish."

He was giving me a ship? I could see it now – traveling to new worlds like I'd always wanted to… But unlike those old dreams, now I'd be doing it alone.

At least this gave me a way out.

"Damien," I called before he slipped out the door. Omitting his title felt natural on my tongue, and he didn't seem surprised by it. "Thank you."

He gave me a small, sad smile. "You're welcome, Aliya."

The door clicked closed, and I didn't even need a moment before I knew what I was going to do.

I was going to leave Callais.

I darted around my room, collecting the things I wanted to take with me: my Nova jacket, my journal which had survived time with the Protective Forces and Nova squad, the pin I'd received from Lord Liseni, and a few extra sets of clothing. It felt weird that I hadn't collected many personal possessions in my time with the Protective Forces or here, but those I did held more meaning than anyone could imagine.

The palace was still quiet as I made my way outside. I refused to meet the stare of anyone I passed because I didn't want them asking where I was going. Not that they could stop me anyway.

I did feel a pang of regret that I wasn't saying goodbye to Adís, Ki'ran, or any of the other guards I'd grown close to in the past months. I knew, however, that they'd try to persuade me to stay. They were soldiers with a duty to protect the king and his citizens. I—well, I had to figure out what my purpose was now.

Making a beeline for the ship – which was obvious as it sat well away from the others parked on the airfield – I ignored the rain. I imagined that it was cleansing me as I started this new phase of my existence.

The ship was small, much smaller than the *Starfire* had been, but it was perfect for me to pilot. I was thankful Caspian had taught me how to fly, but I wished he was here to travel the stars with me.

Shaking my head to clear yet another batch of dark thoughts, I settled into the pilot's chair and started the ship's engines. It vibrated from the powerful hum, begging to lift off the ground. But I didn't take off.

Where exactly would I go? I could literally travel anywhere in the universe, and here I was, uncertain of where my path should take me.

Damien had been right that I didn't want to work under anyone's rule, but something within me still demanded that I protect others. I might have lost the future I dreamed of, but I still had the abilities I'd been gifted. Abilities that could turn the tide of this coming war.

I needed to learn more. Where did the Krech come from? Why

had they been attacking trade ships? Why were they so fascinated with the Outer Rim and Charra?

I couldn't answer those questions by myself, as much as I wanted to remain alone, and in that moment, I knew where I needed to go.

I reached out to grasp the handle for the thrusters and realized I was still wearing the cuff Gunther and Gráinne had created. There was no telling what information it might be transmitting and to whom, and once I left Callais, I didn't want to be tracked or dragged back.

Wrapping my free hand around the cuff, I squeezed with all my might. The clear material groaned, cracked, and then crumbled off my wrist. I stared at the transparent fragments on my lap as I imagined someone in the royal palace panicking when they saw my signal disappear.

I was free.

I started the thrusters and left Callais behind.

Charra was a miserable place. It had been the first time I saw it, but it was even more so now.

The blast that killed a million people months ago affected more than the immediate area. Ash and debris lingered in the air as I landed the ship Damien had given me, and I had to hold a cloth over my mouth when I stepped out and onto the ground.

Hunched creatures covered in rags scuttled away as I made my way down the dirty and decrepit street.

I'd only been here once, but my destination was one that I wouldn't soon forget.

The window of the small shop was still filled with odds and ends. There wasn't a sign indicating it was open, but I could see a light on inside. That was good enough for me.

The hinges squealed as I eased the door open, but the person I was looking for didn't immediately appear. Making my way around the towering piles of junk, I headed toward the counter that I knew sat in the back of this packed room.

Sure enough, the small male waited at the counter. His head was bent as he watched a screen that rested on top of the table. It was, quite literally, the only space on the counter that was relatively clear.

Still unsure that he'd heard me enter, I cleared my throat.

Yornuk's head snapped up, and I was surprised to see the sadness written into the creases of his pointy face. His gray hair was still long and limp, and the glasses that sat on the bridge of his pointed nose were now cracked and smudged. It seemed like hard times had fallen on him, too.

"Oh, Aliya, Aliya, sad times are these." He turned and hopped off the stool he'd been sitting on. Rounding the counter, he shuffled over to where I stood and took my hand. "Your loss is my loss, is the loss for this universe."

Although I wasn't quite sure what he meant, it sounded like he was giving me condolences. "Thank you, Yornuk. I know you knew Caspian well."

"Yes, yes," he said as he bobbed his small head. "The captain and I shared many a good time. But you, you've sought Master Yornuk out. For what purpose is this?"

I took a deep breath. I'd come all the way here, and there was no backing out now.

The Protective Forces failed to keep us safe. The royal guards and fleet failed too. And King Damien… well, he'd failed me the moment he put that needle into my neck.

It no longer mattered. I wouldn't be returning to any of them.

They could call me heartbroken, a deserter, even a traitor.

I didn't care.

There was only one path left for me to take, only one way I could try to help this besieged galaxy.

"Yornuk, I need your help."

Acknowledgements

I love what I do, and it wouldn't be possible without all of you. I'm constantly blown away by the amazing authors and creators I meet, but what floors me even more is when people just like you take a chance on an indie author like myself. So thank you for picking up my books and experiencing this story with me.

As always, thank you to my parents. I'm constantly touched by every one of my author cards that you give away, each time you like and share my writing posts on social media, and each suggestion you give me to improve my writing and marketing. You've supported me so much throughout this entire process, and I don't think I'd be here, releasing a second book, without your love. Thank you for every single thing you do, and I'm so happy that I can share this with you.

Lauren and Adam – I couldn't have finished this book without your help. Your constant questioning about when I was finally going to finish this book helped me completing the writing segment, and the careful editing you provided was invaluable. You caught things I would've missed and helped shape the final product. Yes, even the times that Lauren called something I'd named "stoopid" were somewhat helpful. Somewhat.

To my incredible readers and new author friends – thank you for the endless support you provide, whether you realize it or not. The feedback and reviews I received for *Remade* were hugely helpful in improving my writing and planning process for this book. I'm so thankful for the writing, reading, book-blogging community and countless others who share their thoughts, successes and journeys. You've provided me with inspiration and new tips so I can keep pursuing what I love.

About the Author

Danielle Novotny grew up reading all genres of fiction interspersed with writing poetry and short stories. Inspired by the stories from her youth and many of the ones she reads each year, Danielle began writing in the fall of 2016. A graduate of Brandeis University, Danielle currently resides in New Jersey where she works as an event marketing manager and an occasional cheesemonger at her favorite French cheese store. Her four-legged feline, Milo, continues to be her writing companion – when he's not competing with a laptop for leg space.